BLOOD CRIES

ALSO BY JOHN WEISMAN

Guerrilla Theater: Scenarios for Revolution
Evidence
Watchdogs

BLOOD CRIES

John Weisman

VIKING

VIKING
Viking Penguin Inc., 40 West 23rd Street,
New York, New York 10010, U.S.A.
Penguin Books Ltd, Harmondsworth,
Middlesex, England
Penguin Books Australia Ltd, Ringwood,
Victoria, Australia
Penguin Books Canada Limited, 2801 John Street,
Markham, Ontario, Canada L3R 1B4
Penguin Books (N.Z.) Ltd, 182–190 Wairau Road,
Auckland 10, New Zealand

First published in 1987 by Viking Penguin Inc.
Published simultaneously in Canada

In memory: Robert Rossen

LIBRARY OF CONGRESS CATALOGING IN PUBLICATION DATA
Weisman, John.
Blood cries.
I. Title.
PS3573.E399B55 1987 813′.54 86-45847
ISBN 0-670-81381-8

Printed in the United States of America by
R. R. Donnelley & Sons Company, Harrisonburg, Virginia
Set in Sabon, Univers, and Venus
Designed by Robert Bull

For Syde Kremer, Ema Shelli, a Woman of Valor;
For Susan Povenmire Weisman, Motek Shelli;
and for David and Mikki Halevy, Haverim Shelli

The voice of thy brother's blood crieth unto Me from the ground. And now cursed art thou from the ground . . .

—Genesis 4:10,11

These are not nice guys; these people are trying to prove some nasty things about each other.

—U.S. Federal Judge Abraham Sofaer, instructing the jury in the libel trial of *Ariel Sharon* v. *Time magazine*

PART

ONE

November 1982

CHAPTER 1

On rainy winter nights when the heating was intermittent at best they stayed warm by alternately arguing politics and making love in her cold bedroom that faced away from Mount Zion. Showers were impossible—hot water came once, twice a week at most. So the best thing to do was walk over to the King David Hotel and rent a room for the afternoon, luxuriating in the steamy tile and marble bathroom, soaping each other once, twice, thrice and drying off with thick towels bought with sensitive American skin in mind.

Mornings began early, because it is at dawn and dusk that Jerusalem is at its best. By five they were awake, wrapped in flannel robes, their feet snugly encased in zippered shearling booties. They sipped thick, unsweetened Arab coffee bought from a tiny store on al-Rashid Street where the son of the owner bore a U.S. Marines tattoo, spoke openly of Palestinian rights, and swore the phone was tapped by the Shin Bet. Shutters open, they would shudder in the chill and watch the skies turn from black to indigo, purple to carnelian, ruby-red to rose, finally brightening into burnished handwrought gold over Mount Zion.

They'd munch on toast spread thick with preserves made from strawberries grown in the Sharon Valley, listen to the bells (bells whose dull, metallic thuds had neither the sonorous toll of Notre Dame, nor the deep peal of St. Paul's but a sense, they both concluded, of ineffable, atonal historicity) and debate not the existence of God—it is impossible *not* to believe in God in Jerusalem—but the reasoning behind some of God's more inexplicable actions, specifically, the amount of hot water He seemed to deem sufficient to create for washing, or His approach toward economics. Would Solomon have stood still for inflation of 200 percent the way Menachem Begin did?

Some days he would climb into his Fiat Autobianchi, whose side panels, hood and roof bore rust-flecked scars of dings inflicted while running gauntlets of Arab stonethrowers in Hebron, Nablus, El-Bira and other hotbeds of Palestinian nationalism in what he called the occupied West Bank and she labeled Judea and Samaria, and head north to report on the war's progress, or lack of it, or the latest disturbance in the occupied territories. The nights before he left for Lebanon were generally grim. It was dangerous work and both of them knew it.

This particular day he'd left early for Beit Duqqu, a small Arab town southwest of Ramallah. Electric lines were being strung by the Israeli military authorities in spite of the villagers' opposition to the improvement. To the Arabs it meant yet another step toward absorption into the Israeli state. The Muktar had ordered a roadblock; Jared watched, notebook in hand, as teenaged youths, their faces hidden by scarves and keffiyahs, doused tires with kerosene and lit makeshift barricades on the village's one paved street. While the power company men stood aside, green-bereted border guards were called in along with bulldozers. The protesters were scattered with tear gas, truncheons and heavy-booted kicks—boys, girls, men and women alike roughed up and chased into the bramble-covered olive orchards, or down alongside the slender, winding stream that was the village's drinking water, outdoor laundry and main sewer. A dozen were caught and dragged by the hair into paddy wagons. The bulldozers growled, grated gears, flattened three Arab homes as an example to the Muktar, and half an hour later the powerline poles had been erected.

He drove back to Jerusalem, his eyes still reddened from the gas. Young stonethrowers, who hated him not for who he was but for his yellow Israeli license plates, had dinged a new series of dents into the back panel on the driver's side. A crack in the righthand rear window was another souvenir of the day's events. He drove straight to the office, wrote an account of the incident, and telexed it to New York. Then, still in a foul mood, he stomped out.

It was when he hated the government and its policies most that

Jerusalem provided him with the most comfort. Jerusalem didn't belong to Menachem Begin, Ariel Sharon, or the military administrator of the West Bank. It was God's city; a place in which walking, looking, and smelling evaporated the tensions built up during assignments. Jerusalem calmed his bitterness, soothed his soul.

And so, having dropped an *asimon* token into a pay phone and convinced her to meet him at the Damascus Gate, they spent the early afternoon walking the narrow streets of the Old City, arms wrapped round each other's waists, striding in one-two-one-two lockstep unison, unmindful of tourists and vendors and young Arabs bearing tarnished brass trays of sweet mint tea.

In summer they'd wear shorts, T-shirts and Gali sandals. Now, in the November chill, it was flannel shirt, jeans and tennis shoes for him, and a set of French-made exercise clothes for her—gray hooded sweatshirt and baggy matching warmup pants, topped off with a sleeveless lambskin vest. Her hair, once raven-black and styled to perfection twice a week, was feisty now, a thatch of unruly, thick, luxurious curls flecked with gray. Occasionally, when walking, their shoulders touching, he'd sneak a look at her profile and ponder how wrong he once had been about who she was. He'd smile inwardly and grip her shoulder all the tighter. She'd look at him and laugh out loud. She knew what he was thinking.

Occasionally, through a break in the roofed-over souk, the marketplace, they'd see the sky. When they did, it was her habit to complain.

"That's your fault," she'd say. "See how God is angry today."

Looking up, he could see her point. Gray clouds, moving at tremendous speed, whose angular shapes were living testament to the fierce Unnameable Name—clouds whose character had not changed since Father Abraham himself left the Chaldees of Ur—were assaulting Jerusalem's hills from the northeast.

"God doesn't like what you're writing about Israel," she'd say, "and He's letting you know it."

"God wants the truth about Israel," he'd answer. "It doesn't matter whether He likes it or not."

She'd grunt at times like this.

"Besides," he'd add, "how can you be so sure it's me God is angry with? I think God's bringing His clouds back here after He staged a raid on Gush Etzion or one of the other settlements. It's

Begin and Sharon God's angry with, not me. They use His name more than I do. They're always invoking Him. I'm only a well-paid Jeremiah for a weekly news magazine. It's them God's after, not me."

"Don't be so sure," she'd say, never breaking step or losing the well-oiled syncopation of their one-two-one-two footfalls on uneven paving stone. "You're writing heresy, and God knows it."

A pause. Then, "Let's go for grill. Eat a good kebab and God will forgive you. Buy me a good kebab and I'll forgive you. Buy me a good kebab at Shahin, with pilaf and a salad, and I'll take you home and make you forget God's upset with you."

"I thought it was you who said it's impossible to forget God in this city."

They'd reached the restaurant already. There was no place in the Old City they could not reach in less than ten minutes. They knew the alleys unwalked by tourists, all the shortcuts, and the streets that were less slippery in Jerusalem's winter rains. Heeling smartly to the right, they wheeled inside the narrow white tile grill.

Fuad bowed low and clapped his pudgy hands. "Pasha Gordon, *aufwan*. The beautiful Miss Cooper, *Ahlan W'asahlan*—welcome." He pulled a red and white handkerchief from the back pocket of a pair of patched green trousers and wiped nonexistent sweat from a balding head and sallow, wrinkled, pencil-mustached face. "Coffees, yes?"

They nodded and Fuad disappeared behind a faded floral print curtain in the rear to a cubbyhole where a four-burner bottled-gas stove held a permanently boiling pot of water and cannisters of ground, bitter coffee, cardamom and sugar. Fuad's offer was, of course, a ritual, just as so much of Jared Paul Gordon's life was ritual, or at least had been ritualized. Like the presence of God, ritual was something impossible to escape in Jerusalem.

He had learned this slowly, having previously lived an existence devoid of ritual, historicity, or the undeniable, overt presence of the Unnameable Name. Jerusalem was not Los Angeles, New York, or Washington, D.C. Israel was not the United States. It was impossible to live here and remain blissfully oblivious to what went on—in the region, in the government or the army, in Tel Aviv, Haifa, Caesarea or Beersheva, even on the next street. Israel was a nation of busybodies, gossips, rumormongers. It was as if Jared Gordon had moved in with an extraordinarily large and exceptionally vocal family, a constantly bickering extended family with several branches, some of whom never spoke to each other. And yet a family that, during periods of crisis, came together cohesively despite their differences.

Jerusalem, despite the threefold expansion it had experienced since its unification in 1967, was still a small town. Small enough so that if Jared or Adrian passed up their regular butcher's small stall in the Mahane Yehuda to buy a piece of meat at a shop further down the narrow alleyway off Ez Hayim Street, Nafta the meatcutter would upbraid them for going to the competition the next time he saw them. Small enough so that if they had a dinner party and forgot to invite one of their regular circle of friends, they'd be greeted with forlorn looks the next time they saw whomever it was who'd been omitted. It was a society so close, so familial, that even political enemies could show up at the same party, drink scotch, dance with each other's wives and stand, arms around each other's shoulders, arguing bitterly all night.

"Oh," one would say later, "him, he's a bum, that one, a real no-goodnik. But we were in the Army together. I hate his guts, politically, but we're still in the same reserve unit. Besides—he saved my life in Lebanon in '78."

Jared had come gradually but inescapably to accept changes in the rules by which he lived and worked. Now, when he sat with his colleagues at Katy's, a wood-paneled American-style bar favored by journalists that nestled in a side street close to Beit Agron, the government press center, he talked not about censorship but about the government's internal policies. The censor was a reality of life, someone to be outwitted. The price of frozen chicken, the location of the newest, still undiscovered village on the West Bank to buy cut-rate virgin olive oil, the mind-boggling logistics of dealing with overdraft checking accounts and keeping expense reports indexed to the constantly falling Israeli shekel, and the ominous implications of making material goods like Mercedes sedans, color televisions, General Electric washers and videotape decks into the new "gods" of a society deeply in debt—these were far more serious problems.

Besides, life was good. He lived with a handsome woman who adored him, if not his politics. News stories were easily come by because he'd taken the time to learn the language—not in the pidgin fashion of most American correspondents, but in a two-month course for immigrants at an ulpan, or language school, in Natanya. Sources, he learned, filtered their facts when they spoke English. When they chatted with Jared it was as a countryman, and his reporting benefited from their frankness.

Often, as he wrote—late into the night, working at a portable typewriter balanced on his lap while Adrian took the evening off catching a film with friends at the Jerusalem Cinémathèque—he would experience discomforting and ambiguous emotions. He'd never felt much like The Jew; never revolved his life, as did many of his American friends, around a Jewish existence. He'd grown up assimilated, his parents called it: as an American first (to be precise, an upper-middle-class West Los Angeles American) and as a Jew a distant second, perhaps two days a year. His religious education, what there had been of it, came on Sunday mornings at a chic Reform synagogue on Wilshire Boulevard, where two weeks every December were annually, and rabbinically, decreed as Christmas vacation.

Israel, as he'd imagined it for more than thirty of his forty years, had been a Middle Eastern Lower East Side where Yiddish vendors sold cut-rate bagels and lox and Arabs wore funny headdresses and rode camels.

Israel had been distant and amorphous, something represented by bond drives and form letters from the United Jewish Appeal. Israel was an annual receipt from the Jewish National Fund for the cost of planting trees. Israel was pictures of kibbutzniks or soldiers. Israel was Golda Meir or Moshe Dayan being interviewed in the newspapers or on the nightly news programs. Israel was Entebbe, whose story interrupted Jared's coverage of the United States Bicentennial. It was a tourist brochure with pictures of beautiful, dark-skinned women and handsome young men—the kinds of models he'd seen in ads for Sabra, the Israeli liquor. It was not a place with which he'd ever identified.

Indeed, growing up in Los Angeles, attending Princeton and Columbia University's graduate school of journalism, and then going to work as a reporter, Jared had never identified himself as a Jew. He'd been a part of a minority yet never sensed it. Living here, part of the majority, he often felt more estranged than ever he'd felt in the United States. Their way of life was so blunt, so outspoken. Hebrew was a tongue meant to be shouted, not whispered. What was courteous in America here was interpreted as naïveté or weakness. Here, everything was questioned, scrutinized, debated, while to his Jewish friends back in Washington (and many of those who had emigrated to Israel), Jared's duty was to be Jew first, reporter second. Loyalty toward Israel was more important, they'd tell him—even Adrian would tell him—than loyalty to some grandiose journalistic ideal.

Were they right? Was she right? He'd wrestle with himself, a newsgathering Jacob tussling with Zionist angels whose motives were unclear, and, most often, felt intensely guilty when he published stories that caused his friends—their friends—to regard him more with sorrow than anger. Adrian would sigh and shake her head. She loved him. That he knew. That would not change. But more than love, more than the making of Jewish babies, for which they practiced regularly, she—and they—wanted to convert him into the sort of Jew they were themselves.

And so the rituals, and the arguments, and the subtle pressure of Jew on Jew that caused uncertainty, doubts about his loyalties, and friction. And yet—and yet . . . He'd grown to love the country and the people even as he wrote stories denouncing the government. A government that had, he was convinced, perverted Zionism into imperialism. And yet—and yet . . . He experienced the same excitement as UJA loyalists every time he walked through the narrow streets of the Old City's Jewish Quarter and approached the Western Wall. And yet—and yet . . . He felt a deep sense of historic pride when they visited Adrian's friend Koby Naiderman, in whose family vineyards, first planted near Zichron Yaakov in 1883, he tasted Jewish grapes from soil cultivated by Jews centuries before Jesus was born. And yet—and yet . . . His heart always beat just a bit faster when, flying El Al from London, Zurich or New York, the recorded message "We are now flying over the land of Israel" was played and the passengers invariably broke into song, singing "Le Shana Haba'a." And, living in Jerusalem, he had come to sense the deep bond between man and God, unparalleled anywhere else in the world.

There was something magical, metaphysical, spiritual about this city, this place, this existence, which made Jared question his birthright, his relationship to history and, yes, even his occupation. Things as simple yet complex as angry clouds in slate-gray skies, as walking lockstep one-two-one-two through the souk, as answering the ritual age-old question asked by Ishmael's issue, Fuad, to Isaac's descendant, himself: "Coffees, yes?"

And so they sat at a narrow marble and wrought-iron table in the narrow restaurant and sipped thick, sweet aromatic coffee laced with cardamom pods, until the plates came from the kitchen across the two-yard-wide packed-earth street. The meat was crusted yet sweetly juicy inside. Pushing cups aside, they picked at their grill with aluminum forks, scooping piquant sauce with torn loaves of hot pita bread.

They ate, and God—he hoped—forgave Jared Paul Gordon his sins. They ate, and Adrian Cooper—he knew—forgave Jared Paul Gordon his sins. And afterward, filled with God's blessings and good kebab, they walked one-two-one-two, up David's Street, out through the Jaffa Gate, down the Jericho Road, turned off at the Birket Sultan and climbed the hill to the two-story, nineteenth-century, Jerusalem-stone house in Yemin Moshe, where they turned up the heat—to no avail—shed their clothes, and climbed into bed, the better to practice making Jewish babies.

II SAMUEL 11:2

. . . And the woman was very beautiful to look upon.

"Jared Paul Gordon, this is Adrian Cooper. She spells her name like a man."

"How quaint. So do I." Jared said this reflexively, nodding—politely, he believed—as Sue made the introduction, thinking all the while that Adrian Cooper was very beautiful. Far too beautiful, in fact. Impossibly beautiful. The kind of beauty that meant steady boyfriend or doting husband or both. Wasn't it always that way? He'd noticed her as she walked into Sue Bernstein's Chevy Chase living room, where a sawdust log burned in the fireplace in seventeen colors. Noticed the firm, left-handed grip with which she held her wine, and the gold and steel Rolex on her wrist. She wore a red silk Cossack tunic, and well-worn French jeans tucked into knee-high black leather boots. He was a real sucker for red silk Cossack tunics and boots, especially when worn by someone who looked so good in them.

He caught a whiff of her hair. It was strong hair, healthy, perfect, black-as-raven hair and he was thinking how he'd love to watch her toss it, toss it in a Manhattan-canyon wind; toss it atop Wuthering

Heights; toss it in a Kodachrome forest or an Ansel Adams mesa. As she turned toward him, he could see diamond studs in her delicious ears.

She was speaking. Her lips were moving. But Jared wasn't listening. An X-rated movie was playing in his head: they were rolling in her king-sized bed with slate-gray sheets and a goosedown comforter from Bloomingdale's, and she was clawing at his back and . . . and—Oh, God, she *was* talking. Jared panicked. What the hell had she been saying?

". . . always wanted a son, so he called me Adrian."

There was an uncomfortable pause as she caught him staring at her, glassy-eyed. She sucked in her cheeks and shot him a frosty glance while tapping her boot on the Oriental rug. "Is something bothering you?"

Jared panicked. She was giving him The Look. Only Jewish princesses can do it. It shrivels the privates of Jewish males. "What? I'm sorry. I—ah—my mind was—are you new in town? I don't remember meeting you before."

"I'm a native."

"Are you really? That's even better than spelling your name like a man."

"Why?"

"Because I didn't think there were any native Washingtonians."

Finally a smile that was everything he'd hoped for. "Really?"

"Sure. Everyone I meet seems to have come here during this or that administration. That's how people define themselves: 'I came with Carter,' or Kennedy, or Nixon, Ford. Even the oldtimers call themselves Roosevelt Washingtonians or Truman Washingtonians."

"That's funny." She paused, sizing him up. It was the kind of lull common to singles bars, cocktail parties, and diplomatic receptions in which a decision is made either to continue the dialogue or move on toward something more promising. She reconnoitered the room with a professional eye, evaluating the knots of conversation, then turned back to Jared.

He watched her, inwardly relieved as her eyes told him she was going to stay.

"What kind of non-natives do you meet?"

"Politicians, mostly. Some diplomats. White House types. You're my first indigenous Washingtonian."

"Indigenous! That's a ten-dollar word. You must be a writer. Are you with the Carter administration?"

He was impressed. "No, but I cover it."

She was impressed. "For whom?"

"I'm White House correspondent for *World Week*. And you?"

"A professional volunteer."

Unique. "Where? What? Why? How?"

" 'Just the facts, ma'am.' You *are* a journalist, aren't you? At the Israeli Embassy."

He liked this woman. Not only was she uncommonly attractive, she had a sense of humor too. "Terrific. For whom?"

She flashed him a proud smile and a confident toss of hair that was far better than he'd imagined. "For the cultural attaché. I help coordinate events—concerts and screenings, recitals, lectures. And I do mailing lists, send out letters."

"Sounds fascinating. How do you know Sue?"

"She's a friend of my mother's. They work together on the board of the America-Israel Cultural Foundation. Both my parents are very active in the Jewish community. And you?"

"Blundered into Sue and Bob at a party about six months ago, just after I arrived in Washington to cover Carter. We talked all night. They've taken me under their wing. Keep inviting me to these Sunday brunches so I meet real people."

"Real people?"

"Jews. They tell me I'm too parochial."

A smile. "I see." She looked at him quizzically. "Well, are you?"

"Parochial? I guess so. But that's the job. On the other hand, isn't being around Jews all the time a little bit parochial too?"

"Not necessarily. It all depends on your orientation. The community here is small, and we do all we can to support Israel."

"How?"

"Financially, politically. The embassy coordinates a lot of activities."

"I'd like to learn more about them. Maybe we should have dinner sometime. You could give me some background."

There was no time for her answer. Tall and dark, he swooped in from the den like an avenging angel and put his arm around her waist. It was peremptory, proprietary, and brooked no interference. Neither did his appearance: short hair, muscular, a forward tilt of body that conveyed aggressiveness, and unlikely bright blue eyes that didn't smile. "We have to go."

A pause. "Udi, this is Jared. He's a reporter. Jared, this is Udi. He works at the embassy."

"Hi." Jared offered his hand.

No return. "We have to go."

"So soon? Oh, Udi, I—"

He spoke to Adrian in Hebrew, quick, unintelligible Hebrew. She answered and swung away—then spun back and gave Jared a warm smile. "It was nice meeting you, Jared. Enjoy Washington. Don't be too parochial."

Enjoy Washington? How could he enjoy Washington when this fantasy was being whisked away by an unsmiling Israelite? How could this . . . this somber Semite snatch Adrian in her Cossack tunic right from under his nose before he could schedule even a dinner date?

"Hey, wait!" He lurched toward the vestibule, only to see Udi the Solemn closing the door behind them.

He found Sue in the pantry arranging nova on Wedgwood. "Who the hell was that? She's gorgeous. Where did she go? And what about the Israeli guy? Come on, Sue—tell me."

Sue laughed. "A little anxious, aren't you?"

He realized he was sounding like an adolescent. He shrugged noncommittally. "She's . . . interesting."

"She must be. Adrian's the first woman you've bothered to inquire about in—what—four brunches? Here: take this platter out to the table and let me clean up. Then I'll give you the whole story."

He did as he was told. Then, sitting at the round marble table in the country kitchen, he sipped black coffee and listened. Adrian Cooper, Sue explained, was a Very Committed Young Woman with a Trust Fund. Her father, Felix, a millionaire many times over, informally advised three presidents on Jewish affairs.

Adrian was thirty, Sue told him, divorced, no children, and owned a professionally decorated two-bedroom condo in the Colonnade, over on New Mexico Avenue. "She's always been very independent," Sue said, absently scratching her chin with a vermilion nail. "She was quite the rebel when she was in college—almost a whatchamacallit, a hippie. Then she settled down. Married a lawyer named Allan Jacobson—God, what a wedding. Felix must have had five hundred people. Even the President came."

"What happened?"

"They were married five years, then . . . "

"Yes?"

"It was over. Beverly told me one day. She said Adrian was getting divorced and going to live in Israel. Which she did, for about a year or so. She bought a house in Jerusalem and nobody heard a word. Then, all of a sudden, she turned up. It must have been, oh, six or seven months ago." A significant pause. "Just about the time Udi was assigned to Washington."

Sue nibbled at a piece of cold bagel. "Frankly, Jared, we don't see a lot of her. She has her own friends."

"And Udi?"

He, Sue explained, was the Embassy's assistant air attaché and had been humorless ever since the Syrians shot him down in '73 and he spent three months as a prisoner of war. "Didn't you notice his hands?"

"He never offered to shake mine."

"That's because he's still shy about his fingers. The nails never grew back, and the broken joints didn't heal properly." Udi doesn't fly anymore, Sue said. Not since he was the guest of the Syrians.

"But what about—I mean, you know—Adrian and Udi?"

"Adrian works at the embassy. Udi's wife is overseas . . ."

He understood. Adrian who spelled her name like a man had a thing for married men. He nodded dumbly. "Too bad."

Sue raised her eyebrows. "I didn't know you were so old-fashioned, Jared."

"Neither did I."

"So?"

"So what?"

"Call her. I think you two would get along."

He sighed. "Okay, I'll call," he promised, knowing that he wouldn't. Knowing—thirty-second fantasies aside—that he'd never meshed with Jewish princesses. Especially ones who had affairs with married men. They were too complicated, too demanding, too neurotic. He was incapable of handling their emotional Sturm und materialistic Drang.

He felt out of place at country clubs. He was bad at making . . . reservations.

And Adrian who spelled her name like a man struck him as the archetypal Jewish princess—right down to the trust fund, the gold and steel Rolex and the four-hundred-dollar red-silk Cossack tunic. Damn it. He was drawn to them like a Semitic moth to fire—and every time he was he got boined.

"Call. I know Adrian would like to hear from you," said Sue, not knowing what Jared knew.

Jared's alarm buzzed just before one in the morning and he reached quickly to stifle it. They'd slept away the afternoon and the evening, made love again, then fallen asleep once more. Cautiously, tentatively in the cold, he slipped out of the bed, rubbing her neck when she stirred. He pulled on slippers and padded toward the bathroom, relieved himself and turned on the hot water. After some minutes there was a trickle only a few degrees below body temperature, and with this he washed his privates. Then he brushed his teeth, combed his hair and sneaked back into the bedroom where he donned long underwear, jeans, flannel shirt, down vest, boots and knit watchcap.

From the desk in the foyer he took notebook, camera, tape recorder and a handful of pens, all of which he slipped into a small orange nylon rucksack.

He sliced himself six thick pieces of white bread, buttered them, covered them with slices of yellow cheese and wrapped them in waxed paper. These, too, went into the rucksack.

As quietly as he could, he went down the stairs, unlocked the heavy wooden door and the security gate outside and stepped into the cold. He pulled the watchcap low over his eyebrows, locked both doors and strode up three flights of cut stone steps and along a short street to where the Autobianchi was parked. Looking toward the Old City, he could make out the faint outline of David's Tower in the darkness. The spotlights that bathed the Old City walls, walls built by Suleiman the Magnificent four hundred years before he had been born, had been extinguished, and in the darkness ancient Jerusalem was a shadow among shadows.

He approached the car and quickly looked underneath it. How

fast one learned to adapt here: reporting all suspicious objects; checking under cars for bombs; treating all Arabs as potential enemies. These were some of the not-so-sweet rituals of life.

All clear. He unlocked the driver's side door, slid onto the cold plastic seat, pulled out the choke and started the ignition, praying dampness hadn't killed the battery. The engine coughed and caught. Immediately, without lights, he threw the car into reverse and backed at high speed up the narrow paving stone street. At its apex he U-turned quickly, and drove heedless of the blinking traffic lights toward the Keren Hayesod.

From there he sped on to Ramban, close by the Prime Minister's residence. And then toward Ben Zvi, up the hill past the Turkish Quarter and Foreign Ministry to the Hilton, where he pulled into the parking lot.

The other car was already there: a dull black Dodge Dart with black-and-white Israeli Defense Force plates. In the rear, behind a haze of cigarette smoke, appeared Brigadier General Yoram Gal's round, mustached face. Jared parked his Fiat next to the Dodge and waved from behind the windshield. The general rolled down his window and called in Hebrew: "Come on, boychik—you're late. I have coffee. Did you bring something to eat?"

Jared nodded, shaking the rucksack.

Yoram climbed out of the Dodge. He was not much taller than Jared's five-eight, but a lot broader. His cheeks and forehead were pocked by scars made by grenade fragments; the wide nose had been partially flattened by impact against something hard. He waved a tobacco-stained right hand whose little finger had been shot away and gestured toward the car door. Yoram's garb was anything but military: a black wool turtleneck sweater tucked into a pair of nondescript trousers, a wool jac-shirt and a beret covering a receding hairline.

"Morning," he said. "Been having fun?"

"Always."

"Good. There's nothing like a screw before you go to war, right, Jared?"

"Right on, Yoram," Jared answered in Hebrew. *"Biduke."*

The general's steel-gray eyes smiled in the parking lot's half light. "Let's eat on the road. We've got a long drive."

"Where are we headed?"

"You'll know when we get there."

"Not even a hint?"

"Nothing." Yoram climbed back into his car, pushing Jared ahead of him. "*Yalla!*" he said to the driver. "Let's get the hell out of here."

They sped out of the city to the north, drinking coffee and eating bread and cheese as the car hurled through Ramallah, Nablus, Jenin, and then northwest, along highways unlit except by the lights of an occasional truck or jeep. Inside the car it was hot, and Jared shed his vest. Yoram smoked, silent for the most part, staring vacantly out the window into the void. Half-dozing, Jared watched Yoram watching nothing.

They were so close in many ways, he thought, but so very different. Yoram was only twenty months older than Jared; yet he looked and sounded more like a father than a brother. His thinning hair had gone almost completely gray, a souvenir, he said, of the Yom Kippur War. Yoram's entire adult life had been spent in the Army. At forty-three he was a brigadier general and could, Jared believed, become the IDF's Chief of Staff before he was fifty, given the right political situation. They had met five years previously, when Yoram, then a colonel, had been assigned to Washington as assistant military attaché.

Sue had introduced them, and their professional and personal friendship grew quickly. Jared envied the Israeli's *joie de vivre,* his ability to seek people out and make friends quickly. He appreciated Yoram's advice when he began to cover the Camp David process, receiving telephoned tidbits of inside information from the voluble colonel, who was a member of the Israeli negotiating team.

In return, Jared had been happy to provide Yoram with stories about infighting at the Carter White House, especially the dissension between the State Department and the National Security Council. They'd become close friends who ate and drank and partied together. Jared was a constant guest in Yoram's home. He came and went like a member of the family, showing up unannounced for dinner. He baby-sat for Yoram and Aviva's four-year-old daughter Tamar when Kerin and Sigal, their twelve- and fifteen-year-olds, were out and no one else was available. Often he'd dropped by simply to spend the evening gossiping, watching television, nibbling on olives and drinking scotch. On those nights he'd watch, faintly envious of Yoram's close-knit Israeli family life, as Tamar settled down to sleep across her parents' laps, Yoram absently stroking his daughter's curls as she dozed drooling on his blue jeans.

And yet Jared actually knew very little about his friend, very little about Yoram's business trips, which the Israeli took frequently, and often without warning. In fact, Jared knew virtually nothing about what the gray-haired man whose face bore scars did on a daily basis. Sometimes he'd ask, and get told "It's all bullshit, boychik."

There were the usual rumors, of course: that Yoram was an operative of Mossad, Israel's intelligence service. Or a high-ranking officer in Aman, the Army intelligence unit. But Jared discounted them. Yoram drank too much for covert work. He had a real fondness for J&B scotch. And he had the habit of telling inside stories about Begin and Sharon; he would loudly, lewdly, describe the anatomical peculiarities of Moshe Dayan's various mistresses at embassy parties. He'd point out this or that visiting Foreign Ministry official and whisper conspiratorially to Jared, "That one used to be Mossad, but he screwed things up so they retired him to the bureaucracy." Jared prided himself on his instincts: Yoram was a professional soldier—perhaps a former commando in one of Israel's elite units. But he was no spy.

The roadbed got worse, waking Jared from an uneasy, sweaty sleep. Then it got better, then worse again, and finally it improved noticeably. Without looking, Yoram said, "We're almost there."

Ten minutes later, just after three A.M., they came to a barrier of spikes laid across the road and manned by two yawning MPs in a jeep. Yoram's driver rolled down his window and flashed a pass. The pair of soldiers peered inside. Neither saluted. "Morning, General," they said.

Yoram offhandedly returned the greeting.

The spikes were removed and the car proceeded: first down a straight road for two and a half kilometers, then, after a ninety-degree turn, down another straight road for three or four more. From out of the darkness appeared an unmarked concrete gate house, a squad of heavily armed soldiers, and a gravel-filled truck to block the way.

Yoram hoisted himself out and stretched. A lieutenant in combat gear shook his hand and bummed a cigarette, then peered inside the car. "Morning."

"Morning," said Jared. "Everything quiet?"

"Yes, sir." The young officer turned to Yoram. "We'll have the truck out of the way in a minute." One soldier, whose web-strapped Uzi hung from his shoulder, appeared with a circular convex mirror attached to the bottom of a long pole—it looked to Jared like an outsized dental mirror. Another shone a lantern under the car's chassis while the soldier moved his apparatus underneath, searching for explosives.

The examination complete, Yoram nodded at the soldiers and climbed back inside. "Okay," he said. "I want to go over the ground rules again. Where we are, just which unit we're visiting, the people you'll meet—this is all privileged information. This morning's events must be told only in the way I say they can be told, and when I give you permission to tell them. Everything is off the record."

Jared nodded. What he was doing was in direct violation of his magazine's news policies. Off-the-record reporting trips were forbidden without the prior consent of the Chief of Correspondents or his deputy. But because Jared had been told he would be taken to a secret location and was unable to reveal even that fact, he had agreed. The risk was worth it: he was being promised an inside look at the Israeli military no foreign correspondent had ever had before.

"Okay."

"You've been good to us, Jared. Your girlfriend may not like what you write, but she's a fan of Begin and Sharon's. Her daddy is an old friend of the Prime Minister's. You may piss her off, but that's your problem. So far as the General Staff's concerned, you're on our side."

The car started to move slowly. They had entered a side or rear gate of what Jared now saw to be a huge air base. He made mental calculations about their position.

"We're at Ramat David, right?" he asked.

"My conditions—you're absolutely certain about them? On your word?"

"Sure," said Jared.

"Yes, we're at Ramat David," said Yoram.

"What are we doing here? Am I finally going to get to ride with one of the Air Force's F-4 squadrons?"

"You'll see," said Yoram.

The base was blacked out. Yoram's car proceeded with only its running lights, moving slowly past offices, headquarters buildings, residential streets and maintenance hangars. From the window, Jared could see in the distance a wing of combat-ready F-4s parked in revetments. But Yoram's driver bypassed the pilots' ready-room and squadron HQ, moving smoothly until he came to a pair of sheds, painted dirty brown, at the very farthest edge of the base. Jared could see lights stifled behind thick-curtained windows. The car stopped, and Yoram beckoned him to follow.

They entered the shed to the left. As Yoram threw open the door, Jared winced at the bright lights.

Five men waited inside. Each was dark. Two had mustaches, another the six-day untidy growth of beard favored by Yasser Arafat. The others were clean-shaven. But they were all, Jared realized immediately, Palestinian Arabs. Their appearance, smell, even the way they were smoking cigarettes said it. They dressed like Nablus troublemakers: bell-bottom trousers, pointy-toed shoes and boots, Qiana nylon shirts under cheap leather jackets. And they fondled an assortment of armaments that included Russian AK–47 automatic rifles, hand grenades, and revolvers of the sort favored by Beirut's Moslem street gangs.

Yoram looked around contentedly. "*Bokker tov*—good morning, gang," he said. "This is Jared. He's the one who's joining us this morning."

"Funny," said the Arab with the beard, speaking in perfect Hebrew, "he doesn't look Palestinian."

"Neither do you, Yom Tov," said Yoram. "You look like a *yeshiva bokker*, you know?"

There was general laughter. Yoram started pulling off his clothes and gestured for Jared to do the same. "Yom Tov thinks that's funny," said Yoram. "He's Yemenite—grew up in the orphans' village of Me'ir Shefeya near Zichron Yaakov—and he's spent the best part of his twenty-seven years *shtupping* like a rabbit."

Confused, Jared nodded. Under Yoram's direction he stripped down to bare skin, and was handed an ill-fitting set of clothing much like those worn by the five men.

"The two with the mustaches, they're Yaakov and Yaakov. I call them Koby One and Koby Two—Moroccans. Then here's Amos"—Yoram gestured at the eldest of the five, a clean-shaven man in his late thirties with a tinge of gray in his hair. "And finally, Ze'ev—our little Wolf."

"What unit is this?" Jared asked.

"Call us what you like," Yoram said.

"Are you Saye'eret?"

Yoram shrugged.

"Unit two hundred sixty-nine?" Jared asked. Two-Six-Nine, also known as the General Staff's Special Reconnaissance and Intelligence Unit, carried out most of the IDF's behind-the-lines commando operations.

"Our unit name's not important," Yoram said. "I tell you what, Jared, call us an unidentified group of PLO rebels. Call us the Jihad Brigade."

Again, there was laughter.

"Can't I keep my boots?" Jared was annoyed as his prized Gore-tex hiking boots and thick American socks were taken away and replaced with threadbare nylons and a pair of mud-soiled black leather shoes with what looked like cardboard soles.

"Sorry. And you'll have to leave the rucksack behind, too. No notepaper, no tape recorder—nothing."

"Yoram—why?"

"Because, to put it plainly—" Yoram looked around the room; Jared, to his discomfort, could see the others were amused—"if you should not come back, we can't have any nasty evidence left behind for anyone to discover."

"Where are we going?"

The chunky general grinned. He strapped a Stechkin nine-millimeter machine pistol on a heavy belt around his waist.

"To Damascus, boychik. We're going to Damascus."

CHAPTER 2

Ten minutes later Jared was sitting wedged in the rearmost canvas bench of a Bell 212 helicopter, uncomfortable because of the equipment that lay across his lap and apprehensive over what lay ahead. Yoram sat next to him, cradling a pair of automatic rifles. Like the others, his equipment—right down to the ammunition in the banana-shaped clips for the AK-47s—was all Soviet-made. His identity card showed him to be Major Yusif Ahmed al-Sherif, *nom de guerre* Abu Faradis, a member of Fatah, the largest armed segment of the PLO. The other members of Yoram's squad carried similar documents.

Jared's stomach queased as the helicopter's two jet-assisted engines reached full power and then lifted off the tarmac, leaning into the slight headwind and veering to the right. Straining across Yoram's chest to look out the window, he could see a second chopper following his own.

The two Bells climbed to an altitude of 750 feet, and Jared peered over the pilot's shoulder to see the compass heading on the dimly lit control panel. They were going north by east-northeast, flying above the Hagalil. The air got much colder, and Jared shivered in his thin clothes.

He looked over at Yoram, who had closed his eyes and let his head rest against the window, at Yom Tov in his headphones, who was engrossed in a paperback in Arabic, and at Koby One, who peered vacantly out the forward window into the darkness. No one seemed to show any anxiety. Except for Jared, who found himself scarcely able to sit still. He tried crossing and uncrossing his legs—unsuccessfully, because there was insufficient room to maneuver between the weapons on the floor and those lying across his lap. He exercised his shoulders, cracked his knuckles twice in each direction, and swallowed to relieve the pressure on his eardrums.

Yoram opened an eye. He pulled a headset and microphone on and gestured to Jared to do the same. "Nervous?"

"What do you think?"

The Israeli smiled. "Don't fret, boychik, Yom Tov'll take care of you, won't you, Yom Tov?"

The Yemenite returned a thumbs-up sign. "Sure I will. Don't worry, friend—we won't leave you for the Syrians to play with."

Jared thought of the former pilot he'd met in Washington five years before; thought of the man's hand that wouldn't shake his own. He'd gotten to know Udi professionally about a year after their first meeting. And one night at a dinner given by Israel Aircraft Industries, after more scotch than the Israeli was accustomed to, he'd told Jared and a correspondent from *Aviation Week,* who were sitting with him, some of what had happened.

He was flying an A-4 Skyhawk—not the best of planes, Udi said, and in any case the Syrians were ready for combat in 1973. He'd been hit by a Russian SAM-7, ejected safely, and came down near a small town called Daal. It was the second day of the war, and forty kilometers away Israeli armor was fighting for its life on the Golan Heights. There were no rescue teams available, no chopper commandos or medivacs. He was on his own.

He made it on foot halfway back to his lines before they caught him. The platoon that captured Udi had fun by hog-tying him and removing his fingernails with the wirecutters built into their Soviet-made bayonets. They cauterized the wounds by sticking his hand in the coals of their cooking fire. Later, during interrogation by Syrian intelligence, his fingers were broken. "Slowly," Udi said. "They broke them very slowly."

They were flying very fast and low now, skimming the scrub brush and trees at more than one hundred seventy kilometers an hour. The pilots and crewman in the front compartment worked silently, touching a switch on the control console now and then and nodding wordlessly at each other. They looked like aliens, Jared thought, with their helmets and electronically enhanced night-vision goggles. Had they crossed the Syrian border yet or were they still safe inside Israel? Jared had never particularly thought of Israel as sanctuary—either in the physical or emotional sense. Now, suddenly, he wanted very much to know the precise instant when the unseen border below would be breached; to know exactly when safety would be left behind.

"Where are we?"

Yoram cracked an eye again. "Somewhere."

"Yoram—"

"I could make something up, Jared. I won't. We're somewhere between here and there."

"Don't be patronizing."

Yoram sensed the urgency in Jared's voice. Had it been the right thing to do to bring the American along? All in all the answer was yes; Jared had been cultivated carefully, slowly, over the past four years. He'd shown a willingness to cooperate by sitting on some stories and pushing others, and despite his critical stance on the government and the war in Lebanon, Jared, unknowingly, had been helpful to Israel's military and intelligence communities.

A year and a half before, in July of 1981, Jared had gone to Beirut to interview Yasser Arafat. Yoram gave the infrequent smoker a gift—a good-luck charm, the general had said. It was a cigarette lighter, a solid silver Dupont, inscribed "JPG from YG."

Jared had not known, then or ever, that the lighter contained a transmitting device. Nor had he known that in addition to his guides from the PLO, half a dozen Israeli agents slipped across the Green Line that separated West Beirut from the Mossad command post in Jounieh, the Phalangist stronghold, and tracked his every move from the Commodore Hotel during his three-day visit. The signal emitted by Jared's lighter was sent to a remote-controlled pilotless Israeli Mastiff drone that in turn relayed his position back through a series of microwave stations to a computer at IDF headquarters on Kaplan Street in Tel Aviv. It wasn't that the Israelis didn't know where Yasser Arafat was, most of the time. It was that they wanted to know if he was consistent about where he met foreign journalists.

Jared did his interview, climbed on a Middle East Airlines 727 and flew to Rome to file his story. Six hours after he left, the Israelis bombed the Fakhani District of Beirut, hoping to catch Arafat and his lieutenants in the basement conference room where the Palestinian chairman was holding forth with an East German reporter. The raid killed one hundred sixty-one, PLO and civilians alike. But Arafat escaped.

Then, in September, Jared discovered that Aman, Israel's military intelligence organization, was planting remote electronic sensors in Saudi Arabia by sending commando teams ashore from a missile boat in the Gulf of Aqaba. The boat ran aground on a coral reef twenty-five kilometers south of Al Humaydah. The commandos were evacuated by helicopter, but the vessel sat, in full sight of the Saudis, for three and a half days until it could be unloaded and dragged away by an Israeli naval tug. The Saudis had not wanted to cause an incident—neither did the Israelis, who were flying protective overflights of Kfir fighters from Etzion airbase in the Sinai. Neither nation brought the matter up publicly, although both mentioned the incident to the United States.

Jared heard about the unfortunate boat at a cocktail party given by a visiting American publisher who had just paid a former Minister of Defense half a million dollars for his memoirs. Over kosher hors d'oeuvres in a crowded banquet room of the King David Hotel he heard two Air Force colonels laughing about the Navy's ineptitude and Jared understood their rapid bantering in Hebrew.

When he wrote his piece, the military censor killed it. He was on his way to Cairo, where he'd be able to file the article unhampered, but was intercepted at the airport by Yoram.

"I know what you're going to do," Yoram said. "Jared—as a friend, I ask you not to write this story. It will do no one any good."

"It's news, Yoram," Jared had said. "It's a big story."

"If you print it it will endanger lives," Yoram insisted.

"That's not my problem."

"Look—" The Israeli scratched his chin. "Let's make a deal. Forget about the boat for ten days—then run with it. In the meanwhile I'll get you another exclusive."

"What?"

"Trust me."

Jared pondered the offer. Then he nodded. "Yoram, it better be good."

"It will be."

Jared canceled his ticket, and Yoram was true to his word. Later the same day he produced for Jared a handful of year-old, handwritten documents detailing the Ministerial Committee for Defense's secret debates over whether or not to raid Iraq's Ossirak nuclear plant at El-Taiwaitha, just outside Baghdad.

The minutes chronicled the most intimate details of the bitter arguments in the Ministerial Committee meetings, and showed a side of Israeli politics few had ever witnessed before. When Jared published them, he made headlines and received a bonus from his editor. In the months that followed, Yoram convinced him to delay other stories, stories dealing with preemptive raids to capture Palestinian terrorists, the shipment of weapons to the Phalangist militia in Lebanon, the development of an anti-armor cluster bomb called the Assault Breaker, and the successful testing of an armor-piercing tank shell called *Hetz*—or arrow—designed to penetrate the heavy plates of Soviet T-72 tanks. Each time, Yoram promised—and delivered—substitute exclusive information.

There were also other coups: papers concerning the military relationship between Israel and South Africa; confidential documents outlining a possible strategic cooperation agreement between the U.S. and Israel, and military and intelligence agreements between Israel and Guatemala, Honduras, Costa Rica and Mexico. By censoring himself, Jared got scoops—which kept him and his editors happy. He thought of his relationship with Yoram as journalist/friend to source/friend. And Yoram's motives? Jared never dealt with them.

"Close your eyes," said Yoram. He took a broad hand and ruffled Jared's hair, as a father would do to a five-year-old. "Relax," he said.

Jared looked at the dial of the cheap East German wristwatch they had given him. Four fifty-seven in the morning. Four hours before he'd been leaving Adrian's house. He closed his eyes, wondering if he'd ever see it or her again.

EXODUS 19:5

. . . if ye will harken unto My voice indeed, and will keep My covenant, then ye shall be Mine own treasure from among all peoples . . .

It was two years, almost to the day, between the time Jared met Adrian in Sue Bernstein's living room and the next time he saw her, walking through the lobby of the Laromme Hotel in Eilat. Those two years had taken their toll. Indeed, there are only two ways to work as a journalist in Washington. One is to remain the outsider and report on what happens in a detached fashion. The other is to jump feet first into the social life of the city, to cultivate sources at lunches, dinners and parties. Jared chose the second way—and suffered for it. The pace of his life was chaotic. The White House beat demanded eighty hours a week, working crammed inside a four-by-five-foot cubicle in the press room or a small office at *World Week*'s K Street bureau. Then there were the endless series of lunches and dinners with the Georgia Mafia, deputy assistants, and deputy deputy assistants. In addition to his professional schedule, he managed to follow Bob and Sue Bernstein's advice not to become parochial. He was drawn by them (and by Yoram) into the circle of Jewish life that bubbles just below the surface of Washington society.

As is always the case in Washington, Jared's personal and professional existences overlapped. Jimmy Carter's desire to become the peacemaker of record in the Middle East probably had as much to do with Jared's cultivation of Washington Jews as anything. He found that one can learn more at a dinner at Max Kampelman's house than in a week of Jody Powell briefings—on or off the record. It was easier to glean information from an Israeli political officer over a glass of scotch at an Embassy cocktail party than to wring it out of a defensive State Department apparatchik during office hours.

Besides, Jared was not by any stretch of the imagination an investigative reporter. His background was in covering stories, events, not digging in dusty files for nuggets of information. He had been hired for a slot in *World Week*'s Los Angeles bureau right out of journalism school, not because he was the best and the brightest they could find, but because he had worked for three summer vacations as an unpaid intern there, and because he—like the bureau chief—had gone to Princeton.

After three years of covering entertainment, farm worker strikes and antiwar protests in Los Angeles he was posted to Detroit, where he learned about the auto industry, steel-hauling, and wrote about white urban flight to the suburbs. Then it was Atlanta—where a former peanut farmer whose mother joined the Peace Corps at the age of sixty-five had just been elected governor. Jared discovered that working for a weekly news magazine was similar to being a Foreign

Service officer. No sooner was he comfortable in one post than he was transferred to another.

Still, the system had its advantages. Although Jared had no experience as a political reporter he was assigned to cover Jimmy Carter because he knew Jody Powell, Ham Jordan, Bert Lance, Charlie Kirbo and the rest of the Carter crowd better than any carpetbagging Big Foot correspondent out of Washington or New York. Besides—Carter was considered a dark-horse candidate. The wisdom, as expressed by New York, was that Jared would get some tempering on the road, then—perhaps in 1980—be assigned to a serious contender. Instead, Jared stuck with Carter from the earliest days right through election night, and was moved to Washington when the new President came from Plains.

It was heady stuff. In a matter of months he went from being just another name on the masthead to a writer whose opinions were sought out by his editors, and whose thoughts were plumbed by folks with Presidential commissions on their walls. It had its advantages, too. On his father's desk sat an inscribed color photo of Jared in the Oval Office, the arm of the President of the United States clasped warmly around his shoulder. "To Stanley, whose son knows how hard it was to get here," read the neat handwriting. It was signed "Your friend, Jimmy Carter."

On the other hand, the job had its downside, too. The hours were horrendous; and despite a heavy schedule of parties, receptions and black-tie dinners he had no real social life, no "meaningful relationships" to speak of. There were lots of women available, but nothing ever clicked. So Jared sublimated, substituting power for intimacy, political clout for hugging, and one-nighters for a long-term involvement. That lifestyle took its toll—both on his psyche and his body. In the summer of 1979, while the younger staffers from the White House and Capitol Hill rented beach houses in Rehoboth and Dewey Beach and the Sander Vanocurs and James Restons of the world retreated to cottages on Cape Cod and Nantucket, Jared lay in Georgetown University Hospital wallowing in self-pity—and suffering from a bleeding ulcer.

An operation went with the ulcer: a painful three weeks of intensive hospital care, and the knowledge that he would have a ten-inch scar that looked like a half-inch-wide zipper running down his front.

Jared's parents pleaded with him to come home. His friends volunteered to nurse him back to health, but Jared crawled away like a wounded animal to lair down and heal himself.

Yoram Gal suggested Israel. Jared had been there for three and a half days during Carter's peace mission to Jerusalem and Cairo the previous spring. He was receptive. "Go on, boychik," Yoram urged. "It's September, the most beautiful month. Walk in Jerusalem; eat fish in Tiberias; lie on the beach in Eilat, on the Red Sea. Screw your brains out. I'll find you a soldier girl—a real medic, if you know what I mean, and she'll put you back together again."

It sounded good: he had two months' medical leave coming, and could live in a vacuum—cure himself.

He arrived at Ben-Gurion Airport outside Tel Aviv and took a connecting flight straight to Eilat. The thought of walking in Jerusalem—walking anywhere—was inconceivable. So was the idea of calling "Medic" to Yoram's soldier girl. Jared couldn't face such prospects. He wanted only quiet, solitude, and time to get used to his zipper.

Adrian arrived halfway through his second week at Laromme, carrying the kind of soft Mark Cross luggage used, he thought, by someone who knows how to go away for weekends.

She didn't see him, notice him, remember him as he watched her lope across the lobby and reach up to kiss the head bellman softly on his cheek. No Cossack tunic this time—a red and black plaid cotton shirt in the cowboy style, French tennis shorts and Italian sandals, all topped off by a po'boy cap and a perfect tan.

Jared, pasty, chest still shaved and zipper angry red against white skin, stood silently by and slavered, not daring to say or do anything. What good, he despaired, is a body violated by scalpel before it's healed? Why didn't he have the nut-brown tan and paratrooper physique of those curly-haired Israelis who hung out in the disco cave nightly, their dark skin set off by white shirts open to the navel, necks heavy with gold chains on which hung heavy-wrought chai's. Jared was certain American women came to be seduced, debauched, discovered inch-by-inch by these uniformly handsome men in lounge-lizard uniforms; knew Israeli men had a reputation to be envied, so far as women go. So no-nonsense, almost brusque, in their casual approach, their "You're terrific-looking—want to make love?" attack.

In a way he was relieved to be out of action in the battle for women's bodies, secure in a post-surgical belief that, if called upon for God and Orgasm, he'd fail unfailingly while his Israeli counterparts would perform with the pneumatic reliability of jackhammers.

So he watched, a baseball cap covering his hungry eyes and boxer bathing trunks his wilted libido, as Adrian lay face down at poolside, a sweating glass of Tab with ice and lemon just beyond her fingers' reach. He would pick her up in his binoculars practicing her backhand volley on the tennis courts that abutted the narrow, rocky beach. He would show up in the dining room at seven A.M. and sit till nine, pretending to nurse *decaffiné au lait* and read John le Carré but actually waiting in ambush for Adrian to show. When she did, breakfast usually consisted of orange juice, cereal, milk and four admirers.

It went on that way for almost a full week. Then, one morning as he spied on her as she had an eleven o'clock coffee in the bar with Ari, or Eli, or Ori, or Uri, he overheard her say she'd be leaving on a Sinai trip the next morning (but she'd be back and yes, she'd love to play mixed doubles when she was).

Impulsively, he launched himself toward the concierge's desk.

"There's a Sinai safari leaving tomorrow?"

"There is, Mr. Gordon. It's three days in length, run by the Friends of Nature."

"Can I get a reservation?"

"Let me see." The concierge, Leora, scratched her hairline with a pencil and consulted a dog-eared pad. "There's room for one more," she said.

He sighed. Thank God.

Leora dug into a desk drawer crammed with brochures. "Here's what you need to know," she said, handing him a four-color spread. "One thing—take warm clothing for the night. And oh, yes—take a hat."

"I will, I will. And ask the desk not to throw me out of my room—I'll keep it while I'm gone."

The van came at eight. Adrian, three lusty Swedes, a bush-hatted Australian agronomist who wanted to see the Israeli outback, and an American Jewish prince bedecked in freshly pressed Ralph Lauren safari gear waited impatiently in the shade outside the Laromme's lobby. Jared, reticent, sat inside. When it pulled up he charged through the doors, elbowed his way in first and sat in back, baseball cap covering his face, knapsack on his lap.

Adrian sat next to the driver and made small talk, bantering about someone named Rafi Nelson who owned his own Bedouin resort village in Taba, just south of Eilat. She'd been there once, she said, and met Kirk Douglas. Beneath his long-brimmed cap Jared smiled inwardly. Spartacus in a Bedouin village. Will wonders never cease? Next year she'd probably get to see Charlton Heston, visiting the real-life sites of *The Ten Commandments.*

They drove south along the blacktop, two-lane, coastal road, staring at the multicolored sea to the left and jagged ancient Sinai peaks on the right. The van was not air-conditioned and, windows down, hot air blew in and Jared was glad to have brought oversized sunglasses. From time to time Bedouin encampments could be seen from the road. When they appeared, the prince invariably brought his spanking new Nikon up and snap-snap-snapped away, although how dramatic a three-by-five-inch print of a bunch of black-robed Bedouins, shot at five hundred yards without a telephoto lens, would look in a scrapbook, Jared wasn't altogether sure.

At Dahab, halfway between Eilat and Ras Muhammed, the group transferred to a decrepit, rusting, four-wheel drive army surplus command car that once had been painted white. In the rear were all the supplies for the three-day trip, right down to wood for cooking fires, extra axles, tires, jerry-cans of diesel fuel, sleeping bags and plastic water-barrels. It had creature comforts, too—for spartans: hard bench seats, wooden railings, and hand-holds. The guide, a bronzed fifty-year-old in shorts, sandals, kibbutz cap and a T-shirt from UCLA, mounted next to the driver, introduced himself as Motta, and explained the schedule. They'd be moving inland, going cross-country through wadis and up foothills, stay near an Israeli Defense Force outpost the first night, then move south toward the Monastery of Saint Catherine. The group would camp at the base of the mountain the second night, and make the climb to the monastery at dawn on the third day. Then it would be back to the coastal highway, and Eilat.

Jared's zipper did not enjoy the beating it took in the command car once it left the road and started to climb into the foothills. He thought he'd be sick three of four times during the first half hour, and he sat silent, holding himself in discomfort, as the rest of the group whooped each time the command car took another bone-shattering hit. Then an amazing thing happened: the power of Sinai took over and, except for grating gears and churning wheels, the command car fell silent.

There was, Jared discovered, a purity to Sinai, a starkness, that could not easily be described. Surely it was a place of purification; and he began to see why Moses led the people of Israel into Sinai three thousand years before to harden them for their travails in the Promised Land. He found the absolute intenseness overpowering. The mountains, monochromatic at a distance, came alive at close range, their colors a spectrum going from tan to ochre to rich and regal purple. There was virtually no talk from anyone as the command car jolted and jounced up what Motta said was the Wadi Lig, and the Wadi Humr, until the driver coaxed it, wheezing and steaming, halfway up Gebel el Thabt, a mountain Motta described as third highest in Sinai.

It was there, with capers growing out of the rock and wild peppermint sparse among the scarce soil, they would camp for the night.

And it was there Jared finally spoke to Adrian.

She was engaged in animated conversation with one of the Swedes, a muscular blond with shoulder-length hair tied into a ponytail.

Jared caught her eye and approached. "Adrian?"

She paused and turned. "Yes?"

"Jared Paul Gordon."

"Yes?"

"Jared Paul Gordon—from Washington."

"Have we met?"

He was devastated. "Yes—" He stopped abruptly as she turned away. Motta was speaking Hebrew to her. She answered him, then looked back at Jared. "I'm sorry. You were saying?"

"I write for *World Week*. We met at Sue Bernstein's house about two years ago. You were with Udi Rafieh, the air attaché."

She looked at him vacantly. "I'm sorry. I don't remember."

"We talked about my being too parochial. You were wearing a Cossack tunic and—"

He could see her mental Rolodex spinning. "Sue Bernstein's friend?"

"Yes."

Her eyes brightened. "Of course, of course. I'm sorry—Jared, right? You were new in Washington?"

He nodded. "And you were the native. The indigenous Washingtonian."

"Still using ten-dollar words."

"And you still spell your name like a man."

"I do. What are you doing here of all places?"

"Same thing you are, I guess. Trekking through Sinai."

She smiled her wonderful smile. "How are you?"

"Terrific," he lied. "And you?"

"Terrific too."

"That's—terrific." He laughed self-consciously. "It's been interesting so far."

"Yes. The command car could use a new set of springs."

He nodded. "Did I hear you say you met Kirk Douglas in Eilat?"

"Uh-huh."

"So this isn't the first time you've been to Sinai."

"Actually it is. I've been living in Jerusalem for the past year, and I come down to Laromme about every two months to relax. But I've never taken one of these safaris before."

"No?"

"And, well, you know—the Israelis are going to have to give all of this back soon, what with the peace treaty and all, and I thought I'd better see it while I could."

"Sure.

"It won't be the same when the Egyptians have it back."

"Probably not."

"Well," she said, "it's nice seeing you here. A face from home, I mean."

"Thanks. It's good to see you, too."

She gave him a quick once-over. "You've lost weight. And you're pale."

"Too many hours at the White House."

"That's right—that's right. You're a White House correspondent."

"You know how it is. All work and no play."

"But it must be interesting."

"From time to time. Mostly it's drudgery. Deadlines."

"I see." She paused, wrung out of small talk. "It's much hotter than I expected," Adrian finally said. She'd developed a ring of perspiration around the neck of her T-shirt, on which was printed the logo of The Voice of Peace, a pirate radio station that broadcast rock and roll from a boat in the Mediterranean. "I wish I had a beer."

"Me too. I'll get us some."

"They didn't bring any."

"They didn't?"

She shook her head. "I already asked."

Jared thought for an instant. "Let me see what I can do."

"But where—?"

"Hey, reporters are resourceful." Jared strode toward a path leading down the mountainside. "I'll be back."

She watched him lope off, then turned back to the other campers. One of the Swedes was standing on his hands. The prince was taking pictures. Motta was calling. She waved at him but didn't go over. What she wanted was to be alone, to stare at the purple mountain range and clear sky. She picked a sprig of wild peppermint from a crevice, crushed it between her fingers and inhaled deeply.

"What's happening?" It was Motta.

"Nothing."

"Don't be by yourself. Come, help bring the wood for a fire." He put his arm around her shoulder, oblivious to her sudden stiffening.

She extricated herself. "Please—"

"Okay, okay. I just thought you'd like some company."

"Not now, Motta. Now I want to think." She put the peppermint to her nose. "I just want to think."

Jared scampered down the mountain, following a gravel snake-path that twisted precariously, until he came to the IDF encampment he'd seen as the command car trucked up to the campsite. Even to his unpracticed eye these were not reservists but regular army. And he'd been to enough bases to know that regular army likes its beer.

"Hi," he called to a tall, curly-haired, sand-encrusted non-com who looked up as Jared came upon his jeep.

The Israeli returned the greeting in broken English. "Shalom. You lost?"

"No. I'm with the safari tour up the mountain."

The soldier looked puzzled. "Safari?"

"The tour. Sinai. Santa Catharina."

"Ah—tour. You need something?"

"Do I ever." Jared explained his problem in pidgin Hebrew: "*Havera shelli* —my friend—*rotza beera*—wants beer. *Havera* is—" he made an hourglass with his hands and licked his lips.

"*Hatti-ha!*" the non-com said, twinkling gray eyes smiling. His face was like a raccoon's, a mask of dark skin where his goggles had been and thick beard matted with sand.

"What?"

"*Hatti-ha*—real piece ass," the soldier laughed.

Jared nodded enthusiastically.

"You want beera, and *hatti-ha,* she—" He slung his automatic rifle over a shoulder, made a fist, bent his arm, and gave the universal sign for screwing.

Jared nodded again.

"Good—screw. I help you," he said, walking around to a tent and beckoning Jared to follow. Inside was a huge cooler, in which sat at least a case of Gold Star beer on ice. He looked at the American's pale face, sweaty, unfit body and pointed to a canvas stool. "Sun hot today, yes? Sit. We drink coffee, then you go screw."

Twenty minutes later Jared received a canvas bucket, six cans of beer, and ten kilos of ice. Struggling under the weight, he trudged back up the mountain, cursing his health and Adrian's thirst as he clutched his precious cargo in a clumsy, two-handed grip. The walk down had taken just under half an hour. The climb took him more than twice the time to make the two kilometers.

He arrived sweating and breathless at the campsite to find the group had already begun to eat an early dinner: sandwiches of fried falafel, sliced tomatoes, hunks of cheese and weak instant coffee.

"Hey, what about some dinner for me?" He lugged the bucket toward Adrian.

Without asking, the prince reached for a beer.

"Hey," said Jared. "It's for Adrian."

She saw the bucket and clapped her hands. "My God—you did it!" Her eyes lit up. "How? Where?"

"Professional secret."

She looked at him. "You're a wreck. Here—I'll take care of this. You go dry off. I'll get us some dinner."

Soon they sat away from the group, sipping their hoard of cold beer, eating and talking like old friends. Jared, his head light from his exercise and the beer, began to open up. In a rush of words he told her about the ulcer operation, about Yoram's suggestion to visit Israel, and the need to heal himself.

"Should you be drinking beer?" Adrian asked.

He sipped cautiously. "It doesn't seem to affect me now."

By the time they looked up, it was growing dark. The ridges above were enveloped in shadows that made their rocky starkness menacing. "Can you believe it?" Adrian asked. "Can you believe we're here? Tomorrow we'll see the place where we received the Ten Commandments." Thirty feet away, Motta had built a fire and was leading the campers in song. "It really makes you think," Adrian said.

"About what?"

"About life, and death, and absolutes like God. I mean, we're following in Moses' footsteps. The Sinai hasn't changed since we used to call God Yahweh—the Unnameable Name. There's something universal here. Call it what you will—primeval, commonality of experience, roots. I think you were right to come to Israel, Jared. This is a place where you can be healed."

"How do you know?"

"I know."

They talked some more after that, although the beer started to affect Jared's brain and he never remembered exactly what was said. Somehow, they ended up in sleeping bags side by side, away from the group. Jared slipped into his and watched Adrian as she climbed into hers.

They lay on their backs side by side and watched stars. There was a meteor shower.

Jared nudged Adrian's shoulder. "Look."

She sat up. "What?"

"Just there—" He pointed and aligned her body to his arm. "Meteors—shooting stars. See?"

She nodded.

"Make a wish."

Adrian closed her eyes. She hugged her knees and pointed her face to the stars.

She sat like that for some time, Jared, silent, watching her in the starlight. When she turned toward him there were tears in her eyes and he reached for her. "What is it?"

She pulled away. "Nothing."

"Come on."

She shook her head. "I—"

"Adrian?"

One huge tear rolled down her cheek. Jared struggled out of his

sleeping bag and pulled at his pocket until he retrieved a handkerchief. "Here."

She took it and buried her face in it. Her shoulders heaved.

He moved close, concerned, uncertain, but also fortified by beer. He wrapped an arm around her shoulders. She flinched but did not resist. "Look—what is it? What could be so bad?"

Face still concealed, she mumbled something unintelligible and struggled out of his grasp, burrowing back into her sleeping bag. It was a big sleeping bag and he followed her.

She turned and hit him with her fists. "Get out of here—get out!"

"Adrian—"

"I'm not—I don't—I can't—I—"

He shook her shoulders. "I'm not about to rape you, you know—Christ, I'm not sure that I could. I just want to help."

She pawed at her eyes with the handkerchief and looked him in the face, then calmed down and dry-heave hiccupped. "I haven't been like this with a man in—" Then she started to cry again.

He held her by her shoulders and her forehead dropped onto his chest. His shirt was wet with her tears and he held her, uncomprehending about what had set her off. After some moments the tears passed and the hiccups started again. She shifted in the sleeping bag, turned her back toward him. In a little girl's voice she said, "We all have zippers, Jared."

"You mean nobody's perfect?"

"I mean, what do you know about me?"

"That you're Adrian who spells her name like a man. That you're here, in Sinai. That you have lots of admirers and you like cold beer."

"Don't be flippant. What do you really *know* about me?"

He thought. "Not much."

She turned again. He put an arm out and cradled her head. "I hurt, too," she said. "I'm not whole, either, Jared."

She reached under his shirt and traced his scar. He flinched. She withdrew her hand. He rubbed at her back, hand moving quickly over her bra strap. "What is it? Tell me, please." He wanted very much to kiss her.

As if she read his thoughts she put a finger against his lips. "I'm not ready."

"Trust me." He kissed the finger.

"Would you understand? Could you?"

"What?"

He reached down and kissed her softly on the lips.

"Please, Jared." But she responded and kissed him back. They kissed again, their lips parting and tongues and teeth meeting. Aroused, he traced her back and sides, and was moving his hand over the top of her shoulder when she shook herself free. "No." Fighting herself and him, she turned her back again. "I—"

He kissed the nape of her neck, lifting her hair and touching her softly.

"Tell me. Talk to me."

A shudder ran through her body. He snuggled close, two spoons in a silvercloth. "Last year," she said. "Last year I—I had a breast removed."

He wilted.

Perfect Adrian. Not-so-perfect Adrian. "And?"

She'd felt his body react. "A lump, a biopsy, a tumor—two days later a mastectomy. And—"

He lay silent, listening to her breathing.

"It's hard now. Reconstructive surgery be damned, it's just not the same—it's, it's not being—it's being not whole."

"I know that feeling too."

Adrian said, "I was so numb. I couldn't face my parents or my friends. Nothing mattered. There wasn't anything for me to do in Washington, really. So I came to Israel to heal, just as you did. I holed up in Jerusalem. I sat in my house and cried for three months. It was like being on a retreat in the middle of all those holy sites. I saw nobody. When I did it was always in their eyes—'the mutilated one.' I didn't want pity, Jared."

"What did you do?"

"Nothing. Took long, solitary walks. Had a very short, very unsatisfying affair with a married man who managed to be looking the other way whenever I took my clothes off. That was six months ago. Since then—since then I've been on my own."

"And you came here, to Sinai—"

"I'm not sure why. Maybe it's time to end the numb retreat and get back into the world. Maybe I thought I'd be healed by the desert sun—Moses' chemotherapy." She took Jared's hand in hers and brought it to her lips. "Miracles happen in this desert—you found beer."

He laughed. "You're all right now, though."

"You mean malignancy? I'm fine. But I thought Sinai might heal my soul and—"

"And?"

"Maybe I'd find somebody to heal my body. Except once I got here I couldn't do that. Couldn't deal with sex—a man—in that way. Not yet."

Words spilled out of him. He told her how she'd looked—at the pool, the tennis courts, at breakfast. About his private lusts, his spying, his two-year-old fantasies.

"I want to hold you," he said. "Maybe Sinai can cure us both. It's time to recuperate, Adrian who spells her name like a man."

"Maybe." She used Jared's hand to wipe a tear from her cheek. Then she snuggled down in the down bag and they slept, the fronts of his knees touching the backs of hers.

It was the first night's sleep he'd had without Demerol in more than a month.

A bump. A hand on shoulder. "Jared, we're here."

Jared shook himself awake, stiff kneed and crook-necked. He was suddenly cold. The chopper doors were already open, and Yoram, Yom Tov and Koby were unloading weapons and equipment into a pair of Peugeot sedans that were parked without lights on the smooth, black surface of what looked like a highway.

"Where are we?" Jared whispered to Yoram, who answered in full voice.

"About twelve kilometers from a town called Jdaidet Aartouz," he said. "From here we go by car."

Working efficiently, they stowed the gear; Yoram's squad climbed into the Peugeots, which were driven by a pair of men dressed in Syrian army uniforms. As they headed off into the darkness, Jared could barely hear the whump-whump-whump of the blacked-out choppers' muffled engines as they swept off into the darkness.

"Can you tell me what—where—"

"We're on our way to a highway that leads to a Palestinian camp. We're going to set up a roadblock."

"Why?"

"There's somebody we want to see."

Once clear of the helicopters, the drivers flicked on their low beams, and Jared could see the wadis, scrub brush and wild olive trees along the dusty road. Yoram checked his Soviet Army watch. "We're on time," he grunted. "Even a minute or two early—good."

They drove on in the darkness, although a hint of light was starting to seep over the foothills to the east, bringing the sky from black to midnight blue. All at once the driver swerved the car to the left, turning onto an unmarked dirt road. The Peugeot's suspension creaked under the weight of five bodies and the equipment as the car lurched forward in low gear.

After four kilometers the cars stopped. The men got out. Efficiently, they removed a spiked road barrier from the trunk of one of the cars and laid it across the narrow road. Two signs in Arabic were also removed, and set on pedestals twenty yards each direction from the barrier. The Peugeots were stationed facing back the way they'd come, at forty-five-degree angles to the spikes.

Yoram introduced the Syrians to Jared. "This is Arik and Arik," he said, using the nickname of Defense Minister Ariel Sharon. "They're our ground support staff."

"Mossad?"

Yoram's look confirmed Jared's suspicion.

Jared watched at the squad set up its roadblock. The two Kobys lounged on the trunks of the Peugeots, cocked automatic rifles strung around their necks. Ze'ev sat in the front seat of one of the cars, smoking a cigarette. Yom Tov squinted at his Arabic novel, and Amos had taken one of the bogus Syrians off into the scrub for a private chat. He looked at his watch: six-sixteen. The Israelis waited. Jared found himself starting to sweat, despite the cold.

"If something happens," said Yoram, "I want you to stand behind here"—he tapped the roof of the nearest Peugeot. "If there's shooting, drop—hit the deck at once."

Jared nodded. "Do you expect shooting?"

"You never know what to expect."

Jared felt the need to relieve himself. He started off into the half-light, but Yoram stopped him.

"Not now. There's a car coming. Get to your position."

Jared hadn't seen it, but when he looked, there it was. A small Datsun sedan with only its running lights on was bouncing down the rutted track.

They came alive, but subtly: rifles were not pointed at the approaching car; bodies hadn't tensed. But there was a sense, Jared felt, almost a scent, of the danger. He could smell it on himself.

The car slowed. Now Jared could see that it held three, no, four passengers. It wheezed slowly up to the barricade. Dented and old, its front fender was held on by baling wire, the rearview mirror on the passenger's side snapped off, and stripes of rust where the sidetrim used to be. From his vantage point behind the Peugeot, Jared could see the passengers' faces. There was an older man with a bristly gray mustache in front, next to a driver who couldn't have been more than sixteen. In the back seat were another youngster, perhaps twelve or so, and a middle-aged, plumpish woman who held a parcel—no, an infant—close to her bosom.

Yoram ambled up to the passenger window. "Good morning," he said in unaccented Arabic. "Can I see your papers, please?"

Yom Tov wandered to the far side of the car and looked inside, spitting sunflower seeds as both Arabs and Israelis are wont to do. The Arabic novel jutted out of the breast pocket of his short leather jacket.

Kobys One and Two still lounged on the trunk of the far Peugeot, seemingly taking no notice of the new arrivals. Ze'ev had disappeared.

The man with the bushy mustache handed Yoram a wallet sized identity card. Yoram suddenly snapped to attention. "I'm sorry, sir, for having to ask," he sputtered, "but orders—"

The man inside nodded amiably and held his hand out to receive the identity card back. Instead, Yoram's right hand slipped to the holster on his belt, withdrew the machine pistol, and shot the man full in the face. The shot blew his head apart, and the inside of the far window was suddenly covered with blood. Yoram rolled away from the car. Simultaneously, Yom Tov's AK-47 raked the car from the far side, the two Kobys opened fire at the windshield, and Yoram threw himself back toward the Peugeots.

The inside of the car seemed to implode. Fragments of glass showered the trapped passengers. Calmly, Yom Tov expended his first clip, dropped it into his belt, slammed a new one into the AK-47 and fired short bursts point blank. Yoram and the two Kobys moved quickly behind the Peugeots, as did Yom Tov, who backed away while firing into the car. Then Ze'ev came out of nowhere and ran past the Datsun, flipping something through the shattered windows as he sprinted by. He vaulted the Peugeot and dropped wheezing to the ground.

"Down, goddammit," Yoram shouted—and shoved Jared roughly.

"What—"

The Datsun exploded. Ze'ev's concussion grenade blew its roof off and the gas tank went up, creating an inferno.

Yoram shouted "Let's go!" He threw Jared bodily into the back of the Peugeot and followed himself. Simultaneously, the Syrians started engines, and everyone jumped into the cars, which peeled into the dirt, fishtailed onto the narrow road, and headed back the way they'd come. As they raced off, Jared looked back to see what was left of the Datsun. There was nothing left. He felt sick to his stomach.

The Syrians drove like madmen. Minutes later they were on the highway. Another two minutes and the cars screeched to a halt, their way blocked by the two Bell 212s. Yoram clapped the Mossad driver on the shoulder. "*Todah rabbah*—thanks a lot," he said. "Stay alive. I'll see you in Jerusalem, God willing."

"Your lips to God's ears," said the Syrian, shouting over the chopper rotors.

They threw their equipment aboard and lifted off, skimming the harsh Syrian hills at tree-top level. Yoram slid the hatchway closed, locked it securely and gave the pilot a thumbs-up sign. He wasn't even breathing hard. He snatched a pair of headsets from their cradles, put one on and handed the other to Jared. Smiling, he retrieved the identity card he'd demanded from the Palestinian and showed it to Jared. "Abu Zain," he said, "Arafat's number three. More important, his secret conduit to Abu Nidal and Black June."

"He never had a chance," said Jared.

"What the hell did you want me to do, ask his permission?"

"It was assassination."

"It was military retribution. Abu Zain paid Black June from Fatah's operational funds to assassinate our ambassador to London. We even know how he went to England to oversee the operation. He used a Kuwaiti diplomatic passport to get there. We have the number—we saw the stamps and visa."

They were lifting higher now. The sun poked into the chopper's interior. Yom Tov was engrossed in his Arab novel again. Koby One lit a Lebanese cigarette, crushed it out between his fingers, and prodded the crew chief's shoulder. "Enough of this crap," he said. "Give me a real smoke." The airman nodded toward the uppermost left breast pocket of his unmarked gray multizippered jumpsuit, and Koby One retrieved a pack of Marlboros. He lit one, inhaled deeply and sighed.

"Who else was in the car?"

"His wife, his sons, a driver."

"You killed them, too."

"It had to be."

"It wasn't fair to kill the others."

"Don't be naïve. I swear, you Americans never learn. Because a man comes at you with a knife, you think you should fight him with a knife. You think it's unfair to shoot him. Fair has nothing to do with it—it's war."

Jared sat silent.

"What was I supposed to do? Ask him nicely to step outside and fight like a man? Let everyone else go? Leave witnesses?"

"It was murder."

"What do you expect? To be nice and kind all the time? To be the old-style Jews who were led by their beards to be killed? Bullshit, Jared. I want the Palestinians, the Syrians, the Iraqis, the Iranians to know we can reach them wherever they are—in their bedrooms, on their doorsteps, even on some *forshtunken* road in Syria. I even want them to know we can be as brutal as they. They respect that. For years they took advantage of us—they knew they could blow up our children, kill our women, shell our settlements, and that we'd suffer the attacks before retaliating—to keep Israel's good name, if you will. And when we did retaliate, we'd do it surgically. We lost men, Jared, lost good men protecting Palestinian lives—the lives of terrorists' wives and children. This is war, Jared, war—and you don't always wage war by the Queensberry rules."

"But it wasn't fair. You didn't give him a chance. No matter what he's done he deserved a chance."

Yoram shook his head. "Such a moralist. You're going back to our old philosophers—like Maimonides, who said that if a Jewish army encircles an enemy it must leave them a way out, and not force them to engage in what will be a futile combat. That's a beautiful thought, but it's not realistic. It's a thought bred of the ghetto. It's the musings of philosophers—not guys like me." He lit a cigarette and turned away, staring out the chopper window.

"This wasn't exactly fun for any of us. The fact is, we didn't know he'd be traveling with his wife and kids this morning. We're not perfect, Jared. And I'm not going to justify myself to you—we don't do these things lightly." Then he turned and tapped Jared on the shoulder. "Don't sulk," he said. "You have a terrific story."

"I thought you said I couldn't write about what happened."

"You can write," said Yoram. " 'Dateline, Jerusalem. A senior aide to PLO Chairman Yasser Arafat was killed today by Moslem gunmen thought to be members of a dissident Palestinian faction as he left the Chamoura camp near Damascus, according to Israeli intelligence sources.' I'll be happy to give you all the details you need about Abu Zain. Your magazine will love the story."

"It's a lie."

"Sometimes lies are the best truth."

Yoram peered through the chopper's windshield. "Look," he said, "the Kinneret—the Sea of Galilee. We're home."

Incredibly, Yoram began to hum "Le Shana Haba'a." Yom Tov and Koby One joined him.

Jared knew the song but now the words caught in his throat. The song, he realized—as if he were now hearing it for the first time—was about peace. About children playing with flowers. About sitting in gardens. The commandos sang, their voices strong but reedy through the earphones.

Listening to them, Jared felt emotionally poleaxed; betrayed, as if he had become an accomplice in something so immense, so dark, so heinous, that no showers in the King David's luxurious tile bathrooms would ever rinse him clean again.

CHAPTER 3

The intercom buzzed. Jared ignored it. He'd kept to himself on the long drive back, slouching in the front seat of Yoram's black Dodge while the driver raced through the early-morning traffic and Yoram slept stretched out and snoring in the back. Jared, too, wanted to sleep; he'd been totally exhausted by his experience, yet he found it impossible to close his eyes. Every time he did he saw the Datsun explode; saw Abu Zain's wife and children incinerated. So while the car slalomed around trucks, buses and cars he'd sat up, peering vacantly out the window. The driver, an omnipresent Time cigarette clenched between his teeth, exhaled plumes of smoke through his nose and cursed under his breath at everyone else on the road. From the parking lot of the Jerusalem Hilton Jared drove straight to *World Week*'s bureau, where he waved at the receptionist, declined coffee and conversation, and went straight to his office.

The bureau was in a residential block near Rehavia, a ten-minute walk from Adrian's house. The neighborhood was filled for the most part with the elderly, middle-class Jews of German or Polish ancestry who'd bought their flats when they were in their thirties, the Israeli pound was four to the dollar and inflation was two percent. Now the old pound had been converted into shekels at ten to one, there were fifty-seven shekels to the dollar—570 pounds, and the comfortable but by no means opulent flats that a decade before had cost the equivalent of $7,500 now sold for $80,000—in dollars only.

Once a five-room apartment, the bureau contained four offices—

one for Jared and others for the photographer, Nafta Bar Zohar, the Arab stringer Rafi Taal, who covered the West Bank, plus a spare for visitors. There was a small wire room, in which sat the telex, the computer terminal linking Jerusalem with the home office, the UPI and AP world wires, and AP's Middle East wire. There was a kitchen that held a small butane stove and half-size refrigerator. Three cots were stacked in the corner of the kitchen. They were used when the bureau was manned around the clock, as it had been during the first two months of the Lebanese invasion, and the magazine had sent in five additional correspondents and three photographers.

The living room had been made into a reception area for the bureau's two secretaries, Annie, a Danish Jew who had emigrated to Palestine as a five-year-old orphan just after the Second World War, and Rahael, a stunning, red-haired sabra of twenty-three whom Jared sometimes kidded about being a plant from the Shin Bet, Israel's domestic-security agency. Half a dozen locked file cabinets sat in one corner. The walls were lined with magazine covers chronicling the history of the Middle East, as seen through the magazine's coverage.

Jared's office, the largest, was sparsely furnished: a metal desk with three locked drawers and armless secretary's chair, faced by two Danish modern armchairs; a ratty, frayed copper-colored couch and slatted wood coffee table framed by a pair of decrepit end tables on which sat a lamp and Jared's twenty-year-old electric typewriter. On the wheeled typing table by his desk was a portable Kaypro computer. Behind his desk were three two-drawer file cabinets, across the top of which Jared had laid a series of varnished boards to make a credenza.

The walls of Jared's office were what gave the room its personality. Huge maps of Israel and the Middle East took up one of them; the others were hung with black-and-white and color photographs that had illustrated his articles: the destruction of West Beirut by Israel's air force and artillery; the bloody aftermath of a terrorist attack on a kibbutz nursery; West Bank riots; antiwar demonstrations; dust-filtered shots of armor columns moving north into Lebanon; pretty army girls in short skirts and braided hair; a panorama of Jerusalem in a spring sunset. And other, more staged pictures: Jared interviewing the Prime Minister; Jared with the Defense Minister and chief of staff; Jared and Yoram at Israeli Independence Day ceremonies at the military cemetery on Mount Herzl; a framed picture of the U.S. Ambassador, warmly inscribed; and several shots of Jared, in combat gear, covering the war in Lebanon.

And Adrian. More than a dozen photographs of Adrian, close-cropped portraits and wide-angle shots. Adrian standing windswept near Gamla, on the Golan Heights, where more Jewish Zealots committed suicide than at Masada. Adrian proudly holding two huge bunches of Sultanina grapes in a field near Binyamina. Adrian, framed by the Jerusalem stone of David's Tower in the Old City, her face radiant in a midday smile.

The wall of pictures was both a chronicle of his relationship to and history of his involvement with the country. Documentation of the place's richness and vitality hung framed and juxtaposed with the stark grittiness of the nation's day-to-day reality. There was something about the pictures that was definitive, merciless. Unlike the fleeting images captured by television news cameras, the photographs froze time.

Now Jared sat in his office, his chair pushed back and his feet on the desk, letting the intercom buzz in its annoying tone. Arms folded behind his head, he watched Adrian hold the grapes.

Annie tapped on the hollow wood door. "Jared?"

He sat silent. She rapped again, more insistently this time. "Jared? Adrian is on line two."

"I'll call her back."

Annie cracked the door open and stuck her narrow, high-cheeked face inside. "You two didn't have a fight?"

"No. I just want to think for a minute. Tell her I'm on another line and I'll get back to her."

The secretary nodded. "And New York telexed a query while you were out. They're scheduling a sidebar on Christmas in the Holy Land, and Bill Johanssen wants a story memo from you."

Jared nodded and made a notation on a legal pad. "You'll have it by close of business today, slavedriver," he said, cracking a smile in spite of himself.

Annie nodded. "Good." She paused and peered at him over half-frame glasses. "You look terrible. Coming down with something?"

"Maybe. I don't know. Look—tell Adrian I'll be back to her. No. Better idea: tell her I'll take her to lunch. One o'clock at Venetzia." Jared ended the conversation by swiveling toward the computer. He heard the door click shut and switched the machine on, rummaged in the floppy disk flip file that sat on his makeshift credenza, and found a fresh, formatted disk. He slipped it into the bottom drive and keyed in his word processing program. When it came up, he began typing, his fingers flying.

"On a narrow dirt road near Jdaidet Aartouz," he wrote. He stood up, walked to his map of Syria and measured the distance with a tape pinned to the wall. Then he crossed back to the computer and started tapping again: "roughly seventeen kilometers southwest of the Syrian capital of Damascus, two automobiles driven by operatives of Mossad, Israel's intelligence service, picked up a five-man Israeli assassination squad headed by a veteran senior officer—" Jared swallowed hard. He felt sweat trickling from his underarms. He continued, "Brigadier General Yoram Gal, a former assistant military attaché posted to Washington from 1977 to 1981.

"The hit team, dressed in clothes of Arab manufacture and armed with Soviet-made weapons and ammunition, had been flown to Syria from Ramat David airbase in central Israel by two American-made Bell-212 helicopters. Its target was Chafik Aziz, *nom de guerre* Abu Zain, the third-highest-ranking officer in Fatah, the largest armed group in the Palestine Liberation Organization headed by Yasser Arafat.

"Abu Zain, his wife, two sons and a PLO driver ⟨NAMES TO KOME⟩ were killed when they were stopped by the Israelis at a counterfeit security checkpoint near the Chamoura refugee camp."

Jared hunched over the keyboard, writing quickly, filling in details as he remembered them. When he finished he ejected the disk and pulled a label from his desk drawer. He wrote "Travel Story/Summer Tourism Issue" on it, pressed it down on the disk he'd made, then taped the diskette in its cover carefully between the dust jacket and back cover of a picture book about Jerusalem that sat on his makeshift credenza. From his flip file, Jared plucked another diskette, this one labeled Story Memos. He booted it and pulled a manila file from his bottom desk drawer. Poring over the file, he underlined certain lines on pages of yellow legal paper and then started typing again.

An hour later he walked into the reception area and handed the disk to Annie. "Here's your memo for New York."

"You're productive this morning—and I thought you didn't look very well."

"The deadline kid strikes again," Jared said. "It's the last file on the disk—I slugged it 'Three Kings.' "

She waved it at him. "I'll send it this afternoon. You going to lunch now?"

Jared checked his watch. "Yeah. If you need me I'll be on the PR." He walked over to a shelf under the front window and pulled on a walkie-talkie whose base was plugged into a recharging mechanism. "Or you can call me at Venetzia. But not if you have anything important to say."

"You still think his phone's tapped?"

"Sure. All those *Time* guys go there with their sources. I wouldn't be surprised if the Shin Bet's run a wire into the restaurant itself." He looked at Annie and smiled. "I wouldn't be surprised if Rahael hasn't run a wire into this place. Where the hell is she, anyhow?"

"*Meluim,*" said Annie. "Reserve duty. She's up at that transportation base near Bet Ziev filling out forms in triplicate."

"Isn't that where Zahal"—Jared used the acronym for the Israeli Defense Forces—"loads the blue trucks?" Blue trucks were the trucks sent to Fady Frem's Forces Lebanese, the Phalangist militia. They bore no identifying marks except for the fact that they were painted the same shade of blue as Israeli Naval Forces vehicles. They stood out on the road like sore thumbs, but officially they were "invisible": invisible to journalists, who were forbidden to mention them in dispatches, invisible to the UNFIL forces in South Lebanon, invisible to the Brits, French, Italian and U.S. Marines of the multinational force in Beirut, and even invisible to the Syrians and their Russian advisers, although Jared knew from his sources that Russians, Syrians, Brits, French, Italians and U.S. Marines were, in fact, counting each one.

Annie nodded. "Maybe she'll have some stories to tell when she gets back."

"I hope so." Jared waved as he walked through the door. He galumphed down three flights of stairs and out the back entrance to the building, unlocked the Autobianchi, threw the walkie-talkie onto the passenger's seat, backed the car rapidly into the alley, popped the clutch and fishtailed out toward King David Street, Mamilla and up the hill toward the restaurant.

Adrian was waiting for him, sitting with Mikki Venetzia in the rear of the empty restaurant, sipping a cup of espresso. The good days were long gone now for places like Venetzia, whose prices were as high as any top-flight restaurant in New York or Washington. So Mikki catered to journalists on expense accounts, politicians (for whom he discounted the bill by thirty percent), and American tourists who liked the pink linen, fresh flowers and succulent veal piccata and had no qualms about paying thirty to fifty dollars a head for those luxuries. But, being quiet, it was a good place to go and to talk. Jared often entertained sources there, sitting at a back table and taking notes as they spoke. It was also a special place for him to take Adrian. They had blundered into Venetzia when they'd come from Eilat three years before to be together in Jerusalem.

Mikki had watched them, then, from a distance, as they held hands, stared long, meaningful stares at each other and left half-full plates of his expensive food. He'd grown to know them by name in the five weeks that Jared and Adrian spent in Jerusalem before they went back to the States. And he remembered them when, some months later, they'd visited the restaurant and Jared said he'd been posted to Israel.

The chef's first words had been, "*Metsuyan*—excellent! Now you can open a charge account like the rest of the rich American journalists, and I can begin to make a profit."

"Hi. Sorry I'm late."

Venetzia's forehead wrinkled like a basset hound's as he spotted Jared and a wide smile crossed his face. "Hello, stranger. I was hoping you wouldn't show up and I'd get to have lunch with this one all by myself."

Jared laughed and placed the walkie-talkie on Venetzia's table. "No chance," he said. "Next thing I know you two would run off together and I'd be stuck feeding your in-laws." Mikki Venetzia's Moroccan in-laws were a subject of much hand-wringing. There were a lot of them, and the restaurant's slender profits supported them all. He bent over and kissed Adrian. "Hello, my *hatti-ha*."

Venetzia stood up. "Well, take a table." He laughed bitterly. "Any table you like. I'll get you something to snack on."

"And a bottle of wine," said Jared. "Carmel Chenin Blanc."

"What is this, a celebration?" Adrian prodded Jared's ribs. He was not known to drink wine at lunch.

"Of a sort. Come on, let's sit down." He walked to the rear of the restaurant and pulled back the corner table so that Adrian could sit against the wall. He sat facing her, and waited silently as Moshe, Venetzia's captain, waiter, sommelier and busboy all in one deposited plates of bread and butter, deep-fried Moroccan 'cigars' and chili-spiced, garlic-cured olives on the table, opened the crisp white wine with a flourish and poured without waiting for Jared to taste it.

Moshe withdrew and Jared hunched over the table and took Adrian's hands in his own. "So?" she said.

He looked over his shoulder. Mikki was standing at the small curved bar, talking on the telephone—probably to his broker. The only way anyone made ends meet these days was to speculate on the ballooning stock market or deal in black-market dollars.

"I'm in trouble," Jared said. "I broke a whole bunch of the magazine's rules this morning and I don't know what to do about it. I could be in big trouble."

ISAIAH 51:1

Ye that seek the LORD;
Look unto the rock whence ye were hewn . . .

They came back from Eilat together to Adrian's two-story stone house in Yemin Moshe, inseparable since their first night in Sinai. Just why they were so attracted to each other neither was able to explain. She was exactly the sort of woman Jared had been avoiding most of his adult life. He, in turn, was the personification of the uncommitted Jew, the sort of man she had always thought of as knee-jerk liberal. And yet, as they talked for hours about everything from their hospital experiences to gossip about mutual friends in the Washington Jewish community Jared had come to know, they found they had more in common than they might have thought.

Like their mutual passion for history. Jared had traveled with a woman only once before, and it had been a disaster. They had gone to France, where he wanted to visit museums, castles and cathedrals. She preferred restaurants, discos and nightclubs. Hand-in-hand with Adrian, he explored Jerusalem's historic streets and archaeological sites. He reveled in the fact that she could answer his questions. Those that she couldn't, she looked up in a Hebrew guide book.

Their third morning in Jerusalem she rented a car and, driving like a maniac, sped north through the West Bank, refusing to tell him where they were headed. He sat back and drank in the sights: stone terraces of olive trees and goats that ran free near Arab huts. She pointed out the pre-1967 border as they crossed it near Tulkarm. "See how green it is on the Israeli side?" she said. "That's because the Arabs never gave a damn about making the land work for them."

From Tulkarm she drove north, to Zichron Yaakov, where she pounded on the door of a low stone villa until her friend Koby Naiderman, still sleepy, answered the insistent knocking. He looked at Adrian pie-eyed, then grabbed her in a bear hug and planted kisses all over her face. Then they stood in the doorway and jabbered in Hebrew while Jared waited, feeling like a fool. Finally, Koby offered a big strong paw to Jared and clapped him on the back. "She says you know a lot of Israelis but nothing about the country," he laughed. "She says I should teach you—in one day everything."

And so they drove in Koby's pickup truck to his vineyard, where Jared tasted wine grapes straight from the vine for the first time in his life, and stubbed his foot on a large chunk of stone that, when unearthed, turned out to be a marble section of a Roman column. Hand in hand, they stood atop the bluffs just outside Zichron Yaakov and looked down on the coastal plain where fields of bananas, grapes, eggplant and zucchini stretched as far as the eye could see.

They drove through Zichron's narrow streets, stopping at the home of Yitzhak Naiderman, Koby's eighty-year-old uncle, who filled them with home-cured olives and spellbinding tales of the NILI spy ring, which provided the British with information on Ottoman troop movements during World War I. His cane beating a tattoo on the pavement, Yitzhak walked them up the street from his house and onto the town square. "There," he pointed with the stick, "there's the NILI house owned by Aaron Aaronsohn and his sister Sarah, whom the Turks tortured and raped but still she wouldn't speak." They visited the *yekkev*, the wine cellar built by Baron Edmond de Rothschild before the turn of the century, and in its cool, white-tile tasting room sipped samples of the current vintage, ate salty goat cheese and freshly made tehina dip on pieces of pita bread.

Before they left, Koby took Jared to see the workshed where he welded grape arbors. "You are good together," he said.

"I know."

"Take care of her," the farmer instructed. "She's special."

"I'll try. Right now, she's taking care of me more than I am her."

"Don't try—do. She needs to be with someone."

"But she's so—self-sufficient."

"She needs someone to be self-sufficient with." He rattled a case of tractor parts, rummaging for something. "You're the first man she's ever brought up here."

"I'm honored."

"You're welcome. Ah, here!" The farmer handed Jared an object in dusty cloth.

"What is it?"

"Look and see."

Jared peeled back the wrapping and discovered a piece of Roman mosaic, its tiles colored faded red and blue. "My God—"

"From my Carignan vineyard," Koby said. "For you."

"I can't. I couldn't—"

"Take it. You found a piece of column. This is your reward."

Jared was speechless. He ran back to the house, the treasure clasped like a football in two hands.

Later, in the car, the sun behind them, she said, "Koby likes you."

"Is that important?"

"Very. He's a basic man. To Koby things are black or white—and his instincts are impeccable."

"So today was kind of a test?"

"An audition."

"And I passed?"

"Look at your prize." She tapped the mosaic sitting on Jared's thigh.

"You're the real prize," he said.

They drove in silence for some time. He looked at her profile. "Why did you move here?" he asked.

"I needed somewhere to go. A refuge. Washington was so rootless, Jared. Especially after my divorce. It devastated my parents. Felix and Beverly think of marriage as inviolable. They've been married more than forty years. Then, after Allan and I separated—there was . . . nothing. I wasn't going to move back with them—couldn't face their sighs and all those silences at the dinner table." She paused thoughtfully. "It was an impulse, really. I took a plane, and six days later I bought my house."

"It's a wonderful house."

"I know."

"But not fancy."

"No." In fact, Jared had been surprised at the flea-market character of the place, considering its quarter-million-dollar cost. He'd imagined that Adrian would have had the place professionally decorated. But the house in Yemin Moshe was furnished simply, a mix of Biedermeier, Scandinavian and Turkish market. What made the place so valuable was its view: Mount Zion and the walls of the Old City. Otherwise, it was a house in need of renovation, its rooms cramped, plumbing cracked and insulation nonexistent. Jared's two-year-old fantasy was dashed as well. There were no Bloomingdale's sheets in the bedroom, only white linen and a simple double mattress on a metal frame.

They slept together covered by a wool blanket, touching but not intimate. There was, in fact, an unspoken reticence on both their parts about making love. Neither broached the subject. Jared, for his part, was uneasy about his physical condition. Adrian, too, hesitated because she feared rejection.

On the morning of their sixth day in Jerusalem Adrian took Jared to see the Western Wall for the first time. The sky was cloudless, the sun hot and bright as they walked hand in hand from Yemin Moshe, below the Old City walls and through the Dung Gate, entering a wide plaza that did not exist before the IDF captured the Old City in the Six-Day War.

Jared left her and walked past the stone and chain barriers, clapping a cardboard skull cap plucked from a bin of them onto his head. The old limestone retaining wall towered above him—huge, bleached stones that had originally supported the Temple Mount. Just a wall, he thought, with incongruous sprigs of vegetation creeping out in several places. The religious Jews were there, swaying in Orthodox ecstasy, wrapped in prayer shawls, phylacteries bound around their arms and heads.

He approached, stood next to it and looked up. His eyes caught the sun for an instant, and he was blinded. He touched the Wall for support, palms resting against palm-smoothed stones that somehow remained cool in the autumn heat. He saw spots, and turned to face the stones and rest his head against them. The crack in front of Jared's eyes—all the cracks, as high as could be reached—were crammed with wadded pieces of paper—notes of prayer and request left by thousands of pilgrims. He wanted with all his heart to say something profound, but could not find words.

He stole a look at the Orthodox Jews and, for an instant, envied them their ability to communicate in Hebrew with their God—his God.

His cheek resting against the cool stone, he stood for some time, murmuring over and over the only words of Hebrew prayer he knew—*Shema Yisrael, Adonai Eloheinu, Adonai Echad*—Hear, oh Israel, the Lord Our God, the Lord Is One.

Then he bagan to think—about himself, about Adrian, about the generations of Jews who had lived without being able to rest their cheeks against this Wall, against this pile of stones. He thought of his parents, born Jews, who celebrated Christmas and Easter and gave without thinking to the UJA. He thought of his upbringing, and how devoid of Jewishness it had been. How damnably ill-equipped he was to be in this place, the place Jews had prayed toward and died because of, throughout two thousand years of Diaspora. Jared stretched his arms wide and, touching as many stones as he could, pressed his face against the Wall. Uncontrollably, he began to weep.

A hand touched his shoulder. Jared wiped his eyes with his sleeve and looked up. A soldier in a cardboard skull cap, submachine gun slung over his shoulder, looked him in the eyes. "Okay?" he asked.

He wiped his eyes again and reached for a handkerchief, blew his nose, nodded. "I'm all right."

"Jewish? From America? First time here?"

"Yes."

The soldier was young and dark, and as Jared turned to look at him he saw a suitcase resting on the ground. "First time—me, too," the soldier said. "From kibbutz in the north. I not religious, but want to see. See this place, this history, understand?"

"I know. Me too."

"This place—special. I no religious, but here I pray. Here I pray for all Jews. Here we are all Jews together."

"Yes," Jared said. "Here we are all Jews together."

"You pray with me? You know words?"

"I don't," Jared said, feeling helpless, feeling like an outsider.

"Wait." The soldier turned and from one of the half-dozen Torah stands retrieved a book. "Here words. We read."

"I can't," Jared said, tears welling again. "I can't read Hebrew."

"It's okay—I read—you pray."

And so they stood, the soldier's arm around Jared's shoulder, their heads inclined toward the Wall, while the soldier read the words and Jared wept.

After some time Jared looked up, but the soldier was gone. That was strange: he'd felt the weight of the man's arm on his shoulder all along.

How long had he been standing there? Through his tears, the Wall and the plaza took on strange, flashing colors. He was dizzy and had trouble walking back to where Adrian stood.

"Are you all right?"

"Yes. How long was I there?"

"Half an hour or so."

"Where did the soldier go?"

"What soldier?"

"The one who prayed with me."

"I didn't see a soldier," said Adrian.

"Were you watching the whole time?"

"I think so."

Jared shook his head. "Put it down to a mystical experience."

"That's been known to happen here."

"Even to journalists like me?"

She kissed him on the lips; an outraged passing Hasid clucked loudly and disapprovingly. She laughed. "Especially to journalists like you."

That night, Adrian and Jared made love.

His recovery progressed, as did their relationship. By early October, they started to make plans. His medical leave was ending, and they decided to return to Washington together.

During Jared's convalescence he visited *World Week*'s Jerusalem bureau on an irregular basis. Not out of necessity so much as habit; leave or no leave he was still a journalist, still felt a compulsion to report what he saw and heard. So he filed occasional memos to Roger Richards, *World Week*'s Chief of Correspondents; gossipy monologues that chronicled conversations he'd heard at the lunches and dinners he and Adrian shared with Israelis. Snippets from a party at the home of Teddy Kollek, Jerusalem's energetic ebullient mayor. One-liners from the cocktail hour they shared with Meron Benveniste, who was working on a study detailing how life on the West Bank had changed after 1967. Political musings from dinner with the Speaker of the Knesset. A lecture on Zionist philosophy culled during tea with Aliza and Menachem Begin. Adrian knew them all through her parents and proudly took Jared from event to event to introduce him. She was greeted with the kind of familiarity reserved for close friends. He was impressed. She really *knew* these people. Not as sources, or from press conferences, but as flesh-and-blood human beings.

He thought nothing of his cables to the home office. But three days before he and Adrian were scheduled to leave Jerusalem, he found a telex from Richards waiting for him, inviting Jared to stop by the magazine's New York headquarters on his way back to Washington.

Seventy-two hours later, Jared was seated in Richards's office, sipping Perrier, half listening to the Chief of Correspondents present the view of the world, as he (and the magazine) saw it, and half absorbed by the view from Richards's forty-fifth-floor window, which overlooked the entire southern end of Manhattan. The long and the short of it, Richards said, was that Jimmy Carter was going to be defeated, Ronald Reagan was going to win, and, star correspondent though Jared was, he'd have to give up the White House to the reporter who'd been covering the Reagan campaign.

Where, Richards asked, did Jared want to go? Pentagon? There was a vacancy for the number-two slot. General assignment?

Jared frowned. He didn't want anonymity.

"It would round you out, you know." Richards tapped half-frame glasses on his glass-topped desk.

"I don't need any more rounding out. Come on, Roger, I've covered everything from the Maharishi to ghetto riots. There's nothing I can't write about."

The Chief of Correspondents tapped long fingers together. "I think you still need some tempering."

"Roger—"

"I do. But overseas."

"What? Where?"

"How about Kuala Lumpur?"

"Rog—"

"Tanzania? How about Tierra del Fuego?"

"Give me a break. Come on—what are you really thinking?"

"Jerusalem, Jared. Walter Graff's tour will be up in six months. I read your memos—I liked them. You met a lot of people—important people, even though you weren't on the job. It showed initiative, aggressiveness. We need those qualities overseas. Besides, the move will be good for your career track."

Jared beamed. He considered telling Richards that he'd met those important people only because of Adrian, then thought better of it. "You don't have to convince me. The answer's yes."

"Terrific," said Richards. "It's settled, then?"

"A deal." Jared thought for a moment. "One thing, though."

"What?"

"When we—I—was in Jerusalem, I had a problem with the language."

"Problem?"

"I couldn't speak it."

"So? Neither does Walt Graff. Harry Collins in Moscow doesn't speak Russian. Terry Walters in Cairo doesn't speak Arabic. Besides, everybody important in Israel speaks English."

"I think it would help me to become fluent. Look, Roger, they've got these language schools—ulpans they call them—and it only takes six or eight weeks of study. Oh sure, all the bigshots speak English. But not the people out in the settlement towns, or corporals in the border guard—the kind of people you need to know to really report on a country."

Richards sighed. "I don't really think it's—"

"Come on, Roger. Look, let me have two months' leave. I want to see the region, Cairo, Beirut, Amman—all those places. And study Hebrew. Believe me, it'll help the magazine."

Richards shook his head. "It's never been necessary before, Jared. I don't think the managing editor will pay for it."

"I'll pay."

"What?"

"I'll pay. Just get me the time."

Richards drummed long fingers on his desk. "Okay," he said finally, "take the time. I'll deal with the ME."

Half an hour later Jared and Adrian sat in the "21" Club holding hands.

"Jerusalem? I can't believe it." Adrian held his face with both hands and kissed him. "I can't wait to tell my parents."

"Me too."

"They're going to love you, Jared."

"I hope so."

"They will. I just know it."

"I never really got to know them before. Your father's kind of remote."

"Huh?"

"I'd see him at the big Embassy parties. And he came to the White House for the peace treaty signing. But he isn't like Max Kampelman or Max Fisher or Hy Bookbinder—you know, public. He was never a source for the press."

"He's not that kind of man. He's always preferred a behind-the-scenes role. You know, he was Carter's secret conduit to the Prime Minister just before Camp David."

"The back channel to Begin?" Jared was astonished. He had covered the hell out of the story but Felix Cooper's name had never emerged before.

She nodded. "Poppa was the only one the Prime Minister trusted to get the message straight."

"Incredible. How do you think he'll take the fact that I'm a reporter?"

"He'll love it."

"No, I mean that I'm going to report from Israel."

"But you love Israel, don't you?"

"Sure I do. It's incredible. The people, the energy—the whole place is just unbelievable."

"Then you have nothing to worry about."

"But the magazine's been critical of Israel's policies in the past."

She squeezed his hand. "I know. But that'll change now that you're on the case. You understand Israel, Jared, I saw it in your eyes when you came back from the Wall. I saw it on your face when you visited Koby with me. I felt it when we were in Sinai. You understand Israel, and you'll make the magazine see what you see."

He lifted his glass and touched hers. "I hope so. Cheers."

"L'Chayim, J.P."

"J.P.?"

"I like it better than just plain Jared. It has a ring to it."

"J.P.? It makes me sound like a robber baron. Or somebody on 'Dallas.' "

She pouted. "It makes you sound sexy."

"That's silly."

"No, it's not. I dub thee J.P. Gordon, foreign correspondent."

He laughed and touched her glass with his. "L'Chayim," he said. "To life—and to us."

Their next three weeks were a blur. Adrian spent the time renting out her condo and Jared closeted himself with officials at the State Department and Pentagon, getting briefed on Middle East affairs. Yoram Gal gave the couple a series of dinners in his home to which he invited, in his words, "the who's-and-who's and what's-and-what's" of the Israeli diplomatic and military community.

The Israeli also took Jared to the Embassy, where he happily provided him with a list of contacts in Israel, as well as the grist for dozens of stories.

Adrian and her parents asked about the Embassy meetings, but Jared was reluctant to tell them what transpired. Her father seemed to accept his close-mouthed attitude. "I like a man who keeps his counsel," he told Jared.

Adrian, however, did not. "I am your partner," she said. "I am your friend. I love you. We share secrets. Not very many yet, but some. I understand why you got this"—she drew her index finger down the front of his shirt and traced the scar—"and I don't want you to get another. So, here's my proposal: talk to me. Tell me when you hurt, or when something's bothering you. When you want to bounce an idea off someone, bounce it off me. I'll give you an honest answer. Not for publication, not for anyone except you. And I expect the same. I've fallen in love with you because you're the first man I've ever met who treats me like an equal. My ex pigeonholed me. It was like I was his personal Jewish bauble—you know, socially adept, manicured, and put away between wearings. Allan's a lawyer. Boy, is he ever a lawyer. And you know, not once in the five years we were married did he talk to me about what he did. My father's the same way. Oh—he'd take me to the office when I was a baby, but when I was growing up it was always 'Why bother the little girl with business problems?'

"But not you. You're always complaining to me, thank God, about something or other that outrages you, and I'm always worrying about your complaints. So let's make it quid pro quo: I'll keep your secrets, and you keep mine. I'll disagree with you. I'll argue with you. I'll yell at you sometimes. But I promise, Jared, I'll keep your secrets."

"Okay, and I'll keep yours. I'm keeping some already."

"What?"

"Oh, a couple of things."

"Like?" She grew serious.

"Your age and place of birth."

"What do you mean?"

"When I first met you, you told me you were a native Washingtonian and Sue said you were thirty. When we came through customs I snuck a look at your passport. It says you were born in Great Neck, New York, in 1945. That made you thirty-two when I met you—and no native Washingtonian."

"J.P.—"

"Don't be defensive. I'm just telling you that I'll keep your little secrets."

"I'm not being defensive. I *was* born in Great Neck. Then we moved to New York City and lived there until I was six. Then Poppa moved to Washington. I don't even remember Great Neck, and I hardly remember living in New York. That makes me a native Washingtonian so far as I'm concerned. And, well, I'm—vain about my age. It's a woman's prerogative, you know."

"I know."

"Okay, let's shake on it."

"Shake on what?"

"Our bargain—J.P."

He thought about what she'd said. It was hard to accept. He had never been an open person. Like so many of his colleagues, Jared was essentially a loner, both by habit and by trade. He was sociable, but close-mouthed; personable, but inaccessible. Secrets—his own and other people's—were a way of life. Some he kept. Others he printed. It was not going to be easy to include Adrian.

"But—"

She shook her head. "A deal, Jared. I want a bargain."

He sighed. He offered his hand, feeling imbecilic doing so. She took it in a businesslike grip and pumped it ceremonially once up, once down. "Now, let's seal it with a kiss."

They sealed their bargain with substantially more than a kiss.

But despite the handshake, Jared was still nervous about telling Adrian everything. He had never had that kind of relationship.

Still, shortly thereafter, armed with new passports and visas, their belongings packed and containerized and picked up by Zim lines, and a delivery date set for six weeks hence, Jared and Adrian flew to Rome and then on to Cairo, Amman and Beirut. From Beirut they went to Cyprus, and thence to Israel, where Adrian waited for their belongings in Jerusalem, while he enrolled in a language school in Netanya and struggled for six weeks. Until, one day, he discovered he could speak, read and write Hebrew better than he'd ever thought possible.

The Hebrew was important. It made Jared feel a part of the country. It also helped his reporting immeasurably. He could go to Tel Aviv and sit in Triana, where the head of the Mossad ate lunch two days a week, and speak English to Moshiko the owner while he listened to the Hebrew conversation and made mental notes. Or visit Olympia, Triana's main competition, and eavesdrop on generals from Zahal while they ate labbane with cucumber and garlic and grilled lamb. In the mornings he could browse through the Hebrew press, not having to wait like the rest of his American colleagues for the three-page English synopsis put out in midday by the government press office.

When he went to the Wall, he could take up a book and read the words. For the first time in his life, Jared began to feel truly Jewish, truly a part of his own history.

"What are you going to do? You agreed you'd only write what Yoram said you could write." Adrian lay in bed, the covers pulled under her chin, her head propped up on three pillows. The wine had made them sleepy, and they had napped fitfully for about an hour.

"I don't know. All I know is that what happened today changes everything—my relationship with Yoram, the way I cover Israel, everything."

"Can you not file anything?"

"That's what I'm thinking of doing."

"And?"

"That's fine so long as nothing's leaked to another news organization. If there is, if I get a query from New York, I won't know what to do. If New York wants a piece—the piece they'll want isn't the one I can write. At least not since I know the truth."

"But Yoram's your friend. He wouldn't put you in jeopardy."

"I don't know that anymore. I'm not sure I know anything anymore. I thought I knew him. I thought I trusted him. Now—"

She sat up and hugged her knees. "Talk to Yoram."

"About what? I've got nothing to say to Yoram. I don't think I want to talk to Yoram for a while."

"Maybe if you understood. Maybe there was some reason for what happened. If this Abu Zain really was responsible for the attack in London it could be justified."

"Even if he were, there were the wife and kids."

"War is war," she said. "We're talking about Israel's survival. Sometimes you've got to do, well, nasty things in order to survive."

"That's a horrible thing to say. You can't believe it."

"You don't wage war like a gentleman, J.P."

"Yoram said that, too. I think you're both wrong. That kind of thinking shouldn't apply here, Adrian. The whole reason for this country is so that even a terrorist's wife and kids won't get killed needlessly. God—even Begin talks about the morality of Israel, God help him. That's what gets me so mad: the hypocritical sanctimony of it all. I'm not against the concept of retribution: you kill my kids on some moshav, and I'm going to bomb your guerrilla bases. But here, it could have been done without murder. Take Abu Zain out. Even take his driver out. But leave the wife and the kids alive."

"Aren't you being naïve?"

"I don't think so."

"Not even a little?"

"I'm being . . . idealistic. So what? Isn't idealism what this country's all about? Isn't that what you and everybody else always tell me?" He pulled his jeans from the foot of the bed and started to climb into them. "Look," he said, "I'm going back to the office. I've got to think."

"You mean you've got to sulk."

He ignored the remark. "I'll be home. But late." He shrugged into his sweater and pulled a knee-length parka from a hook on the back of the bedroom door. He walked over to the bed, bent and kissed her on the mouth. "I'll see you. I love you."

Outside, he could see his breath in the chilly, early evening air. It had started to drizzle, and Jared threw up the hood of his parka as he headed up the stone steps toward the street.

He decided not to drive, so trudged until he reached the street that led west toward his office. Rush hour traffic clogged all four lanes in Jerusalem's version of gridlock, and the smell of diesel fumes hung in the drizzle mist. Just south of where he stood, a taxi and a small truck had collided, and motorists stuck their heads out of fogged-up windows to scream curses at the perpetrators.

He walked up the hill, past the King David Hotel, pausing to peer inside the marble, columned foyer. A bus full of Americans had just discharged its cargo in the street, and he watched them struggle with their hand luggage up to the revolving doors. Each of the bags and each of the Americans was tagged, the white cardboard strips fluttering in the chilly wind.

And what will they see? he thought. They'll see what they want to see, what they're supposed to see: a kibbutz or two, a half-day's walk through the Old City, a brief meeting with Jerusalem's irrepressible mayor, Teddy Kollek, if they're from an organization that's contributed enough money to warrant fifteen minutes of his time. They'll get an hour at the Western Wall, where they can pray and have pictures taken at the fount of Judaism, then a quick walk atop the Temple Mount to peer at the Al Aksa mosque and the Dome of the Rock. The buses will take them on day trips to Zichron, where they'll taste wine at the cellars. And then on to Dalyiat al Carmel, where the pro-Israeli Druse live. They'll see Masada, site of the famous TV movie. At the nature reserve at Ein Gedi, they'll see an ibex or two if they're lucky. They'll walk through the Me'a She'arim and buy religious trinkets at twice, three times what they should be paying. They'll go to services on Friday night and Saturday morning and on Sunday it'll be a 'free' day, so they'll walk down Ben Yehuda Street and buy T-shirts and Israeli Army surplus hats, mezzuzahs and gold chai's.

Then they'll climb on their planes and fly back to Philadelphia, or Los Angeles, or Baltimore, or Cincinnati to show their snapshots and tell their friends how wonderful a place Eretz Israel is. And they won't have seen a damn thing.

They'll have seen Potemkin Village Israel. The Israel for tourists, for supporters, for naïfs. The Israel of museums and the Knesset and

Yad Vashem, the Holocaust memorial. And being Americans, Jews, and therefore guilty because they think they're soft compared to the Israelis, they'll accept exactly what they see, exactly what they're supposed to accept. And next year, when Begin or Sharon or any of the others come to raise money, they'll give and give and give.

And what don't the tourists see? They don't see what those of us who live here, who work here, who criticize the government see—the army bulldozing Arab houses in the West Bank, the refugee camps in Gaza, the ultranationalist Jewish settlers from Qiryat Arba swaggering through Hebron with cocked Uzi submachine guns at the ready, the gangs of Sharon supporters bullying their way into Labor Party meetings with clubs, and the slums of Tel Aviv and Or Akiva with their Black Panther meetings and youth gangs. These are no part of Potemkin Village Israel.

The wounded from what Begin called Operation Peace for Galilee—Jared snorted; its real name was first Operation Big Bear, then Operation Big Pine, so named after the Cedars of Lebanon—who lay with head wounds and burns, amputated arms and legs in half a dozen military hospitals, were not on anyone's itinerary. Nor were the kind of mission he'd gone on not eighteen hours ago. Israelis, the visitors were told, are humane, are different, are Jews. We're just like you, the visitors are told again and again: Western democracy; strong anticommunists. Not like *them*—the Arabs. Begin called Arabs "two-legged animals." Zahal's Chief of Staff Rafael Eytan called them "cockroaches in a bottle." But never in front of Americans.

No, Yom Tov and Koby One and Koby Two and Ze'ev and Amos and the two Syrian Ariks were not on the itinerary; never are on the itinerary. They exist, but they're not part of Potemkin Village Israel.

Miracles exist. Jared knew that. Just like the soldier his first time at the Wall. That Israel was a nation at all was a miracle, and Jared took vicarious pride in its existence, in its strength, in its perseverance. He loved the state of Israel. But he also saw its flaws. And somehow, the Israel of the dream was being overtaken by a new reality, a right-wing, fundamentalist, ultranationalist disease, a form of Khomeinism that was infecting the Jewish state, destroying it from within, like a cancer.

He remembered another walk he'd taken with Adrian during their first week in Jerusalem. They'd climbed Mount Zion to visit King David's tomb. They trod along a stone pavement until they reached an arcade, almost a cave, supported by primitive stone pillars. It was, said Adrian, an old inn, and she pointed to iron rings set in the wall where fourteenth century pilgrims' horses once were tied. From the depths of the tomb itself they could hear wailing: Oriental Jews had come to the grave of the biblical forefather to mourn. They descended, and looked, and marveled. Then they walked out through the heavy iron gates of the Dormiton Church, built by German Benedictines early in the twentieth century, shortly after the Ottomans gave the site to the German Emperor Wilhelm II.

Across the road was a low stone building with a narrow stairway going down to a wooden door. Above the entrance was an inscription in Hebrew. Adrian translated it: "The blood of your brothers cries out."

She almost balked at entering. Then she clutched Jared's hand and together they went through the door. The low-ceilinged chamber they entered was musty and dim, lit by a few bare bulbs and candles. White stone tablets lined the walls; each was engraved with the name of a city, town or shtetl that had been destroyed by the Nazis during the Holocaust. Dust-coated glass cabinets held relics of the Nazi extermination. A wild-eyed, small, elderly bearded man reeking of cheap tobacco approached.

"Shalom. Tourists? Americans?" His skull cap was frayed; a wrinkled, gray-tinged white shirt was tucked carelessly into trousers of an indeterminate color that were shiny with age. Wrinkled thumbs hooked into clip-on suspenders.

"Yes," said Jared. "What is this place?"

"*Martef Hashoah*," said the man. "Chamber of the Holocaust." He came up to face them, and Jared squirmed in discomfort at the man's opaque left eye.

"Can we look around?"

"You must. You must see and remember." He put gnarled hands on the smalls of their backs and propelled them toward one of the white stone tablets. He pulled at a string and a bulb came on. "This was my town," he said. "In Transylvania. Now it is dust. Now there is nothing except"— he pointed at himself—"what remains in here." He did a little dance. "They took us away in the spring. To music. The *goyim* played music as they marched us to the station, fi-fiddle-

fiddle-um-dah. Beautiful music." He pulled at the string and extinguished the bulb. He walked to a display case, pulled a handkerchief out of his pocket and swabbed at the dusty glass.

"Americans almost never come here," the man said. "I am not on the tours. Not approved. On the tours they go to Yad Vashem. They don't come here. They don't give me money. Me—I did this myself. Gathered these things myself. I live here"—he pointed to a cot in one dark corner of the chamber.

Jared looked at Adrian. She was pale—gray in the yellow light—and beads of moisture had formed on her upper lip. He took her hand. She shook herself free. There was panic in her eyes as she stood, her gaze riveted on the old man. He understood—they'd wandered into a madman's den.

"You think I'm"—the old man punched his forehead with his thumb—"a crazy old *Zhid* living in his room of memories?"

A silence followed. Adrian searched for a tissue. She wiped at her mouth, put it away, then took Jared's hand. Her palm was clammy.

"Possible," the old man said. "But who wouldn't be crazy after this? I'd be crazy if I weren't crazy, if you get what I'm saying." He shook the dusty handkerchief out then blew his nose into it. "That's why you must look and remember, and tell others to come here. Tell the Americans to get this place put on the tours."

He looked at Jared and Adrian, who stood mute, clutching each other's hands. "Young and in love? Good. Make Jewish babies. Make Jewish babies to replace those that were lost." A sigh like a body punch seemed to start in his toes, move through knees, thighs, diaphragm, lungs, heart and thorax, ending at quivery lips. "Aieee. All those beautiful Jewish children." He looked them over, evaluated their ages. "You could have been them. They could have been you." Adrian shuddered at the thought. Jared found something on the dusty floor to stare at.

"Come and see," the old man wheezed. "Come and learn what human beings can do to other human beings. Learn the limits of humanity." He sighed another long, groaning sigh. "Learn, and hope is possible. Forget, and despair is inevitable."

Under his watchful good eye they wandered, pausing at the relics: prayer books, yellow cotton stars, sections of rusted barbed wire and inmate uniforms, urns containing soil—perhaps ashes, even—from Dachau, Bergen-Belsen, Treblinka, Buchenwald and Auschwitz. The little man preceded them and followed them, turning lights on and off as they walked through the chamber. "Learn this," he said, his knuckles rapping a case. "This is our duty. To remember. To tell the story. Not to forget."

"We won't forget," Adrian said, fumbling in her purse, crumpling three five-hundred-shekel notes into a ball, and stuffing them into the man's waiting hand.

The money disappeared into the pocket with the handkerchief. "You mustn't forget," the man said. "To be a Jew today means to testify, to bear witness—to what is, and to what has been."

"We will," said Jared, reaching for his own pocket until he felt Adrian's hand on his arm.

"Go back to America. Testify. Bear witness. Tell your rich American Jews who don't put me on their tours. Take an oath to testify. Testify! Testify! Be witnesses. Make Jewish babies."

In the days after that excursion, Jared couldn't get the little man out of his mind. He'd asked Adrian to go back to the *Martef* with him but she refused, a flash of panic in her eyes when he brought up the suggestion. So Jared had gone back by himself one afternoon, drawn as if by a magnet up the dusty road across from the Dormiton Church and down the narrow stairway. He looked up at the inscription above the door and then, taking a deep breath, pushed it open.

The chamber was still dim and the room lined with the dusty white stone tablets. But the cot was gone. And the little man was nowhere to be seen. Another guide, a middle-aged man who spoke almost no English, showed Jared through the rooms, and held his hand out for a donation when Jared left. Jared tried asking where the little man with one good eye had gone, but received only shrugs and quizzical looks in return. He'd mentioned the whole thing to Adrian, who told him to put it out of his head.

But the little man's words had stayed with Jared. And now, walking on the wet pavement, he knew what had to be done. He reached the office building. He pushed the button for the elevator, waiting impatiently for it to arrive. On the second floor, the lights were out and he fumbled for the *minuterie,* the button that turned the hall light on for just long enough for him to open the five locks that secured the bureau door.

Inside, he flicked on the reception area light, bolted the door behind him, went to check his box for messages and saw that Annie had transmitted his Christmas story memo to New York. He walked into his office and saw that the Kaypro was still on. Damn, he thought, he'd forgotten to turn it off before he'd left for lunch with Adrian.

Jared reached for the picture book on his credenza and peeled off the back cover. The diskette cover was still taped neatly in place; but the disk was gone.

They had been here, whoever they were. And *They* knew he could just sit down and write the whole thing over again. So he had been left a message, a signal: *We* can break into your office, and *We* can turn on your computer, and *We* can take our time and look around until *We* find what *We* want. Then *We* can read it at our leisure, and take it with us when *We* go.

It was a sign, an omen, a portent. But it wasn't the only one.

In quiet panic, he read the single sheet of paper that had been left neatly centered on his desk. It was a confirmation copy of a story sent to New York. It bore his computer password and his byline, and was directed to the magazine's newsdesk, just the same as all of Jared's articles. It was written in Jared's style. It was datelined Jerusalem.

A SENIOR AIDE TO PLO CHAIRMAN YASSER ARAFAT WAS KILLED TODAY BY MOSLEM GUNMEN THOUGHT TO BE MEMBERS OF A DISSIDENT PALESTINIAN FACTION AS HE LEFT THE CHAMOURA CAMP NEAR DAMASCUS, ACCORDING TO ISRAELI INTELLIGENCE SOURCES.

He took the paper and in fury ripped it to pieces. Took the picture book from the credenza and flung it at the opposite wall, knocking down half a dozen framed photographs that crashed and scattered sharp glass shards on the marble floor.

Rage gave way to numbness. Jared pounded the metal case of his word processor in impotent frustration. The dispatch was the perfect blackmail. It could cost him his job—his whole future—if the magazine ever found out he hadn't written it. It was the one secret he could never share with Adrian. Or anybody.

In a daze, Jared crossed the room and knelt, staring at the shattered picture of Adrian and the grapes. He put his head in his hands and wept.

PART TWO

March 1983

CHAPTER 4

They'd gotten a cat. Actually, the cat had chosen them. It showed up in December, mewling and scratching on the wood shutters outside the living room. Jared opened the window, then the shutter, and the cat, scrawny ribs marimbalike through eggshell colored fur, jumped inside, shook its wet fur on their one good Turkish rug, grudgingly accepted a saucer of milk from Adrian and then immediately went to sleep in front of the electric heater as if it had been doing so for years. When it still hadn't moved on after two weeks, they figured the relationship was going to be permanent, named the creature Pilgrim, and had took it to be spayed.

Now, almost three months after it had first arrived, the cat had not yet left the house. They would leave the door open; it would approach the sill, sniff the air outside and then, disdainfully, reject the possibility of venturing any further. It was definitely a house cat. It knew not to sharpen its claws on the furniture; it accepted meekly the flea collar Jared had pouched from New York; it liked being rubbed and tickled and even brushed. And it got fat. Fat from the milk Adrian fed it. Fat from the scraps of veal and fish sent by Mikki Venetzia. Fat from its taste (newly acquired, Jared thought) for brie cheese, carefully trimmed of the rind.

The cat did not like Arabs. Visitors would come and go and Pilgrim would, according to her mood, be either playful or distant. Except for Arabs. It arched its back at Arab delivery boys, caterwauled from the safety of the second-story window at the West Bank laborers who were installing a new drainage pipe in the street outside and hissed at the Bedouin washerwoman from East Jerusalem who came once a week to do the laundry.

It made no distinction about social class, either. It spat at the editor of *Al Fajr,* the Arab-language East Jerusalem newspaper, when he came to dinner. And one rainy Sunday when Rafi Taal, *World Week*'s Columbia University–educated, Brooks Brothers preppy Palestinian stringer, came over to pitch Jared on a story about Bir Zeit University, accompanied by two of the school's department heads, the cat screeched at them and bared her teeth, then ran away to glower from the top of the cabinets in the kitchen, coming down only after they had gone.

"I wonder how she senses it," Jared said, bribing Pilgrim from her aerie with a chunk of the precious brie that had just been brought from Paris by an accommodating colleague.

"Maybe she once belonged to Meir Kahane." Adrian watched as Pilgrim poked her nose over the top of the cabinet and twitched whiskers at the proffered treat.

"Maybe she's a linguist. Maybe she can differentiate accents. Let's try." Jared held out the brie and imitated Rafi's Arab accent: "Nice cat. Good Pilgrim. Do you want some ridiculously expensive cheese?"

The cat leapt nimbly down, caroming off two shelves, an open silverware drawer and a kitchen chair, then stood on its hind legs to nibble its treat from Jared's fingers.

"I guess not."

The phone rang and Adrian went to answer it. She came back some seconds later, agitated. "It's for you."

"Who is it?"

"Yoram Gal."

"Tell him I'm out."

"I said you were here."

"Tell him I'm busy."

"You tell him."

"I don't want to talk to him."

"Then you tell him. Look, Jared, you haven't spoken to Yoram since November. You're going to have to face him sometime."

"I will. But not today."

She shook her head and went back into the living room. From there she called: "He says it's important. Really important."

"Who's he going to murder this time?"

"What? I can't hear you. He says he's going to hang on till you come to the phone."

"Damn him. Okay—tell him I'm coming." Jared rinsed his hands and wiped them, taking his time. Then he walked into the living room and took the receiver from Adrian.

"Hello."

"Hello, boychik," came the familiar voice. "Long time no see."

"I've been busy."

"So I read. You wrote a nice wrapup on the Kahan Commission. Really nailed Sharon and his goons on Sabra and Shatila."

"I only wrote what was true."

A pause. "Jared, we have to talk."

"I'm not sure we have a whole lot to say to each other, Yoram."

"You're still mad."

"I'm not mad. I'm upset. No—yes—I am mad. I'm damn mad."

"Let's talk about it."

"There's nothing to say."

"Bullshit. There's a lot to say. At least give me the chance to clear the air. We've known each other too long."

"But obviously not that well." Jared stared across the room. Bells on Mount Zion began to toll.

"Jared?"

"What?"

"We have to talk. You and Adrian come for coffee this afternoon."

"We have plans."

"Cancel them."

Something in Yoram's voice made Jared agree. He turned to Adrian, cupping his hand over the mouthpiece. "Okay with you if we drive to Yoram and Aviva's?"

"Herzlyia? I thought we were going to see *China Syndrome* at the Cinémathèque."

"He says it's important. I think we should go."

She sighed. "First you tell me to say you're not even home. Now we're driving an hour to Herzlyia. Honestly, J.P., I wish you'd make up your mind."

"I think we should go. We'll make it back for the late show. I promise."

"Okay—just give me a couple of minutes."

He took his hand from the mouthpiece. "We're on our way."

"Bye-bye, bye-bye." Yoram abruptly rang off.

Jared cradled the receiver, wondering what Yoram wanted of him now.

The two solitary figures on the beach walked side by side, hands in the pockets of their windbreakers, leaving sneaker tracks in the moist, low-tide sand. The water was insolent: foamy gray-green waves breaking far out with an ominous roar. A cigarette dangled from Yoram's lips, and as he walked he inhaled the smoke and let it come out through his nose. In summer, the place would have been awash with surfers—surfing was Israel's latest fad—and tourists working on their Mediterranean tans. Now it was desolate as they walked north from the Acadia Hotel, past boarded-up fish and falafel shacks, empty lifeguards' chairs and rental cabanas. Yoram's black, gray and whisky-colored dog, Othello, bounded ahead, chasing the scolding sea gulls that floated low in the slate sky, and rushing into the water to retrieve pieces of miscellaneous flotsam, worry them momentarily, then abandon them again to the surf.

Finally the dog ran to Yoram, a three-foot length of two-by-four in his mouth, his yellow eyes wide with anticipation. Yoram sighed, pried the wood from Othello's teeth, and threw it as far as he could out into the surf. The dog kicked up sand as he charged into the water.

"Good Othello," Yoram called as the dog wallowed in chest-high water and pounced on the wood. He was a big dog: a mixture of German Shepherd, Boxer and Rottweiler that combined, Yoram was proud to say, the worst qualities of each. Already it had cost him more than a thousand dollars in insurance premiums and ten times that amount in payments. At the age of six months the animal had gotten loose and mauled two teenagers on their way past Yoram's house. It was no house pet, but a trained attack dog. Why it was friendly, even affectionate, to Jared and Adrian neither of them understood. But it was. Of all Yoram's friends, they were the only ones who could open the eight-foot iron gate and walk to the front door with neither a bark nor a growl from Othello, who kept watch from the first floor terrace, ready to gnaw unwary intruders.

The dog was back now, wet and happy, with the two-by-four chomped between massive jaws. It came up to Jared and nudged him with its flat Rottweiler's head. Jared pulled on the wood, twirled it above his head and threw it out into the water. Soundlessly, the dog went after it.

"He's grown."

"He's eating me out of house and home. Eighteen months old and he weighs sixty-five kilos. The vet says he'll go to seventy by the time he's two."

"How do you get him to the vet?"

"We drug him."

"That must be fun."

"It's wonderful. Schlepping him into the car is a real joy. And you don't want to be around when he wakes up. Othello with a hangover is a unique experience."

"I can imagine."

"Jared—I . . ."

"What?"

"I owe you an apology. I understand why you were hurt by—"

"Hurt? I was furious. I'm still furious. You broke into my office. You know damn well what happened. I'm vulnerable, Yoram. Really vulnerable because of what you did. That's more than 'hurt.' That's intimidation. That is dirty tricks."

"You never filed the real story about Abu Zain."

"How could I? You saw to it that the magazine got your version first. Then when the *Times* swallowed your lie and my editors saw it there was nothing I could do. Nothing I could do and still have a job."

"What does Adrian think?"

Jared paused. "I haven't told Adrian."

"Told her what?"

"That it was you, not me, who filed the story."

Yoram nodded.

"Why, Yoram? Why the hell did you screw me like that? What in God's name did I ever do to you?"

"What if I'd said to you that we needed our specific version of the events in Syria made public?"

Jared rubbed sand off his hands onto the thighs of his jeans. "You know how upset I was about what you did to Abu Zain's family. I'd probably have told you to go screw yourself."

"And?"

"I'd have sent the real story to New York."

"If you had, the censor would have pulled your credential."

"It would have been worth it."

"You're being naïve. Worth it? Not to be able to work in Israel? To have to pull up stakes and transfer out?"

"Some stories are worth that kind of risk."

The Israeli nodded. "I agree. But not that one."

"So you say you saved my credential by forging an article?"

"I'm not saying I forged any article. But in one sense, yes: by letting you know—how to put it—certain things. You made a bargain with me and you were going to break it. You promised you'd write only what was agreed on. What would it have meant if you'd had to move? What would the consequences have been—to you, to Adrian?"

"We'd have dealt with them."

"Maybe. But it would have put a strain on your relationship. With Aviva it's different. Three years in Washington, a year in London. Moving from base to base when we were younger. She's used to it. But we've been married eighteen years, we can take the strain of pulling up stakes at a moment's notice. I'm not so sure you and Adrian could do that right now. You're not married, after all, although you should be. Besides, you're better off here. You're doing a good job here—"

"What does that mean, Yoram? That I'm following the party line—whatever it may be? That I write only the stuff your people want me to write? For God's sake, you've used me."

"And you've used us. Nobody's forced you to write anything. You knew good stories when you came across them, and you wrote. If you think you've got a reputation as a propagandist, forget it. The government doesn't think very highly of you. I was at the Knesset last week and your name came up in the dining room. One of our lawmakers referred to you as a known liar and enemy of the state. Another called you a self-hating Jew."

"I take those as compliments."

"I would, too, if I were you—and knowing from where they came."

Jared watched as a gull swooped and dove toward the water. He turned toward the general. "Yoram, we're dancing around the point. Why did you ask me here?"

"Because I have a story for you."

"You've got to be kidding. I wouldn't believe it."

"This is serious."

"You've said that before."

"Hear me out, Jared. Then make up your mind." Yoram turned and whistled at the dog, who ran panting and smiling from the water. "*Artza,* Othello. *Artza!*—down." From the deep pocket of his windbreaker, Yoram pulled a heavy leather leash, which he snapped onto the dog's choke collar. "Good Othello. Heel."

The animal stood and walked at Yoram's thigh. Looking far down the beach, Jared saw why Yoram had leashed the dog. A jogger was descending the long flight of concrete steps that ran adjacent to the Sharon Tower Hotel. Othello's nose went up in the air, his ears flattened and he began to pull at the leash. Yoram dug his heels into the sand and jerked him back. "Heel, you sonofabitch."

Yoram waited until the jogger passed them, scrunching sand and chugga-huff-huff-huffing in the direction of the Acadia. "I've come on some information," he said.

"Disinformation? More PLO 'rebels' murdering high-ranking Fatah officials and their children?"

Yoram stopped and turned toward Jared. The dog sat and stared up at the men, responsive to the American's abrupt tone and the vehemence of his master's voice. "Get something through your head, boychik. What I do, I do. I told you—I don't have to justify myself to you. War is war. You don't—you don't—have to like it. But it's the real world." He reached in his pants pocket and pulled out a pack of cigarettes, extracted one, placed it between his teeth, replaced the pack and then lighted the cigarette, drawing deeply and exhaling through his nose.

"Look—we—I—made a mistake by taking you on that raid. I know that now. I'd hoped you'd see fit to do me a small favor. You didn't. However it happened, the story we needed out, got out. Nobody's been hurt by what got into your magazine. Nobody knows the real story—"

"You made sure of that."

"I did?"

"Don't play the naïf with me, Yoram. I know the real story, but what happens if I go to New York and tell my editors, 'Sorry, guys, it was all a big mistake. I broke your rules by agreeing to conditions I've been specifically forbidden to accept without your permission. Now I want to tell the truth.' Goddammit, Yoram, I'd be out on my ass. Now tell me what difference *that* would make to Adrian and me. It wouldn't be a matter of not working in Israel. It would be a matter of not working anywhere, anyplace, any time."

"That won't happen."

"No, it won't— I've got to keep my mouth shut. But how sure can I be that you'll keep yours closed? Or that you won't want some little favors from me from time to time? You know what I'm talking about, Yoram. Plant a little disinformation here and there. That's blackmail—boychik."

"You think I'd do that to you?"

"Dammit, Yoram, you've already done it to me."

"And so now when I tell you there's something you should know about, the information is suspect."

"Wouldn't you feel the same way?"

"Not if I'd known the source as well and as long as we've known each other. Not until I'd heard what he had to say."

Jared thought for a moment. Then he raised his palms. "Okay, okay. Talk. Yoram. I'm mad, but I'll listen."

The general sighed and began walking again. "You know my unit."

"Yes."

"Since you came out with us, we've undertaken three similar missions. It doesn't matter where, or who, or what. They were successful—well, two of them were successful. On the most recent one we lost a man."

"One of the people I met?"

"Yes. The one I called Ze'ev. That wasn't his real name, of course."

"I'm sorry."

"So was I. He was a good man. He earned his keep."

"And?"

"We brought him back and buried him. It was reported as a training accident. Most of the time families know when somebody belongs to units like mine. But nobody's supposed to talk specifically about where they go or what they do. There are too many possible compromises. It's a small country. Word gets around."

"Like the missile boat story?"

"Precisely," said Yoram. "In certain circles it's hard to keep secrets. Anyway, I paid a condolence call on Ze'ev's family. They have a cottage in the religious part of Neve Yaakov, a small place but comfortable. Four rooms. One of the reasons to go there was to make sure he hadn't left any papers behind. You know how it is: you stuff a memo in your pocket, and all of a sudden the maid is reading your operational plans, or your loudmouth mother-in-law is telling her friends what a great guy her daughter married because he's leaving on a secret mission to Iraq. You remember when the raid on Ossirak was cancelled the third time? You know why? Ezer Weizman's son-in-law Danny was a pilot on the mission. He told Ezer's daughter Michal about the schedule—pillow talk—and she told her old man, who runs to Begin and screams bloody murder. Ezer raised so much hell with Begin they had to reschedule."

"I remember. Sure. So?"

"I went through his dresser, and his desk, and then went out to the bomb shelter. Most of the time that's where our people store their heavy weapons. Who the hell wants RPGs or AK-47s sitting around the house? His stuff was there, all right. But there was more. Claymore mines. Three kilos of K-4 plastique. Two dozen hand grenades. Fuses. Timers. The place was a munitions factory."

"My God."

"Everybody's god, boychik. I locked it up, brought back some satchels and loaded everything into my car, told the family that it was all in order, and drove off. Now, I ask myself, what the hell is Ze'ev doing with enough explosives to level a couple of apartment houses? So I go back to the unit and I start looking through our ordnance records. Then I checked against inventory."

"And the stuff's been stolen?"

"Right."

"What was he going to use it for?"

"I don't know. I called a friend of mine in Shin Bet. Nathan Yaari, a man who used to serve in one of my units. I started to tell him the story, and he says not to go any further on the phone, that he'll meet me in person and we'll talk about it. So I met him. It turns out that Nathan knows about Ze'ev. Knows what Ze'ev had been doing—the stealing—and then he tells me, 'I can't do anything about it.' "

"Can't?"

"We were walking on Ibn Givrol, two blocks from my office. Strolling like a couple of boulevardiers. And I say, Nathan, what do you mean you can't do anything? And he points up—to the sky—and says 'We have orders not to interfere.' "

"You're kidding."

"Jared, you remember the bombings of the Arab mayors?"

"Uh-huh."

"And you know how far the investigation went?"

"It went nowhere. The rumors were that Achituv quit as head of the Shin Bet because Begin held the investigation back. No preventive detention, no phone taps, no informers. Does this thing with Ze'ev have something to do with those bombings?"

"I don't know," said Yoram. "But anything's possible. Look, Jared, I've steered you off some stories and on to others. Sometimes I've misled you. But that's the real world. I do what I do—and I make no apologies for it. But here we have something different. Here we have Jewish terrorism, and I find out that the Shin Bet's hands are tied, and worse, that a major—that was Ze'ev's rank—a major in my unit, might have been involved."

Jared stared at the Israeli. "And that bothered you, as opposed to what you do for a living?"

"I've got no moral problem with assassination when it's carried out as a military operation," said Yoram. "I even understand when the PLO hits one of our attachés, like in Washington, or Paris, or wherever. A military target is a military target. But what we've got here is different: it's the Jewish equivalent of pure terror operations. Like what the PLO did at Ma'alot, or the slaughter on the Tel Aviv highway in 1978. Or like the time before the War of Independence when Begin ordered the Irgun to roll a barrel of explosives into a crowd of Arabs at a bus stop. Pure terror I can't condone—by Arabs, or Irish—and especially by Jews. So what can I do? I can call you."

"I—"

"I don't really know what to think. Sure, there've been whispers, and we've had instances when some idiot who belongs to one of the self-defense groups at a settlement takes an extra clip of ammo or two. Or we're told that a submachine gun has been lost—and we know it hasn't. But this—I run a tight group. And if Ze'ev could skim these explosives from me, he had to have some help. I'm working on that problem, boychik. What I think you should do is look at the subject too."

Jared whistled. "It's a hell of a story, Yoram. If people would be willing . . . to talk . . ."

They swung back, walking south again, until they reached a deserted restaurant named Daboush that sat adjacent to a steep flight of concrete steps. Yoram unstacked one of the plastic chairs that sat by the boarded-up counter and pushed it next to a table. He motioned for Jared to sit, then got another seat for himself.

The two of them sat quietly for some moments, watching the gray-green water attack the beach. The dog lay with his head on Yoram's tennis shoes, tail brushing the sand.

Jared watched his friend watching him. Despite the anger he felt, the betrayal, there was an intrinsic bond between himself and Yoram. In a perverse way it had been forged even more strong because of the mission to Damascus. Despite the revulsion he'd felt at the time—felt even now—at what Yoram and his unit had done, there was also in Jared's mind a grudging admiration, even a sense of pride, at their efficiency and planning. It was the sort of feeling many American Jews felt upon hearing about Israeli military triumphs: a vicarious thrill, a communal sharing in the victory. It was a primal, undeniable emotion, and it bothered Jared deeply.

He watched as Yoram lit another cigarette. Then he took the pack, shook out one for himself and lighted it.

"You know what makes me mad?" the Israeli said. "What really makes me furious?"

Exhale. "What, Yoram?"

"It's the state of mind these days. I was against Lebanon. You don't wage a war to change the political map of the Middle East—which is what Sharon did. Arik misled the General Staff. He misled the Cabinet. He played two ends against the middle—and then when he got caught on what to him was a minor point, the killings at Sabra and Shatila, he tried like hell to duck the responsibility. Now Kahan and the commission have him cold. But you know what, boychik? He'll wriggle out of it. Sooner or later, if he's not stopped, he's going to be Prime Minister. Then—watch out. Then it's the Ansar POW camp for all of us."

"You say you're furious," said Jared "But until now, Yoram, you kept your mouth shut. You've all kept your mouths shut on the General Staff. So long as things were going your way, it was okay not to talk. Not to look too hard. Where was Zahal when Sharon was making his plans? Where were the whispers to the good guys in the Cabinet? Now you tell me I should look into Jewish terrorism. Okay, maybe I will—it's an important story. But it's really a job for the Hebrew press. Where the hell were *Maariv* and *Ha'aretz* and the *Jerusalem Post* when the Arab mayors were bombed? Where were they when all of us who drink at Katy's knew there were Jewish terrorists in the woodwork?"

Yoram nodded in agreement. "You've got a point. But I swear to you, Jared, I didn't have the foggiest idea that there were Zahal people—operational people—involved."

"Dammit—that's what I'm talking about, Yoram. You didn't give a damn until you found there were Army people involved. That's just not good enough. And I'm not just talking about terrorism. You guys have a wonderful way of working. You could call it networking. It happens here, it happens in the States. Remember how we met? Through the Bernsteins. They're what you call active Jews, right?"

"Sure."

"And the crowd of Americans you saw socially in the States. Active Jews?"

"By which you mean?"

"Committed to Israel. I've seen the lists at the Embassy in Washington: Active Jewish Community. Names, phone numbers—a whole society that can be mobilized about as fast as Zahal can put reserve units in the field. You need people to call their congressmen? There's the list. You need someone to write a protest letter to *The Washington Post*? There's the list. They're all there: money raisers, money givers, influence peddlers. People like Max Fisher, or Max Kampelman, or Adrian's father."

"What are you getting at?"

"I'm not stupid, Yoram. I covered Carter—and I saw the pressure you guys put on him during the peace negotiations and when the fight started over the sale of F-15s to the Saudis."

"There was nothing wrong with that. As a matter of fact, it wasn't us Israelis who were given an office in the U.S. Capitol. It was that lovely Saudi prince—Bandar—who got one during the fight over AWACS."

"I don't want to argue about lobbying," Jared insisted. "I'm talking about something else."

"What?"

"That most of these supporters—as well as most mainstream American Jews—don't ask too many questions about Israel."

"Questions?"

"About motives. About morality. About the direction Israel is going. They support Israel—whether it's Labor in power or Likud; whether it's Begin and Sharon, or Ezer Weizman or Dayan, or Rabin. They don't ask questions."

The general scratched his chin and exhaled smoke. "Perhaps not."

"Perhaps? Perhaps? Yoram—let's put our cards on the table. When I wrote the Arafat profile a year and a half ago, Adrian and I went back to the States for some time with our families. You should have heard what our friends said. What her family said. 'How could you do it?' and 'We thought you were a friend,' were the two most prevalent comments. They thought I'd talked to the devil himself. It became more than an article. It was something that a 'good Jew' would never have written. Or the time I pulled together the stuff about the bombing of Ossirak. You gave me that material, Yoram. You wanted it out in the open. But we got a phone call from Adrian's father that burned my ears.

"You know what he told me? He said that by embarrassing Begin I was being subversive to Israel and putting Jews everywhere in danger. He said that Jewish journalists have the obligation to be positive, not critical, of Israel. And he's not the only one I heard from. Boy—talk about the Jewish lobby. . . ."

"Okay, I accept your point. American Jews are uncritical. So what? Israel needs the support. Does it matter how we get it?"

"Of course it matters."

"Does it really? This isn't Washington, Jared. Damascus is twelve minutes' flying time from Tel Aviv. If the Russians bring SS-21 missiles in they could hit us before we're able to launch defensive air strikes."

"I'm not talking about legitimate defense, Yoram. I'm talking about the way the country's moving. And it's moving to the right.

Do you think most American Jews really know what's going on here? Really understand the battle for the soul of the country that's being fought right now? I don't. And what upsets me is that I'm not sure that you guys want them to."

"That's unfair."

"Is it? I think you're satisfied with dollar Zionists and influence peddlers. That you feel it's enough so long as the Felix Coopers of the world give money— Do you realize that in the past twenty-five years, Adrian's father has given about fifteen million dollars to Israel? That's cash, Yoram—that's real dough. He built a whole school at the Technion, and three dormitories at Hebrew University, and paid for the College of Social Studies at Tel Aviv University—and a hell of a lot more, too. Adrian's even got her name on some buildings. But Felix is more than a money-giver. He's well-connected politically at home, he's a big Republican fundraiser, he goes to the White House. There are more subtle things he can do than just give money, if you get what I mean."

Yoram drew deeply on the cigarette, then flicked it away. "We need support. These are good people."

"Agreed. Nobody's accusing them of doing anything evil. But where the hell were they after the Arab mayors were bombed? You know what Felix told me? That it was done by the Arabs themselves to discredit Israel. And believe me, nobody in the current government has done anything to dissuade him from that opinion."

"It could have been true."

"Sure it could have been true. But when it turned out that Bassam Shakaa and the others were attacked by Jews, Begin and all the rest have been slow to react. And where's the pressure from people like Felix? Nowhere. They turned their backs."

Yoram sighed. "What's your point, Jared?"

"My point is that Israel as we knew it is dying. Come on, Yoram—be honest. Look at the alliance Begin's forged with the Christian right wing in the United States."

"Jerry what'sisname?"

"Falwell. Yeah. Look, Jerry Falwell is a fundamentalist Christian, a right-winger, who has no endemic love for the Jews. In fact, Jewish organizations have been complaining about him for years. On the other hand, he's someone who believes that the United States should recognize Jerusalem as the capital of Israel. He wants Jewish control of the Temple Mount. So Begin appears with him in public. Begin courts him and the other fundamentalists—including the one who once said God doesn't hear the prayer of a Jew. Now a fair number of American Jews are beginning to say, 'Maybe Jerry Falwell isn't so bad, after all.' That maybe the Moral Majority isn't so bad, after all, despite its politics!

"And why? Because the Moral Majority supports Israel. And why does it support Israel? Because it's in the Moral Majority's narrow interest to do so—right now. Maybe because they want the United States to become a Christian nation; then they'll have a place to send all the Jews, once it does. Or, maybe, it's because they think that if they support Israel—not all of Israel, but the Begins and the religious zealots—they'll throw out the Arabs, rebuild the Temple, and the Messiah will come."

"You're right," said Yoram. "There's even a place near Jerusalem where they're making garments for the priests to wear when the Temple's rebuilt."

"I know. And American Christian fundamentalists are helping to pay for it."

"Well," said Yoram, "they've got a persuasive argument. They tell the Jews, 'You say the Messiah hasn't come yet. We say he's coming again. So let's build the Temple and see who's right.' "

"An irresistible argument." Jared laughed in spite of himself.

"Very fundamental." Yoram stood up. Othello yanked at his leash. "Let's go back to the house," the general said, tossing his cigarette into the sand. "I think you should meet Nathan Yaari and hear what he has to say."

They were in what Jared called the Modified Wagon Train Position: six people, three men, three women, separated according to sex, sitting on Yoram and Aviva's L-shaped sofa and two straight-back chairs. Israelis invariably pulled their chairs into a circle at cocktail parties. None of your Washington or New York style standing up and moving around. No 'Power corners' or 'Dominant positions'—just the chairs, in a constantly expanding circle. You sat and talked while rooted to the spot. It made arguing better because it was impossible to walk away from a fight.

Jared claimed the crook of the sofa, a cup of Turkish coffee—

cafe botz in Hebrew—balanced on his lap. To his left was Yoram, who was playing with the curly mop of hair on his daughter Tamar's head. To Yoram's left, sitting on a creaky dining room chair, was Nathan Yaari, Yoram's friend from the Shin Bet. Adrian, Aviva Gal and Nathan's wife Ziva shared the long leg of the sofa. Outside, Othello, who had been chained securely, bayed and growled. He knew there were strangers in the house, and he didn't like it a bit.

The house the dog guarded was a two-story chalet-styled bungalow that sat on a narrow side street in Herzlyia-Bet, half a mile from the ocean, on a bluff above the main highway between Tel Aviv and Haifa. Yoram had built an eight-foot-high wall around his small lot, and closed off the driveway with an iron fence of the same height. Like many similar buildings in the neighborhood, Yoram's home was filled with ersatz Scandinavian furniture. The living room's focus was the huge German-made television set that sat catty-cornered facing the couch. The marble floors were covered with Israeli copies of Oriental rugs, and the coffee table was scarred by Yoram's cigarette butts and the rings left by Tamar's habit of spilling her juice. A gas heater pumped warmth from the center of the room toward the couch.

Even though the furnishings were spare, there were books crammed into low, teakwood cases, and a plethora of art on two of the walls. The dominant piece was a three-by-four-foot collage by Tumarkin, depicting the Yom Kippur War. Called Kilometer 101, it was warmly inscribed to Yoram and Aviva by the artist. There were a dozen other pictures as well: oils by Itamar Siani, the Yemenite artist; Shmuel Katz's prints; and a huge Moreh drypoint.

Another wall was reserved for Yoram's military souvenirs—plaques from the Pentagon and from Sandhurst, a diploma from the U.S. War College, insignias of the units Yoram had served with or commanded in Zahal. And there were half a dozen photographs that pictured the general over the span of five wars.

Yoram had called Nathan Yaari from a pay phone outside a drugstore three blocks from his house on the way back from the beach. "You know who this is?" he had asked into the receiver. "Good—come for coffee. The usual living room."

Twenty minutes later the Yaaris had arrived, driving a beat-up Citroën station wagon.

"I heard you two weren't speaking," the Shin Bet agent said as he pumped Jared's hand. He was a big man, barrel-chested and bulky, but not fat. His massive hands were callused; despite the season, he had a deep tan that set off his short-cropped, gray-streaked blond hair.

"We weren't," said Jared. "But you know how it is—friends—"

"I understand."

They made small talk for the first half hour. It was uncharacteristic for Yoram. But Jared had the feeling that he was allowing Yaari to sense him out. It also gave them the chance to eat. Ziva Yaari had brought hotly spiced pickled eggplants, done in the Yemenite style. Aviva served pita bread and labbane seasoned with olive oil, cucumbers and fresh garlic. The six of them lapped up the mixture with much licking of fingers. Finally Yoram spoke: "So, Yaari, what can you tell us?"

"Tell you? About what?"

"About the investigation."

"What investigation? There is no investigation. Those *ben zonim*"—he used the idiomatic for sons of bitches—"have put a cap on it. Nothing. *Klum*. We don't even talk about it in the office anymore. Why? Because it doesn't do any good, and besides, some sonofabitch will probably overhear us and put something derogatory in our personnel records."

"He's getting an ulcer over this," said Ziva.

"An ulcer? It's going to give me a heart attack." Nathan scooped up the last of the labbane and sucked a dribble from a big index finger. "But our hands are tied. That's the thing—we have no problem getting permission to tap reporters' phones, but not fascist sons of bitches like Rabbi Kahane and his hooligans from Kach, or that little Khomeini from Qiryat Arba, Moshe Levinger."

"Aren't you being unfair?" asked Adrian. "Nobody's proved they've done anything wrong."

Nathan smiled at Jared. "Yoram told me you live with a real Likudnik." He looked at Adrian. "You're wrong," he said. "We've known since 1980 that half a dozen Jewish terror cells existed. They bombed the Arab mayors. They've shot up Palestinian schools. You know what they call themselves?"

"What?" asked Adrian.

"TNT. *Terror Neget Terror*—terror against terror. But we haven't been able to move against them because your papa's friend Menachem Begin won't let us do our jobs."

"I always thought your job was to catch Arab terrorists."

"It is," said Nathan. "And we do. We're pretty damn good at it, little girl. But more than that—it's supposed to be to catch *all* terrorists."

Adrian bristled. "You're saying that the government keeps you from doing your job?"

"In a way."

"That's ridiculous. Besides—if you know about this TNT group, you're not the only ones. The story would get out. Look at what happened in Lebanon. Israel was slaughtered in the world press. The American networks broadcast lies. People are just waiting to give us a bad name."

"The problem," said Nathan, "is that, sometimes, we deserve it."

"But why always us? The Syrians killed thousands at Hama, and nobody said a word. Khomeini executes Kurds and Bahais and nobody says a word. Over a hundred thousand people are killed during the Lebanese civil war, and nobody says a word. The Saudi judicial system is medieval, and nobody says a word. But whenever one lousy Palestinian is roughed up during a demonstration in Judea or Samaria, it's front-page news."

"That's because Israel is a democracy," said Jared. "It has a free press—most of the time."

"Right." Adrian tapped her coffee cup for emphasis. "Which is a fact you seem to overlook, J.P." She stared at Nathan Yaari. "I'm no fan of Kahane, and I don't care for Moshe Levinger either. But I'm for a strong Israel. And you can't stay strong if you aren't unified."

"But the truth, little girl. What about the truth?"

"The truth is that we spend too much time flagellating ourselves over picayune matters. The central issue is the survival of Israel."

"The bombing of three Arab mayors isn't whatchamacallit—picayune," Yaari argued. "Unless you think that attempted murder is trivial."

"I don't. But Israel's survival is more important than those three men."

"If there's been a cover-up, it should be exposed," insisted Jared.

"You don't help things by washing your dirty laundry in public," said Adrian.

"You sound like your father," said Jared.

"Well, he's right." Adrian leaned forward. "I didn't agree with your Arafat interview, or the way you covered the war."

"What about the way I covered Abu Zain?" Jared shot Yoram a quick look.

"You did what you had to do. You agreed to Yoram's conditions and you filed the story you both agreed on."

"But it was a lie."

"It was good for Israel," Adrian said vehemently, missing the glance that passed between Jared and Yoram. She stood up. "You three patriots can continue your discussion without me. I'm going for a walk. I don't need to listen to any more of this trash."

"I don't think you should get yourself mixed up with Nathan Yaari." Adrian sat scrunched up in the front seat of the Autobianchi sucking on a piece of hard candy.

"Look," said Jared. They were driving past a new housing development on the outskirts of Ramat Hasharon. "Over there—to the left. You know, three years ago those were carrot fields. You used to be able to buy fresh vegetables. Now the farmers are gone, moved to the West Bank where the land's cheap."

"Don't change the subject."

"I'm not changing the subject. I'm not starting the subject."

"Sometimes you're a fool."

"Why?"

"Because you're so naïve. Listening to Nathan Yaari peddle that Peace Now, anti-government crap. He should know better—he's Shin Bet."

"What's that supposed to mean?"

"All that bull about Jewish terrorism. The Shin Bet has its hands full making sure Arabs don't blow up buses or kidnap solders on their way home for leave. Those are real problems—the whole idea of Jewish terror is overblown."

"What about the Palestinian mayors?"

She drew her legs under her and leaned against the window. "That was wrong. I never said it was right. But it's not the norm. It was never condoned by the Prime Minister. He told my father."

"And that's gospel?"

"He wouldn't lie to Poppa. They've known each other too long."

Jared grunted and gunned the car onto the highway heading south toward the Jerusalem interchange.

"Well?"

"Well, what? Begin wouldn't lie to your father? Just like Yoram wouldn't lie to me, right? Well, who knows. You know. Or you think you know. Me—I'm not so sure." He slowed for a traffic light at the Petah Tikva interchange and saw two girl soldiers waiting at a kiosk on the far side, thumbs outstretched. When the light changed he swerved across three lanes of traffic and stopped, reached across Adrian's body and opened the door. "Where to?"

"Jerusalem."

"You're in luck. We'll take you all the way." He ignored Adrian's nasty look. Hitchhikers would put an end to arguments, indeed to all but the most perfunctory conversation. She might not have wanted it, but Jared welcomed the prospective silence. It would give him a chance to think.

Sullenly, Adrian stepped out into the damp chill, tilted the seat forward, and allowed the girls in their bulky khaki parkas—*dubonim* they were called—to crowd into the tiny rear seat, duffel bags clasped to their bosoms like children, semiautomatic weapons—this pair were military police—stowed securely underfoot.

"You will be sorry you ever listened to Nathan Yaari," she said as Jared floored the accelerator. "Just mark my words, J.P."

CHAPTER 5

"Poppa?!" Adrian's voice rose two octaves in excitement. "Where are you?" She laughed vigorously into the phone. "That's wonderful. That's fantastic! We'll be right over." She slammed the receiver down and waltzed Jared around the living room. A unilateral truce had been declared, a ceasefire in the argument that had begun in Herzlyia. "Poppa's here. He got in two hours ago and he's been calling. He's at the King David and he wants to see us for dinner."

"What brings him?"

"Business. The bank."

Jared nodded. Felix Cooper, because of his three-decade friendship with Menachem Begin and his long, and generous, support of the Jewish state, had been able to cut through vast quantities of red tape to establish the first privately owned, full-service, American-Israeli bank with multiple offices on three continents. Given spiraling inflation in Israel, and the precariousness of the stock market, which resembled a financial soufflé, Jared had written the idea off as soon as Adrian's father had mentioned it.

But Cooper was both an optimist and a shrewd businessman. Opening U.S branches in New York, Los Angeles and Dallas, he beat the bushes for domestic business in every area from silicon chips to oil development, scouring the Jewish communities for accounts, and stressing the fact that a majority of the bank's investments would be made in Israel. He inveigled and cajoled the Israeli Embassy, until—at the urging of the Prime Minister's office—they transferred three of their seven major accounts to the bank's luxurious headquarters in a glass-and-steel tower Cooper built at the corner of Connecticut Avenue and L Street in downtown Washington. He bought a four-story townhouse on Brook Street in London's Mayfair district, which he converted into European headquarters and offices. Using his friendships in Israel, he sought out a solid portfolio of high-tech industries to support through loans. And—perhaps most wisely—he named his institution Eagle Intercontinental Bank, so as not to draw attention to its Israeli connections.

Miraculously, Jared thought, the bank, capitalized at twenty-five million dollars, had quintupled its initial investment and began running in the black in its sixth month. Now Cooper visited Israel regularly. Sometimes he brought Adrian's mother, Beverly. But on most trips he came alone, staying two or three days in Jerusalem to be near Adrian, and commuting in a chauffeured Chevrolet to Tel Aviv, where the bank's Israeli headquarters took up fifteen thousand square feet on the bottom two floors of an office building Cooper financed next to Diezengoff Towers, or to branch offices in Haifa, Beersheva, Metulla and Eilat.

They dressed rapidly, Jared changing from jeans and sneakers to polite gray slacks, a dark green cashmere turtleneck sweater Cooper had once brought him from London, a blazer and loafers. Adrian primped for half an hour in the bathroom, and then selected a paisley silk dress, high heels and a short red-fox jacket.

The effect, Jared noted, was more Chevy Chase than Yemin Moshe. "Don't we look like a couple of tourists," he chided amiably as they swung through the King David's revolving door and marched arm in arm through the colonnaded lobby.

Cooper was waiting for them in the semidarkness of the wood, tile and beam-ceilinged bar, dwarfing a small rectangular table, which he almost upset as he rose to greet his daughter and Jared. He swallowed her in a bearhug, big arms clasping and lifting Adrian right off the ground. "Pidge, oh, it's so great to see you." He smiled and grasped Jared's hand and arm firmly. "You too, Jared. It's a blessing to see you both."

"What a surprise." Adrian settled into the terra cotta velvet settee and snuggled under her father's arm. "What brings you?"

"Business. As usual. You know me—any excuse to see you. Some deal with a kibbutz making semiconductors near Beersheva, and I said to myself, 'Why do it by phone?' So here I am, for a two-day trip. I'm not even going to get jet lag." He waved a waiter over. "Another scotch for me, on the rocks with a twist, soda on the side. And what'll you two have? Listen, we'll have a couple of drinks here, and then I've got reservations in the grill downstairs. I know you two don't get American style steaks too often, and besides I've got an early day tomorrow. So I just thought—if it's okay with you, Pidge—we'd eat here?"

Jared ordered a Campari and soda. He liked Felix Cooper, honestly enjoyed and respected the bluff, loud-spoken Polish immigrant who had started out repairing radios and irons in a storefront on Manhattan's Lower East Side. By the early 1930s Cooper was making his own brand of irons in a small factory in the Long Island "sticks." A few years before World War II he relocated in Long Island City, in Queens, closer to transportation, and began manufacturing photoelectric cells—the result, Cooper once said, of a fortuitous tip from a business acquaintance.

"I didn't know what the hell I was doing," he'd told Jared. "I was the youngest of five kids, and the only boy. I had to drop out of school when I was fifteen because my father, God rest his soul, died of pneumonia, and it was up to me to support everybody. You know what I did? I carried oysters—schlepped oysters at this place on the Lower East Side called Billy the Oyster Man's. Twelve hours, thirteen hours a day I worked, and for pennies. There's all this talk about pulling yourself up by the bootstraps, Jared. I'll tell you something—I was too poor to buy the boots."

Educated or not, Cooper was a natural salesman. He secured himself a series of lucrative defense contracts during the war, building bomb sights and rangefinders for the Army Air Corps and financial security for himself. When the war ended, he enlarged his Long Island City plant and began to make semiconductors and connectors for the embryonic space industry. Then, abruptly, in 1951, he sold his business and took his wife and daughter to Washington. "I got bored, so I moved," was how he put it.

In the capital, Cooper invested in real estate. He bought a twenty percent interest in the area's first three shopping malls; he developed tract housing in suburban Maryland; he built apartment houses. He prospered. Simultaneously, his stature in the close-knit Jewish community grew. An outsider, he both charmed and bought his way in:

he donated both his time and his money generously to Jewish charities. He became president of the largest synagogue and chairman of the local chapter of the Zionist Organization of America, and spent as much time supporting the new state of Israel as he did selling three-bedroom, one-and-a-half-bath Colonials in Bethesda.

Jared had occasionally seen the Coopers at functions in Washington, although he hadn't socialized with them. But he knew Cooper's influence in the Jewish community was tremendous. He was a man whose involvement guaranteed the success of a charity dinner or fund-raising drive. Crowds parted when he entered a room. He was a friend of presidents, who dined in the private White House living quarters. In Israel, he was entertained by a series of Labor prime ministers, although he preferred quiet evenings in Menachem and Aliza Begin's modest Tel Aviv apartment. It had even crossed Jared's mind—fleetingly—that one of the reasons Jared himself did so well in Israel was the fact that he lived with Cooper's only child. Sure, he represented five million influential American readers. But he also had Cooper's indirect *protekzia*.

Now seventy-four, Cooper had a private net worth that ran into the scores of millions. He'd set up a private foundation to support his philanthropic activities, sold off his companies, and devoted himself entirely to what he called his retirement hobby, the bank, which had opened its doors thirteen months before.

To Jared, Cooper was unique. He had never met anyone so single-minded in his devotion to Israel. In Washington, it was all Cooper talked about. He was a well-read man, but politics didn't interest him unless there was a connection to Israel. His universal criterion for what went on in the world, what happened in the United States and what took place in the Washington area was simple and direct: "Is it good or bad for the Jews?"

Even his home reflected Cooper's attachment to the Jewish state. Jared's parents, Stanley and Muriel, lived in a stylishly minimalistic, faux-adobe-and-red-Spanish-tile-roofed hacienda in West Los Angeles. They decorated in soft pastels and earth tones, accenting with fashionable relics of the Camino Real and Western-inspired art purchased during week-long trips to nueva Santa Fe. Felix and Beverly Cooper had filled the mock-Tudor castle that sat on nine acres in Potomac, Maryland, with Judaica, Israeli art, and four-by-six-foot tapestries designed and executed by Maskit.

Jared's father, a surgeon, was a two-day-a-year man at Temple Beth-El on Wilshire Boulevard; he owned neither skull cap nor prayer shawl. Felix Cooper never missed a Sabbath or festival service at Washington's Adas Israel congregation. He wrapped himself in a huge, classically thick black-and-white wool tallit with much the same ecstasy he experienced as he cheered his beloved Washington Redskins from a private box high above the fifty-yard line.

After three years of listening to Cooper voice his passionate love of the Jewish state, Jared began to understand the depth of Adrian's unquestioning devotion. "Is it good or bad for the Jews?"—it was something that had been inculcated in her as long as she'd been alive.

She was, in so many ways, he thought, her father's daughter. Physically, she resembled neither of her parents closely, except for her mother's violet eyes and a smaller version of her father's nose. But in character, in outlook, in the way she approached life, Adrian was a carbon copy of Felix. Conservative both politically and financially, she was generous philanthropically. She, like Felix, shied away from the emotional in order to pursue the literal. They were both loyal, strong-minded (even pig-headed sometimes). But also honest in an old-fashioned way. Cooper often did business on the basis of a handshake. Adrian had done the same when she'd made her bargain with Jared before they'd moved here.

The waitress served their drinks. Jared raised his glass and smiled at Cooper. How American Jews changed in Israel. In Washington, Cooper wore blue suits and white-on-white shirts. Here he sported an open-necked, loud print silk shirt, plaid jacket and a gold-embroidered *kippa*—a skull cap. In Israel no one looked strangely at men wearing skull caps in five-star hotels. In New York or Los Angeles or Washington, it would have made Cooper an object of discussion. Yet to Jared the donning of a *kippa* only when in Israel bore the taint of faint hypocrisy. If one believed in such things, he thought, they should be done all the time. The Unnameable Name, after all, sees you wherever you are.

Adrian's father clinked Jared's glass with his own. "L'Chayim. So, still causing trouble?"

"Cheers." Jared sipped his drink. "That's what I'm paid for."

The elder man shook his head. "I talked to Ariel Sharon this afternoon. He was going to join me until he found I'd be taking you to dinner."

"Snubbed by the ex-defense minister? I didn't know I rated."

"It's not funny, Jared. This is a small country. You need all the friends you can get."

"Not that kind."

"Come on, be sensible. He told me he's thinking of suing you for libel after what you wrote about him and the Kahan Commission report."

"He's already suing *Time*. Isn't that enough?"

"You came down on him pretty hard."

"I came down on him? The Commission came down on him. 'Indirect responsibility' is what they said. Let him sue—he won't prove malice by *Time*, and he won't prove it by me."

"But to blow it up so much? What do you call it?—hype the story."

"Come on, Felix. I told the truth. I reported the facts. Nothing more. I simply said that there were a lot of unanswered questions. And there are."

"You know what the problem with Jared is, Poppa?"

Cooper looked at his daughter. "What?"

"I think it's a case of familiarity breeds contempt."

"Oh, for chrissakes." Jared was annoyed.

"It's true. Remember Sinai, and Jerusalem that first time? You loved Israel."

"I still love Israel."

"You have a hell of a way of showing it."

"I can be critical and still love it."

"You're not critical—you're vindictive. I see it in your articles. I see it in the way you talk about the government. Ever since we came here, you've taken a negative approach. In your eyes, Israel can't do anything right."

"What is it they say?" Cooper interrupted. "Good news is no news?"

"That's the way it is in *World Week*," Adrian said. She took Jared's hand in hers. "What about the good things, J.P.? What about Koby's vineyards, and making the deserts bloom, and all the high-tech industry, and the fact that Israel is the only democracy in the region? And what about Jerusalem? You love Jerusalem. When the Jordanians occupied the city you and I couldn't visit the Western Wall. But now every religion has freedom of access."

"So?"

"So the last story you wrote about Jerusalem wasn't about freedom but censorship, when *Al Fajr* tried to publish a PLO press release and the military censor forbade it—and rightly so."

Cooper shook his head. "More dirty laundry about Israel. That's the problem, Jared—" He put his head back, finished the scotch and ground an ice cube between his teeth. Glass in hand, he signaled for another round. "I know you have the best of intentions, but everything you write seems to give Israel's enemies something to be happy about."

"I can't be concerned about that."

"You're a Jew. You have a stake in this country."

"That can't affect what I write."

"It can't help but affect what you write. Answer me this: Does the state of Israel really mean something to you?"

"You mean emotionally?"

Cooper nodded.

"I just said it does. You know we both love it here."

"Then, as a journalist, how do you reconcile your emotions with what you write?"

"I don't."

"Bull."

"I don't."

"That's horse puckey, Jared. You can't help but make choices. From where I sit, you've done one of two things. Either you're being harder on Israel because you're a Jew and you hold the Jewish state to higher standards, or you're uncomfortable with being a Jew and somewhere in the back of your mind you want to appease the *goyim*."

"Dammit, Felix, that's a preposterous syllogism. You're giving me the original 'when did you stop beating your wife' line. You're saying I write what I write either because I'm Jewish and I report by Jewish—in other words, higher—values, or because I'm a self-hating Jew and I don't."

Cooper looked at Adrian and laughed. "Syllogism! A ten-dollar word from the writer. You may think it's preposterous, but that's how it looks to us back in the States. You all but call Ariel Sharon a murderer, but you go to Beirut and write a complimentary profile of Yasser Arafat, the *shmutz*."

"Complimentary?" Jared was outraged. "I was so critical I was warned never to come back to Beirut. I grilled him about the PLO's five billion dollar budget. I asked him about the drug smuggling that Fatah's been involved with. I wrote about PLO terror operations. That's hardly complimentary, Felix."

"You called him a *moderate*, for chrissakes."

"He is—compared to some—compared to Abu Nidal or George Habash he's—"

"He's a god-damn ter-ror-ist," Cooper interrupted, accenting each syllable by rapping his glass on the table. "That's not the only thing, either. Remember what you wrote about the Lebanon war? You said it was tearing Israel down the middle. You wrote that Sharon misled the Cabinet and the General Staff; that the war wasn't fought to end Lebanese-based terrorism, but to rewrite the political map of the Middle East."

"That's all true!"

"All I can tell you, Jared, is that Menachem Begin told me differently. And when Ariel Sharon came four months ago and spoke to the national council of the UJA—and I was there—he swore that Operation Peace for Galilee was undertaken only to destroy the terrorist bases in Lebanon—and there wasn't anybody at the dinner who didn't believe him. Me included."

"Of course he'd say that," Jared sputtered. "That was his whole spiel—at the start of the war and now. I'll bet he didn't talk about the Lebanese Shiites either."

"Shiites?"

"I go to Lebanon, Felix—you don't. And the same Islamic fundamentalists who welcomed the Israelis with flowers and rice ten months ago are going to start shooting at them pretty soon. Sharon tried to give Lebanon to his Maronite Christian friends—except he couldn't deliver. Now we're going to see all hell break loose."

"You can't be serious. Look at the talks, Jared. There are normalization talks going on between Israelis and Lebanese. Lebanon'll be the second Arab country to sign a peace treaty with Israel."

"It won't happen. The Syrians won't let it happen. The Shiites won't let it happen."

"You see?" said Adrian. "This is what I have to deal with every day from him."

Jared shook his head. "Facts are facts. The Shiites haven't been taken into account either by the Americans or the Israelis. And they're different from the PLO. The PLO likes to attack civilian targets; they're basically cowards. Shiites aren't afraid of making themselves martyrs. That's a historic fact—just look at the way Iran's gone in the past five years."

"Bull." Felix rapped the table with his glass. "There'll be a peace agreement."

"Maybe," Jared said, "but it won't last. And everybody here knows that. Everybody sane, that is."

"We didn't hear anything like this from Sharon. As a matter of fact he was optimistic."

"Then he lied."

"Sharon's a hero. A general. He wouldn't lie. Not to us—not to Jews."

"I don't believe you're so naïve." There was an uncomfortable pause. "Look, Felix. Let's just drop it, okay? I'm really happy to see you here. Let's just drop the politics and enjoy ourselves. Bring us up to date on what the bank is doing."

Cooper nodded. "Good idea." He sucked an ice cube out of the bottom of the glass, crunched it and squeezed Adrian's shoulder. "Okay, Pidge, enough. Let's go down to dinner and you can tell me what you've been up to over a good steak. I've got a proposal for you, too—something I think you'll jump at."

They were walking home, the one-two-one-two of their normally well-oiled syncopation out of beat, their shoulders tapping paradiddles against each other. Jared's hands were jammed in his pockets, his body hunched against the wind. "I think it's a lousy idea to work for your father," he said.

"Why?"

"Because you're doing just fine as you are. What do you need a job for?"

"For me, Jared—for me."

"You don't have any experience."

"Poppa said I can learn as I go."

"It's not a game, Adrian, it's not the same as volunteer work—"

"Precisely."

"—And we don't need the money."

She stopped abruptly and turned to face him. "You're not listening. It has nothing to do with money—it has to do with me. It would be the first time I've ever had a job—a real job, a full-time job."

He took her hands in his. "But Adrian, we'll never see each other. Commuting to Tel Aviv every day. Both of us with long hours. Life just won't be the same. Besides, we only have one car."

She shook him off and turned, walking slowly down the hill. "You heard Poppa. The bank will give me a car. And it's not the car that's bothering you. It's that life won't be the same. I won't be home all the time. I won't be at your beck and call any more. That's what you're really afraid of—my having my own life."

"That's a bunch of crap."

"Is it? Is it really? Think about it. No more afternoon walks in the Old City. No more fooling around whenever you want—"

"Whenever *I* want? I thought it was whenever *we* wanted."

"Okay—whenever we want. The thing is I won't be available to you the same as I have been. Which is another reason for taking this job. Dammit, J.P., we've settled into the same pattern my marriage settled into: you work, I sit at home. I'm a housewife—except I'm not a wife. So what does it make me? A houselover?"

"That's silly. You've got friends. You keep busy."

"Precisely—I keep busy. Around the house. And go shopping with friends. And have lunch. And we make love. Isn't that kind of existence a little Jurassic these days? I did graduate from Sarah Lawrence, you know—I did major in history. And I don't *want* to 'keep busy.' I want a job. And this *is* a job, but not just any job. It's a job with Poppa."

"But you're unqualified. He's throwing you a bone. He won't let you do anything. He's just giving you a title and an office."

"That's unfair."

"It's the truth, Adrian."

"It's the truth as you see it, J.P."

They were taking the long way home, walking along a path bordered by flower beds that led past the Montefiore windmill. Just beyond the old structure was a low stone wall. Adrian stopped and sat on it, facing the Hinnom Valley and Mount Zion. She patted the stones and Jared settled next to her, his arm protectively around her shoulder in the chill night air.

"Okay," he said. "Explain the truth as you see it."

She stared at the lights across the way. "This is the first time my father has ever dealt with me as an adult, J.P."

"Huh?"

"He always shut me out, never told me anything. I was never allowed to be a part of his business life—never really knew what he did, or how, or how it was going or anything."

"And you think it's going to be different now?"

"Yes." She turned toward him. "My parents and I have had a complex relationship, J.P. It hasn't always been, ah, stable."

"You seem to get along just fine to me."

"We do—now. But there were times . . ."

"What happened?"

She looked away. "Things."

"Such as?"

"It's very complex, Jared. I don't want to go into it right now."

He shrugged. "Up to you."

"Trust me—the job is very important."

"Even if you won't really be in a position to make decisions?"

"You don't know that."

"You're not a banker, Adrian."

"So what? I don't need an economics degree to run an office or check out companies the bank wants to lend money to."

"But—"

"And I can learn on the job. Poppa didn't say this was going to be easy, J.P. He said it was going to be a challenge."

"I still think he's throwing you a bone."

"You've got so little sensitivity." She shrugged his arm off and stood up. "It doesn't matter what you think. I'm going to take it." She wandered along the wall, trailing her hand on the stones.

Jared followed, scuffing the soles of his shoes on the smooth stone walk. "Do what you want."

She turned to him. "Besides—it probably won't affect our schedule that much, now that you've got that important new earth-shattering project you cooked up today with Yoram and Nathan Yaari."

"Project?"

"All that malarkey about Jewish terror. For God's sake, J.P., the press has already been so rough on Israel. Why do you have to go out and concoct more dirt?"

"I'm not making anything up. It's a story that's out there."

"Says who? Says Nathan Yaari. How do you know you can trust him?"

"I don't. I'll check him out just like I check all my sources out."

"I have the funny feeling he's going to check out just fine."

"Why?"

"Because he's peddling a story that fits in with your magazine's preconceptions."

"That's silly."

"No, it's not, J.P. *World Week* has always been hostile toward Israel. I told you that the day you accepted the assignment here. You were going to change things—or so you said."

"I have changed things. Our coverage of Israel is balanced. It's fair. It's better than *Time* or *Newsweek*."

"Not by much."

He caught up with her and took her by the arm. "Come on," he said. "Give me a break. You want me to become a propagandist for Israel. That's not my job, you know. It ain't my job to do Israel good—or bad. Just to tell people what's going on here."

"Sometimes—"

"Sometimes what?"

"Sometimes I think for all the times you say you love this country, I never see you do anything to prove it in print."

"Oh, Christ. That again?"

"I mean it. You've always been negative in your reporting, but in the past few months you've really gone off the deep end."

"You can't be serious."

"I am serious. When was the last time you wrote a positive story about Israel?"

"The Kahan Commission report story was positive."

"Only to you."

"What about the West Bank settlements piece?"

"It made Jewish settlers look like land-grabbing carpetbaggers."

"I did that sidebar on the Israeli press—showed how vital and free it was in comparison to the Arab press. That was positive."

"You had to drag in, what—two, three paragraphs about how ruthless Israelis are about censoring the Arab newspapers in Judea and Samaria. Nothing positive there."

"Okay, okay. The Christmas piece about Bethlehem."

"In which you managed to bring up—let me see if I can quote

you correctly—'Uzi-toting fanatics from Qiryat Arba' who broke up a peaceful Palestinian Christian demonstration."

"That's what happened. What was I supposed to do, lie?"

"You know something? The only story I can think of is one in which you did bend the truth a little—the one you filed as a favor to Yoram. And that only appeared because *The New York Times* ran a similar piece and the magazine had your file on hand."

"That really tells you something, doesn't it?"

"What?"

"That whenever I tell the truth, you don't like it." They had wandered down along the Mishkenot Sha'anannim below the windmill and stood facing a pile of metal and stone, a peace memorial, built by Abbie Nathan. "Well, here's some more truth you're not going to like. I never filed that story."

"What?"

"I didn't even write it."

"I don't understand what you're saying."

"I'm telling you I never filed anything on the Syrian raid. Yoram—or his people—did. They broke into my office and sent it to New York."

"They forged—" She drew in her breath. "That's why you were so mad at Yoram."

He nodded.

"Now I'm beginning to see."

"See what?"

"Why you've been writing all this trash lately. It's revenge."

"My God, you're myopic. Don't you see anything? Can't I tell you anything? Adrian, watch my lips move. I—am—simply—writing—what—is—going—on—here."

"And now to get back in your good graces, Yoram is trying to peddle you this sensationalistic garbage about Jewish terrorism."

He took her arm but she pulled away. "My father's right about what makes you write what you write about Israel," she said. "I think in your heart of hearts you're a self-hating Jew."

"You can think whatever you please." The blood drained from Jared's face. "You can think anything. I don't care. I'm going to the office."

"At this hour?"

"I—"

"Jared—we have to talk."

"About what?"

"I want you to understand. You have to understand."

"Understand?"

A tear formed in the corner of her right eye. "There are—it's—oh, J.P., it's so complex. I have to make you see why I have to work with Poppa. Please don't leave, J.P., please."

"Hey," he said, "the self-hating Jew already understands. Poppa's little girl is just following orders. Take any goddam job you want, Adrian. Do what the hell you want. I don't care. I'm leaving."

"If you go, Jared—if you walk out on me like this—you'd better think about it."

He wheeled and headed up the hill. "Oh, I have thought," he shouted over his shoulder. "I have thought."

CHAPTER 6

If winter was a time for angry prophets' skies and pedestrians' shoulders scrunched tight against the chill winds that whipped out of the rough Judean wilderness, then spring belonged to the shepherds. Warmed by a beneficent sun and encouraged by a living palette of multihued wild flower buds, hundreds of teenaged Arab goatherds from Ar Ram or Shufat in the north, and Silwan, Sur Bahir or Bayt Jala to the south moved their flocks across rock-strewn pastures, scrawny yellow and black dogs yapping and nipping at the hooves of nannies heavy-uddered with milk.

The city, too, changed with the change of the seasons. The Mahane Yehuda's jerrybuilt stalls filled with a rainbow of fruits and vegetables; and shoppers, no longer having to fight the cold and the wet, paused during their buying to gossip or joke with the vendors. Walking became a way of life again, heavy shoes and *dubonim* gave way to sandals and light sweaters. Business picked up at the cafés on Ben Yehuda Street where tables and chairs, stored in basements for the winter, reappeared overnight with the speed of West Bank settlements. Laughter, muffled in the cold season behind closed doors and heavy drapes, now once again became an integral part of the city's sounds—the shrill cries of children in playgrounds, the ecstasy of religious *heder* students discovering new meaning in an obscure Talmudic passage in the Me'a She'arim; even the muezzins' discordant taped calls to prayer, floating on the springtime breeze, seemed less ominous to Jewish ears.

And, oh, the babies. It was as if every young wife in the vicinity had given birth during the winter months. From villas, town houses, flats, out they poured, thousands of strollers filled with smiling, gurgling cherubim whose mothers and grandmothers pushed and wheeled and pinched and cooed over double, triple and quadruple infant chins.

Meanwhile, over at the corner of King George Street and the Jaffa Road, the ritual evening courting games began once more in earnest. Pimpled youths, not yet of Army age, clustered in twos, threes and fours to lick ice cream cones, gobble pizza or falafel and ogle the twos, threes and fours of nubile *hatti-hot* who paraded in skin-tight imitation French jeans, bulky oversized sweaters and double-dipped mascara. Those *hatti* hot eyes, however, were hot only for the lean and hungry-looking soldiers who strolled on patrol, berets at rakish angles, rifles strung across their necks horizontally in the Russian style so that, as they walked, they rested their arms as if on balance beams.

If spring was the season of birthing and mating it also was the season of building, of construction. Huge, lumbering flatbed trucks filled with bricks or the rose-tinged Jerusalem stone quarried to the north and west of the city clogged narrow streets as they crawled toward scores of new housing sites. Scaffolding went up: skeletal shrouds for hundred-year-old houses scheduled for revitalization, modernization and speculation.

Every day some thirty thousand Arabs came from the West Bank, walking, hitching, jostling and cramming onto scores of dilapidated diesel buses whose blue or white license plates made them prey to long security checks on the main roads to the city. They would come, by the thousands, to stand at what had become known as Jerusalem's new slave market: the Damascus Gate in the city's Eastern sector, where Jewish contractors driving panel trucks pulled to the curb, pointed fingers, and selected who would work and who would return home empty-handed and hungry.

Jared sat in a small Arab café on Sultan Suleiman, sipping sweet tea with mint and watching the human sea ebb and flow a hundred yards away. A brown Mercedes 280 SEL pulled into the living surf; its driver pressed a button and the passenger-side window eased down a crack. He called something out. Immediately three young men, knitted fellah caps on their heads, fought for position to jump in the back seat. Two made it, each pummeling the other. The Israeli turned, grasped the one closest to the open door by the collarless neck of his shirt, and tossed him back into the crowd. Window up, car doors locked electronically, the car gunned into traffic and disappeared up the Nablus Road.

The young man sharing Jared's table wiped a shiny paper napkin across his full beard, not quite erasing all traces of the powdered sugar residue of a sweet bun, and shook his head. "Depressing, no?"

"Depressing, yes."

"It could have been me, you know."

"What could have been you?"

"That poor fellah—swept away to do a day's work at someone's villa for five hundred shekels. Scrubbing a Jew's floors. Cleaning bathrooms. Gardening."

"And instead, you hire your own domestic help, and eat at Venetzia?"

The Arab nodded. "It's amazing what a graduate degree in journalism from Columbia will do for you. I still wonder, though—how close I came to being one of them." He nodded toward the eddying crowd across the wide, divided avenue. "Ahh—the authorities arrive."

Two mounted policemen wheeled large gray horses toward the edge of the crowd, flicking their mounts with batons. The Arabs edged back toward the gates of the Old City, hampered by construction barricades. Whistling, the police broke the pool of would-be workers into puddle-groups, catching half a dozen by the scruff of the neck and issuing fifty-shekel summonses for loitering.

"A real-life slave market," said Rafi Taal bitterly. "Better, even. This one's swept under the rug before the first tourists arrive. No evidence of what's gone on. And the American Jews walk unhassled into the Old City. What do you call it?"

"Potemkin Village Israel," said Jared.

"A lovely image, and so true. How come it's never been in print?"

"The right story hasn't come along yet."

The Arab nodded. "Perhaps so." He lapsed into silence and watched as the last of the non-working stragglers were dispersed. "How's Adrian?"

"Okay. Working hard."

"I haven't seen much of her lately."

"It's the hours. She's gone by six-thirty, and doesn't get home until after eight."

"It must do wonders for your domestic life."

"We'll survive." Jared sipped at his tea. In fact, he was not so sure what would happen to his domestic life. It was not Adrian's job alone that had caused a rift between them. It was something he could not put his finger on, a new fault line in their emotional topography that daily grew wider and wider. They shared a house, a life, the cat. And yet these days he felt cut off by Adrian, banished from her thoughts, emotions, goals.

Her job didn't help matters. Newly chic in half a dozen Valentino and Armani dresses after a quick buying trip to Rome, financed by a five-thousand-dollar advance on her salary, she'd thrust herself headlong into the bank's operation. Felix had given her the title of Managing Director, Israel; despite a complete lack of experience she had, indeed, begun to manage and direct. Felix, of course, was no fool. He'd given Adrian not only a title, but two assistant managing directors—with MBAs from Harvard. They did the real work. Adrian went to lunch a lot and busied herself designing a new logo for the stationery, hiring an advertising agency and taking meetings with big-name Zionists. She came home every night to kick off her Guccis or Papagallos, lugging a spanking new Vuitton attaché case bulging with documents that were sometimes read and sometimes not, but never went unflaunted.

And with each new self-delegated responsibility, Jared felt, she moved further and further away from him. It wasn't just the fact that she now earned more than he. Nor that she had her own set of commitments (as likely as not she'd eat dinner in Tel Aviv—business, she'd say—and come home just in time to plop exhausted into bed). Their social life suffered; no time for dinner parties these days. So Jared was reduced to seeing friends by himself, either at their homes or at cafés, bars, restaurants. There were no more long walks through the Old City, no shashlik lunches at Shahin. And in their time-consuming, disparate business schedules, the scheduled business of making Jewish babies had become almost forgotten.

Still, there was his work. He shuttled back and forth to Lebanon, where he covered the normalization talks, reported on Israeli reaction to the bombing of the U.S. Embassy in Beirut, filed thousands of words on Secretary of State George Shultz's shuttle diplomacy and

Begin's grudging acceptance of the American plan for Israeli troop withdrawal from Lebanon. Repeatedly (but unsuccessfully) he tried to interest his editors in an article about the growing resentment of Shiite Moslems against the Israeli Army. In the summer of 1982 the IDF had been seen as liberators. Now they were just another in the endless list of occupying armies that came and bivouacked and upset the fragile status quo. There were rumors that sometime during the coming summer Israel would pull its troops back behind the Awali River, leaving most of South Lebanon under the guns of the Shiite and Druse militias, or the heavy-handed oppression of the Syrian Army.

There was not much progress on his long-term project. Yoram Gal and Nathan Yaari had given him some leads. But Jared's editors weren't interested in Jewish terror. Like most executives, they based their understanding of foreign events on what they were fed by government officials, what they read in *The New York Times* and saw on the nightly television news. Jared knew that the Lebanese situation would never be solved without Syrian participation and involvement. But his editors felt they knew better: briefed by the Secretary of State during a private, off-the-record lunch, they bought the Administration's line completely. Jared filed a story on the arrest of four armed religious Jews who tried to penetrate the tunnels under the Temple Mount. But the Jewish terrorist story was spiked by a senior editor in New York named Johanssen. He cabled Jared to drop a subject of minor importance and to concentrate on the real issues of the day: the upcoming Lebanese peace agreement, and the effect Begin's aggressive land-confiscation policies would have on U.S.–Israeli relations.

And so it was that Jared found himself sitting in an Arab café at seven in the morning with Rafiq El Taal, M.S., Journalism, Columbia '77, who supported a wife, three children, his father, and his wife's parents on the twelve hundred dollars a month *World Week* paid him (plus mileage and expenses) as its West Bank stringer.

"Well." Jared signaled to the waiter, threw a handful of coins into his tea saucer and stood up. "I think we should go to work."

Rafi Taal nodded and scraped his chair back from the table. He could, Jared thought, have passed for a Kurd or Moroccan, with his beard and thick shock of longish black hair. Still, Taal managed to maintain an air of Ivy League yuppiedom. His open-necked white shirt was tucked into nicely aged chino trousers whose plain bottoms fell neatly just above a pair of Bass Weejun penny loafers, properly scuffed. The requisite reporter's notebook—No. 800, reorder from Stationers, Inc., Richmond, Va., U.S.A.—was in his left rear pocket. The top of a Cross pen shone from his shirt. Only his accent and his identity card betrayed him: the accent was unmistakably Palestinian; the identity card made him subject to search and seizure at IDF roadblocks—as did the blue license plate on his beat-up Renault, into which he and Jared now climbed.

The ignition caught after several tries and Taal threw the car, choking and belching smoke, into gear. They bucked into traffic, waved off an approaching donkey cart long enough to make a U-turn, and swung onto the lower part of the Haneviim. From there, they made their way through rush-hour traffic around the center of the city, skirting the narrow, triple-parked streets, until they caught the main Bethlehem road going south.

At the Gillo exit they headed up what had once been a wadi. Now it was a four-lane blacktop access road cleft by concrete planters filled with rust-colored soil and young palm trees and tended by squads of solicitous Arabs. But instead of continuing to the center of Gillo with its banks, supermarket, auditorium and small shops, Rafi veered onto an unpaved dirt road; it wove alongside the heavy stone walls of the fortresslike settlement, and into the Arab village of Sharafat.

It was to be another in what seemed to Jared an endless series of interviews for a piece about land appropriation on the West Bank. Rafi had found a family, the Sallemehs, whose sole support, four dunam of olive trees (about an acre), had just been bulldozed so that a new underground water tank for Gillo could be installed. The story would write itself, actually. But now he had to go through the motions. He would ask questions, Rafi would translate. He would get answers, Rafi would translate. He would make scribbles in his notebook. They would leave. His story would be published. The government would complain. Adrian would call him a self-hating Jew. Nothing would change. And in another six months, that same dumb-ass senior editor in New York would suddenly get the bright idea to do a feature on Israeli land appropriation on the West Bank, and the whole meaningless cycle would start over once again.

The morning progressed precisely as Jared thought it would.

Actually, the Sallemehs were better than most. He was a young man of about thirty-five, with an earnest face and a sense of fatalistic humor about what had happened to him. She was beautiful in the classic Arab sense: a strong face and flawless bone china complexion which was set off (quite magnificently, Jared thought) by the red, white and green kerchief worn bound around her head in traditional Palestinian style. He made a quick note for Nafta Bar Zohar to come and take a few pictures. These weren't your normal caterwauling Palestinians. They were a family whose pictures would evoke some sympathy from an American audience. They looked like, well, like the kinds of neighbors who shouldn't have had their olive trees bulldozed. He spent more time with them than he should have, tracing their family history back before the War of Independence—the 1948 war, Mahmoud Sallemeh called it—to the time when Sallemeh's great-grandfather bought the olive grove from an absentee Turkish landlord.

It wasn't until shortly before eleven that he arrived back in the office. Annie told him that someone named Nat had called—she said it was a voice she didn't recognize—and had left a message asking to meet Jared at twelve for lunch "at the usual place." "Does that mean I can reach you at Venetzia?"

"Nope."

"Where, then?"

"I'll be on the beeper." Jared rummaged through his desk drawer and attached the device to his belt. "See you later."

"The usual place" meant a drive down to Tel Aviv and a long, meandering walk through the city's old Carmel Market to make sure he wasn't being followed. It also meant that Nathan Yaari finally had some new information.

Jared left the Autobianchi in an underground car park near the intersection of Ibn Givrol and Carlebach, equidistant from Zahal headquarters and the wholesale farmers' market. From there he worked his way due west, taking several cutbacks and zigzags, until he arrived on King George. There he jumped a bus, rode for five minutes, got off at the last minute near Pines Street, flagged a taxi and rode to Magen David Square. He ambled there for a few minutes, looking at the posters for coming attractions in the movie house, window-shopped at a delicatessen, and then wandered across the bustling street and disappeared into the crowded alleyways of the Carmel Market. He checked his watch: twelve twenty-five. He was late.

To the tourist's eye the *Shuk Ha'Carmel* is a place of chaotic disorder, of produce, meats, fish, cheese, olives, breads, all sold hurly-burly amidst the shrieks of street hawkers peddling counterfeit audio and video cassettes, stolen radios and TVs, jewelry from satchels, and exotic T-shirts. All of this is simultaneous with other, more established shops: toy vendors, suitcase dealers, leather goods and clothing stalls. But to Jared's practiced gaze it had a definite Levantine logic.

First came the clothing stalls, cassette vendors, and fruits and vegetables. Bakeries sat cheek by jowl with T-shirt hawkers. Delis and butchers, of course, were located alongside tables of wind-up toys. The side streets were reserved for meat and poultry, the secondary alleyways for spice, dry goods and legumes kiosks, each of which blended its own recipe for Yemenite *kawaij*—the all-purpose pepper-enriched spice that was used to bolster soups, meats, fish, poultry, coffee and tea—or *zatar*, the Arab blend of coriander, sesame, salt and cumin into which one dipped chunks of round, olive-oil-soaked bread. The expensive goods were closest to Allenby; the cheapest at the market's southernmost tip, where beggars clustered to scavenge the garbage piles of half-rotted produce, and half a dozen flower dealers hawked their wares under each other's noses.

Jared found Nathan at their usual contact point: sampling hard, salty Arab goat cheese at a kiosk at the corner of Zion Street, just above "Turkey Butchers Row." He paid no attention to the Shin Bet man but rapped on the counter, bought a hundred grams for himself and then started down past the butcher shops, peering inside to watch as the dexterous knivesmen stripped carcasses to make *schnitzel shel hodu*—turkey cutlets. Nibbling on the cheese he walked west again, stopping to buy fresh *kawaij maroc* in a brown paper sack; he continued south, then west, descending past metalworking cubicles and shoemakers, seamstresses and tinsmiths, working his way into the *Kerem Hataimini*, the Yemenite Quarter. When he reached the small doorway of the Zion restaurant, he descended the three steps, waving at Shmuel, the diminutive, curly-haired Yemenite who managed the place.

"*Zion—b'bayit*—Is Zion around?" he shouted over the din of

waiters calling orders and customers arguing. The tiny place, two rooms, twelve tables, was crammed with market workers.

Shmuel pointed at the ceiling. "Upstairs."

Jared slipped behind the salad counter. Waiters were ladling mounds of humus, tehina, eggplant babaganough and Turkish-style marinated, chopped vegetables onto small plates, scooping bowls of garlic-laden olives, and spooning red-hot pepper sauce into aluminum dishes. He went through a concealed door, up two flights of stairs, through another door, along a passageway that connected two buildings, and then down a flight of stairs. At the end of a narrow hall he was confronted by a heavy metal firedoor that had no handle.

He knocked three times, then twice, then three times again. The door eased open. Nathan Yaari stood behind it, smiling.

"*Bokker tov*—good morning. I didn't think you were going to make it."

"And miss one of Zion's good meals?" Jared eased past the burly Shin Bet agent and let him close the door. Then he took Yaari by the shoulders. "It's been a while. I worried you wouldn't call."

"Why call if there's nothing to say?"

"Just to stay in touch."

Yaari shook his head. "You Americans." Then he smiled. "I understand, Jared. Working the sources by staying in touch, right?"

Jared nodded. He walked over to the louvred window and peered down into the street.

"Don't worry." Yaari poured himself a small cup of *kawaij*-infused coffee. "We're alone. Zion sees to that."

"He runs the neighborhood, doesn't he?"

"Just about. Nothing goes on he doesn't know about. And, good fortune, he happens to be my wife's cousin's cousin."

Jared sank into a pumpkin-colored overstuffed velvet sofa and looked at the painting that dominated Zion's office. It was a six-by-nine-foot canvas depicting Operation Magic Carpet—the exodus of the Yemenite Jews from Aden in 1948. He watched as Yaari lit a cigarette, sat at Zion's desk, and put his feet up.

Finally the Shin Bet agent spoke. "We have something for you. But it has to be handled delicately."

"Okay."

"No—delicately. With kid gloves. You're going to have to protect me on this."

"Tell me about it first."

"Off the record."

"You know how nervous I get when I hear those words from people like you and Yoram?"

"It has to be."

"I'll protect you, I'll protect you. Just tell me the story on background," said Jared, pulling out his notebook and a pen.

"We got a break in the bombing case—the Nablus and Ramallah mayors. Remember I told you that we were forbidden from pursuing it with the same, ah, energy, as we use in Arab terrorism cases? Anyway, I bent the rules a little bit. We set up a surveillance team in Qiryat Arba. Good men—quiet guys—who knew how to do a job. And they got their feet in the door.

"There's this asshole named Katzblum. A real militant . . . you know? The kind who likes to carry his Uzi all the time. We knew about him because the bus from Jerusalem was stoned outside Beit Jala last year. He, the schmuck, opens the window, fires three clips into the hills, and a couple of the shots ricochet; they come back through the bus and wound a Jewish student and his mother. So anyway, we're keeping an eye on this Katzblum.

"We discover that he fools around. Such a religious man, too. I tell you these Orthodox hypocrites will be the death of me. Now get this—he's having an affair with his neighbor's wife. I mean, the wonderful chutzpah of it all. Not only coveting his neighbor's wife—but *shtupping* her too.

"Now, here's the best part. The surveillance team gets pictures." Yaari brought his feet off the desk, opened a briefcase, and tossed a brown envelope at Jared.

Jared opened the package, spreading half a dozen photographs on his lap. He laughed and whistled. "Wonderful shots. He didn't even take his *tzitzit* off."

"He's a religious man. Notice how his *kippa* is all skewed around. There's another shot—it's not here—where he's holding onto his *kippa* for dear life while he's going down on her."

"Who says the religious don't know how to have fun?"

"Not me," said Yaari. "I learned a few things from these pictures, believe me."

"What happened?"

"Here's the incredible part. We took the pictures to Katzblum.

Showed them to him. I did it myself—in a friendly sort of way. I said, 'Katzblum, I'm not going to quote 'Leviticus' to you. I won't be like that. But here you are with your putz stuck someplace it definitely should not be stuck. And your wife won't like these pictures at all. Not to mention your neighbor, who may be religious just like you, but also is a reserve paratrooper who's stayed in shape.' "

Jared laughed conspiratorially.

"And you know what? The schmuck says nothing. Mute. He just sits there in his living room and stares at the pictures. So I say, 'Look, Katzblum, there's a way to keep this quiet. We know you know who's doing what to whom. We know you have friends—not bad guys—just people who feel strongly about Judea and Samaria. The next time you all get together, we'd like you to wear a little microphone to the meeting. Just in case they say anything interesting. And if you do this little favor for us, we'll burn the pictures and give you the negatives.' "

Yaari ambled to Jared's sofa, wiped each of the prints with his handkerchief, packed them in their envelope and replaced them in his briefcase.

"And then you know what? He refused. He threw me out of his house. Then he called up the Qiryat Arba leadership and told them he had a problem with Shin Bet. So they recommended a lawyer to him. He goes to Jerusalem, where he sees the lawyer—this Eliezer Ben-Canaan guy who represents a lot of the West Bank settlers. They have a conference, and then—would you believe—the two of them march up to the Prime Minister's office. They actually get an appointment. And Katzblum tells his story to Begin, and the next day I get an official reprimand and I'm ordered—ordered!—off the case. The Prime Minister's office tells me that I'm pursuing something that could be deleterious to the welfare of the state of Israel."

Jared whistled.

"You bet it's worth a whistle."

"Can I confirm any of this?"

"I bet Ben-Canaan would give you something. He's always blowing his own horn."

"What about Begin's office?"

"You know that baldheaded twenty-five-year-old Yeshiva-bokker runt who takes Begin's notes?" Yaari used the Hebrew for dwarf—*gammad.*

"Yankel Grupnik? Sure I do."

"Buy the *gammad* a drink. He likes to drink. His tongue gets loose."

"What about Katzblum?"

"That's up to you. The only thing is that you have to protect me."

"But that's hard. I could only have heard the story from you. Or someone in Shin Bet."

"Not necessarily. If you started inquiring about Shin Bet abuses, started talking to the Hebron and Qiryat Arba crowd about religious harassment—and you sounded sympathetic—I bet something would open up."

"Possibly."

"Of course it would. These guys like to brag about how they have a line to Begin, about how important they are. The only thing is, when you call Shin Bet we're going to deny the whole story. Probably censor the piece, or try to."

"I can get around it. Let me worry about that end."

"You're the journalist. I'm only a poor whatchamacallit—shoegum."

"Gumshoe."

"Gumshoe." Nathan Yaari pointed to his rubber soles. "Gumshoe." He pressed a button on Zion's desk. "Let's eat. How about a big bowl of oxfoot soup and some kebab?"

An hour later, well fed and a little sleepy from the heavy food, Jared slipped out of Zion's back door and wandered back up the hill toward the market. He caught a bus on Allenby, rode it north on Ben Yehuda and transferred to another on the corner of Bograshov, alighting near the Habima Theater. From there he walked east until he came to the corner of Ibn Givrol and Carlebach.

He decided to stroll to *Maariv*'s offices two blocks away and visit a friend there, a columnist at the afternoon daily who had helped him set up appointments with West Bank settlers in the past. Jared was meandering up the street when he noticed two black Mossad Chevrolets with their multiple antennas pull up to the Olympia restaurant across the wide thoroughfare. The first was a security car, with four agents carrying automatic weapons. The second had curtained windows. Both were heavily streaked on their lower body panels and wheels with the dirty red-brown mud Jared knew to be common to southern Lebanon. He stood in the doorway of a tobacconist's shop, watching as the security men checked out the restaurant then returned to open the door of the second car.

First to climb out was Yoram, in combat fatigues and maroon paratrooper's beret rolled up in his epaulet. Then came a tiny, round-faced, pasty-skinned man with darting eyes behind thick glasses, dressed conservatively in a black suit, black tie and white shirt. It was Menachem Navor, nicknamed Mandy, Mossad's number-two man and one of the prime architects of Israel's policy of selective retribution against Arab targets.

The blood drained from Jared's face as a third passenger in the second car emerged. It was Adrian.

He heard her come in; heard the locks being secured and the creak of footfalls ascending. He'd been waiting three hours. Preparing. "Hi."

"Hi. You're up late."

"Just waiting for you. Good day?"

She gave him an impersonal kiss on the mouth. "Busy. What about you?"

"Nothing special. Did some interviewing for the West Bank story. Want anything to drink? Some wine, maybe?"

"Just juice."

"I'll get it for you. So—anything special go on today?"

"The usual. One nice thing: we're going to be the first bank in Israel to run American-style promotions. You know, gifts for depositors. Mind if I join you?"

"Not at all. I was just reading."

He put a marker in the book and peered at her. "So business is okay?" He headed for the kitchen.

She flopped onto the sofa, kicking off her shoes, and massaged her feet. "I talked to Poppa today. He says that if we keep up this pace, I'll be bringing home a big bonus at the end of the year."

"Terrific." He gave her a glass of orange juice and watched as she sipped it slowly.

"It is terrific." She took another swallow. "He relies on me."

"That must be tremendously satisfying."

"Now you're sounding petulant. Don't begrudge me this, J.P. Please. It's important."

"More important than me?"

"What the hell does that mean?"

He raised his palms toward her. "I'm sorry. I didn't mean . . . It's just that we haven't had a whole lot of time together lately."

"That'll change. I know it'll change. And besides, I seem to remember a four-month period last year when you were hardly home at all."

"That was a war, Adrian."

"So is this, Jared—in its way."

"What?" He stared at her. Her face was a mask. She set the glass of juice down. "Nothing else to report?"

"Not really. The usual paperwork."

"No meetings?"

"Huh-uh. Boy, I'm starved." She headed for the kitchen, followed by the cat. "I never got away from my desk all day. Had to cancel a dinner with Chaim Levy from the World Zionist Organization." He could hear her putter. Heard the rustling of pot and pan. "I'm going to make an omelette. Want something?"

She was lying. He knew it. The question was, did she know he knew? "No thanks, I ate."

"How's the West Bank story going?"

"All right. Rafi and I spent the morning near Gillo. I should have things finished by the weekend."

"What?"

"Finished by the weekend. Listen—if I can get it done, how about we go away for a couple of days? Drive up to Galilee. Maybe to Vered Hagalil, or Safed?"

She poked her head through the kitchen door. "Oh, J.P., I'd love to, but I'm going to have to work straight through. I told you, I got caught up today with desk work, and now I've got to finish this proposal for the WZO by Sunday morning. That's when we rescheduled the meeting."

He nodded. "Okay. Just a thought."

She smiled. "A nice thought." She disappeared back into the kitchen.

"Thank you," he called after her. "I tell you what—maybe if

you have to work on Sunday I'll come down to Tel Aviv. We haven't been to the Olympia in ages. I'll take you to lunch."

"That would be wonderful, I've missed going there."

"Maybe I'll call Yoram and Aviva."

She came back carrying a plate of eggs and a slice of buttered bread, followed by the cat. "Why?"

"We haven't seen them lately."

She made a face. "I don't want to see Yoram."

"Why?"

She sat on the sofa, put her feet up and balanced the plate on her lap. "I told you. I thought he was peddling you a bad story. And I think he's ambitious and self-serving. He's not a nice man, J.P. You were right about him."

"Right?"

"The Syrian mission."

"You defended him."

"I know. But . . ."

"But?"

She took a forkful of egg and chewed on it slowly. "He's cold, Jared. Manipulative. He'll do anything to get what he wants."

"That's a big change from you. What happened?"

"Nothing. I've been thinking, that's all. I guess I hadn't realized the truth about Yoram until the last time I saw him—"

"When was that?"

"You know, when we went to visit them in Herzlyia and met that Yaari character. I think your instinct was right, J.P. I think Yoram uses people."

"Is that from firsthand knowledge or woman's intuition?"

She stared at him, egg paused halfway between plate and mouth. "You're grilling me."

"Am I?"

"Yes. And I don't like it. What are you getting at, J.P.?"

"I saw you today. With Yoram and Mandy Navor. At Olympia."

"And?"

"You lied—you told me you were at your desk."

"So?"

"I thought we were going to be honest with each other. We made a deal a long time ago."

"I forgot—you're right: I was at Olympia. So what? It slipped my mind. I've got a lot of things on my mind these days."

"Such as?"

"Things. There's a lot of pressure on me with this job. I don't have to talk about it, Jared. There are things you haven't told me—"

"Like?"

"The time Yoram forged your story. That you were going to be in Tel Aviv today."

"It just happened."

"Did it—or were you following me?"

"Don't be asinine."

"Just who's the asinine one here, Jared? You with all your silly suspicions, or me?"

"There's an obvious answer to that question, but I'm not going to say it."

"God, you make me furious."

"And you make me furious. We never spend time together. You're always busy—you drop into bed and fall asleep. I don't think we've slept together in three weeks. It's always the bank, the bank, the bank. When the hell do I get equal time?"

"Don't try to change the subject—it's not my fault, Jared. I put up with you when you went to Lebanon. My God, you'd disappear for weeks at a time to heaven knows where. And I'd be waiting here like some—some—*bimbo*—for you to come back. Did I open my mouth? Did I complain? Did I do anything? And now, I finally have a job—maybe it doesn't mean anything to you, but it does to me, and all you do is bitch and complain. And you're suspicious, too. You don't trust me. You know what I think?"

"What?"

"I think you played dirty pool. A dirty reporter's trick. You followed me. Followed me! And now you tried to catch me up. You knew where I was all the time, and you tried to get me to—" She jumped to her feet, inadvertently upending the plate of eggs onto the rug. The cat went at the food. "Oh, damn you, Jared. Damn you! It wasn't fair to follow me—"

Jared pulled his handkerchief out and knelt to mop up the mess. Adrian went straight for the bedroom door and slammed it. He scooped the eggs back onto the plate and followed her, to hear her turn the bolt on the inside of the door.

"Adrian—"

"Just leave me alone."

"Adrian—"

"Get out—get out. Go away, Jared."

She wanted him out? Okay—he'd get out. Sleep at his office. Live at his office. She could do what she goddam wanted to do. Meet with Yoram and lie about it. She could even screw Yoram for all he cared. Maybe she was even now. Yoram kept mistresses. He was attractive, charming, lascivious. It was not impossible.

And yet he was torn. Perhaps he should stay; wait her out. He always escaped to his office when they had a fight. The office was a refuge, a womb—it was his in a way this house could never be. But the battlefield was here in Yemin Moshe; it was here that he'd have to make a stand, sooner or later.

So tonight he'd wait. Jared rapped on the door. "Adrian!" Tonight he'd confront her. "Come on, Adrian, open the door."

He pounded on the solid wood. Goddammit—their lives were coming apart. Despite his anger he didn't want that to happen.

"Adrian, please open the door. We have to talk."

Silence. He put his ear to the door. He could hear muffled sobbing.

"Please?"

No response. Dammit. Well, it wasn't his fault. He wasn't the one who'd lied. It was Adrian. She had lied to him—a baldfaced lie. Was it the only one? Was it because of Yoram? Were they—was she—oh, Christ.

"Okay—to hell with you," he shouted through the door.

Reporter's tricks? She hadn't seen anything yet. Not in their lives and not in his work. He'd find something. A good story to write—not some crap about olive groves being appropriated. Let her work twenty-hour days at the bank, or wherever the hell she was spending her time. He'd go to Qiryat Arba. He'd see the *gammad* for a drink, two drinks, three.

Reporter's tricks? She hadn't seen anything yet.

PART THREE

June 1983

CHAPTER

SWWM:JERU/3 NYK 25 MAY 1983
TO: NEWSDESK FOR: WORLD
FROM: JERUSALEM BY: J. P. GORDON
SLUG: GOVT INTERFERES IN JEWISH TERROR INVESTIGATION

—MILITARY CENSOR HAS NOT CLEARED THIS COPY—

THE BEGIN ADMINISTRATION HAS ACTIVELY DISCOURAGED THE SHIN BET, ISRAEL'S INTERNAL SECURITY ORGANIZATION, FROM PURSUING PERPETRATORS OF TERRORIST ACTS AGAINST ARAB PALESTINIANS, ACCORDING TO INFORMED SOURCES HERE.

A HIGHLY PLACED SOURCE IN THE PRIME MINISTER'S OFFICE CONFIRMS THAT LESS THAN TWO MONTHS AGO A SHIN BET OFFICER WAS REPRIMANDED FOR INVESTIGATING THE POSSIBLE CONNECTION BETWEEN A MILITANT WEST BANK SETTLER, AZRIEL KATZBLUM, AND THE 1980 BOMBING OF THE PALESTINIAN MAYORS OF RAMALLAH AND NABLUS. KATZBLUM, AN IMMIGRANT FROM THE UNITED STATES, IS A MEMBER OF THE GUSH EMUNIM—THE BLOCK OF THE FAITHFUL—WHO LIVES IN THE MILITANT RELIGIOUS SETTLEMENT OF QIRYAT ARBA, JUST NORTH OF THE ARAB CITY OF HEBRON, IN THE OCCUPIED WEST BANK.

KATZBLUM'S LAWYER, ELIEZER BEN-CANAAN, CONFIRMS THAT ≪THE SHIN BET MADE SOME INQUIRIES WHICH WE CONSIDERED IMPROPER, AND A COMPLAINT WAS FILED WITH THE APPROPRIATE AUTHORITIES.≫ BEN-CANAAN, WHO HAS DEFENDED A NUMBER OF MILITANT

JEWISH WEST BANK SETTLERS, WOULD NOT CONFIRM THAT HE WENT TO THE PRIME MINISTER'S OFFICE.

(MORE)

PAGE TWO JERU/3 NYK 25 MAY, '83

SHIN BET AUTHORITIES DECLINED TO CONFIRM OR DENY THAT ANY OF THEIR OPERATIVES HAD BEEN REPRIMANDED IN THE KATZBLUM CASE, OR EVEN THAT KATZBLUM HAD BEEN UNDER INVESTIGATION.

IT IS KNOWN, HOWEVER, THAT KATZBLUM, WHO HAD COME TO THE ATTENTION OF SECURITY FORCES WHEN HE FIRED A SUBMACHINE GUN AT A BAND OF PALESTINIAN ROCKTHROWERS DURING A BUS TRIP FROM JERUSALEM TO QIRYAT ARBA LATE IN 1982, WAS UNDER SHIN BET SURVEILLANCE.

IT IS ALSO KNOWN THAT KATZBLUM AND HIS LAWYER SOUGHT—AND RECEIVED—AN APPOINTMENT WITH PRIME MINISTER MENACHEM BEGIN ON MARCH 13.

INDEPENDENT CONFIRMATION OF THIS WAS ACHIEVED BY CORRESPONDENT WHO SAW WITH HIS OWN EYES THE PRIME MINISTER'S APPOINTMENT BOOK WITH APPROPRIATE NOTATIONS. THE MEETING TOOK PLACE BETWEEN FOUR-FORTY-FIVE AND FIVE-FIFTEEN IN THE AFTERNOON.

SINCE MENACHEM BEGIN BECAME PRIME MINISTER IN 1977, AND APPOINTED ARIEL SHARON AS MINISTER OF AGRICULTURE AND SETTLEMENTS, THE GOVERNMENT HAS TRIED ITS BEST TO PLAY DOWN INCIDENTS OF JEWISH TERROR DIRECTED AT ARABS.

(MORE)

PAGE 3 JERU/3 NYK 25 MAY, '83

BUT SIGNS OF INCREASING JEWISH TERROR ACTIVITY DISTURBS SECURITY AUTHORITIES DESPITE PUBLIC DENIALS. IN RECENT MONTHS HIGH-RANKING OFFICERS IN THE ISRAELI DEFENSE FORCES (IDF) HAVE NOTED WITH ALARM THE PURLOINING OF MUNITIONS FROM A NUMBER OF ARMY BASES AND UNITS. ONE TOP IDF SOURCE SAYS THAT THE MATERIAL INCLUDES LAND MINES, CLAYMORE BOMBS, HAND GRENADES AND HIGH EXPLOSIVES. IT IS THOUGHT THAT THE STOLEN ORDNANCE IS BEING SIPHONED TO JEWISH TERROR GROUPS.

BUT INVESTIGATIONS HAVE BEEN STYMIED. ONE SHIN BET OPERATIVE WHO REQUESTS ANONYMITY SAYS THAT HE HAS BEEN ORDERED TO ≪STAY AWAY≫ FROM COUNTERTERROR OPERATIONS

EMANATING FROM WEST BANK SETTLEMENTS, OR THOSE THAT MAY BE TACITLY ENCOURAGED BY RABBI MEIR KAHANE'S ≪KACH≫ (*THUS*) ORGANIZATION.

RM 0725
EWWX

"Of course they're denying it!" Jared screamed into a bad intercontinental connection. "It makes them look like the hoodlums they are." He cupped his hand over the receiver and called to Annie. "See if you can get me a better line to New York."

He cursed the echo. "No. Yes. I see. What do you mean they're talking about a lawsuit? The stuff was solid—golden. I had sources. I saw Begin's goddamn appointment book, for chrissakes."

He wrinkled his forehead and frowned. "Well—no. Not the book itself. A Xerox of the page. No—I wasn't allowed to take it with me. Dammit, Roger, there are some times when things like that are impossible. No—no, no, no. I won't tell you who my sources were—not on this phone. Not on any phone from this country.

"Yes—yes. I can catch the red-eye tonight. I'll see you in the morning. Sure. Straight to the office. I'll be there by nine. Yes—with all my files. Bye." He slammed the receiver down and bawled into the next office for Annie to make his reservations, cursing the luck that had caused him to have to work for the next three days straight.

Nafta Bar Zohar stuck his head into Jared's office. "Problems?"

"Begin's office is denying my terrorism piece. He called it—wait a second, I want to get it right—'blood libel and an unequivocal fabrication.' "

"That's what I like about Begin—he's so wishy-washy." Bar Zohar toyed with the three Cannon F-1s that hung around his neck while he planted thick bifocals firmly atop his head. "We talked about that one, Jared—you got it cold."

"Sure I did. But New York is getting cold feet. You and I know how it is when Begin puts the pressure on. But those assholes in New York don't. They don't realize it's all rhetoric. So all those editors who love you to stick your neck out for exclusives disown the same story they sent you a hero-gram for last week if Begin so much as sneezes. Roger Richards wants to see me in New York tomorrow.

He's talking about a 'clarification' for next week's issue. Dammit, this story is righteous, Nafta, right down the line."

He punched at the telephone, waving as Bar Zohar left grim-faced. "Adrian, it's me. No—I gotta go to New York. Tonight, dammit. The Prime Minister is making a stink about the Jewish terror story. Okay, okay—I'll see you at home later. If there's anything you want me to take to Felix, bring it with you. I love you too."

By the time he climbed out of the taxi and slogged his suitcase up the elevator, stowed it with Roger Richards's secretary, unpacked his notes and waited for admittance to the Chief of Correspondents' office, Jared had been awake thirty-five hours. He'd wanted to go to his hotel to shower, shave, and put on a New York meeting suit. But the El Al flight had uncharacteristically arrived two hours late. So instead of a breeze through customs and a half-hour cab ride at six A.M., Jared wormed his way into the city at morning rush hour, going directly to *World Week*'s editorial offices on Fifth Avenue.

Gratefully, he accepted a Styrofoam cup of coffee from the secretary and sipped it, pacing the pastel-carpeted antechamber. He felt grungy and uncomfortable in clothes that were wrinkled from the flight and a shirt that stuck to his back. He had been bumped by the airline from his last-minute-reservation business-class seat in favor of a U.S. Senator whose connections at El Al were better than Jared's. So Jared sat in steerage for thirteen hours, wedged between a Hasidic youngster who got airsick and a New Yorker who snored.

What made him feel even worse were the three men who greeted him formally in the opulent but minimally decorated office. Richards, senior editor Bill Johanssen, and senior writer Tom Small, the team that had transformed Jared's copy into an article, were at their clean-shaven best. Richards was working in shirtsleeves: bespoke English shirtsleeves. Tom Small's jet-black hair was slicked down, still wet from his early-morning workout at the New York Athletic Club. Johanssen's trademark suspenders this morning were narrow red stripes on chrome yellow, almost too bright for Jared to take.

It was a grave tactical error, Jared realized, not to have stopped at the hotel to change. So much of what went on at headquarters revolved around style, not substance. The building that housed the magazine's eleven hundred employees was structured to reinforce a rigid caste system: it culminated with the corporate executives on the forty-seventh floor, and began in the subterranean mailroom two floors below ground.

For factotums, there were posters and modular wall units. Writers and low-grade editors did better: private offices, lithographs and carefully tended plants. Senior writers and editors had lithos, too—but theirs were signed and numbered. And executives' suites, custom-painted, featured oils by Rauschenberg and Stella and furniture from Roche-Bobois. And yet, despite the overt splendor of Roger Richards's forty-fifth-floor office, there was a coldness, an impersonal patina to the place that caused Jared to shiver as he was ushered through the door.

The man he faced belonged to all the right clubs, frequented the best tailors and sipped chablis at the trendiest restaurants. He summered in the Hamptons and wintered in St. Barts. Richards's world view was developed on the squash court where he played with his social equals, at the bar of the "21" Club—or from reading the confidential memos on which correspondents and bureau chiefs worked for hours so that he and the other top executives could titillate their friends with gossip from the capitals of the world. Indeed, Jared, like many of his colleagues, realized early on that he could win favor and advancement not through reporting alone, but by dispensing tidbits to the news panjandrums who controlled his professional existence.

Oh, Richards played at being a journalist. He toured the bureaus once a year: Concorde and limousine junkets to Paris, London, Rome—even Moscow. He came with an entourage, like a senator or a general. He met all the right people, hobnobbing with prime ministers and Junta leaders. But he never caught the whiff of gunpowder, the scent of poverty, the odor of the masses.

And the other two? Faceless bottom-liners, probably. Ambitious Ivy League WASPs with lean and hungry looks, recruited from competing publications, who sparred and feinted with each other using not épées but staff writers. Jared stole a quick look at Small and Johanssen. Sure, they had to work together, and they no doubt played squash twice a week. But they probably hated each other's guts, spending much of their time looking for weaknesses that could be used during corporate in-fighting. For all the magazine's vaunted clout and circulation, these two could have been junior oil-company executives, bankers, or associates in a large law firm. They had none of the journalist's grit, none of the reporter's dog-eared informality.

They were cyphers—highly paid cyphers, but cyphers nonetheless. They respected power only when it tallied with their neatly defined concept of how power should look and sound. And Jared, grimy, rumpled, and sweaty, fit none of their preconditions. Compared with his superiors, he looked like an office boy; from the look of them they were about to make him feel like one.

Richards motioned him to sit in the middle of a seven-foot sofa. Small and Johanssen took the Mies van der Rohe leather-and-chrome chairs that flanked it. Richards, tan and fit, sat in a judge's chair behind his nine-foot-long wood-and-glass desk, a full ten feet across the room. They all stared at Jared.

Jared stared back. He realized, to his perverse amusement, that these three could have been struck from the same die pattern, right down to their tasseled "success" loafers from Paul Stuart. He'd known Roger Richards for almost two decades, but still had trouble recognizing him in a room of his upscale colleagues. He looked at Johanssen and Small. God, how they tried to fit in—jogger lean and Nautilus fit, with unlined, tanning-room faces and lab-rats' eyes that blinked reflexively whenever they spoke in what Jared supposed passed for aristocratic drawls.

Finally Richards spoke. "I hope you had a pleasant flight."

"I'm here."

"We're glad to see you." The Chief of Correspondents coughed a small, tactfully embarrassed cough. "But we have some, ah, problems, Jared."

"The piece has no holes in it, Roger. I brought my files."

"I'm happy you feel that way—and I hope you're right. But we think there may be cause for a clarification. And it's not just this piece I'm concerned about—But we'll deal with that later."

Jared started to interrupt, but Johanssen, pulling at his suspenders, cut him off. "The Israeli Consul General delivered a personal message from the Prime Minister unequivocally denying your story."

"I'd expect him to."

"So would we." said Richards. "But he—well, I seem to be getting ahead of myself. First, I should say that we want to go over your documentation, talk about your sources, see how much of the piece is defensible. Then we can deal with what the Israelis have to say."

"How much? How much? It's all true, Roger."

"Jared, Jared." Richards looked across the room over the half-frame glasses that sat perched on his button nose. "Don't be defensive."

"I'm not being defensive. I'm telling you the truth: the story is righteous."

Tom Small snorted. "What about the appointment book?"

"I told Roger—I saw a Xerox of the page that had the appointment with Ben-Canaan and Katzblum."

"How do you know it was a Xerox of the real page?"

"It was Begin's assistant who showed it to me."

"Oh, come on," said Small smugly. "He's the one who's making the complaint on behalf of the Prime Minister."

Jared's eyes widened, shocked. "Yankel? Yankel Grupnik is making the complaint for Begin?"

Richards nodded.

"Then he's doing it to save his butt. Someone must have seen him with me, or saw him Xerox the appointment book."

"We thought of that," said Johanssen. "But—and this is painful, Jared—Yankel Grupnik not only has denied ever meeting with you or discussing Jewish terror with you—let alone giving you any information about the Prime Minister's schedule—he also has done something unprecedented. He's faxed us four pages of the Prime Minister's appointment book at the suggestion of Mr. Begin himself. They blacked out some names, but during the time period you cited in your piece"—he walked to Richards's desk, squinted at a sheet of yellow legal paper and looked up, his eyelids fluttering Morse code—"four forty-five to five-fifteen on March thirteenth, there is no appointment with Katzblum and Ben-Canaan. Those pages, which we've had translated by an independent firm, show that on Sunday, March 13, the Prime Minister attended a Cabinet meeting, met with a secret committee of the Cabinet—its name was deleted by the censor—then had lunch with his son. The afternoon was spent in more meetings: economic committee, finance committee, a U.S. congressional delegation, and a briefing by his military aide. That takes us to five P.M., and no sign of your Mr. Katzblum or Mr. Ben-Canaan."

"Grupnik's lying. He sent you a forgery."

"Do you actually believe that?" Johanssen pointed an accusing finger at Jared. "I warned you not to pursue this story. But no, you went ahead, and look at the mess it's gotten us into."

"Grupnik's lying. To save his ass. He sent you a damn forgery," said Jared.

"If it is, then show us the real document," said Tom Small. "We've got a Xerox—where's yours?"

"I saw the real document—the Xerox. Yankel made a copy of the page." Jared flipped through his notebook. "Here—I interviewed him on May twenty-second. Took him for drinks at a Bulgarian restaurant—Jonathan's—near his house in Tel Aviv. He says—quote—'They were in. They came to see the old man, screaming about persecution. Ben-Canaan flatters Begin—talks about how great the old man is for Israel and for observant Jews, how he's going to be as important to Israel's history as Ben-Gurion, how Begin's peace treaty with Egypt makes him a world-class peacemaker. Begin listens attentively. Smiles. Begin is sitting in the armchair in his office. His hands are folded over his belly. He looks like a happy *zeda*'—that's grandfather in Yiddish. 'Ben-Canaan tells Begin that Shin Bet has fabricated a case against Katzblum—made up evidence including damaging pictures that are photo-composites—only because Katzblum believes in the idea of a Greater Israel, and the Shin Bet men are Labor Party intellectuals who hate what Likud has done and want to embarrass the Prime Minister.'

"I ask Yankel: 'Did they show Begin the pictures?' Yankel says, quote, 'No—they just told him about them.'

"I ask Yankel: 'Why wouldn't Begin ask to see the pictures?' Yankel says, quote, 'He trusts Ben-Canaan. Also, Begin has a soft spot for the settlers and the religious. He's never taken a hard line against *kana'ut*—zealotry—when it's practiced by Jews. Don't forget—Begin's told the story of Pinchas before.' "

Richards said, "Pinchas?"

"He was an ancient priest," Jared explained. "Pinchas saw one of the children of Israel commit an immoral act with a Midianite woman in sight of his congregation. He became so enraged that he grabbed a spear and impaled them both. Later, God spoke to Moses and told Moses that Pinchas's act was forgiven because Pinchas had committed *kana'ut*—zealotry—for His sake."

Johanssen asked, "Why would he tell you this?"

"Because, underneath it all, he's jealous of Begin. He's a little guy whose life has been spent in Begin's shadow. He's an apparatchik who wants to make himself important. So he becomes a source. He spreads rumors and insults behind Begin's back; he leaks documents. He's a tiny, bald man with a drinking problem. They call him '*gammad*'—the dwarf—maybe he's trying to live down to the image."

"The problem," said Johanssen, "is that you don't have a piece of paper in your hand—and we do. You're a good reporter, Jared. But when you make a charge like this you've got to have evidence. Right now, the evidence we've got contradicts what you wrote."

"But he wasn't the single source. I heard it from the Shin Bet agent who was reprimanded."

"Who is that?"

"I'm not sure I can tell you."

"Why?" Richards asked.

"He talked to me in confidence. I promised not to use his name."

"Jared—" Johanssen pulled nervously at his suspenders. "We've got a serious problem here. The magazine's credibility is at stake. I understand your need to keep sources confidential. But in this case we've got to know who he was."

"Will you abide by his rules?"

"What?" Johanssen said.

"His request—confidentiality."

Small and Johanssen looked at the Chief of Correspondents for guidance. Finally, he nodded. "Yes," said Richards. "We'll keep his name out of it." The other two then nodded in agreement.

"His name is Nathan Yaari. He works out of Tel Aviv. It was his unit that set up the photographic surveillance of Katzblum. Yaari went to Katzblum with the pictures."

Tom Small crossed and uncrossed his legs. "How did you meet him?"

"At someone's home."

"Whose?"

"It's not important."

"It might be. Whose?"

"Let him go on," said Richards. "How well do you know him?"

"Pretty well. I've seen him half a dozen times in the past three months. Everything he's ever told me has checked out."

Richards nodded. He smiled at Jared. "He sounds reliable," he said approvingly.

Jared smiled back in relief. "He is."

"Good," said Richards. "Then why don't you call him now and reconfirm."

"What?"

"Just call him and ask him to confirm the story again. It's not much to ask from a reliable source."

"He won't—not over the phone. He believes his phone is tapped. His career would be over if they found out he'd talked to me."

Richards smiled again. Now Jared saw it wasn't a friendly smile. "Oh, Jared, just try, will you?"

"Roger, you don't understand. In Israel you don't talk over the phone like that."

Small pouted. "You're really paranoid, aren't you?"

"This has nothing to do with paranoia. You don't understand how things are in Israel. They tap phones. They follow you. They—do things."

"Jared," Richards pointed at the console phone on the coffee table. "Call—or I will."

Jared looked at Richards. The son-of-a-bitch would do it, and Nathan would be fired—or worse. "Damn you, Roger." Jared pulled a loose-leaf address book from his briefcase, looked up the number and punched it into the phone. Richards picked up one extension, Johanssen another. They waited silently as the connection was made and the phone in Israel beep-beeped.

Nathan's voice came onto the line. "Ahllo?"

Jared knew what he had to do. Instead of his normal Hebrew, he spoke rapidly in English. He said, "Hello? Nathan Yaari, please."

"Ahllo. This Yaari spicking."

"Nathan Yaari—this is Jared Paul Gordon."

A long pause. "Who?"

"Jared Paul Gordon—remember me?"

"No. Have we met?"

"I'm working on a story about Jewish terror."

"A writer?"

"From *World Week* magazine. I called you about the Katzblum case."

"I don't recall it."

"I called you about Azriel Katzblum."

"I never met you. I never talked to you. I don't know you. Why are you calling? How did you get my name? Where did you get my number?"

"The Prime Minister's office has complained to my magazine. They say the story we published about Begin meeting with Katzblum and Ben-Canaan is a lie. They say that the Shin Bet was never told not to investigate Jewish terror. They say—"

The line went dead.

Richards and Johanssen hung up their receivers. The room was very quiet. Jared found the imperfections in the woodgrain base of Roger Richards's desk suddenly fascinating.

"He denies talking to you," Richards said.

"What do you expect? His line probably is tapped."

"He denied knowing you," said Johanssen. "Now can't you see the problem we've got?"

Richards tapped his desk with the eraser of a pencil. "Look at things from our point of view. You write a story, based on interviews with two major sources—one of whom you say showed you a document but wouldn't let you have it. When the government of Israel protests, the man you say was your prime source is the one who does the protesting. Not only does he do that, he also provides evidence that contradicts what you wrote. Then you call your other major source and he denies knowing you. What the hell are we supposed to do?"

"Something else," said Tom Small. "The Israeli Consul General called yesterday. He said—quote"—Small flipped through a legal pad on his lap—" 'Gordon is unabashedly anti-Begin in his reporting. Gordon is not objective when it comes to the Prime Minister's policies. Gordon's circle of left-wing sources use him to vilify the Prime Minister and promote the Labor Party.' End of quote."

"That's absolute horse shit," Jared snapped. "What I write has nothing to do with my own beliefs—whatever they may be—and you all know it."

"Perhaps," said Johanssen. "But look at it from our side. We have to defend the magazine's reputation for objectivity. I've checked, Jared—you haven't been very complimentary to Menachem Begin over the past couple of years."

"Nobody ever complained before. You guys were falling all over yourselves when I gave you the Baghdad bombing stuff, and the Mossad in Central America, and the real story about how Sharon misled the Cabinet during the Lebanese war. None of those pieces was very complimentary to Begin. It wasn't my idea to do three pieces in one year on Begin's aggressive land confiscation policies in the West Bank, either." He looked at Johanssen. "You're the one who assigned those gems, Bill."

"*World Week* has never had the threat of a lawsuit from a Prime Minister before," said Richards.

"It's bullshit. They'd never sue. They're covering up," Jared insisted. "I nicked them good on this one and they're trying to save themselves. So they tell you I made up the story. But it isn't true. I didn't make anything up. I don't make anything up. I write what happens—no more, no less."

"Sure you do," said Small.

There was an embarrassed pause. Finally, Roger Richards spoke.

"Which brings me to something else, something that made us look very closely at your Jewish terror story." He opened the file drawer of his desk and retrieved a magazine page. "Jared, look at this."

Jared rose. He walked to the desk, his eyes following a plane as it coasted high overhead on its way up the Hudson River. Then his gaze fell on the tearsheet under Richards's manicured finger.

It was a two-paragraph story. The headline read: "A CRUNCH IN THE PLO?" It was the piece Yoram had filed under Jared's name.

Roger Richards said: "Did you write the file on which this article was based?"

Jared was silent. He could feel the thumping of his heart. He hoped no one else could hear it. They had him. He was finished. His mind flashed on Adrian—what would she say? And on Yoram—the sonofabitch—and on—

"Well, did you?" Richards rapped his pencil on the article.

Jared stood mute, staring at the page, hoping it would disappear.

"What about it, Gordon?" Small pronounced Jared's name with an icy emphasis on both syllables.

"It has come to my attention," said Richards, "from what we in journalism call an unimpeachable source—and confirmed by another—that the file upon which this article was written was a fabrication."

Oh, jeezus, I told Yoram I'd be out on my ass if the truth ever surfaced, Jared thought, his mind racing. And what did the sonofabitch tell me? He said it would never happen. He said nobody would be hurt. He promised. Oh Christ, he said—

Richards's voice was insistent. "Is this story a fabrication?"

Jared nodded his head. "Yes."

"Tell us what happened," said Richards.

Jared felt more vulnerable than he had ever felt on the dirt road near Jdaidet Aartouz. He returned to the sofa and dropped, cracking his knuckles. "I—" He stared at his three interrogators, playing for time by taking a swallow of his coffee, only to come down with a fit of hiccoughs. The coffee came back through his nose, onto his shirt and Richards's gray and dusty rose carpeting. He grabbed for a napkin—there was none—then tried unsuccessfully to swab the stains with his handkerchief. He wiped at his soiled shirt, his eyes darting wildly around the room as the other three stared disdainfully. Once, at Princeton, while taking a test in his sophomore year, he'd farted loudly, uncontrollably, in the silent room. His classmates had stared at him the same way. It had taken him a year to live down the mortification.

He found it impossible to concentrate. Instead, his mind—brain impulses skewed by shock—flashed random pictures: Yoram pulling the Stechkin from its holster and firing; Adrian in the sleeping bag; himself, standing with Jimmy Carter in the Oval Office. Even his first school prom . . . the band was playing "The Limbo Rock" . . . the lyrics reverberated in his head.

How lo-o-o-w . . . could he go-o-o?

He stifled an hysterical impulse to giggle—or scream.

He took as deep a breath as he could muster and tried to slow his racing pulse. "I didn't write the story," he said. "I don't know who did—maybe the Army, maybe Mossad. It wasn't me." He focused on Richards, trying to detect a hint of sympathy in the man's face. He was greeted by stone. So he told about the raid and the preconditions Yoram Gal had imposed. He described his anger at the brutality of the assassinations. He explained about writing a true account of what had happened, and how he discovered the phony dispatch that had been sent under his byline to New York.

"You should have called. You should have told us," said Richards.

"Goddammit to hell, you really steam me," said Tom Small. "Just where are your loyalties, anyway?"

"I was going to . . ."

"Were going to what?" Richards stood over Jared.

"I was going to tell you. It was just—there was no time to call before we went out. They wouldn't let me call. The ground rules were set—it was a calculated risk. Then afterward—"

"Afterward?"

"I wanted to tell you, I did—really. But then they filed the piece under my byline, and I never . . ."

Johanssen interrupted. "Let me try to crystallize the situation," he said. "You breach our published news guidelines—you do have a copy of them, Jared, because we give them to all our employees—by accepting conditions for covering an event that we specifically say may not be accepted without the written consent of the Chief of Correspondents or his deputy.

"Then, in violation of our guidelines, you become an observer to what you have just described as a brutal act of political assassination. Is that correct?"

Jared nodded numbly.

"Then, when someone—you say now you do not know who—filed a forgery, a story you now tell us was a complete fabrication, and filed it with your byline, no less, you neither informed us, nor contacted us to warn that we were being used as a conduit for disinformation."

"Yes."

"This," said Johanssen, "stretches the imagination."

"It's the truth," said Jared.

"I'll tell you what I think is the truth," said Tom Small. "I think you did a favor for your pals in the Israeli Army. I don't think there was a forged file. I think you made the whole thing up because they asked you to. And now you've been caught with your hand in the cookie jar."

"We're faced with a real problem," said Richards. "You admit to one lie. Now the Israeli Government says you have lied again—that what you sent to us was—and here I quote from the Prime Minister's telex as transmitted by the Israeli Consul General here in New York—'untrue, fabricated and designed to bring ignominy on the sovereign state of Israel.' How should we deal with this, Jared? You tell me."

"I don't know. I really don't."

"Well, neither do I," said Richards. "I have to admit, Jared, you've got us in a quandary." He stuck the half-frames on his high forehead and faced the huge window. "Go check into your hotel. Take a shower. Get some sleep. Be back at three—we'll have come to a decision by then."

He wheeled and faced the reporter. "I'm sorry, boy, truly sorry. You've done some fine work, but now . . ."

He watched as Jared slumped from the office.

"Fire the s.o.b.," said Tom Small after the door closed. He turned to Johanssen. "We should can him. We should make an example—"

"Certainly that is a possibility," said Richards, interrupting. "But I'm not sure we should do anything irreversible. First of all, *World Week* can't be seen as firing someone because the government of Israel—or any government—doesn't like what they write. Even if we were to fire Gordon, we couldn't do it now—it'd have to wait until after this affair's blown over. Second, let's just suppose that Gordon is right; that he got caught up in something over which he had no control. Let's speculate that, for argument's sake, the Israelis are using him; or that Begin's people set him up.

"Let's suppose that the Jewish terror story is true, and we retract it. And a month from now, or two months, or six, or a year, we discover that Gordon was on to something. Well, we'd look like asses. Worse—the magazine could be accused of knuckling under to the Jewish lobby. Submitting to pressure from Begin." He shot the white French cuffs of his bold-striped English shirt. "*World Week* doesn't submit to pressure."

He smiled coldly at his subordinates. "Think of those possibilities, gentlemen. And then think what the reaction on the forty-seventh floor would be if we acted precipitously."

He pointed to his ceiling, two stories above which sat the magazine's top echelon of executives. "I can see myself in Arnaud's office now, holding my head the same way poor Gordon did in here. I can see Arnaud Henri Leclerc dropping my head out the window of the Editor-in-Chief's office. And if my head goes, boys, so do yours."

He ambled to the window and looked at the logjam of traffic on Fifth Avenue. "It's a long way down," said Roger Richards.

"Suggestion." Bill Johanssen stretched lengthwise on the couch, his feet on one of its arms. "He takes a leave of absence."

"That's one alternative," said Richards. "What do you think, Tom?"

"I still say we should can the sonofabitch right now. He's an embarrassment."

"I'm not ruling that option out." Richards opened the door to a concealed wet bar, took a chrome thermos pot out, and set it on the coffee table by the couch. He retrieved three mugs and saucers emblazoned with the magazine's logo, took one of them and poured himself some coffee, which he carried carefully to his desk.

"I admit what Gordon's done is a firing offense. But he's got a few things going for him, too. He's had as many or more exclusives in the past two years as any of our correspondents—"

"And how many of them were planted by his Israeli pals?" Small asked, reaching for the carafe. "You know how Jews stick together."

"We don't talk like that at *World Week,*" said Richards. "Besides, it doesn't matter. Gordon's stories checked out. They put us out on the cutting edge. *Time* and *Newsweek* had to run to catch up. That makes them"—he pointed toward the ceiling—"happy. And I happen to know that Arnaud likes Gordon's reporting. He says that Gordon hits a lot of long balls."

"Agreed," said Johanssen. "Arnaud's always calling to see whether Gordon's done something that would rate inclusion on the publisher's notes page."

"If that's the case," said Small, "why not let Arnaud make the decision?"

"You haven't been here very long, Tom," said Richards. "Maybe that's the way things work at the *Times*—it's not what happens here. Here we make the decision at our level, and then give it to the Editor-in-Chief as an action memo. He either approves or disapproves. If it's the latter, we try again."

Johanssen reached to pour himself a mug of coffee, which he balanced on his chest. "Another option—probation, with a demotion to researcher."

"Possible," said Richards. "With positive aspects. First, it keeps

Gordon under our supervision. We can send a temporary bureau chief to Jerusalem to control his assignments and monitor the results. Second, it lets him know that we're watching him. And third, it keeps him from jumping ship."

"Not that anyone would want him if we leaked anything about the fake story he wrote," said Small.

"I don't see how you can be so positive he wrote it," said Richards.

"It had to have been him. Who else?"

"Wait just a second," said Johanssen, "didn't the *Times* have something similar, Tom?"

"I don't remember," Small snapped defensively.

"You were deputy assistant foreign editor."

"I don't remember. We ran a lot of stories—I can't remember them all."

Richards pushed a button on the intercom that sat on his glass and freeform wood desk. "Maggie?"

"Yes, Mr. Richards?"

"Punch up the *New York Times* index for last November. See if the *Times* ran a piece about the assassination of a PLO official named Abu Zain. If they did, pull it up."

The trio sat without talking. Then the intercom buzzed. "Yes it did, Mr. Richards. No byline, just three short graphs, datelined Tel Aviv. Do you want me to read it to you?"

"Just the top, Maggie, please."

"Quote: 'Special to *The New York Times*. Tel Aviv, November 16. A high-ranking PLO official was assassinated yesterday near Damascus by dissident Palestinian gunmen, according to Israeli intelligence officials,' graph. Do you want me to continue?"

"No thanks, Maggie, that'll be all." Richards looked over at Tom Small. "Well—five days before we hit the stands. Did Gordon plant that one on you guys at the *Times*?"

Tom Small shrugged. "Okay, so he didn't write it."

"No," said Johanssen, a contented look on his face, "and we're not going to can Gordon to make up for your mistakes at the *Times*, either. I vote for demotion and probation."

"I agree," said Richards. "Tom?"

"Okay, okay—make it unanimous. But I'm gonna keep an eye on the bastard."

"So are we all," said Richards. "Now let me earn my money and draft something for Arnaud. You guys are dismissed."

Jared stood under a steamy shower, his body feeling the effects of a seven-thousand-mile plane ride, the emotional pummeling of the morning's meeting, and the aftershock of three shots of straight vodka he'd downed shaky-handed as soon as he had checked into the hotel. Even though the cascade was as hot as he could stand it his body shivered and twitched as the water drenched him.

At least he'd kept his word—tried to protect Nathan Yaari, although if the Shin Bet agent's phone was tapped, poor Nathan was in for more than his share of trouble. No—they were covering up on the terror story, which made him believe all the more strongly that he was on to something. And he had resources to go to—sources the government wouldn't be able to compromise. Damn the magazine. Let them fire him—he'd do the terror story on his own.

But there were even more important things to discover than why the terror story had come apart. He closed his eyes under the hot downpour and tried to ravel out who had told Roger Richards about Abu Zain; who had killed his professional life.

Richards said he had it from one unimpeachable source, and confirmed by another. It was possible that one of Richards's pals at CIA had done the confirmation. The Chief of Correspondents had once worked at Langley, and he still had a lot of friends there. But the primary source had to be Israeli. Who? It wouldn't have been Yoram, because it was in Yoram's interest to keep the story secret. But who else knew?

Annie, perhaps. No, Annie didn't know the file was a forgery—unless she'd been the one to send it. Was *she* the Shin Bet plant? Or was it Rahael? No—impossible. Rahael had been on *meluim* when he'd gone out with Yoram. Begin's office? Very possible. But Jared doubted that anyone in Begin's office knew about the false story. Somebody would have had to give it to Begin. Ariel Sharon, perhaps. Jared had heard rumors about a back-channel intelligence operation initiated by the former Defense Minister to gather his own political information. Arik could have slipped a juicy tidbit to Begin.

He let the hot water relax his tight neck and shoulders. The Shin Bet was a more likely possibility. Jared accepted as fact that the office phones were monitored, so the story would have been intercepted when it was sent. And the Shin Bet had to be upset over his latest piece.

He turned off the water and toweled himself dry, shaved, took three aspirin, and walked into the next room to check his watch. Noon. Three hours. They'd fire him. Of course they would. The old joke—you'll never work as a journalist again. Only it wasn't a joke. God—what the hell was he going to do? What the hell was he going to tell Adrian?

Adrian.

Adrian knew.

Adrian knew Yoram had planted the Abu Zain story, because he'd told her. But why? No, the idea was preposterous. He laughed out loud. A ten-dollar word from the writer. He pulled the covers off the bed, flipped the TV on, turned the sound off and set his alarm for two. Shivering, he crawled between the sheets and lay there for some time, staring blankly at the screen as the noontime newscast annotated the latest mayhem befalling the Big Apple.

He wondered whether he could wangle himself some sort of a book contract before the story of his firing came out. How long would they give him? How much severance? Could he convince them to put out a story saying he hadn't been fired—only that he had decided to resign? Where would he find a literary agent? How would he—what—if—oh, goddammit, goddammit, goddammit to hell.

He poured another quarter inch of vodka into the bathroom tumbler that sat on the bedside table and downed it; felt its warmth on his empty stomach at once. Maybe he could get a job on the copydesk of the *Jerusalem Post.* Or as a stringer for one of the European newspapers that used part-time Jerusalem-based help. Or move to Rome, to Paris, to London. Write novels. That would show them. He'd become a best-selling author. Spy novels, based in the shadowy Middle East. Or nonfiction: the Mossad against the world. Secret assassination plots. A sequel to *The Hit Team* that would really blow the top off Israeli intelligence operations. A novel about an American reporter sandbagged by the Mossad—and how he got the story out anyway.

The Mossad.

The goddamn Mossad.

Adrian. What the hell had Adrian been doing with Menachem

Navor? And why did she lie about being stuck at her desk all day when he had seen her on her way to lunch at the Olympia? Why had she lied to him? She knew about the Abu Zain story. She did, she did—he'd told her.

Adrian and Yoram? It was possible they were—no, it was impossible. But—he poured himself more vodka and swallowed, grimacing—she'd had affairs before. When he'd first met her she was with Udi of the damaged fingers and the wife in Israel. And—hadn't she told him about a short affair with a married man? It wasn't impossible.

What the hell did he know about Adrian anyway? That her father was a millionaire many times over who owned a bank in Israel and had advised four presidents on Jewish affairs. That his contacts in Israel were broad; he knew everyone from the Prime Minister to Moshe Levinger, leader of the Gush Emunim, and Adrian benefited from his friendships. That she spelled her name like a man, and she'd been born in Great Neck, which was out on Long Island. But she hadn't lived there—she'd lived at Fifth Avenue and Seventy-fourth Street in Manhattan until she was—what? Five? No, six? Then the family had moved to Washington.

Why? Why had Felix sold what had to have been a successful business—Felco—it was called Felco and it was in Long Island City—to make the move?

He rolled onto his back and stared at the ceiling. He closed his eyes. What else? She'd seldom talked about her childhood, never told stories about what it was like growing up, never talked about her childhood friends. Jared still kept in touch with people he'd known in grade school. He had a past. But Adrian? Adrian existed entirely in the present.

Adrian knew, dammit. He'd told her.

He'd told her. And he knew precious little about her; precious little about a woman with whom he had been living for more than three years.

Jared's head began to spin. He opened his eyes and looked at the pictures on the silenced screen. Another day in New York. Another murder. Another victim.

He watched a gurney being loaded with the body, the attendants struggling with the weight as they carried the corpse down a flight of stairs. For that one it was all over. Only the shell was left—no life, no breath. A picture flashed on the screen. The smiling face of the victim, taken from a high school yearbook or a parent's mantel. Why were the victims always smiling?

He closed his eyes. Jewish terrorists also struck smiling victims. The schoolgirls in Ramallah. The youngsters in Hebron. The Arab mayors.

I Samuel 25:3
Now go and smite Amelek, and utterly destroy all that they have, and spare them not . . .

The bright June morning in 1980 when it happened, Jared jumped into the car and sped north along the crowded road to Nablus. He knew Bassam Shakaa; liked the crusty humor—if not the radical political views—of the outspoken Arab, a former Syrian Baath Party activist, who openly defended the PLO's most violent elements, suffered house arrest and the threat of deportation, while all the time preaching Palestinian and pro-Syrian propaganda to any foreign journalist who would visit his stone house on whose flat roof stood a wrought-iron TV antenna built in the shape of the Eiffel Tower.

When Jared arrived, Bassam's legs had already been amputated and the round-faced little man with the pencil-line mustache was sleeping off the anesthetic in a room protected by Arab police and Israeli border guards. Outside, the network cameras had arrived. The crush was on: correspondents offering fifty-dollar bills for pictures, photographers shooting the crowds—and each other. Reporters milled in the street, now thick with troops to guard against wholesale rioting, and interviewed passersby.

He cajoled his way into the room. Jared knew these people and they knew him; knew he came regularly to sit with Bassam over Palestinian coffee reduced six times in brass pots of decreasing size. They knew he'd pushed his way past Shin Bet agents into Bassam's house, his photo taken from across the street where they sat on perpetual stakeout. They thought of Jared as a friend. And so, having donned a white doctor's coat he had liberated from a handy closet, he slipped into Bassam's room.

The place reeked of disease; an ineffable, indescribable smell of disinfectant, bandages, and misery choked him. A young, bearded Israeli doctor in operating-room greens was there, mask hanging croplike around his neck. He stood shaking his head over the pulpy stumps, looking down at the thick-swathed bandages.

Jared closed the door behind him. "How is he?"

"He'll live. But without his legs." The doctor gave Jared a second look. "Who the hell are you?"

"Jared Paul Gordon. I'm a friend of Bassam's."

"How did you get in here?"

"I told you—I'm a friend."

"A reporter?"

"Yes. Can I talk to him?"

The doctor shrugged. "You're here."

"It's okay to talk to him then?"

"When he's awake, for just a minute. But no questions."

"Okay," Jared pulled a steel chair across the marble floor to the bed and sat, waiting and watching. Bassam's face was puffy and mottled, blanched gray by the shock of what had happened. After some minutes the Palestinian moaned. Cracked an eye. Moaned again. The doctor put a hand on his shoulder, leaned down and whispered into the mutilated man's ear. Bassam's eyes widened, then closed. He rested in silence another quarter hour. Then he opened his eyes and saw Jared.

Incredibly, he smiled. A squinty-eyed madman's smile. "Jared—*Ahlan W'asahlan*."

"Bassam—"

"No questions," the doctor insisted.

Bassam waved him off. A weak hand hampered by intravenous lines gestured toward the stumps. "You see? They blew my legs off to separate me from my Palestine," he wheezed. "My legs are gone but I am rooted more firmly to the ground than ever." The Arab smiled again, the smile of a man who has won a great battle. "They tried—and they failed," he said, and a hoarse laugh or cough escaped blistered lips.

They talked for some minutes, Bassam characteristically talking sedition, revenge and wild accusations against the Prime Minister. The doctor nervously watched and listened—probably, Jared thought, taking mental notes for the Shin Bet—until finally Bassam waved the American off. "Good-bye," he said. "Salaam, Jared—shalom." He smiled the martyr's smile again: he knew he'd won, although what he'd won Jared was not exactly sure.

Still, when Jared filed his article later that day he wrote: "The Israeli government is faced with a real dilemma. What, after all, can you do to a man who's just lost his legs? Even harder—what can the Israelis do to a man who's just lost his legs—and smiles?"

"I saved your ass today, Gordon." Roger Richards twirled the olive in an empty Martini glass, thrust it in his mouth and chewed.

"I know you did, Roger, and I'm grateful." Jared watched the Chief of Correspondents as he swiveled away from the desk and faced the picture window.

"Self-interest, really."

"Bull."

"No—truth. I hired you when I was L.A. bureau chief. I sent you overseas. If one of my guys screws up, it's my behind as well as theirs."

Jared pulled the lemon peel from his Perrier on the rocks and chewed on it.

Richards's chair turned noiselessly toward Jared. "Make no mistake, Jared—you screwed up."

"I admit that on the Abu Zain story, Roger. But—"

"Even if I believed you were right on Jewish terror, there's nothing I can do. You've got no evidence; you don't have a single document. Both your major sources deny knowing you. What the hell am I supposed to do?"

"Stand by me. Back me up."

"I backed you up by not canning your butt. Look, Jared, here's what happens. Next week we issue a clarification. We admit that some of the story was not verifiable but that the gist of it—that is, there's been a rise in Jewish terror—is correct and we stand behind it. The lawyers like that approach. The Israelis say it'll appease the Prime Minister, and Arnaud wants to go with it."

"So it's all done and done."

"In effect, yes."

"And what about me?"

"You go back to Jerusalem. But as a researcher, not a correspondent. I'm posting Jerry Atkins as acting bureau chief."

"Jerry? He covers local politics in New York. He doesn't speak the language. He doesn't know a thing about Israel."

"It's in the magazine's interest to keep a low profile for a while." Richards rose, his long legs carrying him to the wet bar where he refilled his glass from a pitcher in the small refrigerator. He gestured toward Jared's glass, but Jared shook his head.

The Chief of Correspondents plucked two olives from a small jar, ate one, dropped the other into his drink and went back to his desk. "There's no bargaining. You go back as the number-two man. You write what Jerry Atkins tells you to write. No more, no less. He pre-edits your copy, and then sends it to me. And if I'm happy I'll pass it on to the newsdesk."

"You're cutting me off at the knees."

"I'm saving your career. Your ass was on the line. There were other possibilities, too. We could have transferred you back here. Know how many bylines you'd have in a year? One, maybe two. Not to mention the whole editorial staff looking over your shoulder. Think what you want, Jared—you may not believe it, but this way we show the Israelis we're not backing down. We send you back to Jerusalem. At full pay, too, I might add. Except you keep your head down. No Jewish terror; no secret army operations. No Mossad assassinations. No fighting with Menachem Begin and Ariel Sharon. You just do what you're assigned."

"And if I come on something big?"

"You keep it to yourself—unless you've got all the documents, and they're authenticated, and you've got witnesses willing to be quoted on the record. As far as the magazine's concerned, we don't want to see a single piece of copy from you with the words 'sources' or 'officials' or 'secret documents.' "

"Jeezus—"

"That's the way it is, Jared."

Jared drained the Perrier. "You know," he said, "the last time I passed through London I had dinner with Marty Knight. We got to talking about covering wars for *World Week*—him in Vietnam and both of us in Lebanon. You know what he told me? He said that in Vietnam, when all hell broke loose and they were in real deep shit, everybody knew that if they got hold of the Chief of Correspondents—it was Harry Grey then—everything would be okay.

"Marty said you just knew that somehow a big white helicopter with *World Week* magazine in letters three feet high would show up above whatever free-fire zone you were stuck in, and Harry would be up there calling down 'Don't worry, guys, I'm here!' Marty said knowing Harry would be there kept a lot of guys sane in Vietnam.

"Then we started talking about Lebanon, about the times he was working out of Beirut and I was working out of Israel, and the Syrians and the PLO and the militias were putting guns to our heads and we both got caught in some really messy ambushes.

"And you know what, Roger? Marty and I decided if we sent up a flare—if we really were in trouble—the first thing you'd do would be write Arnaud a memo. Then you'd have a meeting. And then—maybe a couple of days later, you'd send Johanssen or Small or one of your other flunkies to find whatever pieces of us were left."

"That's not funny, Jared. Or fair."

"Maybe not, but it's how we feel. Look, Roger, when you're out there on the line, when it's all happening, you gotta know that somebody is going to back you up; that somebody's gonna take the heat. Otherwise, what the hell's the use of taking chances, huh? Maybe you did save my ass, Roger—maybe I don't care about my ass anymore."

Richards stared at the correspondent across the top of his half-frames. "I'm disappointed you feel that way," he said. "It's not true. I backed you as far as I could. I backed you as far as your evidence allowed me to."

"That's what I mean," said Jared. "Here's the subtext of what you're telling me: Go back to Jerusalem. Follow up on Jewish terror—just don't get the magazine involved. Be a good little boy. Don't get into trouble. Keep your head down—rewrite Begin's press releases. Then, if you've got something incredible, and you've got all the pieces, maybe we'll think about using it."

"I haven't said anything like that."

"It's what you mean."

"If that's what you think," Richards took a sip of his drink. "Take off, Jared. Get the hell out of here."

CHAPTER 8

There was no problem spotting his suitcase as it came off the Eastern shuttle at Washington's National Airport: it was the only aluminum three-suiter in the batch, scarred from hundreds of thousands of miles of travel; dented from bouts with hostile baggage handlers in Beirut, London, Rome, Cairo, Paris and Tel Aviv. It sported three dozen hotel stickers, and, on each side, a foot-long label three inches high bearing the logo of the magazine in bright blue letters. Jared hefted the Halliburton from the conveyor and struggled up the escalator toward the Avis counter.

The Coopers had offered him their guest suite and one of the cars, but Jared declined, explaining that he wanted to stay closer to the magazine's offices downtown. He drove to the Four Seasons Hotel in Georgetown, claimed his room, and sat down with the telephone, address book spread open on the bed.

"Felix? It's Jared. Yeah—I just got in—yeah, the Four Seasons. Hey—expense-account time, you know how journalists always travel first class. Sure—brunch tomorrow is fine. I have a package from Adrian—oh, she told you. She's terrific. Just fine, except you're working her too hard." He rang off. He'd see Felix's whole crowd at brunch. They probably couldn't wait to jump his bones over the Jewish terror story.

He checked his notebook and dialed a number in Silver Spring. The phone rang five times, then a husky voice answered.

"Hello?"

"Dvora? This is the magazine writer. I used to live here. Now I live in Jerusalem. You remember?"

There was a pause on the line. Then, "Of course. Hello, Mr. *World Week*."

"I'd like very much to see you. Can we meet? Can we talk?"

"Of course we can. It's lovely to hear your voice."

"Yours, too. Remember where we first met for a drink?"

"Yes."

"I'll see you there. When would be convenient?"

"Now."

"I'm on my way." He replaced the handset, stuck the notebook inside his sportcoat, locked the address book in his suitcase and hung a Do Not Disturb sign on the door on his way out. It would take Dvora half an hour to drive from Silver Spring to the bar on Connecticut Avenue above Dupont Circle—plenty of time for Jared to walk leisurely from Georgetown.

Dvora Lavi was not listed on the State Department's protocol list. She enjoyed no diplomatic immunity. She was a civilian secretary in the Israeli Embassy's political section. She was also, however, one of Mossad's covert operatives in Washington.

Of medium height, olive complexioned, with dark eyes and henna-red hair, the forty-three-year-old sabra had been in Washington for two full tours, and was six months into her third. Her English was virtually unaccented now, her lifestyle a mix of American disco and Israeli coffeeklatches. Unmarried, she lived alone in a modestly furnished one-bedroom apartment in an unremarkable Silver Spring high rise, through which passed, according to rumor, a constant series of good-looking younger men.

She was no beauty. Her face was prematurely lined. By fifty, her skin would develop the leathery patina that caused large numbers of Israeli women to have face lifts. She had prominent, uneven teeth and thin lips that rolled back over them when she smiled. And yet there was an animal magnetism to her, a voluptuous Yeminite earthiness that was tremendously seductive. Her laugh was unabashedly loud; her style often *outré*. She wore clothes that advertised her body, and had the habit of touching whomever she talked to.

Jared had met her through Yoram. He'd been her dinner partner at one of the parties Yoram and Aviva had given during the Gals' Washington assignment. He liked the way Dvora talked, the way she gestured, punching the air with an omnipresent cigarette. And she was knowledgeable: she knew a lot more about the ins and outs of Washington than your average embassy secretary. Jared thought of dating her, but Yoram warned him off.

"Slurp," the bulky officer said.

"What?"

"She'll eat you alive."

He'd laughed. "What's so bad about that?"

"I don't mean that way—although if *shtupping* were money she'd be a millionaire."

"What, then?"

"You'd be playing with fire."

"How so?"

"Trust me—she's hot, that one. Stay away. Don't get involved."

So Jared had not gotten involved, but he hadn't quite stayed away, either. Dvora became someone to hang out with in off-hours, a woman he could call at the last minute and take to dinner parties if his date cancelled. From time to time she'd visit him at his English basement in Georgetown, bringing a bottle of Israeli wine from the Embassy's commissary, and they would sit talking politics and listening to music. She invited him to a few of the charity banquets Israeli Embassy staffers invariably got tickets to. He, in turn, gave her the rare experience of attending a State Dinner at the White House when he received one of his three invitations from the Carters to be a guest. They'd sat across from a Georgia banker in formal double-knit and his moonfaced wife, who drawled, upon hearing that Dvora was an Israeli, "That probably means you're a spy of some kind, right, darlin'?"

Dvora smiled and laughed. "Oh, absolutely," she said in her throaty voice, "and you—you're the Vidalia Onion Queen, yes?"

Still, the more Jared got to know her, the more he grew to believe that she was more than she appeared to be.

Final confirmation came shortly before the ulcer operation that ultimately led to his assignment to Jerusalem. It was at the Israeli Independence Day party, an annual event at the home of Delores and Harry Yuppman. The Yuppmans owned three auto dealerships in Virginia and a shopping mall near Landover. They were strong Zionists with an immense house—and more than willing to foot the bill for three hundred guests, a dance band, and kosher catering once a year, so that the Embassy could save its money for better things.

Jared went alone to the party. He'd had to work late and wasn't sure he wanted to drive the twenty miles to the Yuppmans' Virginia mansion. At the last moment, however, he decided to go. Usually there was information to be gleaned at parties such as this one. And it would be a chance to talk to the Ambassador—not to mention the smattering of State Department and White House types, high-level lawyers, lobbyists and former officials who were sent pro forma invitations. Instead of driving, he cabbed out, figuring he'd catch a ride home with someone he knew.

At about midnight he found himself having drunk more than he'd expected to, in the company of Benjamin Ben-Ami, commercial attaché. Ben-Ami was a dead ringer for Tweedle-Dum or Tweedle-Dee. Jared knew—as did a large number of people in official Washington—that Mr. Dum (or Dee) was not, as his calling card pronounced in neat raised script, a commercial attaché. He was the Mossad's chief of station. Ben-Ami himself virtually made no secret of it. Indeed, about the only thing he tried to conceal, and even this he botched, was that his name was neither Benjamin nor Ben-Ami but Maurice Goldberg, an emigré Rumanian, and not the native-born sabra he bragged of being.

Still, Ben-Ami had become a good source of Washington gossip for Jared, who'd cultivated the intelligence officer during expensive dinners at Washington's best French and Italian restaurants. Ben-Ami had a brandy habit, a loose tongue, and an abiding distaste for the Carter administration, based on his own short experience in Washington, as well as the Mossad's psychological profiles of the President, the Secretary of State, and particularly the head of the CIA. Indeed, the station chief loathed Stansfield Turner, whom he not-so privately accused of trying to wreck the historic partnership between CIA and Mossad that had been nurtured from the time Allen Dulles ran the Agency and James Jesus Angleton headed Langley's Israeli desk.

Ben-Ami's loose and acid tongue had gotten him into touble. He couldn't get an appointment with Admiral Turner. Zbigniew Brzezinski wouldn't see him, either. The CIA's current Israeli desk officer, an Arabist named McCoy whom Ben-Ami incessantly, and publicly, referred to as "McGoy," thought he was a drunk and has-been. Pressure had been put on Tel Aviv. There had even been an angry phone call from Stansfield Turner to his Mossad counterpart, Yitzhak Hofi, known as Hakka. And now Ben-Ami was facing imminent recall.

On this particular evening, Ben-Ami had decided to drink himself into a stupor, and had put away a considerable, even a remarkable, amount of Three Sevens Israeli brandy by the time Jared found him at one of the Yuppmans' four bars.

"Nu, Goldberg?" Jared tapped the Mossad station chief on the elbow. "What goes?"

"Ben-Ami, Ben-Ami. There is no Goldberg."

"As you wish. Mr. Ben-Ami." Jared bowed elaborately. "Any interesting information pass through your hands lately?"

"Commercially speaking, I can tell you that we're about to score a breakthrough. Put that in your magazine, Mr. Jared Paul Gordon. It's front-page news. A cover story."

"I'll call it in immediately," Jared slurred. "Get me to a telephone. No, Ben-Ami, I mean real *information*."

"Information? I don't deal with it any more." The Israeli poured himself four fingers of Three Sevens and downed it straightaway. "She does." He pointed at Dvora, who was leading a hora line fifty feet away. "Here's some real information: she's cut my *baytzim* off. She's wearing my nuts around her neck."

"I could think of worse ways to go." Jared took the Israeli's bottle and gave himself a generous dollop.

"You, maybe. For me—feh. And life was so good here, too. Expense account, French restaurants. My own car. Now—" he shook his head and rubbed his ample stomach. "Now, it's back to falafel and tehina. I hate falafel and tehina."

"That's treason."

"None dare call it treason. What kind of a country is it anyway where you have to buy spareribs under the counter? Where they prefer herring to caviar? Where it costs fifty dollars for a decent bottle of cognac?" Ben-Ami took the bottle back. "It's her fault I'm recalled even before my first tour's over. They'll tell you it was my choice. Not so, my boy—not so." With that, the Israeli lurched off toward a buffet table where a whole turkey was being sliced for finger sandwiches.

Jared nudged his way into the hora line next to Dvora Lavi and slipped an arm around her waist. "I need a lift home," he shouted over the music. "Bring a date tonight?"

"No, you can ride with me." Circles of sweat were forming under the armholes of her silk blouse. "But I want to dance yet a while."

Jared nodded and withdrew. He wasn't up to dancing. An hour later he held the door of her beat-up Chevy for her, then went around to the passenger's side as she reached across the front seat and opened the lock.

She buckled herself in, stashed her cigarette in the ashtray and turned the ignition. "It was a good party. *Shiga-on!*—terrific."

"They always are." He waited as she backed onto the Yuppman driveway, reversed and headed toward the main road to Washington. She switched the radio on and loud rock and roll filled the car. "Goldberg's going home, he says."

"Why do you call him Goldberg?"

"That's his name."

"His name is Ben-Ami."

"If you say so."

"I don't say so. It's his name." She retrieved the cigarette and inhaled deeply.

"He says it's your fault. Says you cut off his *baytzim*."

She laughed her throaty laugh. "Does he?"

He nodded. "Did you?"

"Me? How could I?"

"I don't know. Maybe you're his boss."

"Don't be silly. Everybody knows about Ben-Ami. Ben-Ami's not a very successful attaché."

"Or chief of station."

"Or what you will."

"And you?"

"I'm a successful secretary."

"Nothing else?"

"Would I tell you if I were?"

"Probably not. You didn't even flinch when what's-her-face, the Vidalia Onion, called you a spy."

"Why should I have flinched?"

"Because it's true—says Goldberg."

"Ben-Ami."

"Ben-Ami." Jared put his head back and closed his eyes. "I drank too much."

"Sleep. I'll drive."

He let himself drift off, surrounded by music and cigarette smoke. When he awoke, they were in an underground garage. "Where are we?"

"You looked beat. I'll give you a backrub."

Why the hell not. "Fine by me."

Hours later, after the backrub, after the lovemaking, she rolled over and said: "You know, we should talk from time to time. I could help you."

He laughed. "You are Mossad."

"I'm a secretary—with big ears."

"That would be *secret*-tary, wouldn't it?"

She was sitting in the bar when he arrived, sipping a cup of coffee. Three unfiltered cigarette butts with her lipstick on them sat in the ashtray. He kissed her cheek and ordered a beer. "Hi, long time no see."

She kissed him on the lips. "Hi. How's Jerusalem?"

"Fine. Busy. How's Washington?"

"The same." She exhaled smoke through her nose. "What brings you here?"

"I had business in New York. The magazine."

"The Prime Minister's upset with your magazine."

"News travels fast."

"Word has it you're in big trouble."

"With whom?"

"The Prime Minister and his friends."

"That's nothing new."

"It could be dangerous."

"Dangerous?"

"Not personally—professionally. There are people who think you're on thin ice."

"Your people?"

"Some people." She stabbed her cigarette out, extracted another from a leather case and held it out for Jared to light. "Thanks."

"I need help, Dvora."

"I'm happy to oblige, Jared—if I can. Ask."

"I was set up." He sipped his beer, bummed a cigarette and told her about the Abu Zain story, about the leak to the magazine, about his meeting in New York.

She nodded sagely. "What does that tell you?"

"That I'm on to something. But where to go?"

"You know," she said, "some people at the Embassy keep their fingers on things like this even though the government doesn't, ah, officially sanction them to do so."

"I've learned."

"Let me check things out. I'll call you. Where do you stay?"

"Four Seasons."

"Nice place." She smiled conspiratorially. She pinched his arm. "Big beds."

"Adrian would kill me."

Crow's-feet gathered around Dvora's eyes as she laughed. "Probably. If she found out. How is dear, sweet, rich, little Adrian?"

"Running her father's bank. Lunching a lot. Three weeks ago with Yoram and Mandy Navor."

Dvora frowned. "Did she tell you that?"

"No."

"How do you know?"

"I saw her—I was across the street from Olympia when they went in. Why should Adrian go to lunch with Mandy Navor?"

"I have no idea. Look—Jared, let me make some calls. Maybe I know someone who'll be of help in this other matter. As for Adrian, you have to ask her." Dvora put her cigarette out, took another and lighted it. "I have to go. I'll leave you a message—unless I show up personally." Jared's eyes clouded over and she laughed. "Does that make you nervous?"

"Tempted."

"Good."

He put the call off until the last possible moment. At half-past nine he dialed the Potomac number. "Felix, I can't make it for brunch. I apologize, but it's impossible. Something's come up."

"Jared—is anything wrong?"

"No. Nothing's wrong. Just business."

"Can't it wait? We told everybody you'd be here at twelve-thirty."

"I'm sorry—no, Felix."

"Beverly will be very disappointed. She's worked so hard. And all that food, nova and sturgeon . . . fresh bagels she went out herself at eight this morning specially to buy for you. My God, Jared, we invited the ambassador. And all your friends, Bob and Sue Bernstein, and the Yuppmans, and Barry Weiss who's Ronald Reagan's Jewish expert, and Shmuel Tzur from El Al, and Colonel Evan, who took Yoram's place. They'll all be here to see you. And everybody wants to hear about Adrian." Cooper's voice took on a tone of familial reprimand. "Is business so important you can't even show up for a few minutes? This isn't right, Jared. You gave your word."

"I have a meeting. I can't put it off. It just came up."

"With whom? I'll call."

"I can't say, Felix."

"Secrets yet? Jared, this isn't right. How am I going to explain to Beverly? What'll I tell Adrian?"

"Tell them I told you how sorry I am. Look, Felix, this wasn't my idea."

"Whose was it?"

"I told you—I can't say. Look, I'll make it up to you. Really. Felix, I have to go. I'll be in touch before I go back, I promise. I'll call you from New York. I'll leave Adrian's package for you with the concierge here at the Four Seasons."

"You're going to New York?"

"I've got to make the noon shuttle. I'll call you. I'm really sorry about this. Love to Beverly. 'Bye."

He rang off before Cooper had a chance to reply. He sat on the edge of the bed and wrung his hands. "He's pissed."

Dvora swung him around and pulled him on top of her. She put his head between her breasts and moaned when he kissed a nipple. "Listen, business before pleasure."

"Easy for you to say."

He rolled off and lay alongside, running a hand down her rib cage and flat stomach to the mounded thatch of black hair and rubbed gently. She nudged his face lower, spreading her thin, muscular legs apart.

Later, in the shower, she returned the favor. "How often do your sources do this?"

"Ah-aiee! Not often enough." He grabbed at the towel rack at the end of the tub to support himself.

She stood up, wet red hair plastered against her scalp, and pressed against him. "I have good news and bad news."

"What's the bad news?"

"The bad news is that I'm famished and you better feed me. The good news is that I have some names for you," she said. "People who may be helpful."

He took her shoulders. "Who?"

"Not so fast. It's going to cost you." She slipped out of the shower, toweled semi-dry and headed toward the king-size bed. "Order room service. Fresh orange juice, French toast and bacon. Espresso. Then you come here and—you know."

He stepped into the bedroom dribbling water onto the gray rug. "You know why they say Israel's a wonderful place to visit? Because it's every day a holiday and every night a Yemenite." He laughed and jumped wet into the bed, grunting as she wrapped her legs around his waist.

"Hey," she protested, "you were supposed to order first!"

He finally got around to calling room service just as she was taking her third shower of the morning. Unlimited hot water was still something she, like most Israelis, counted as a luxury.

There had been no love professed between them in bed, only the passion of the moment, the resumption of an old and friendly relationship that had been, three years before, guilt-free. He'd slept with Dvora perhaps half a dozen times, and in each instance it had been a decision based on animal attraction and momentary opportunity. They'd never become involved in each other's lives. There was nothing complex about their relationship. They were friends. Occasionally they slept together, sometimes they traded information.

This time, however, he was paying a new and inestimably higher emotional cost for Dvora's body—and her assistance—one that caused him a certain amount of discomfort. He felt a gnawing sensation that he'd betrayed Adrian. It was the first time he'd cheated on her. In Israel, cheating on wives and girlfriends was a way of life. Jared had stayed away from it simply because he'd had no reason to go to bed with anyone but Adrian. Unlike Yoram, whose current mistress was a girl-soldier lieutenant at Zahal headquarters, or many of his other friends who kept *hatti-hot* stashed away for late-morning assignations, nooners, cocktail-hour quickies and evening *shtups,* Jared was the constant and consistent lover.

And so now he found that he had trouble making small talk as he stood, shirtless, folding clothing and stuffing it in his well-worn suitcase and Dvora laughed and joked from behind the shower curtain. He couldn't concentrate on Dvora; instead he thought of another shower curtain, at the King David Hotel, and how Adrian looked as she soaped and lathered and rinsed off in the steamy tile and marble bathroom.

Still, on the one hand, there hadn't been much of that soaping and lathering and rinsing off lately. And, on the other hand, he'd earned some solid information: two names, two phone numbers, and two introductions handwritten in Dvora's precise and neat Hebrew script.

The door buzzer rang. "Room service's here," he shouted at the bathroom's open door.

"Finally. What took them so long?" She ran to the closet, grabbed his Burberrys trench coat and wrapped it around herself. "Am I presentable?" She flashed him.

"Quit that!" He laughed and turned the latch. His expression froze. Felix and Beverly Cooper stood in the doorway. They were bearing food.

"We couldn't let you leave without at least saying hello," Beverly said.

He watched her smile calcify as she looked past him.

CHAPTER 9

The magazine kept a permanent room for visiting correspondents at the Dorset Hotel on Manhattan's West Fifty-fourth Street. Jared took a cab there directly from the airport. He stashed his belongings in the nicked mahogany dresser, tossed a bunch of dirty shirts and underwear into a paper laundry bag, and piled his papers on the small desk. The room was seedy genteel; more like a London club than a New York hotel. Writers didn't mind staying there, although when executives from the magazine's sales offices visited New York they were put up in the Towers of the Waldorf Astoria, where the magazine kept another, far more regal, set of accommodations.

He knew he ought to call Adrian; her parents had no doubt already burned up the phone lines to Jerusalem. They'd stood in his doorway like a couple of mannequins, blurted an apology, thrust the basket of food into his arms and run off. Dvora had laughed. Jared hadn't.

But he didn't call Adrian; he felt unable to cope with recriminations right now. So, instead, he bought a four-pound Sunday *New York Times,* opened the arts and entertainment section, and read the movie listings. Then he went downstairs. He dropped his laundry at the bell captain's desk, sauntered over to Times Square and sat through a mindless Chuck Norris movie twice. When he finally emerged, stupefied, he walked up Seventh Avenue to the Carnegie Delicatessen, bought himself a tongue sandwich, a container of cole slaw and two bottles of Heineken beer to go, went back to his room and ate sitting cross-legged on the double bed while he read the *Times* and watched television simultaneously. He swallowed a sleeping pill with the last of the beer, dropping into a drugged but deeply therapeutic sleep.

He slept late Monday morning, awakening at eight-thirty, groggy right through his shower. At nine he called the New York City number Dvora had given him. The phone was busy. He waited five minutes, then dialed again, tensing when it was picked up after three rings.

"Hello?" A woman's voice. A thick Israeli accent.

Jared spoke in Hebrew. "Is Avram there?"

"*Lo, Avram lo b'bayit. Mi-zeh?*—Avram isn't here. Who is it?"

"I'm a friend from Israel. Where is he?"

"At work. Do you want to call him?"

"I'd like to see him."

"Ahh. And your name?"

He used the name Dvora had given him. "Shem Tov."

"He's at the store. Dynamic Sports, on Fourteenth Street."

"Good. I'll call him there."

"Wait—if he comes home—can he call you?"

"No, I'll call back if I don't reach him. Thanks. 'Bye." Jared rang off, picked up the phone book and looked up the address. He dropped his room key at the front desk, went through the revolving doors, turned east on Fifty-fourth Street and walked to Fifth Avenue, where he elbowed aside a pinstriped banker and caught a cab downtown.

Dynamic Sports was located just off the northwest corner of Fifth Avenue and Fourteenth Street, a storefront set into a white brick apartment house that was undergoing renovation. To the east was Union Square, with its small park hemmed in by heavy traffic. Looking west, Jared saw sidewalk vendors and an unbroken line of cut-rate furniture and clothing stores, discount outlets and record shops that stretched to Sixth Avenue and beyond.

To the south lay Greenwich Village and lower Fifth Avenue, with its million-dollar co-ops and trendy restaurants. Here, however, sandwiched between the Village and Chelsea, was a narrow belt of stores that provided a gaudy reminder of the time Union Square had been one of the city's prime shopping areas for the lower middle class. Fifty years before Jews had shopped here at Ohrbach's before it moved uptown, and Klein's. Now Puerto Ricans and emigré Hondurans, Marielito Cubans, Salvadorean refugees and illegal Nicaraguans bought drugs in Union Square's wasteland park and crowded into stores whose E-Z credit terms were announced in Spanish.

Jared peered inside. He pushed open the door.

"Good morning. Can I help you?" A gangling redhead in designer jeans and a rugby shirt accosted him.

"Just looking. Is Avram here?"

A jerk of thumb. "Behind the register."

Jared looked to his left. The man was about thirty, dressed in jeans and an open-necked shirt unbuttoned low enough to reveal opaque black chest hair that ascended unchecked across his neck and chin, metamorphosed into matted untrimmed beard, and finally melded into ragged curly locks. "Avram?"

"Yes."

"Hi. My name's Shem Tov. I'm a friend of Dvora's. Dvora Lavi."

"So?"

"I wondered if you could spare me a few minutes."

"I'm busy."

Jared looked around the empty store.

"I don't have time to talk."

"Dvora said—"

Avram interruped. "I don't care what Dvora said." He gave Jared a careful once-over. "You work with Dvora?"

"No, just a friend. She said you could help me. She sent you this." Jared offered up a sealed envelope, which the bearded man opened with his teeth and read.

He tore the message into little pieces, scattered them somewhere behind the counter, and sighed. "Okay—" He called to the redhead that he was taking a break, and motioned Jared to follow him out the door.

Walking east, then south, saying not a word, Avram led Jared to a steamy-windowed coffee shop on University Place near Tenth. Motioning toward a booth in the rear, he scooched across the padded plastic bench, ordered coffee, and lit a cigarette, offering one to Jared.

"Thanks."

"You're welcome."

"So, how do you know Dvora?"

Jared answered in Hebrew. "She's an old friend."

"I'd rather speak English if it's all right with you," Avram said.

"Sure."

"I speak Hebrew at home. We're in America—I speak English in public."

"Okay."

"What's your name? It's not Shem Tov."

"Jared Paul Gordon. I'm a magazine writer."

"Jared Paul Gordon, Jared Paul Gordon. Of course—Jared Paul Gordon from *World Week*. I didn't know Dvora hung out with anti-Semites."

There was a pause while the coffee was served. Jared chose to disregard the comment. "You came back . . ."

"Three months ago. I needed a change. I made aliyah when I was eighteen. Thirteen years ago. Did my time in the Army. Got married. Worked."

"For whom?"

"Nothing special. At Ampal—I assembled refrigerators."

"Dvora says—"

Avram hunched over the table. "Dvora says a lot of things."

"She says you can tell me about something called TNT."

The other man leaned back in the booth, crossed his arms and exhaled smoke through his nose. "Why should I know anything about TNT? I'm no explosives expert."

"Not TNT explosives. *Terror Neget Terror* organization. Terror Against Terror."

Avram scratched under his beard, found something on his chin, probed, squeezed, examined, and discarded it on the leg of his jeans. "I don't know what you're talking about."

"Dvora says—"

"Look, *Mr.* Jared Paul Gordon, I don't know what you're talking about. You walk into the store and give me a note that says I should go have a cup of coffee with you. So here we are. And first thing out of your mouth is some crap about TNT. Frankly I don't give a goddamn what Dvora says. Who cares what secretaries say, if y'know what I mean." He lifted the thick coffee cup in a meaty hand, blew across the top and sipped. "You—big left-winger—I know you hate Begin—you come and you start asking questions. This is none of your business. Dvora says a lot of things. Why should I even talk to you?"

"Because Dvora says you're a decent guy. Dvora says you left because you didn't want to get more involved than you were."

"Involved? I'm not involved."

"Let's stop the cat-and-mouse, Avram. I've got friends. You might not believe that, but I do. And I could go back to Israel tonight and call them. They'd run your name tomorrow through a certain computer in Tel Aviv we both know about—it's called 'Springs' if you remember—and then I'd jump a plane back here and show you the printout. It would be a waste of time and money. Dvora says you're a decent guy—so be decent. Talk to me. I'm not planning to bring you into it. Whatever you tell me's off the record—not for attribution. I won't use your name. But you know things that could help. I need help."

"You never wrote anything good about Begin. But since I've been back here I'm beginning to think that some of the things your magazine prints are pretty close to the truth. The problem, *Mr.* Jared Paul Gordon, is you. You've got a wild hair up your ass for Israel."

"What?"

"Your stories are slanted. When you wrote about Lebanon, all you talked about was the resentment the Lebanese felt against the Israeli invaders. That's bull. I was there: they greeted us with rice and kisses—the Shiites and Druse as well as the Christians."

"That wasn't true for very long."

"But it was true at first—and you never wrote it. Your reporting on the war was like that asshole Timmerman—he should go back to Argentina, the *putz*—whom we rescued, brought to Israel, and then he gives the whole country the shaft, saying it's worse than Argentina." Avram stabbed out his cigarette, lighted another, inhaled deeply and jabbed a forefinger in the direction of Jared's chest. "You're a *putz* too. You may speak Hebrew; you may live the high life in Jerusalem or Herzlyia or Kefar Shemaryahu or any of those places where you rich assholes live. But you don't understand a frigging thing."

"Such as?"

"What the country is and where it's going and why. You're a Peace Now liberal. You don't know any real people."

"Real people?"

"Real Jews. You come from the United States to live a couple of years in Israel and you live well, too, I know—and the only people you ever meet are liberals. Professional liberals, Army liberals, kibbutznik liberals, political liberals. And when you run into what you call hard-liners, well—you think, you believe, you choose to believe that they're political exceptions. Well, they're not. We're not."

Avram's vehemence was jarring. Jared tried to ease the pace. "Okay, Avram, tell me. Explain to me."

"I'm not sure you're worth it."

"How the hell can I learn if you don't?"

The Israeli laughed—a short, cynical guffaw. "Learn?"

Jared nodded.

"Okay, Mr. Jared Paul Gordon, welcome to the University Place Coffee Shop *heder*. I'll start from the beginning. You and I probably didn't grow up alike. You're from—not New York—where?"

"Los Angeles."

"I'm from Brooklyn. You wealthy?"

Jared hesitated. "Comfortable. My father's a doctor."

"Mine's a grocer. You grow up religious?"

Jared shook his head.

"I didn't think so. Well, I did. When I was growing up in Brooklyn getting my ass kicked by the wops and the *schwartzers* we were all taught that Israel was the realization of a dream. I lived my life around Israel. Made up my mind before I was bar mitzvah I'd make aliyah. Tell me, Mr. Jared Paul Gordon, was your ass ever kicked by a *schwartzer*?"

"No. I wasn't bar mitzvah either."

"I didn't think so," Avram said bitterly. "You're not the type. So anyway, I went—in 1970, right after high school. Finished ulpan in October, then went straight into the Army. I made Egoz—"

"Golani Brigade's reconnaissance unit?" Jared's opinion of the Israeli changed. Only one in a hundred made the elite commandos.

Avram nodded. "We were the best. I wore the brown beret with real pride. Then came the war. I fought the Syrians. God—they were tough, the bastards. I'd never thought of Arabs as tough, but those guys were murder. Anyway, I came through it alive, got out of the Army in '74, started university, got married and dropped out. Found my job at Ampal. We lived in Samaria, in a development town, and I took the bus to work. Two and a half hours a day on the damn bus. We did okay, I guess. My folks sent money—Batya's parents don't have much—and we survived. For us, it was enough just to be in Israel.

"But there were things that disturbed me. Things I saw. I'd do my reserve duty in Judea or Samaria. I knew how the Arabs prospered, the way they never did under the Jordanians. They took Jewish jobs—they work cheaper than Jews—took Israeli pounds and converted them to dinars and sent the money abroad. It was like we were being raped. Here were Arabs, living better than they ever had, sending money to their relatives in Jordan or Syria or Lebanon, and that money—Jewish money paid by Jews—ending up in PLO bank accounts.

"And you know what made it worse? The government condoned it—encouraged it even. 'Let the Arabs in the occupied territories expand their economy,' they told us, 'it'll be good for Israel.' Well, that was a load of bullshit. And the only one to fight it was Begin. Even in the mid-seventies, I liked what Begin stood for. After all, it was Labor: Golda, Dayan, Peres, Rabin, that beached whale Abba Eban with his *forshtunken* Oxford accent—all those crooks—who let the Arabs get at us first in '73. They screwed up. Begin wouldn't have.

"So when Kach was formed, I joined. Meir Kahane makes sense."

"How?"

"He tells the truth. He calls the American Jewish leadership pygmies and dwarfs—which most of them are. He doesn't give you any of this sanctimonious bullshit about live and let live. He wants Jews to be just like anyone else: human beings with their own country. Germany for Germans, France for the French, Ireland for the Irish—and Israel for the Jews. Oh, how you're looking at me—'How can he say such things? How can a Jew talk so tough?' Don't interrupt, Mr. Jared Paul Gordon—*Sheket!*—shut up! Don't interrupt with your left-wing brotherhood crap. The Arabs? I know all I need to know about the Arabs. They have Kuwait, Saudi Arabia, Oman, Syria, Iraq, Jordan, Lebanon, Morocco, Algeria, Tunisia, Libya, Egypt, Yemen, Sudan—lots of places.

"Us? We've got this tiny speck of land; and the whole world wants us to share it. To give most of it up!

"Thing about it is, Kach isn't made up of crazy people. It's made up of people who want to preserve the Jewish state—people like me."

"Then why did you get out? How come you're not relgious any more—you're not wearing a *kippa*."

"I stopped being religious—observant—when I was in the Army. You're making a big mistake if you think Kahane and Levinger and the rest of the patriotic nationalists only attract religious fanatics. Go to Metulla; sit in cafés in Bet Shemesh or Afula; listen to people talk—not your corrupt, effete Labor Party intellectuals, but real people—real Jews. Have you been to Bet Shemesh? To Afula?"

"Not recently."

"Listen to him—'not recently,' he says. Liar! You were *never* to Bet Shemesh, never sat in the cafés or even visited the *forshtunken* Givat Sharett, where the rich ones live and think they're in Tel Aviv or some other highfalutin place. You never went—you don't have the face for it, or the guts. If you ask me, you only read Amos Oz in *Davar*'s magazine."

He watched Jared's eyes lower toward the coffee cup then raise to meet his own again.

"Listen, Mr. Jared Paul Gordon, I've been to Bet Shemesh, and you know what they say there? They say that Peres and the rest of Labor are faggots—weaklings, with no guts to stand up to the Arabs. And they say so in Afula and Binyamina and Holon and Ashdod and Yavne and Kefar Sava and all those places you frigging American, Hellenized, assimilated left-wing liberal Jews don't dare to stick your noses."

Jared took a deep breath. "So you're saying Kahane appeals to these people because he represents strength?"

"Strength? More than strength. Kahane knows how to deal with Arabs. He wants them out. Let the Arab countries take them back, just like Israel took in the Jews who lived under Arabs. For example—I married into a Kurdish family. My father-in-law, Zadok, lost an arm fighting in the War of Independence. You know how he came to Eretz Israel? He *walked*. He and his father and his mother and his two brothers *walked* from Kurdistan to Palestine. As the crow flies, that's about 1,500 kilometers. Except they didn't fly like crows. And by the time they reached Jerusalem one of the brothers was dead and Zadok's mother was dying.

"They left their home in 1940 and arrived in Palestine in 1942, when Zadok was nine. Before he was bar mitzvah he was smuggling arms for the Hagganah. And in 1948, he was fifteen, and he got wounded in the fight for the Kidron Valley. His father died in the alleys of the Old City.

"My father-in-law's no religious fanatic. He belongs to Tami. But he also supports Begin, and he's leaning toward Kahane. And you know why? Because he grew up under Arab rule. He saw his relatives die. He deals with Arabs—he speaks better Arabic than he does Hebrew—but he wants them out of *his* country. And there are thousands and thousands like him—Yemenites, Moroccans, Algerians, Syrians, Iraqis—all the Jews who grew up under the Arab thumb. What the hell does Labor know about Arabs? Labor's a corrupt bunch of Russian, Polish and the worst—German Jews—*Yeckes*—who did nothing but talk brotherhood while they screwed people like my wife's family and gave Jewish jobs to Arabs.

"You want to know what attracted me to Kach? Reality did. Four million Jews against a hundred million Arabs."

"But you left, Avram."

"Sure."

"Why?"

"Inflation, the economy—like they say, it used to be that at the end of the month you had a little salary left over. Now at the end of the salary there's a lot of month left over. I left because of lots of things."

"Such as?"

Avram hunched over the table, ground his cigarette out in the tin ashtray, lit another, and shrugged. "Things."

"Look," said Jared. "I understand where you're coming from. But there must have been something that made you uproot your family. Kurds are close-knit—my friend Shimon who runs Chez Simon in Jerusalem is Kurdish, and I think if his son-in-law picked up and brought his daughter to the United States he'd fly here in a minute and drag them back by the neck."

"So you know a token Kurd. Good for you, Mr. Jared Paul Gordon." Then the expression on Avram's face softened and he nodded. "It's a problem. Batya misses her family a lot. But right now . . ." His voice trailed off. He focused on the coffee that lay untouched at his elbow. "Right now, it would be, uh, hard to go back and live."

"Because?"

"Call me a hard-liner," said Avram. "I am—and I'm proud of it. But there are certain areas where I draw the line."

"Such as?"

"Random violence. You know, when you're asked to do certain favors, well, some of them are okay. Like when I did my reserve duty, there were people who'd ask me to bring home extra ammunition. Once I lost my Uzi—on purpose. But lately, it was getting a little heavy."

"How heavy?"

The Israeli slipped into quiet Hebrew. "Heavy. Claymores. Grenades. Timers."

"And?"

"Look—in for a penny, in for a pound. They've got you both ways. Cooperate, or when the crunch comes, you're the one whose name's given to the Shin Bet."

"Who's the 'they,' Avram? TNT?"

"I won't talk about TNT and I won't give you names. I don't care what Dvora wrote. But I can tell you this. When you get back, keep your eye on Hebron. Go down to Qiryat Arba."

"I've been there."

"Maybe you have, maybe you haven't. I mean really get to know the place."

"Why, Avram?"

" 'Why, Avram?' " He mimicked Jared's California accent. "I thought you knew about Israel, Mr. Jared Paul Gordon. Because that's where the real action is. That's where the patriotic nationalists are going to stand and fight. First in Hebron. Then afterward in Nablus and Umm Al Fahm and Jenin and the rest of the cities where those *jukim* live."

"Jukim?"

"The Arabs, schmuck. Cockroaches." The Israeli shook his head in disgust. "Look—that's it. No more, huh? I only talked to you because Dvora's been good to my wife and me and I owe her. I told you—you're not my kind of Jew."

Jared placed two dollar bills under the saucer of Avram's coffee as the Israeli slid from the booth. "I understand," he said awkwardly.

Avram shrugged, his palms wide. "And keep my name out of it.

I want to go back, y'know. It's not good for Batya here. She needs her family."

Jared watched the Israeli go, then pulled a reporter's notebook from his jacket pocket and reconstructed as much of the conversation as he could.

He sipped his cold coffee. He was disturbed by what Avram had said. No—he hadn't been to Bet Shemesh. He didn't know anybody from Afula or Holon or Yavne. Maybe to Avram he and Adrian lived in Potemkin Village Israel. He didn't have a lot of friends among Oriental Jews, either. He knew Mikki Venetzia, but had never been invited to Mikki's home. Or to Shimon's. Nor had they visited him and Adrian in Yemin Moshe.

"You're not my kind of Jew," Avram had said. "You don't know any real people—real Jews." What the hell kind of Jew was Avram's kind of Jew? What the hell is a real Jew?

It bothered him. Avram bothered him—Avram wasn't Jared's kind of Jew, either. For years he'd been uncomfortable with overtly religious Jews, or Jews who wore their Jewishness on their sleeve, like those who joined Hillel in college and were active. It was as if they'd wanted to set themselves apart from the mainstream of campus life; create a social and cultural ghetto that excluded everyone but them.

These days in Israel, they were doing the same thing: the Hasids in their enclaves; the militants in their settlements. They created ghettos for themselves. They'd built Israel to escape the heritage of the ghetto, to escape the ghetto itself. But what was Israel these days? Jared's sorry conclusion was that it was becoming the world's largest, most well-armed ghetto-state.

And what was "his" kind of Jew? Who was a "real" Jew, anyway? Yoram Gal? Nathan Yaari? Adrian's friend Koby Naiderman, who grew grapes and suffered because the harvest had been bad for two years running? His secretary, Annie? The old people walking in Rehavia? The soldier at the Wall—if the soldier had ever existed? Adrian? Felix? Bob and Sue Bernstein? The madman at *Martef Hashoah*? Avram and his pals in Kach?

Was he himself a real Jew?

But weren't they all real Jews? It came down to that—it was all of them or none of them. Jared believed so. It was just that *they* didn't.

They kept trying to get bills through the Knesset narrowing the definition of who is a Jew. Only the Orthodox would be considered real Jews if they won. *They* had neglected the Ethiopian Jews for years. Falashas, they called them—outsiders. When Ethiopian Jews made aliyah they had to go through a ritual conversion—had to immerse themselves in the mikvah before they'd be accepted as "real" Jews by the Chief Rabbinate.

Jared shook his head. And yet it had been Ethiopian Mossad agents who slipped into Uganda to clear the way for the IDF's rescue of the hostages at Entebbe—Ethiopian Jews who, shunned by Israel's religious leaders, had still risked their necks to rescue hostages simply because those hostages were Jews.

He didn't doubt Avram's sincerity. Nor the man's passion. Nor the truth of what he'd said. It was just that Jared's truth was different from Avram's. The Unnameable Name had not molded Avram and Jared from the same clay. Only their Creator remained consistent.

Yet that was impossible: God had created every man in His image. "When God created man, in the image of God created He him." Any other interpretation would be *hillul ha shem*—a desecration of His name.

But what? How? Why?

It was all too confusing, too frustrating, too bewildering. Things were happening too fast. Jared was losing control. He needed time. And there were other questions, questions about Adrian, about Felix, about the bank—about Adrian's lunch with Yoram Gal and Mandy Navor.

But where to start? What was the line from *Alice in Wonderland*? You start at the beginning, and go on until you reach the end. Then you stop. So he knew in part where to start: Long Island City and Great Neck. The beginning. That's where Adrian had been born, where Felix once had his business.

Jared put his notebook away and, shrugging into his trenchcoat, walked out of the coffee shop and strode north on University Place. At Thirteenth Street, he came upon an Avis car rental office. He walked inside, plunked his credit card on the counter, and ten minutes later was sitting behind the wheel of a bronze Ford Thunderbird.

CHAPTER 10

Jared drove through heavy traffic, cursing the cars that cut him off, swerved dangerously close in front of him and ran red lights. Israel was known for its mad-dog drivers but this, this was worse than Cairo. He missed the turnoff for the Midtown Tunnel, being unaccustomed to New York's capricious system of one-way streets and avenues. At Fifty-eighth Street and First Avenue he turned west. The map they'd given him at the car-rental counter showed he could get onto the Queensboro Bridge from there. But the entrance was closed; it took him half an hour to negotiate two gridlocked blocks to Third Avenue. He crept north, then east on Ninety-sixth Street, gunning the car onto the East River Drive, carefully edging into the left lane so as not to miss the Triboro Bridge turnoff. At the toll booth he brought the roadmap up and plotted his route with his finger, while the attendant fumbled for change.

Despite having memorized the way to Great Neck, Jared promptly got lost as soon as he hit the Grand Central Parkway. Stuck in the right lane, he was crowded by a taxi onto the Brooklyn-Queens Expressway access road. It took him south. He was supposed to be driving east. He cursed his luck, and the taxidriver, swerved onto the first exit road, and discovered himself on Northern Boulevard in Queens. He pulled to the curb and studied the map. He was better off than he'd imagined: Northern Boulevard ran to within a couple of miles of Great Neck.

The question, of course, was what he'd find once he got to Great

Neck. Jared was no investigative reporter, not one of those patient souls who relished the thought of spending weeks sifting through documents to find a kernel of truth in papers of incorporation or transcripts of congressional hearings. But he had the practiced eye of a good observer. His reportorial strength lay in his ability to look at a situation, report it accurately and analyze it coherently. He understood the ebb and flow of politics; after his years in Washington he was able to sift rhetoric for subtext and truth. He was a good interviewer, and—although he'd never known it before Lebanon—a gifted battlefield reporter.

But this was something new: to go into a place he'd never been before, looking for who knew what, and trying to discover . . . something. The need to chart unknown waters without clear-cut goals made him uneasy. And in any case, even if he found something, he hadn't the faintest idea what he'd do with the information.

He peered through the windshield at the factories, warehouses and used-car lots that lined the pot-holed boulevard. The very size of everything in America was so different, so immense. He'd been gone less than three years and still, every time he returned, he was struck by the larger-than-life scale of American society, American commerce, American industry.

He wondered how Avram's wife was adapting to New York. Not well, probably. Israelis liked everything close. They shopped at neighborhood markets, stayed near home, didn't travel well. Well—not quite true. The rich ones did—the ones who made their money on the stock market, wore designer clothes and carried back everything from refrigerators to videotape players—traveled very well indeed. You could see them in Los Angeles, Phoenix, Washington or Orlando, the proud possessors of VUSA tickets, hundred-pound suitcases—and things. Things, things, things. Disposable diapers.

Traffic thinned. He chuckled to himself. Question: How do you know you're on El Al? Because everyone stands up for the entire flight and the overhead bins are crammed with cases of Pampers and Huggies and Luvs. God—to have the Pampers concession at the El Al terminal. He'd make a million. To hell with journalism. Why put up with crap from editors when you can make a fortune dealing in crap itself.

A building caught his attention at—where was he?—Forty-ninth Street. Art Deco glass, white bricks, rounded corners and scalloped cornices. Five-foot-high letters proclaimed the company's name. FELCO. Jared squealed the car across five lanes of traffic, U-turned, and parked in front of the three-story structure. FELCO. It was Felix Cooper's old company—this was where Felix had made his photoelectric cells.

He got out, walked to the front door and peered through the glass into a small frosted-glass walled lobby. A circular staircase rose in the rear. He stepped back and read the brass plate to the left of the heavy glass doors. FELCO INDUSTRIES, a Division of Grunwald, G.M.B.H., Frankfurt.

He whistled. So Felix had sold out to a German company. No—that was impossible. Felix had a pathological hatred of the Germans. He never forgave them for the Holocaust, never lost an opportunity to remind his Jewish friends who drove BMWs and Mercedes that they were contributing to the economy of a country that once had tried to eradicate Jews from the face of the earth. So Felix could never have sold out to Grunwald. He'd sold the company to someone, who had ultimately sold out to the Germans. He'd ask Felix.

Grunwald, Grunwald. It was an old German electronics company. A multinational: radios, televisions, computers, semiconductors—even phosphates and petrochemicals. Defense work, too, for NATO and for the U.S. government. But the company had a blot on its history. Like Siemens and Krupp and a lot of others, it had been an integral part of the Nazi war effort during the Second World War. Grunwald had helped build the concentration camps. It supplied high-voltage electric fences and ignition systems for the gas crematoria. There were contracts, documents—photographic evidence of the slave laborers who'd died building them. Jared had seen it at Yad Vashem.

He pushed open the thick, green glass door and wandered into the lobby, looking at color posters of the semiconductors Felco was currently manufacturing. Then he mounted the circular staircase, entered a paneled reception area and found himself in front of a curved wood desk behind which a young black woman sat.

"Good morning. Can I help you?"

"Just looking, if that's all right. I think this place used to belong to my girlfriend's father—I was driving by and the sign caught my eye."

"Sure," the receptionist said. "When did your girlfriend's father own Felco?"

"Sometime in the fifties, I think. How long has it been run by Grunwald?"

"Gee, I'm not sure—a long time."

"Is there anyone here who knows?"

"I don't know. Maybe our office manager."

"Could I talk to him?"

The receptionist shrugged. "I guess so. Who should I say is calling?"

"Jared Paul Gordon."

"And you represent?"

"I'm just here on my own, but I'm a reporter for *World Week*."

The receptionist lit a cigarette and punched a button on her console. "Hattie, there's a Mr. Gordon from *World Week* out here. He wants to see Mr. Stewart. He says his girlfriend's father used to own the company." She nodded. "I'll tell him." She looked at Jared and smiled. "Have a seat. He'll be with you in a minute."

Soon, Jared was shown into a small office where a bald man worked in shirtsleeves behind a worn metal desk. "Yes?"

Jared told his story. The man nodded, noncommittally, and smiled. "I wish I could help you, but I've only been here three years myself."

"Is there anyone who might know?"

"I don't think so. There was a bookkeeper I think who'd been here forever, but I never knew her. Someone once told me she was hired just after World War II, but . . ."

"Do you remember her name?"

"I'm afraid not."

"Is there any way of finding it?"

"Personnel might have it. Wait." He dialed an extension on the old rotary phone. "Doris, this is Mr. Stewart. We used to have somebody—a bookkeeper, secretary—she retired a couple of years ago—who'd been here forever. Is there any way of locating her name?" He paused. "End of 1981, I think."

He cupped his hand over the receiver. "She's checking the pension records."

Jared waited. "Fine. Good. Sure. Thanks." Stewart hung up the phone. "She was a secretary. Her name's Harriet Fusco Mercaldi," he said. "She retired in November 1981. Date of hire July 1946."

"Where is she and where can I find her?"

"I'm afraid I can't help you there. I'm not allowed to give out addresses."

"Even to a reporter?"

Stewart smiled. "Especially to reporters. But I guess it would be okay if I told you to look in Bensonhurst."

"Where's that?"

"Brooklyn. Near Coney Island."

Jared nodded. He rose. "I will. Thanks."

Back in the car he scanned the map again. This time, however, he traced his route with a pen, then wrote the turnoffs into his notebook before he started the ignition and wheeled into traffic.

Forty minutes later he was standing at a pay phone next to a bowling alley on Avenue U, in the shadow of an elevated train station. He'd marveled at the El as he drove under it. It was the first New York elevated train line he'd ever seen except in movies like *King Kong* and *The French Connection,* and as he drove under its pylons and girders he found himself excited by the rumbling overhead, and strained to catch a glimpse of the trains as they passed.

There were sixteen Mercaldis in the Brooklyn phone book, although none of them was listed for Harriet or H. Jared had no idea which ones lived in Bensonhurst. He wrote all the names and numbers into his notebook, dropped a quarter into the phone and dialed the first number, a listing for A. Mercaldi. There was no answer. The second number—Anthony V.—was busy, as was the third. The fourth picked up but hung up abruptly when he asked for Harriet. He tried number two again. This time he got through. A man's voice answered.

"I'm looking for Harriet Fusco Mercaldi."

"She doesn't live here."

"Do you know where she lives?"

"Who's calling?"

"Jared Paul Gordon. I think she used to work for my girlfriend's father, and I'd like to talk to her. Who's this?"

"Anthony Mercaldi. You say your name's—"

"Gordon. Jared Paul Gordon. My girlfriend's father is Felix Cooper, and I'm looking for Harriet Fusco Mercaldi."

"How do I know you're not some kook?"

"You don't, I guess. Look, do you know Harriet Fusco Mercaldi?"

"She's my aunt."

"Terrific! I tell you what. I'm at a pay phone at the corner of"—Jared looked up—"Avenue U and Forty-seventh Street. If you could call her and say I want to talk about Adrian and Felix Cooper I'm sure she'd say it was okay. Then you could call me back here—or she could."

"You sound a little nuts to me, but okay. What's the number?"

Jared read it off. "I'll get back to you," the man said.

Jared leaned against the wall of the bowling alley and waited. Five minutes passed, then ten. He'd almost given up hope when a blue and white Pontiac sedan pulled up behind his car and a man waved at him. He walked over. "Jared Gordon?"

"Yes. Who are you?"

"Anthony Mercaldi. My aunt says she'll see you. Follow me."

The Pontiac cruised under the El, then turned onto Fifty-fifth Place, heading south on a narrow street of two-story frame houses. Halfway down the second block the car turned into a driveway. Jared pulled in behind.

The Pontiac's door opened. Mercaldi hoisted himself from behind the wheel. He wasn't a big man, but a brawny one; he wore pressed blue jeans and boating shoes and a short-sleeved plaid shirt that hung out over his belt. As he reached back across the front seat to retrieve a golf jacket, Jared saw the butt of a pistol flash under the shirt. He stopped cold. Mercaldi saw his reaction and reached into his shirt pocket. Coming up with a well-worn black leather case, he opened it and Jared saw a police shield. He smiled. "You're a cop."

Mercaldi nodded and replaced the case. "You're lucky you got me," he said. "I was just on my way to work and my aunt's phone isn't listed under Mercaldi. My uncle died five years ago. Now she lives with her son-in-law and my cousin Patsy. His name's Genovese."

"Are there any other Mercaldi relatives?"

"Sure, my mom and pop. But you'd have a hell of a time getting anything outta them. Come on—follow me."

Mercaldi led the way to the side door of the white frame house and entered without knocking. "We're here, Aunt Harriet," he called. Jared looked around. The room was sparsely furnished: a Colonial-style sofa and easy chair, a Barcalounger that faced a console TV set, a Formica dinette set (white table and four padded plastic and chrome chairs) and a high chair completed the room's decoration. The walls were bare. Jared heard floorboards creak above his head. Mercaldi motioned for him to sit, but the reporter jumped to his feet as a tiny, dark-haired woman in a flowered dress came into the room.

The policeman picked her up to give her an affectionate kiss on each cheek and lips, then spoke to her in rapid Italian. She laughed. She looked at Jared. "Mr. Gordon?"

Jared extended his hand. "Jared."

Her grip was firm for someone less than five feet tall, her hand dry. "Jared. It's a nice name. You've met my nephew Anthony. Isn't he a doll?"

Jared smiled. "He's been very kind. You're very kind to see me."

"You said the magic words," she said. "Felix Cooper."

"You knew him?"

"Oh, yes. A wonderful man. So generous and kind—"

"You worked for him a long time?"

"Oh, yes." She smoothed the front of her dress and clasped short-fingered, red-nailed hands at diaphragm height like an opera diva. "Mr. Cooper hired me in 1946. The war was just over and jobs were hard to come by. You're too young to remember, but that's the truth. So Mr. Cooper, God bless him, hired me as a receptionist, and then I went to secretary school, and—oh, just listen to me go on." She tittered. It had been years since Jared had heard anybody titter. Words came out of her in a torrent: "Would you like something to drink? Please sit down. What about you, Anthony? How is Mr. Cooper?"

Jared waited until she'd sat in the armchair and then plunked himself onto the sofa. Mercaldi took the Barcalounger, which he double-clutched into High Recline. "Thank you, no, I'm okay. Felix's doing just fine—living in Washington."

"And Mrs. Cooper? She was always so kind."

"She's fine, too."

"How wonderful. And you—you're little Adrian's boyfriend?"

Little Adrian. How quaint. "You *knew* Adrian?"

"Oh, yes—of course—he used to bring her to the office all the time. Such a sweet girl. An angel. And her eyes, so big and beautiful, violet eyes, just like Elizabeth Taylor's. I'll never forget them. I never saw such eyelashes."

"She's still beautiful."

"Where is she?"

"We live in Jerusalem."

Her eyes went wide. "Jerusalem? In Israel? Oh, it must be exciting. All those religious shrines. But isn't it dangerous? I'm always seeing stories about bombs and terrorists on the television."

"It's not as bad as they make it out," said Jared. "Actually, it's pretty dull most of the time, Mrs. Mercaldi."

"Harriet—please call me Harriet. You're Adrian's boyfriend, after all." She paused, giving Jared a maternal once-over. "And what do you do?"

"I'm a writer for *World Week*."

"We have a subscription!" She scrambled out of the chair. Jared rose but she motioned him back. She walked into the kitchen and emerged waving the current issue. "See? Now I'm going to have to look for your stories. Oh, it must be exciting. To have your name in the magazine every week, to be able to speak to important people. You must be very good at what you do."

Jared blushed. "Well . . ."

"No, you have to be very good if you work for *World Week*. It's better than *Time*. Anthony's good at what he does, too. He's got twelve commendations. He's going to be a sergeant next year." She smiled at her nephew, who blew her a kiss.

"She's a piece a work, isn't she, Jared? My aunt Harriet's a piece a work."

Her eyes flashed in a delighted smile, and Jared caught a hint of the energy she must have had twenty or thirty years before. She turned to him. "Why were you looking for me? I mean—it's been years since I saw Mr. Cooper or Adrian."

"It's, well, sort of a chance thing," Jared explained. "I'm here on a visit, and I was driving out to the Island, and I happened to see the building, and I stopped, and on a hunch I asked if anybody knew Felix—he's told me so much about Felco—and one thing led to another, and here I am. It's just luck, I guess."

"Well, what a lucky day for me, too. To meet Adrian's boyfriend."

"Thank you."

"And even a famous writer. And you'll have to say hello to Mr. Cooper for me when you see him. You have to tell him that Harriet Mercaldi says hello. Tell him Harriet Fusco Mercaldi—I was married just before he sold the company and maybe he won't remember my married name."

"I will," said Jared. "When did Felix sell out, anyway?"

"Oh, I'd say in nineteen fifty—let me see—fifty-one. February of nineteen fifty-one is when Grunwald took over."

"*He* sold to Grunwald?"

"Oh, yes—he and Mr. Grunwald were very old, dear friends."

Jared nodded noncommittally. "Really."

"Oh, yes, and—"

"Excuse me," Jared interrupted. "So Felix sold Felco to Grunwald directly?"

"Well, really sold it back to Grunwald. You see, they'd been in business together until the war. It was Mr. Grunwald who gave Mr. Cooper the opportunity to expand and make photoelectric cells—at least that's what I understand." She poked at short curly hair sprayed firmly in place. "But that was all before my time. I wasn't hired until 1946, you see. Just before Mr. Cooper brought Adrian home."

"Brought Adrian home?"

"You know—home—from Germany. Mr. Grunwald found her in one of those camps and Mr. Cooper adopted her. She was an angel, just an angel from heaven."

Jared thought: The sky is falling. He kept a straight face and nodded. "How right."

"So you have to tell Adrian hello from me. Hello from Harriet Fusco Mercaldi. Mr. Cooper used to bring her to the office and let her play. You know, I was the receptionist—there was a round rug that Mr. Cooper had had specially made for the lobby—it had the company seal on it with the globe and the big letters F-E-L-C-O around the border—and Adrian would toddle around the rug and I'd teach her to spell the letters. And the names of the countries on the globe and everything. And I'd watch her—she was so cute—and now she's all grown up, and she has a boyfriend." She shook her head. "It all goes so fast, you know. Time. It seems like only yesterday little Adrian would play and I'd pick her up and give her a million kisses. I wasn't even married then."

Numbly: "Oh?"

"I'm a grandmother now, three times over," she said.

"Congratulations." He had started to shake. His head was pounding. He could feel the pulse in his wrists, arms, neck, temples. He had to get out. "Well—I . . ."

Anthony was looking strangely at him. The policeman pulled himself out of the Barcalounger. "Hey, Aunt Harriet, I hate to break up this reunion but I gotta get to work," he said. "I'll walk you to the car, Jared."

Jared swallowed. He was beginning to sweat. He could feel the moisture on his forehead, his chest, his arms. "Thanks."

Harriet Mercaldi stood up and gave Jared her hand. "Please tell Mr. Cooper hello."

"Sure."

"Harriet—"

"Fusco Mercaldi." He finished the sentence and swung around, looking for the door, for an escape. It had become very hot and he had to breathe cool outside air. A hand closed on his elbow. Anthony Mercaldi was guiding him toward the door. Jared remembered his manners and turned. "Thanks—it was good meeting you."

Outside, Anthony walked him to the car, his big hand never losing its grip on Jared's elbow. "You okay?"

"Yeah—sure. I guess I forgot to eat dinner or something last night. I just got a little light-headed in there."

Mercaldi backed Jared up against the side of his rented car and looked him in the eyes. "Light-headed my foot," he said. "You're in shock."

Jared shook himself free. "No—I'm okay," he insisted. "I just needed some air."

"Listen, Mr. Reporter, I see things. Like last night I was working a stabbing out in Brownsville. And the mother of the kid who got wasted took a look at the body and she let out a scream you wouldn't believe. The kinda scream that doesn't say little Pepe's hurt—it says little Pepe's dead. You just did the same thing in the house—except you did it without making any noise."

"No—I'm okay," Jared said.

"Sure you are," the policeman said. "All I wanna know is who died, Jared?"

"Nobody—really. I'm okay. It was just a little hot in your aunt's house."

Mercaldi patted his cheek. "If that's what you say, Mr. Reporter. Just so you're okay to drive."

"I'll be fine." Jared climbed into the car and turned the ignition. He waved at Mercaldi. "Thanks—a lot, really."

"Any time."

Jared found his way to Manhattan, raging at the heavy traffic that kept him stuffed inside the Brooklyn Battery Tunnel and nauseated by diesel fumes for twenty minutes. It took him another forty to weave uptown. At the Dorset he abandoned the car, threw the keys at the doorman and bolted for the elevator. His hands were so unsteady it took him three attempts to unlock the room.

He was still trembling as he dialed the operator and asked for an international line. "Israel." He gave the number.

He heard the phone ring. Adrian's voice said "Hello."

He swallowed the vodka he'd poured into his bathroom tumbler. "Harriet Fusco Mercaldi says hello." He heard her suck air as if she'd been gut-punched. He hung up the receiver.

When the phone rang some minutes later he didn't pick it up.

PART FOUR

July 1983

CHAPTER 11

Jared tugged at the uncomfortable, bulky flak jacket fastened securely around his torso and tried to shift the weight of the khaki rucksack that hung between his shoulders. A pebble got inside his boot and he called out to the sergeant commanding the eight-man patrol to wait while he extracted it.

"*Rak-shnya*—wait a couple of seconds." He found a boulder by the roadside and sat on it, pulled off the Gore-tex hiking boot and turned it upside down. "Ahh."

The sergeant, a lanky, thirtyish reservist named Yossi, took off his helmet and ran a hand over his matted curly hair, his unshaved cheek and chin. "Tired?"

"And hot," said Jared.

"Hot? You haven't seen anything," Yossi grunted. "For you, it's like a vacation here in the 'North Bank.' Three or four days, then you go back to Jerusalem to drink beer and play with the girls. Us—I've been here three weeks now and they'll probably extend me another three. How the hell I'm going to support my family this year I don't know."

Jared nodded. Like the rest of the unit, Yossi had been called up to spend his *meluim*—reserve duty—in Lebanon. At home he ran a small grocery in Netanya, a store that was presently closed because both Yossi and his partner had been mobilized at the same time. Here he was a squad leader whose patrol moved north and west out of Sidon along the southern banks of the meandering Awali River to guard against Palestinian infiltrators and Shiite guerrillas.

There were thousands of Israeli soldiers like Yossi in Lebanon; most were equally nervous and discontent. What Ariel Sharon and Chief of Staff Eitan once promised would be a short, decisive campaign had turned into a war of attrition. The Shiites and Druse who originally welcomed the Israelis had turned mean. In the first days of the war there had been rice, kisses and flowers showered on IDF troops, who had been greeted as liberators. Now, there were landmines, sniper fire and sullen, blank stares. The Israelis reacted strongly. Villages were destroyed, their inhabitants forcibly moved to new locations. The Arabs struck back with car bombs and isolated attacks. Each day that the occupation continued, more Israelis were sent home wounded or killed.

At Beirut's airport in the north, Jared found the situation not much different. U.S. Marines were finally coming under hostile fire from Druse gunners who controlled the high ground to the east of the runways. Like the Israelis, the Marines had at first been welcomed. But as the Americans gave more and more support to the Christian-controlled government, they received less and less support from the Moslem slums that abutted Beirut International. From their high ground in the Chouf, the Druse could shell Phalangist positions in Christian East Beirut and the Marines in their bunkers surrounding the airfield. To the northeast, Shiite militias built mortar emplacements, dug slit trenches and fired off occasional rounds at the Marines, the Druse, and the Maronites in East Beirut.

Just like Israel, the United States became caught up in the deadly game the Lebanese had been playing for generations. But for American military personnel it was a new and confusing game: one without rules. The Marines, accustomed to rules in everything from football to warfare, became, most often, its biggest losers—evacuated to hospital facilities on the Sixth Fleet ships that sat ten miles offshore, or shipped in body bags to Rhine-Main Air Force base in West Germany for the long trip home.

Still, for Jared, Lebanon—despite the dust, despite the heat, and despite the danger—was an escape. He'd spent three of the preceding four weeks in Lebanon, either with Zahal patrols or up in Beirut, trying to get a handle on the fragile political situation. Anything was better than Jerusalem—even the snipers, RPG ambushes or car bombs that made reserve non-coms like Yossi nervous about stopping long enough to allow Jared to remove a pebble from his boot.

He had thought about not returning at all. Debated staying in the United States and looking for another job, or telling Roger Richards that an assignment in the New York bureau was acceptable. But Israel was like a magnet: the country drew him back. It was the most complex, the most perfectly imperfect place he had ever seen. There were so many questions, and so few answers. At first he thought he'd figured the country out, understood its moods, deciphered its dynamics. Learned what made its people tick. But he realized now he hadn't. He'd only touched the surface—felt the heart beating, but not opened up the chest and touched the pulsating organ. Every day in Jerusalem he learned something new, about the Israelis, and about himself. In Los Angeles, Detroit, Atlanta and Washington he had been an observer: professional, detached, disengaged from the stories he'd covered. In Israel he was . . . a pilgrim. Every story was a lesson. Every day a new shard of truth was unearthed to be painstakingly brushed and carefully examined. Emotionally, Jared was unwilling to give up those journalistic luxuries. And, despite his anger, his resentment, and his sense of outrage, he also was unwilling to give up Adrian.

But what was she hiding? What secrets did she and Felix share? He tried to answer those questions on the long intercontinental flights that took him from New York to London, Paris, then Vienna, where he dug through decades-old dusty files about concentration-camp victims and the few orphaned children they left behind. The records were sparse; Jared learned next to nothing. He dug up what he could about Grunwald, trying to find evidence that would help explain the company's fifty-year relationship with an American multi-millionaire. Though he found less than he expected, he found enough to make him enraged over what he began to think of as Felix's hypocrisy.

Not that he'd expected to discover the whole truth. Indeed, taking the long route back to Jerusalem was one way to put off confronting Adrian. As much as he wanted to see her, hold her, tell her that he loved her, he also wanted to slap her silly; shake her until she broke.

It was all so . . . stupid. Living a lie like that, when it wouldn't have made any difference at all. So she'd been born in a DP camp. So what?

There were more ominous possibilities gnawing inside Jared as well. Adrian had lied about herself. She'd betrayed their relationship. Was she capable of betraying him to the Prime Minister because she believed what he was doing was wrong? Was she having affairs behind his back? Was she—oh, Christ, anything was possible.

He rented a car in Vienna and drove to Frankfurt, did a day's worth of research, then climbed on an El Al flight to Tel Aviv, and tried to sleep. It was impossible. He thought about what had happened to him, and about Adrian, and—briefly—settled on murder as a possible solution. At Ben-Gurion he commandeered a taxi and drove to Yemin Moshe. It was late evening when he arrived. He paid the driver and stalked toward the house, his aluminum suitcase clunking as he half-carried, half-dragged it down the cut-stone steps.

Quietly as a commando he opened the wrought-iron security gate. Then he kicked in the front door. She must have heard the wood give way, because she screamed and came running down the stairs.

"You bitch!" He threw the suitcase in her direction and started for her.

She retreated up the stairs, scrambling away from him. The cat got caught under her feet, and she stumbled. "Stay away from me."

There were tears of rage in his eyes. "How could you—"

"How could I? How could *you*—you son of a bitch. How dare you go off and sleep with that whore the first chance you get?"

"What about you?" Jared demanded. "Who the hell have you been screwing, huh? Yoram? Mandy Navor? The goddamn Prime Minister himself? What the hell story have you been giving me for the past three years? I thought we weren't supposed to have secrets!"

He turned on his heel and descended for his luggage, closing the ruined door as best he could. He came up, his heavy suitcase banging against the railing. "Do you know," he screamed, "do you know what I found? Your father was in business with the Nazis! Yeah—Felix Cooper, the world-class Jew, the big pal of Menachem Begin, the generous benefactor and philanthropist. Felix Cooper did a lot of business with the Nazis. Not only before the war, either. Afterward, too—when the whole world knew what they'd done to the

Jews. Jeezus, he probably just couldn't wait until 1945 so he and his pal Grunwald could be partners again!"

He tossed his suitcase into the living room, where it landed with a thud on the rug. He spun the combination lock and opened it up, grabbed a thick sheaf of Xerox copies and threw them in her direction. "It's all there," he said. "Records—in London, Paris, Vienna. Who Grunwald was, what he did—it's all on paper."

"He was never a Nazi. Poppa said so."

"Did he? Well, if Grunwald wasn't he sure had a lot of friends who were. What the hell do you think he was making from 1937 until 1945—hair dryers? Grunwald made equipment for the camps, Adrian. For Auschwitz, and Buchenwald, and Bergen-Belsen, and Treblinka. You know about those places, don't you?"

She looked at the strewn documents, silent.

"Don't you?" he screamed.

She picked up the cat and stroked its head.

"And then for Felix to go back into business with Grunwald after the war? It's inconceivable. And you know what? He wasn't the only one. I checked it out, Adrian. A lot of American Jews did business with Germany, right up until the day Roosevelt declared war. And afterward . . ."

He sucked air into his lungs. "And then there's you—"

"What about me?"

"You never told me—"

"To hell with what I told you or I didn't, Jared. What I told you is my business, not yours."

"That's not the bargain we made."

She glared at him, a wounded animal. "I—"

"What, Adrian?"

"I—"

"What? What? Come on, tell me." He collapsed onto the sofa, arms crossed. "Tell me. I'm all ears."

"You wouldn't understand."

"Oh, wouldn't I? Come on, Adrian—I'm a very understanding kind of guy."

"Don't do this, Jared."

"Don't do what? Learn about the woman I've lived with by talking to a retired secretary? That's no way to have a relationship, Adrian, no way."

"Then end it."

"What?"

"Then let's end it, Jared."

He could consider throttling her, even killing her, but not leaving her. "Don't be asinine."

"I'm not being asinine. I am what I am—that's it. I don't need you. I don't need anybody."

"That's not true."

"It is true. I was alone once. I can be alone again."

"Adrian—"

She kicked at his suitcase and stubbed her toe. "Dammit to hell. Get out, Jared. Get out of my house."

"You bitch." Stunned, he picked up his suitcase. He was mad, but he hadn't wanted to end things; just to shake her up a little. Make her tell the truth. "Look—Adrian . . ."

"You smug, self-satisfied sonofabitch," she spat. "Who the hell do you think you are, judging me? Checking up on me as if I were some . . . some . . . *factoid* in one of your stories? You're always saying you love me, Jared—well, love isn't fact-checking. Love is absolute. Unconditional." She tossed the cat gently toward the kitchen and turned her back on Jared. "Get the hell out of here."

"All right, goddammit—I'm going." Fifteen minutes later Jared checked into the Kings Hotel, a block and a half from his office.

He threw himself into his work—what there was of it—with a vengeance. But despite long hours staring at the screen of his word processor, he couldn't think of much besides Adrian. He moped around the office. When he finished he would buy take-out food and sit in the hotel room, listening to the short-wave radio. Some days, when he knew she was down at the bank in Tel Aviv, he would go to Yemin Moshe and retrieve his clothes, piece by piece, surreptitiously searching the house for signs of other men and relieved when he found none. At night he often found excuses to walk past the Montefiore windmill. He'd swing down the three flights of cut stone steps and stare up at the freshly repaired front door and the lights of her house. Often he thought of going inside. But he didn't. He paced and stared and paced some more, then wandered over to Katy's or the Goliath, where he would drink a whole bottle of red wine and stagger back to his single bed at the hotel. He was angry and confused. He was lonely, desolate and miserable.

As if it weren't enough that his personal life had collapsed, there was the stigma of his demotion, too. Begin made sure the whole country knew by mentioning Jared's presence—though not his name—during a debate on Lebanon at the Knesset. Dressed in his usual black suit, white shirt and black tie, Begin paused during his remarks to point an accusing finger toward the press seats.

"Up there," the Prime Minister intoned, his voice heavy with vibrato, "sits a known liar; a slanderer of the Jewish state, whose magazine, which I will not deign to mention by name, has seen fit to render its own journalistic judgment upon his head by placing this known liar, this traitor, on probation."

Jared had sat, his face red and frozen in a half-smile, taking notes. Half an hour later, he walked into the Knesset's dining room, took a cup of coffee and a piece of fruit on a tray and walked over to a group of Israeli correspondents. They told him their table was full, although two seats sat empty and piled with briefcases. He shrugged and walked to another, where three of the photographers who regularly covered Knesset sessions sat. As he placed his tray on the table, they gathered their cameras hurriedly and left.

He sat by himself, sipped his coffee, and peeled his apple with a knife, cored it, cut it into neat eighths, and consciously dawdled over each morsel so that by the time he'd finished, the last section he ate had turned brown. He knew everyone was staring at him.

That afternoon, as he left the Knesset's press parking lot, the guards—who'd seen him scores of times, and even called him by name—delayed him half an hour with an unprecedented search of his car. They removed the back seat, checked under the spare tire and inside the air filter. They went through every page of Jared's notebook and then took him into a concrete blockhouse where they strip-searched him. They refused to give any reason for what they did.

The ordeal did not end there. When the nine o'clock news came on that night, Begin's remarks about him were televised, the camera panning from the Prime Minister's outstretched finger to Jared, eyes lowered, self-consciously taking his notes. The newscaster went on to recount *World Week*'s story, the magazine's clarification, and Jared's demotion. The video behind his voice-over script showed a telephoto shot of the Knesset guards rummaging through Jared's car. The whole thing had been a setup.

Jared expected no less from Menachem Begin and his supporters. What he had not bargained for was the chilly reception he got from his regular contacts in the Labor party. Before he'd been summoned to New York they'd slipped him tidbits, returned his phone calls, met him for lunch or dinner. Now he couldn't get people on the phone. Opposition politicians made excuses not to share a table with him at Venetzia. Even the American reporters with whom he hung out at Katy's seemed cool to his presence. They didn't turn their backs when he came by—nothing so overt. But they didn't talk to him with the same collegial informality that had been their style less than a month before, displaying a reserve that subtly let him know they disapproved of what he'd done.

He began to feel like a leper.

Nathan Yaari was impossible to contact. Whenever he called the Shin Bet agent's home, never identifying himself by name, either Yaari hung up on him or Ziva curtly informed him that her husband was not in the house. Jared finally drove down to Tel Aviv and left a message at Zion's restaurant. But there was no response. Poor Yaari—he'd probably been transferred to Gaza or Metulla by now.

Worse, there was Jerry Atkins. Roger Richards's acting bureau chief arrived in Jerusalem ten days after Jared, and in his first six hours he turned the bureau upside down. Jared's belongings had been moved from the big office to the small one, his maps and photographs unceremoniously piled in the corridor. Now, in their stead, hung two huge posters from old New York mayoral campaigns, warmly inscribed by John Lindsay and Ed Koch, plus a boxing card from the old Madison Square Garden featuring Rocky Marciano in a heavyweight title defense.

The changes were more than cosmetic. Atkins, a pot-bellied bachelor of fifty who wore rumpled tan wash-and-wear suits, frayed blue button-down shirts, stained striped ties, penny loafers, and a straw porkpie hat, was an ex-Marine who had seen combat in Korea and an old-fashioned political reporter. Though he was not particularly liked by the squash-playing, chablis-drinking editorial hierarchy that ran *World Week,* he was trusted by them. He did what they told him, offended no one, and changed the slant of his writing in line with their opinions. And no writer at the magazine could turn out a file faster than Atkins. He was a good field soldier who knew how to work the phones and get the boiler-plate one-sentence quotes with which *World Week*'s editors liked to pepper their articles.

If Roger Richards wanted *World Week* to keep a low profile in Jerusalem for the next few months, Jared thought, then Jerry Atkins was a perfect choice. He would answer Richards's queries promptly, but show no initiative ferreting out new stories or new angles to old ones. His files would be based on press releases and calls to official spokesmen. He would not challenge the editors' preconceptions about the region. Indeed, like most of the journalists who came to Jerusalem without any knowledge or understanding of the Middle East, Atkins took the obvious path preferred by his editors: he followed the lead set by the American administration.

So Jerry Atkins arrived in Jerusalem with his canvas suitcase and campaign posters, believing, as did many American policymakers, that U.S. policy toward Lebanon was credible. Like Ronald Reagan, he saw Lebanon not as a Middle East problem, but as an element in the ongoing U.S.–Soviet conflict. And, like the American President, Atkins believed—without any facts to support him—that Amin Gemayel could unify his fragmented, Balkanized country, and that the U.S. could help him do it through military assistance. In Korea his Marine experience had proved to him that armed strength could hold the line against Communism; if it could be done there it could be done in Lebanon.

One day after he appeared, Atkins assembled the resident personnel and laid down a series of new rules for *World Week*'s Jerusalem bureau. Starting with what was to be covered, and what was not.

"Policy. We cover American policy. I don't give a damn about your socioeconomic bullshit or your religious-ideological crap," he said, jabbing a chubby finger in Jared's direction. "There's no difference between covering Israel and covering New York City. It's all policy. What's the effect on the U.S.? How does it help Reagan beat the Commies? If we know those things we'll know what's going on.

"And military. We cover Lebanon. The American involvement. That's what readers want. They want to know who the scuzzballs were that blew up the American Embassy. They want to see how our training program's beefed up the Lebanese army. We gave 'em—whaddizit?—two hundred million for weapons?"

"Two hundred and ninety million," said Jared.

"Whatever. And—whaddizit?—sixty M-48 tanks—"

"Sixty-eight," said Jared. "Sixty-eight tanks."

"Whatever," said Atkins, annoyed. "Exact numbers aren't the point. The point is we gotta show 'em how the money's being spent. They want to see how we're gonna make Lebanon safe for democracy."

"Safe for what?" Jared asked, incredulous.

"Democracy." Atkins used his hand to slick back red hair going gray at the temples, then wiped it on his trouser leg. "You remember democracy, Jared? Land of the free? Home of the brave? Well, the Christians are gonna make Lebanon democratic if we give 'em the chance. I saw the Defense Minister at a reception last night, and he told me so. And if Moshe Arens says it, who the hell are you to question him? Moshe Arens himself told me—shook my hand and told me—'Give the Lebanese Christians a chance,' he said."

" 'Give 'em a chance'? My God, Jerry—I'll tell you about democracy, Lebanese Christian style. Last time I was in Beirut I was stopped at a Phalange checkpoint. They handcuffed me to their Mercedes while the officer called the spokesman at Forces Lebanese to check out my credentials. In the ditch next to me were three bodies. Palestinians. You know why they died, Jerry? They died because they flunked the tomato test."

"Huh?"

"The tomato test. Sometimes Palestinians try to pass as Lebanese—it's easy to get forged papers—and the Phalange has an interesting way of sorting out who's Lebanese and who's not. They ask about tomatoes. Palestinians pronounce the Arabic word for tomato 'bandura.' The Lebanese pronounce it 'benadura.' The guys in the ditch got it wrong. That's Phalangist democracy for you—a goddamn tomato test."

"Whaddya, whaddya, giving me lip? Don't give me lip, Jared. Just do what you're told. You think I like being here? Geez, they uproot me on five days' notice after I rented a house on the Island for the summer and everything, and I'm living out of a hotel that doesn't even have room service twenty-four hours a day, and it costs me twenty-five bucks for a lousy bottle of scotch—and now you're going to give me lip because you want to do things your way? Can it, Jared. I don't want to hear about any goddamn tomatoes.

"You want a memo to spell it out? Okay—I'll give you a goddam memo. I don't want to hear about tomato tests, or mullahs, or Jewish terror. You want to write about those things you do it on your own time—not mine. You're a researcher now, and you'll do exactly what you're told. You're on probation."

So Jared filed Jerry Atkins's three-line memo in his desk drawer and did what he was told. He packed his combat gear, called a contact at Zahal headquarters, and went to Lebanon. But instead of hanging out with elite troops and bantering with colonels, he was shunted off to minor reserve units and forced to travel with second-rate patrols like Yossi's. He visited the U.S. Marines in their bunkers and he went to Beirut, sneaking in and out of the ruined city by a convoluted route that led him from the Coast Road up through the mountains; cut back by the airport through U.S. lines, met *World Week*'s Shiite driver Kazim inside the terminal; and then, hunkered down in the passenger's seat of Kazim's beat-up Mercedes, while the grizzled Lebanese, jaw set like an old bulldog's, threaded the needle by the militia roadblocks at the Kuwaiti Embassy, snaked along the Corniche al Mazzra, and then careened up the hill toward the Commodore Hotel.

He interviewed Walid Jumblatt, the Druse leader, and Nabih Berri, the head of the Shiite militia Amal. One of its larger gangs, the Murabitoun, controlled the streets closest to the Commodore, where most of the West Beirut–based foreign press was headquartered.

Berri was an interesting type, Jared decided. He'd lived in the United States—his ex-wife and six children were still in Dearborn, Michigan, just outside Detroit. In many ways Amal was the same kind of umbrella group as the PLO. It, too, was made up of factions that ran the political spectrum from centrist to radical.

Somehow, Berri—with Syrian help, one of Jared's few remaining Mossad sources told him—managed to control them all, from Islamic Amal, based in Baalbek and headed by a young fanatic named Hussein Muzawi, to the Murabitoun gang which, Jared concluded, was in it for lucrative protection scams and petty drug-running more than any ideological or nationalistic commitments, to Hezbollah, the Islamic Party of God run by Mahmoud Fad'allah. Or were there two Hezbollahs? Fad'allah's bunch and another, more shadowy element that was controlled directly by Iran? He put his findings down in a four-page file and left it in Atkins's in-box.

But Jerry Atkins wasn't interested in Nabih Berri. Or the Murabitoun. Or either of the two Hezbollahs.

"They're all geeks," he told Jared. "What I want—what New York wants—is to know how the training is going. When will the Lebanese army come together? What's Amin Gemayel going to ask for when he visits Reagan? How much more aid? How many more tanks?"

He shook the four-take story in Jared's face. "This stuff is horseshit, boyo. I told you—I wrote you one goddamn memo about what I wanted from you. Whaddya need, another? Who the hell cares what some Shiite mullah preaches in some damn mosque in South Lebanon? So what if there was a one-day strike in Sidon last week? And this Fa-la-la guy is off the deep end. The story is policy, not some religious fanatic. The story is what the Israelis are going to do next month, and how they're going to coordinate their withdrawal with Amin Gemayel, so the Lebanese army can fill the vacuum."

"They won't fill it," Jared insisted. It's going to be chaos up there. Once the Israelis pull out the Shiites and the Druse will be at each other's throats, the Palestinians are going to start infiltrating back into South Lebanon, and it's going to be a mess."

"Don't give me lip, Jared, okay? Just do what the hell you're told. I want to know what the Israeli army is going to do. So go to Lebanon and look around and tell me what's going on. This week's story needs color—so get me some color."

Jared pulled the nylon laces tight and double-tied his boot. "Okay," he said, "I'm ready."

Yossi pointed an index finger straight up and made a circle. "Okay, guys—let's move." He watched Jared stand, then turned and started moving slowly up the road, Uzi submachine gun slung muzzle forward over his shoulder, the non-com's finger on the trigger and his hand wrapped around the 'lemon squeezer' safety. "So—" Yossi spoke without turning around. "How do you like Lebanon these days?"

Jared unscrewed the top of his canteen as he walked and took a swallow of tepid water. "It's changed."

"You bet it has." Yossi pointed toward the northeast. "The Syrians still got—what?—sixty thousand men in the Beka'a?"

"Sounds about right."

"And that whore Gemayel—still he talks like he's the leader of a country." Yossi laughed bitterly. "The sonofabitch isn't even the mayor of Baabda. You heard that the friggin' presidential palace got shelled by the Druse last week? Two mortar rounds hit the bathroom where the Lebanese chief of state takes his presidential craps."

"I heard." Jared replaced the canteen and pulled out his notebook and a pen. "Hey," said Yossi, "don't quote me."

"I won't, at least not by name."

"You can call me 'a disgruntled Israeli non-com' if you want, but don't get me in trouble. It's bad enough I agreed to take you along with us."

"I got permission."

"I know you did. But then Ezra what'sisname the escort officer got the runs, and I wasn't supposed to let you come along alone."

"Ezra? He said it was okay. I brought you a pass from him."

"Paperwork?" Yossi snorted. "The army's gone crazy, you know? It used to be everything was word of mouth. These days, if it's not in triplicate it doesn't exist. Sure, I've got your pass right here—" He patted the breast of his flak jacket. "But what happens if you trip and break your ankle, or you fall into the river or something? It's still my ass."

"Don't worry, I've been out with patrols before."

"Yeah. But not with me." The non-com squinted into the dry underbrush, and paused. He raised his hand. "Hold it." He motioned to the corporal, Avi, a burly kibbutznik with a full-faced beard, pointing toward the roadside. Jared could see nothing awry.

"Recent?" Yossi asked.

"Maybe." Avi pulled the cigarette out of his mouth, pinched the lit end and field-stripped the butt, scattering the tobacco and grinding the paper ball into the road surface with the toe of his boot.

"What's up?" asked Jared.

"Somebody's been here lately," said Avi.

Yossi said. "Let's be careful." He slipped the safety off his submachine gun. The others did the same with their weapons.

Yossi moved ten meters ahead of his squad, taking the point, his Uzi sweeping the road. Jared followed, walking—as he had been instructed—squarely in the midst of the squad. He looked left and right and kept an eye on where his feet were about to fall on the dusty, rutted road.

He paid no attention to a muffled 'whump' that came from behind a hillock to his left. But Yossi did. Screaming "Mortar!" the non-com dove for the opposite side of the road.

Avi, the corporal behind Jared, body-blocked the American, knocking him sprawling into the thorny underbrush. Jared tried to stand up and see where the fire was coming from but Avi lay on top of him. There was a muffled explosion; thirty yards behind them a puff of smoke showed where the round had hit.

"Everybody okay?" yelled Yossi. "They're over there—ten o'clock behind the hill. I'm going to take a look." He started to move then stopped and shouted at the Moroccan private on whose back was strapped a radio. "Get us a chopper gunship," he yelled. "Get us some backup!" The private pulled a map from his pocket and started calling coordinates into the receiver.

Jared rolled from under Avi. There was blood on the American's face where his cheek had been scratched by a thorn. He watched Yossi scramble across the road.

There was another 'whump' and another puff of smoke, this time much closer.

"Shit," said Avi. "They're bracketing. Let's move." He called to Yossi, "We're behind you," and launched himself in a crouching run behind the sergeant, his Uzi raking the underbrush on full automatic fire.

Yossi screamed, "Hold your fire, goddammit. Let's wait until we've got something to hit," but he was too late. The machine gunner had already locked and loaded and he sprayed the opposite hillside. Panicked, the others joined in with Galil automatic rifles and Uzis.

Yossi made himself heard above the gunfire. "Hold it," he screamed. He stood up and waved his arms. He pointed to the machine gunner. "You—Amos—asshole—up there—" He indicated the crest of the opposite hill. "Barak, Hillel—Yoni—with him! Benny, Teddy, Avi—and Jared—with me." He pointed toward a small wadi snaking up around the crest of the hill, flanking the position from which the mortar fire seemed to be coming.

"Okay, okay—go-go-go!" The first four moved quickly in a crouching run across the road, scrambling through the thorns and up the hill. They moved crablike, dodging forward and then side-to-side. Yossi watched them. When they were a hundred meters from the crest, he pointed toward the wadi. "Let's go-go-go!"

Jared was the last to move. He stumbled getting to his feet; he made it halfway across the road when he heard another 'whump.' Instinctively he dove for cover, trying to hide himself in the rut of the road.

Then the round hit. Jared, on one knee, could see the puff of earth and white smoke where it impacted, not too far from him.

A baseball bat whacked him on the upper arm and knocked him onto his back. He rolled to the right, away from the pain and saw that his khaki shirt was daubed with blood. He started to his feet but the baseball bat clubbed him again—except this time it was a burning bat.

He thought he heard himself screaming "Oh shit, oh shit," and watched as a hand—was it his own?—tried to cradle his left arm, which was bleeding profusely—how could it be, so much blood in so little time?—a wash of blood, a flood of sticky red, soaking the entire length of his arm between shoulder and wrist, then puddling on the road surface. Oh God it hurt.

He had no idea where he was. Adrian—where the hell was Adrian?—he wanted Adrian. Oh, God, she didn't even know where he was.

Avi came back for him. He grabbed Jared by the collar of his flak jacket and dragged the hysterical American across a ditch and through a thicket of brambles, eased Jared's rucksack off, then propped him upright against the knotty trunk of a wild olive tree.

"Get a medivac," Avi shouted at the radioman. He ripped open a pouch on his combat kit. Jared screamed when he heard the Velcro. It sounded as if Avi was tearing the flesh from his arm. The corporal bit open a package of white powder, drizzling it over Jared's wound. With his assault knife he sliced the rolled sleeve of Jared's safari shirt upward from the bicep and gingerly cut it off at the shoulder. "I think it hit a vein," he called. He pulled a roll of gauze out of another pouch.

Jared tried to struggle to his feet. Avi knocked him back against the tree with his knee. He slapped Jared's face. "Come on, baby, it's not that bad."

He yanked Jared's arm skyward. Jared screamed and tried to pull it down.

"Shit!" Avi slapped Jared's face again, the blood on his hand smearing the American's cheek. Jared, wild-eyed, screamed in incomprehensible English into the bushy beard.

Avi answered in Hebrew. "Journalist—asshole—hold it up. Let me fix it—understand?" He triple-layered a meter of gauze wrapping and wound it tightly around Jared's upper arm. "*You*—you understand me?"

"*Ken! Ken*—Yes!" Jared screamed. "*Ken-ken-ken-ken*-yes-yes-oh God it hurts. Yes I understand oh lord oh God oh please, Adrian, Adrian, please Adrian."

"We've got to go after the fuckers," Yossi shouted. He looked at Jared writhing on the ground. "Avi and Benny stay with him. Teddy—with me. Benny—get that frigging chopper."

"Oh, jeezus it hurts," Jared screamed in English.

CHAPTER 12

JEREMIAH 8:19
Behold the voice of the cry of the daughter of my people from a land far off . . .

He came with the regularity of the seasons and sat to my father's right. Poppa's friend, Erwin Haberman. I called him Uncle Erwin. Even as a five-year-old, I knew there was something . . . different about him. First of all, there were his eyes—eyes like embers, their burning darkness always misted, as if by ashes. Eyes that bored into my brain, searching for . . . something. Oh, his eyes were terrible eyes, I knew that. Even as a little girl I sensed that behind Erwin Haberman's eyes lay unspeakable secrets.

He was one of those people who, if you see them once you never forget them. A widow's peak of dark hair that often fell into his eyes, to be brushed away with a stroke of his hand. A prominent nose, high cheekbones and veins that stood out from the sides of his forehead. He always wore a black suit, white shirt and a black silk tie. When he took off his jacket there, against the white shirt, were red elastic suspenders clipped to the band of high-waisted trousers.

He was as tall as my father, but ascetically thin—a real beanpole (Momma called him a skinny marink, *though not to his face). He moved quickly, furtively, like a fox or a squirrel, his eyes darting right-left, left-right as if to scent possible danger. I was fascinated by the way he ate. He pre-cut everything, then speared it with a fork held in his right hand. His left arm curved protectively around the plate, as if one of us might steal the food.*

He came three times a year: Passover, Thanksgiving and New Year. The other 362 days I had no idea what he did or where he went, where (or how) he lived, or whether or not he had suspenders other than those cheap elastic red ones. He showed up half an hour before we started dinner, sat to Poppa's right, ate his gefilte fish quickly, slurped the chicken soup noisily (and always held out the bowl for more), finished his plate and had seconds before the rest of us were half done. And then he'd sit, staring into space. His body was with us but his mind was in another universe. He always had three portions of dessert. How he could eat so much and be so thin I never understood. He ate like a man wth a tapeworm, or like someone who might never get another meal.

After dinner, he and Poppa would disappear to do business. I knew they were doing business, because they went into the small guest bedroom off the back hallway where Poppa had a kind of office, and where Poppa and I did our own weekly accounting of my allowance. So after dinner we would all push our chairs back from the table—ornately scrolled chairs covered in hand-stitched tapestry with roses—and Momma and I would go into the parlor and I would stand on a stool and peer down at Fifth Avenue, down at the people walking in the early evening, down at the cars as they moved along, and the double-decker buses as they chugged to a stop at the next block uptown.

I loved the buses, loved to ride uptown to the Metropolitan Museum. Loved to ride downtown to Bergdorf's and Saks and Best's, my hand clutched firmly in Momma's kidskin-gloved fingers as we sat. I'd scramble for the window seat and I'd point when we passed the zoo. "Momma," I'd say, "can we go to the zoo today?" I loved the animals even though they were in cages and animals shouldn't be in cages. Momma would always let me pull the bell cord, too, when we came to our stop. When Poppa and Uncle Erwin would finally emerge from doing whatever they did, Uncle Erwin would shrug into his black jacket, Poppa helping him. And then they both would put on their coats and hats and they would go walking. If the weather was warm, I would go out onto the terrace and, bracing myself on the wrought-iron railing, I could watch them as they crossed

Fifth Avenue and went north along the patterned sidewalk, then disappeared into the park at Seventy-sixth Street. Two figures in black coats fading into the evening as, arm in arm, their faces turned toward each other in deep conversation, they strolled along the narrow curving asphalt path that was lit by iron lamps that made yellow pools of light every few yards.

I don't remember when I asked but I must have asked because I was an inquisitive child. "Who's Uncle Erwin?" I must have said.

"Poppa's friend," Momma must have answered.

I knew she didn't like Uncle Erwin very much because she seldom talked to him, despite the fact that she talked to everybody—even strangers on the bus, and saleswomen in the stores, and people we'd just met in the grocer's or at the butcher shop on Madison Avenue. My mother was a very talkative woman. But not with Erwin Haberman. Before dinner, after he'd arrived, we would all sit in the parlor, eating nuts, and my father would have one drink of scotch, sipping slowly from a tiny cut-crystal glass. Uncle Erwin would drink only water, or coffee. I never saw him touch alcohol. And he would talk to Poppa—talk to him in a language that neither my mother nor I could understand, and we would feel left out. He would call me over and look me in the face with those dead-ash eyes, and touch my hair and my cheeks, and he would ask me about my school, and my friends, and what it was like to go to the museum, and he would tell me how pretty I looked and ask if the dress I was wearing was new. And when I'd answer him he would smile, and nod, and speak to Poppa. But he almost never talked to Momma. Never asked her the same kinds of questions he asked me. To her, it was the bare minimum: "Hello," or "How are you," or "Thank you, it was a delicious dinner," or "Good-bye." I knew that it was Poppa he'd come to see.

So Uncle Erwin came, and Uncle Erwin went. He was a mystery—except to Poppa. He was as much a fixture at those three annual family dinners as Hiram, the colored man married to Virginia, our maid. Hiram clomped around the dining table when he served because he had a wooden leg which I once demanded that he show me. (Momma caught me asking him to show it and she got very angry but Hiram said it was okay because there was nothing wrong with showing off your wooden leg especially because it was a gov-

ernment leg, given to him when he'd lost his real one in the war.) And he rolled up his black trouser and there it was—rounded, tapered wood that he let me rap my knuckles against.

And then one Thanksgiving Uncle Erwin Haberman didn't sit at his accustomed place. Nor on New Year's Day. Nor Passover. And soon thereafter Poppa broke the news.

We were moving from Fifth Avenue, from the only home I could ever remember, and I'd never ever see Gillis the doorman again (he had buckteeth and looked funny when he smiled but I never laughed at him—well, yes I did but only once), or Andy the elevator man who gave us our mail, or Mr. Willy the super who had a big black and silver German Shepherd dog that Momma said I could never pet because he might bite me but I did pet him and he didn't. Or Mrs. Willy who used to give me cookies. And I'd never ever ride the double-decker Fifth Avenue buses or go shopping with Momma at Saks and Best's and Bergdorf's, or be able to visit the museum and its beautiful pictures, or ride to my school on East End Avenue on the big silver and green Campus Coach Lines bus every morning, sitting next to my best friend Diane Robbins who lived on the next block at 745 Fifth Avenue and whose apartment I knew as well as my own. It was all going to be over. We were moving to Chevy Chase, Maryland, wherever that was, to begin a whole new life.

I didn't want a new life. I was perfectly happy with my old one and I cried when Poppa broke the news. I cried as I'd never cried before. And I cried some more when they came—big Irish redhaired men who smelled of beer, Momma said, wrinkling her nose—came with boxes and crates and barrels, and they took apart the apartment and packed everything I'd ever known into those boxes and barrels and crates, and I knew—I just knew—that we'd never see any of it again.

I stood in the middle of my denuded room; stood looking at the wallpaper without my pictures. Looking at the carpet, pale where my dresser and my bed and my table had stood, the indentations of furniture legs evidence of what had once been. Poppa came in and picked me up. "Adrian—Pidge—it's time to go." And I beat him with my fists and cried and cried because I didn't want to. He started to carry me out but I grabbed for the doorknob and would not let go. Gently he pried my fingers from it and carried me sobbing to the elevator. It was weeks before I forgave him for uprooting me.

I didn't understand why we were moving. Of course, there were a lot of things I didn't understand for a long time. I was a child.

Until Rome. Until I was nineteen, a sophomore at Sarah Lawrence, and visiting Rome for the first time. And I saw him—Uncle Erwin—in the street.

It was one of those United Jewish Congress escorted tours for teenagers. Two weeks in Israel, followed by three European capitals in fifteen days. Twelve of us—all girls—and a chaperone, masquerading as the tour guide. Momma booked it for me and sprung it as a surprise during spring vacation. I thought she was crazy. I was nineteen, a grownup in my own estimation, and the thought of—well—a chaperone, was just a little much. And the people. I was the oldest one by eons. Little girls, high school seniors and college freshmen, and I was about to go into my junior year and this was crazy. Three of my friends from college were going to Europe by themselves and I was so mortified at what Momma had done I couldn't bring myself to tell them about my own summer plans.

I chafed and pouted and put up a big protest, but in my heart of hearts I was excited. Even with the chaperone, it was my first trip overseas; the first time in my life I'd be on my own. Every summer until that one we'd spent in Washington, where I whiled the time away at the Woodmont Country Club's swimming pool and signed the chits with Poppa's account number. Or we traveled as a family: to Los Angeles once, to the Bahamas and Puerto Rico in the winters.

So I got myself a passport, and in June we drove up to New York and stayed at the Plaza, and saw Hello, Dolly *and ate at Sardi's Restaurant and the "2l" Club, and then they put me on the plane and waved good-bye. Israel was wonderful, too. It was so different from anything I'd ever seen before—everybody was Jewish but they weren't like our friends at home at all. The signs were all in Hebrew and I couldn't read them. The Israelis were so informal, too. They all wore open-necked shirts, and I knew I'd brought too many clothes because I never wore a dress, only shorts and sandals and my Lacoste shirts. And the streets were filled with young people, tanned and healthy looking.*

We stayed at the King David Hotel. In the evenings, we could look from our windows across No Man's Land and see the walls of the Old City turn to gold; see the sun reflect off the roof of the Dome of the Rock, and even—if we looked hard enough—see the Jordanian soldiers in their red and white keffiyah headdresses as they moved along the walls. I bought a kibbutz hat and a gold Star of David on a lovely chain and ate Middle East food for the first time, and wrote dozens of postcards to my friends, and even got to call my parents long distance and listen to their voices echo and echo.

I considered myself a seasoned traveler by the time we arrived in Rome. It was so different from Israel, because you had to dress up all the time, and the streets were all dirty (our first day we actually saw a man relieving himself in an alley) and the smell of diesel fumes seeped into our small bus. But it was all oh, so wonderful, even with our chaperone making sure that we didn't get picked up by the boys in tight jeans and loose, V-necked sweaters that they wore without any shirts underneath, gold chains with big, heavy crosses around their necks. The chaperone—her name was Esther, and she had thick legs and wore Red Cross shoes—had let us meet Israeli boys. But these swarthy, Christian Romans were off-limits.

We stayed at the Ingleterre, on Via Bocca di Leone, three hundred and fifty-seven steps from Gucci. (I know—I counted each one of them. More than once.) It was our last full day in Rome and we'd seen the opera at the Baths of Caracalla and the Forum and St. Peter's Square and I was on my way to Ferragamo to buy four pairs of flats. Navy, bone, tan and yellow. I was just coming out of the hotel, into the cobblestoned piazza, and there he was, Uncle Erwin, crossing right in front of me.

It was him. It had to be him. The same black suit. The same ferret face, high-cheeked, and the veins, more pronounced than ever, standing out from his forehead, and those eyes, those ember-eyes darting left and right. As he passed me he brushed the hair out of his eyes and I knew it was the same man who'd come to dinner at our apartment in New York a dozen years before.

He moved with deliberation through the crowded piazza, a package wrapped in brown paper tied with twine carried like a football under his left arm. It's amazing, I thought, how you can go half around the world and run into someone you know—someone you haven't seen in years and years.

I started to call out but for some reason I didn't. I watched, mesmerized at the sight of him. What was Uncle Erwin doing here? After all these years how incredible to see him. I forgot about my flats and followed as he strode along Via Bocca di Leone, threading his way through the late-morning shoppers and tourists. He turned left on Via Vittoria, then right onto the Corso, and I thought I would lose him if he ran and caught one of the smelly orange and white buses that roared along the crowded avenue. But he didn't. He walked, shoulders hunched, the package under his arm, up to the Piazza del Popolo, cut across the traffic and continued up a wide street, past what looked like an official building, and then suddenly veered into a café. I watched from across the way as he stood at the counter, ordered a coffee and swallowed it in a single gulp.

Then he was off again, in the same direction. I followed, wondering when would be a good time to catch up to him and say hello. He turned right, and proceeded up a steep hill, then turned left into a narrow street. I followed, increasing my pace until I was almost running. But by the time I came to the corner he had disappeared.

I found myself in a small piazza. Straight ahead, three narrow streets came together, a florist's wagon at their apex. To my right were stores: a café, what looked like a delicatessen (although I was sure that no such thing could exist outside New York), and a drugstore. I peered inside the café. Three men in blue smocks, cigarettes dangling from their lips, were laughing loudly. One of them blew a kiss at me and I ran away, up the street, toward the corner.

An arm shot out from a doorway—I hadn't even noticed it—and grabbed me. I screamed.

It was Erwin Haberman. His face was angry. Contorted. He shook me and spoke in Italian. I began to cry. He looked at me.

"Uncle Erwin?" I sobbed.

He dropped his hand from my arm, leaving white marks where his fingers had been.

"Uncle Erwin? It's me—Adrian Cooper."

"My God." He took my chin in his hand and looked me in the eyes. "My God—I thought—"

"It's me," I said. "I saw you when I was coming out of my hotel, and . . ."

"You've been following me," he said. "For a long time. Since the Corso."

I nodded my head. "Uh-huh."

He nodded too, revealing uneven, yellowed teeth. "Little Adrian Cooper."

"Not so little anymore. I'm in college."

"And in Rome."

"A tour. We came three days ago from Israel, and we leave tomorrow for Paris, and London, then home. By boat, Uncle Erwin—I'm sailing on the Queen Elizabeth. *It's been wonderful so far, and I—" Then I stopped myself. "But you! I haven't seen you in ages—not since you used to come to the house for Passover."*

"And Thanksgiving," he reminded me. "And New Year's Day."

"I remember. And now?"

"Here. In Rome. For the past seven years."

"Do you work here?"

"Of course."

"What do you do?"

"I work—for the Jewish Agency."

"Is that like the United Jewish Congress? I'm on a Congress tour."

"Good for you. Something like that." He looked me up and down. "You're all grown up."

I laughed. "You look the same. The same as when you used to do business with Poppa."

"Business?"

"When we lived at Nine-thirty-six Fifth Avenue. The two of you used to go into that little office down the back hall next to the guest room, where I got my allowance, so I always guessed you had business with him there, and—"

He cut me off. "Adrian, Adrian." He touched my cheek. "Why stand here? My flat's around the corner. Come up and visit. You can tell me about yourself, about how you've been, and what you're doing. You can tell me about Felix—it's been years. Come—the housekeeper will make us coffee." He shook his head. "Little Adrian Cooper, after all these years. My God."

We climbed the stairs and I waited while he pulled a huge bunch of keys on a gold keychain out of his pocket and inserted three, one at a time, into a heavy wooden door at the end of a dark hallway. He reached in and flicked on a light. "Antoinetta? Antoinetta?" He let loose a rapid spray of Italian, took me by the shoulder and nudged me into the vestibule.

"This way." We walked through a set of French doors into a long, narrow, dark living room. He pointed at a sofa and motioned me to sit, while he went to the windows and drew back a set of heavy

velvet drapes, flooding the room with light. "Better, hah?" Setting the package down on a coffee table, he pulled a straight-backed chair from the dining room where I saw a table piled with newspapers, files and documents, and sat facing me. Suddenly, he got up and disappeared. I looked around the room. It was very European, filled with antiques and there were oil paintings on the walls. Although I had been hot outside, sweaty even, after my long walk, Uncle Erwin's living room was cool.

He reappeared, carrying a silver tray on which was a pot of coffee, two cups and saucers, a sugarbowl, spoons and a plate of cookies.

"Antoinetta keeps hot water," he explained. "She knows I like my coffee. I probably drink too much of it, but at my age I don't worry."

I waited as he poured carefully and handed me the cup and saucer, then held it on my lap while he served himself.

"A cookie?"

"No, thank you. I've been eating too much lately. The food's so good here."

He took one for himself and popped it into his mouth. "I can't resist," he said. He had another.

"You're still so thin. I remember. Momma used to call you a skinny marink.*" I giggled as his eyebrows raised. "Well, she did. You used to eat and eat and eat, and you were always thin."*

"Well, maybe she was right—maybe I am a skinny marink.*" He smiled but did not laugh, and I realized I had never seen him laugh.*

"Do you still wear red suspenders?" I blurted out.

"What?"

"Wear red suspenders. You used to. I remember. Whenever you came to the house you would take your jacket off and you'd have on red suspenders clipped to the top of your pants."

He unbuttoned his shiny black jacket to show me. "Still," he said. "You have a good memory."

"That's what Poppa says."

"You call them Momma and Poppa, not Beverly and Felix?"

"Huh?"

"Momma and Poppa."

"Of course I do. What else could I—"

His eyes, those burning eyes, narrowed. "When did they tell you?" he asked. "They did *tell you—"*

I knew what he was going to say. I'd known it the instant he asked whether I called them Beverly and Felix. Maybe it was something I'd known instinctively as long as I could remember. Except no one had ever put it into words before. Put a name to it. But Erwin Haberman did.

Adopted.

Adopted Adrian.

The hints had been there. My friends' family albums had pictures of their mothers pregnant—but not mine. And snapshots of tiny babies, I didn't have any. And once, when my parents were away and I was alone with Virginia I snuck into their room and I went through my mother's drawers and I found, in one of her handbags, a folded, yellowed clipping from a magazine. It was a poem, and it was titled "The Joy of Special Children," and I think it was then that I knew something was not . . . not right.

"Years ago," I lied with what I hoped was a carefree wave of my hand. "They told me years ago." I held the saucer with my left hand and reached for the cup with my right and started to sip, but the saucer started to shake and I would have spilled the whole thing on myself except that Erwin Haberman moved so quickly and took them out of my hands, resting them gently on the coffee table next to his package.

I looked at him, thinking the only thing worse than being a child and told that you are adopted is being a nineteen-year-old and being told you are adopted. In the instant I looked at him I became an orphan. No family. No heritage. No roots. Totally alone in the world.

Isolated in a way no one else ever could be. And betrayed . . . by . . . them.

They did it to me. I hated them. Momma and Poppa. Not Momma and Poppa anymore. Beverly and Felix. My adoptive parents.

The strangers who took me in.

Them.

He must have been watching my face. "Cowards." He said it more to himself than to me but I knew about whom he was talking and I wasn't having any of it.

Tears welled in my eyes. "They're not. They told me. That I'm adopted. See? I said it. I said it. I knew. I've always known."

He waited, silent, as the tears came. He said nothing, but pulled the white handkerchief out of the breast pocket of his coat and handed it to me. Watched while I cried, and cried, and blew my nose and cried some more.

When there could be no more tears, when I was cried out, empty, devoid of anything, he spoke.

"I tried to tell them," he said, brushing the forelock out of his eyes. "The sooner you explain these things the better it is. But you know your father. So pig-headed. And she—worse than he is."

I watched his face. It was a pained face, an anguished face; as he spoke to me the veins on his forehead bulged and pulsed. He bore into me with those unrelenting eyes, looking inside me as he told me everything I didn't want to hear. Things about refugee camps, and displaced persons, and Zionist agenices, and German businessmen who had used Jewish slave labor in their factories later trying to atone for their sins, and American Jews who were the partners of those guilty German businessmen, and Jews helping each other, and finally his words enveloped me like the waves at the beach when I was tiny and we still lived in New York and they used to take me to the Lido Beach Hotel for the summers and I played in the sand.

His mouth just . . . kept moving and his words washed over me like surf, and then the colors in the room faded and I began to sweat, and I got quite cold, and not just Erwin Haberman's suit, but everything in the room turned black and white, even the oil paintings, and his words were like an inescapable undertow and I slipped into a blackness I'd never known before and I thought that I was dying.

Adrian awoke sweating and teary and kicked herself out of the bedclothes, her legs tangled in the comforter, the cat scurrying for safety from her sudden thrashing. She had fallen asleep in her clothes; now they were clammy with moisture, and she was chilled. She looked at the bedside clock. Three-thirty A.M. She blew her nose, shed her dress and underclothes, pulled on her robe and slippers, and padded into the kitchen, the image of Erwin Haberman's face still peering at her until she turned the light on and the sudden brightness made it go away. She lit a burner and, after checking to see there was water in the kettle, set it to boil and watched until steam rose through the spout. The cat rubbed against her leg, and she bent down to ruffle it behind the ears.

She spooned Nescafe into the biggest mug she could find and

poured the water, stirred, dropped the spoon into the sink and took the coffee into the living room. She opened the shutters and stared across the Hinom valley at Mount Zion, bright in the clear night and setting full moon. She blew across the top of the mug and sipped cautiously.

For years she hadn't thought about Erwin Haberman. Until five nights ago, when she'd had the dream. This was the third time she'd had it since. Why?

For years, the secret had been . . . safe. There was a bond of silence between herself and her parents. She'd had no bad dreams, no nightmares. No one suspected anything. She was her father's daughter; her mother's child. The secret went unspoken. Life went on—as if nothing had happened. And yet like her cancer, the secret lay dormant, festering until, until—oh damn him, damn him, damn Jared for finding out.

Damn him, he knew, and their relationship was over. It was over because he knew, and he'd do . . . something with the secret. Use it against her. How many times had she wanted to tell him? Dozens? Scores? Hundreds? But it had never been . . . the right time. Never the opportunity she wanted.

Besides, he *would* use it against her. That's what Felix said. He'd said it about her husband, too. "Why tell Allan anything? Why wash our dirty laundry in public? He'll only use it against you—against us. What he doesn't know won't hurt him."

He'd said the same about Jared. "He'll only fling it back in your face," Felix said. "What he doesn't know won't hurt him." But this time Felix was wrong. It *had* hurt Jared. For the first time, Felix had given her bad advice.

Or had he? Jared said he loved her, but he'd left her anyway. He said he wanted to make Jewish babies but he'd been to bed with that bitch, Dvora. And then—to go to London, and to Vienna, and to Simon Wiesenthal. To check up on her. Oh, damn Jared. Damn him.

Maybe Felix was right. The evidence was plain. Hadn't Jared walked out without a fight? Wasn't he willing to leave—hadn't he wanted to leave—because of who she was? He hadn't called, hadn't said a word to her since the day he'd snatched up his suitcase, thrown it into his car, and roared off. She knew where he was. At the King's Hotel. Or in Lebanon. She had checked with Annie. At least Annie hadn't deserted her. She called Annie every day to see how Jared was, where he was; and Annie told her.

This week he was in Lebanon. A three-day reporting trip, Annie had said. But now it was five days and Annie hadn't heard a word. She'd called the IDF spokesman, she said, but never heard back. Adrian called Yoram. But the general was out of the country. Even the well-connected assistant managing directors at the Bank hadn't been able to find out anything.

Oh God, it was all over. Jared had left her. There would be no Jewish babies. Not with Jared. He'd take the last of his clothes and go and she'd be alone again. As alone as she'd been that morning in Erwin Haberman's apartment in Rome. Adrian finished the coffee and thought about making some more. Instead, she went to the bedroom and took the comforter, bundled it back to the couch, wrapped herself in it and lay staring at the window.

The bells would ring soon. Perhaps, when it began to grow light, she'd be able to sleep.

It was wrong, all wrong. She'd wanted Jared to tell her everything was all right. To tell her it didn't matter who she was, where she'd come from. Instead, he'd left. Deserted. Bugged out. She'd wanted so much to hold him that day he'd come back; be held by him. But she hadn't. He hadn't. It was impossible. Make Jewish babies. That was what the crazy old man at *Martef Hashoah* said. Crazy old man living with dust and ashes. Crazy old man with one good eye, which looked at her in the same way that Erwin Haberman's eyes had once pierced her very soul.

Were her parents in the old man's urns? Her real parents? . . . Down in that chamber with the yellow stars and pieces of soap? Erwin had told her, in Rome, that they were dead. Ashes. Dust. She'd fainted in Rome. She'd almost fainted in the *Martef*, too—thank God for Jared. Make Jewish babies with Jared, the old man had said. But damn him, Jared *knew*. And he'd use it against her. Wouldn't he?

Pilgrim settled at her feet. Adrian closed her eyes, listening to the cat's even breathing, feeling its heartbeat through the soles of her slippers.

She cracked her eyes. It was bright daylight. The sun above Mount Zion refracted through the window, making crazy patterns on the Turkish rug.

She blinked and raised her head. Jared was sitting in the armchair, watching her sleep. He was dirty and unshaven. His face was bandaged.

Was there madness in his eyes?

She bolted to her feet. "J.P.—?"

"Miss me?" he asked.

She burst into tears and started toward him. Then she stopped. His shirt was covered with mud—no—dried blood, and his arm—a heavy cast from shoulder to wrist. "What's wrong—what happened?"

"I love you," he said.

CHAPTER

He asked no questions about the state of their relationship; she volunteered only that she'd decided to nurse him back to health. There was no problem about medical leave. Roger Richards was only too happy to grant a month of it, even though Jared's wounds were not serious. The mortar fragment had nicked an artery and chipped a bone near the elbow. But healing, the doctors said, would be complete, with no loss of movement in the arm.

For a week Jared stayed in bed, dozing on Demerol and complaining about the pain. Adrian was solicitous but remote. She plumped his pillows but would not look him in the eye. She cooked him whatever he wanted but eschewed all but the most rudimentary conversation. She took his phone messages but slept on the sofa. Three nights running Jared awoke to hear stifled crying from the living room. But when he padded out, groggy from the drugs, to comfort her, she feigned sleep.

Potemkin Village Adrian.

She was as omnipresent in the stone house that faced Mount Zion as the Unnameable Name, and equally as unapproachable. He cajoled and complained. He railed against the Prime Minister. He muttered obscenities about Ariel Sharon. But Adrian would say nothing, would neither defend her father's friends nor the policies she had always supported. He could not shake her up or penetrate her reserve. It was like living with a zombie.

By the sixth day of enforced bed rest Jared had a serious case of cabin fever. He was delighted when Yoram Gal showed up unannounced with a Purple Heart medal—part of his prized collection of American military souvenirs—and pinned it to the chest of Jared's pajamas.

"Welcome to the club, boychik. I tell you, I go off to Guatemala for a month to help the heathens fight Commies and look what happens. You decide to become a hero and end up flat on your ass."

Jared smiled wanly. "Thanks a bunch."

Adrian came into the bedroom. "I'm going shopping." She looked at Yoram. "I can report that shrapnel hasn't affected his appetite. I'll be back in an hour or so. Do you mind staying with him?"

"I can take care of myself," Jared protested.

"Sure you can."

"What's so hard? Look." Jared struggled to his feet and began to straighten the bedclothes. He wrenched his arm and sat down again quickly, wincing with the pain.

"That's real good, J.P." Moving with the cold efficiency of a ward nurse, she pushed Jared back into bed, fixed the covers, neatened the pillows and patted his cheek. "Yoram, will you stay?"

"No problem. I'll babysit the patient. But don't be too long. I've got to be at the Defense Minister's office in a couple of hours."

The general watched Adrian leave before he turned to Jared. "No kiss? She's not very friendly these days."

Jared stared at his friend. He was genuinely happy to see the Israeli, but puzzled at his sudden appearance. Despite Jared's cordial reception at Yoram's house when he'd first met Nathan Yaari, he and Yoram basically had lost touch since the general took him to Syria. Indeed, Jared felt that much of the familial closeness they'd enjoyed since their days in Washington had evaporated. Yet, with Yoram sitting there on the bed it seemed so easy, so simple, to slip back into their old relationship. The banter, the gossip, the inside jokes.

He wondered what Yoram wanted. "We've had a few problems," he said noncommittally.

Yoram nodded. "So I heard. But you're together now."

"Temporarily. She's helping me get back on my feet."

"Don't lose her, boychik."

"Why?"

"She's better than you deserve."

Jared lay back and stared vacantly at the ceiling. "Probably," he sighed.

"God, you're morose. Feeling bad, huh?"

Jared nodded.

"You got what you deserved."

"Huh?"

"For going out on patrol with the *forshtunken* reserves. It wouldn't have happened in one of my units."

"You're probably right."

"Of course I'm right. Planning—it's all in the planning. These reservists don't know what the hell they're doing. All they want is to finish their month's duty and go home. And who can blame them?"

Jared fingered the medal. "Yoram . . ."

"What?"

"When I got back, I called Yaari. He won't talk to me."

"Not won't, can't. Already it's been bad. They had his phone tapped. They were listening when you called him from the States."

"I figured. What happened?"

"Demoted. Transferred. He's working as a chauffeur-bodyguard now, for the Minister of Tourism."

"You're kidding?"

"I wish I were. He's not angry, understand. He wanted the story to get out. And even though your magazine issued a clarification, the Israeli press is sniffing around. Besides, Yaari's a persistent sonofabitch. He's keeping his hand in, believe me. I had coffee with him yesterday, by the way, and he told me to tell you he appreciates the way you handled things in New York. It could have been a lot worse. Your phone call didn't give them absolute proof that he'd been the leak. Still, the story was enough to screw him. There were only a couple of dozen people who could have told you. He was one of them. So . . ."

Jared shifted in the bed. "I undersand." Yoram lit a cigarette and offered it. "Thanks. Can I talk to Yaari? I'd love to see him."

"Of course. But we have to be careful. Maybe you and Adrian can come down to Herzlyia. I'll arrange something."

"Yoram—"

"What, boychik?"

Jared paused, uncomfortable.

"Come on—anything you want—you're the wounded person."

Jared settled back into the pillow and exhaled smoke. "This is between us—just us."

The general nodded. "Okay."

"I was in Tel Aviv. In the spring. You and Adrian and Mandy Navor went to lunch at Olympia."

Yoram nodded but didn't answer. He took a cigarette, tamped it on his watch and lighted it.

"Adrian lied, Yoram. Adrian lied about that lunch."

Yoram exhaled smoke through his mouth and reinhaled it through his nose. "So?"

"What's up? I mean—since we're *mano a mano*."

"Privilege of the wounded?"

"Something like that."

"Look—" he paused. "What were you, worried?"

"Kind of."

"There's no 'kind of.' Either it was yes or no."

"Yes, then."

Yoram shook his head. "It was nothing. It was business."

"With Mossad? Adrian?"

"Sure. Mossad has to keep checking accounts just like the rest of us."

"Checking accounts?"

"Rest assured, Jared. Your little *hatti-ha* isn't *shtupping* Mandy Navor—or me, and more's the pity. She's not a deep-cover Mossad agent either. But her father's got a big bank. And he's willing to do the state of Israel a favor now and then."

"And Mandy Navor?"

"Mandy was representing his friends in the Phalange. They've already opened a liaison office here—you know what'sisface the spokesman—"

"Elie Awad?"

"He's the one. So now the *Kataeb*"—Yoram used the nickname for the Phalange—"they want to open information offices in Washington and New York. But they need a line of credit. And Felix's bank . . ."

Jared interrupted. "Felix gave it to them?"

"*Biduke*." Yoram nodded. "Precisely."

"Because Mandy Navor, who runs Mossad's liaison with Phalange, asked Adrian?"

"Right again." Yoram tapped Jared on the chest. "You know, you should be a reporter—you've got a nose for the facts."

"You wouldn't know it from the way they're treating me lately."

"Who?"

"Everybody. *World Week,* the guys in the press office, other reporters. It's like I'm a nonperson."

"The demotion?"

Jared nodded. "And the one thing that really steams me—really frustrates me—is that I've got no idea who the hell . . . you know I've gone over it again and again . . . who the hell could have leaked the Saye'eret raid story to my editors?"

"What? Somebody leaked my Syrian operation?"

"Yoram, *that's* what almost got me fired. The Jewish terror story was bad enough. The *gammad* cut me off at the knees when he sent a faked version of Begin's appointment book to New York. Even so, that story was righteous. Somehow I think I could have convinced them. But then Roger Richards said he had two sources who told him about the bogus telex after Jdaidet Aartouz."

The general's eyes narrowed. "I didn't know."

"You've been out of the country. We haven't spoken." Jared rubbed at the cast on his arm. He itched but he couldn't reach the spot. "How many people knew, Yoram? How many?"

Yoram rubbed his mustache. "Me, some people in my unit, maybe a couple of dozen others."

"There was someone else."

"Who?"

"Adrian. Adrian knew."

"Come on, boychik. Be serious."

"She lied to me about the *Kataeb*'s bank account."

"She signed a paper. An agreement to keep it quiet."

"She lied about . . . other things."

"Other things are between you and Adrian. For God's sake she loves you, Jared. Don't be a fool."

"Then how did they learn about the forgery? It wasn't in your interest to leak it."

"There are lots of possibilities. The Prime Minister's office could have found out. Or Little Rafi Eitan, who runs the nuclear program—he's got his own intelligence network, too. Or Sharon—he's not above things like that, either. It would be one way to get you out of their hair permanently, and don't think they wouldn't like to do it. Look, Jared, I don't have to tell you your phone is tapped. Or that there's probably a bug in your office. Who knows—maybe my phone is tapped too, and somebody heard something. There are lots of possibilities. But I can't believe it was Adrian."

"I'm happy you can be so sure."

"Don't be a schmuck, boychik."

"What the hell am I supposed to think? I was sandbagged, Yoram. My ass was grass. And now—"

"Now you're sounding like a wounded crybaby," the general barked. "You lie here like a little king. Like the *Katanchik*—the little fellow—" Yoram used Ariel Sharon's favorite nickname for King Hussein. "Waited on hand and foot, and feeling sorry for yourself."

"So?"

"So I gave you your medal. Now get off your butt. Go back into action like a soldier. Okay, they sandbagged you, Begin and the rest of them. But the story you wrote was—what do you say?—on the money."

"I know that."

"So, run with it. Screw the editors, and that potbellied *ben zona* they sent to take your place. You know what you have to do. Screw the acting bureau chief and his memos."

"What?"

"Come on, Jared, don't play cat-and-mouse. I know what Atkins told you. But screw him. Go for it."

"How did you—"

"These things get around," Yoram said. "Word even has it"—a sly smile crossed the general's face—"that you secured a couple of introductions to TNT from an old friend of yours in Washington." He watched as Jared's face grew red. "Word has it you've only used one of them so far."

Jared said nothing. How the hell did Yoram know what Dvora had given him?

The answer was that Yoram knew because Yoram knew lots of things. That was one of the fascinating elements of Israeli society. There was an informal inner circle to the state of Israel, a group of perhaps three or four hundred of the country's elite politicians, officers, intelligence personnel, and professionals who, among them, knew the details of practically every top secret cabinet decision and classified military plan in the Jewish state.

How could it happen? The answer lay in Israel's size. The country was so damn small it was only logical that, within a five-to-ten-year age span, people of a certain type and background knew each other from the Army. All eighteen-year-olds endured the hell of basic training together. But then came the separation. Most went into regular Army service. But the *crème de la crème*, the ones from the best kibbutzim and old-line families, tended to volunteer for elite units: pilot school, the commandos, Saye'eret, or Armor. They were the ones selected for officer's training. And the best of the young generation were trained by the best of their elders.

The Army was the key. It was both Israel's great equalizer and the creator of its elite. So whether you were a forty-three-year-old general or a Knesset member, an industrialist, scientist, doctor, or intelligence official, if you'd served as a pilot or an officer or in an elite unit you knew a lot of people. You had connections. And when you ran into them it was only natural to gossip.

Jared propped himself up in bed and looked at Yoram. Yoram knew about Dvora. Of course he would: Yoram was one of the people who counted in Israel. He had access to a level of secrets he would not know in most countries of the world. The United States had more than a thousand brigadier generals, most of them paper-pushers or bureaucrats. In Israel there were less than fifty; each had clout.

"You're a real piece of work, *mon général*." He worked a finger under the wrist of his cast and tried to scratch an unreachable itch. It was probably a cat hair. Pilgrim had taken to sleeping in the bed with him and it was driving Jared crazy.

Fact of life one: the Israelis who count know all the secrets. Fact of life two: Yoram was one of them.

He tried to keep a poker face. "So?"

"So use the second letter you got from your friend."

"And where am I supposed to use it?"

"Hebron, boychik. Hebron."

Jared thought: What the hell does he want from me now?

CHAPTER 14

"You can't go to Hebron. You can't go anywhere—you can't even drive."

"I'll take a cab."

"That's ridiculous, J.P."

"It's not. It's something I want to do. Have to do." Jared stood half-dressed in the bathroom, scrubbing his teeth with a toothbrush. "I feel like a vegetable. I haven't been out of the house in more than a week. It's not like I was seriously wounded or anything."

She tapped the cast on his arm. "What's this, chicken liver?"

"That's a cast. Just like the one I had when I fell off my bike in the fifth grade. Same arm, even. It didn't keep me from going to school."

"But you're not going to school. You're going to the West Bank."

"So?"

"So it's different. It's dangerous. What if something happens?"

"It's not dangerous. Besides, nothing is going to happen. I just want to go to Hebron and take a look around." He replaced the toothbrush in its holder and walked back into the bedroom, pulled a shirt out of the dresser, and tried to shrug into it.

She followed him, watching as he struggled with the left arm. "Oh, good Lord," she said, taking a pair of scissors and slitting the sleeve so he could pull it over his cast. She rolled the cuff neatly just above the elbow. "You see? You can't do anything yourself."

She exhaled. She sighed. She pouted. "I'll take you to Hebron."

"It's not necessary. The magazine has Zvika. He's a capable driver and he owns a nice cab."

She looked him in the eye in a way that told him she wasn't going to be put off, as she threaded his belt through the loops of his bluejeans. "Zvika won't roll your shirtsleeve for you if it falls down." She kicked off her high heels, unbuttoned her striped silk shirtwaist dress and headed toward her closet.

She was a no-nonsense driver. Jared appreciated that. He sat in silence as she took the big Chevrolet smoothly around the S-curves of the Hebron Road south of Bethlehem, south of the Dahisha refugee camp, past the Kefar Ezyon interchange and along the straightaway leading to Mu'askar El Arrub. His notebook, autofocus 35-mm camera, tape recorder and a handful of pens sat in the orange rucksack between his feet. Dvora's letter was folded into his back pocket along with his wallet.

Jared had insisted that they remove the large-type, bright yellow "Foreign Press" placards in Hebrew, Arabic and English from his Autobianchi and transfer them to Adrian's car. "Sometimes it helps, sometimes it doesn't. Usually it works at roadblocks. But if the Arabs want to stone you"—he tapped the cracked rear window of his own car—"they'll do it."

Now, as the morning sun beat down unhampered by clouds, he was happy they'd taken the Chevy with its air conditioning. The road was not crowded; Jared stared out the window as they passed terraced hillsides filled with olive trees and scrub brush, grape vines and tomatoes, fig trees and date palms. They drove in silence, Adrian self-consciously keeping her eyes on the road ahead while Jared sneaked glances at her. West Bank towns were like Jordan or Lebanon—archetypally Arab. They were simple compared with the fortresslike Israeli settlements. Jews preferred high-rises with textured stone facades. Arabs built flat-faced buildings with metal-shuttered shops on the ground floor and one or two levels of apartments above.

The refugee camps, too, had the look of Lebanon to them. Unlike the sun-dried-brick, Jordanian-built camps just south of Jericho, which had stood since 1948, Dahisha was a sprawling slum of jerrybuilt one- and two-story buildings less than a decade old, that began at a barbed wire fence adjacent to the Hebron highway and expanded eastward for more than a kilometer like a dirty puddle of urban blight.

"It looks dangerous," Adrian said as they drove by. She increased the pressure of her foot on the accelerator.

"No worse than Sabra or Shatila," Jared answered. "And fewer bomb factories. But a lot of the problems are the same: disease, filth, no education, no future, and Dahisha's got something Sabra and Shatila didn't have for a long time, a military occupation that breeds hate."

"So Dahisha is Israel's fault? Why is everything always Israel's fault, J.P.?"

"It's not always Israel's fault. It's simply a cycle that nobody's seen fit to break. Not Labor and not your father's friends in Likud."

"Then what's the answer?"

"I'm not sure there is an answer. I'm not even sure what the questions are." He pointed out the window at a knot of young Arab men sitting at a roadside café. An Israeli jeep patrol was checking identity papers. "What do they know about Israelis except as occupiers? And what do the Israelis know about the Arabs?"

"What do you mean?"

"It's been sixteen years since the Six-Day War. The generation of Israelis that's grown up since then—the boys and girls who are going into the Army now—know nothing about the pre-war borders. For them, the West Bank is a reality of life. It's where most of them do their Army duty. It's where the cheap labor comes from. It's where you go to buy vegetables and fruit at half the price of the Mahane Yehuda or the supermarkets. And the Arabs who live there? Non-persons. The first days, first years, of the occupation were different. At least that's what Yoram and his generation tell me. The soldiers treated the Arabs as people, treated them with respect. But now—dragging demonstrators by the hair; shooting them. It's different."

"But the Arabs," Adrian said. "The Arabs are different, too. Bombing, rock-throwing, setting up barricades of burning tires. Last week Arabs stabbed that yeshiva student Aharon Gross in Hebron—killed him right in the street. They throw grenades at Jewish settlers. And what about the cars that get stoned in Ramallah or Nablus or Tulkarm? The people in them aren't soldiers. They're not part of the occupation force, they've just got the wrong color license plates. So don't the Arabs bear some of the responsibility? Or is it only the Jews?"

"No, it's not only the Jews. But look at it from their side. Just like the Israelis, the current generation of West Bank Arabs has grown up knowing only Israeli occupation and expansion. Look at the settlements. We're not talking about tent colonies—they're cities. Self-contained cities. And now Moshe Levinger wants to take over Hebron—well Hebron's a sacred city to the Arabs. It's also probably got more Islamic fundamentalists than anyplace on the West Bank. You know, Hebron's so conservative there's not even a movie theater. How do you think they feel about Jews—*kippa*-wearing ultranationalists who carry machine guns and take over vacant Arab apartments in the name of a Greater Israel. You can't expect them to like it?"

She swerved gently around a curve and slowed to a crawl behind a huge, gravel-filled truck. "Like it, no. But even Jewish settlers have to be better than what Jordan did for nineteen years. Hussein is a repressive little ant. He squeezed the West Bank like a lemon as long as he had it." Adrian checked the rearview mirror, swung the car into the passing lane and gunned it past the truck. "Come on, J.P., I read the economic reports these days. Arabs on the West Bank—including Hebron—are making more money than they ever did before. Their life expectancy has gone up. There's better health care and education than under Jordan. There's electricity in most of the villages now. And running water. Why can't they appreciate what's being done for them? Why can't they give Israel just an ounce of credit?"

"Because they live under military rule. They have different license plates so they're stopped at roadblocks. They don't have the same rights as Israeli Arabs. Their identity cards are checked—you saw the soldiers back there. Sure, their lives may be better. But they're being made better in an unacceptable way. You know what the Arabs, the Palestinians, call themselves? *Samed*. It means steadfast, persevering."

"So what's the answer?"

"Like I said, I'm not sure there is an answer anymore. In 1967, if Moshe Dayan had had the guts, he could have expelled the Arabs from the West Bank just after the war. Oh, there would have been an outcry, but it could have been done. But Labor was weak in the knees. It was preaching coexistence in those days.

"Thing is, Labor never figured out what the hell to do with a million and a half Arabs. Never answered the basic question of how they fit into a Jewish state. The answer to it is, that they don't fit."

"You're sounding like Meir Kahane, Jared. That's exactly what he's been saying for years."

"I'm beginning to think that Kahane's solution may become a viable alternative for a lot of Israelis soon."

"That's crazy. He's a fanatic, a crazy man. He doesn't have any real political power."

"Not yet—but wait. Next election, he'll take a couple of seats. The one after that, maybe five or six. After that, who knows? He may become as powerful as the religious parties are in the Likud coalition."

Adrian grunted. "You're such an alarmist. No real Jew would vote for a man like Kahane." She slowed the car as they came to the Beersheva interchange just north of Hebron itself. She slalomed slowly around an Army roadblock on the southbound lane, waving to the soldiers. They directed the Chevy past a long line of heavy Mercedes trucks crammed with vegetables and dry goods, stretch-chassis diesel taxicabs with West Bank plates, and private cars driven by Palestinians. Some Arab drivers had unpacked their cargo for inspection. Others waited to have their papers checked.

Jared pointed. "See?"

"It's for their own protection. Someone might have put a bomb in the load at a rest stop."

He shook his head. "Bear left at the fork up here," he instructed. "Go slow down the hill."

Jared glanced up to his right. High above the city stood the Israeli military headquarters, a huge, rectangular edifice of dirty gray-brown stone, surrounded by barbed wire and topped with a bristle of antennas. Moshe Levinger, the fundamentalist rabbi who had founded Qiryat Arba, had staged a sit-in there from 1968 to 1972. Now Levinger was a squatter once again. He had moved his family from the pastel-accented prefab houses of Qiryat Arba—that sat high on the hills overlooking Hebron—to the belly of the beast itself, a tiny, crowded apartment in the center of Hebron's covered, bustling Arab casbah.

He, his American-born wife Miriam, and a handful of Jewish fanatics had decided to reclaim Hebron, with its seventy thousand Arabs, as a Jewish city.

Levinger based his occupation on biblical history as well as historical reality. Hebron held the tombs of Abraham, his wife Sarah, and his sons Isaac and Jacob. It was the city in which Samuel anointed David King of Judah. And for more than 2000 years it was a seat of Jewish learning. But Hebron also is a city revered by Moslems. While Jews call out in prayer to *Avraham avinu*—Abraham our father—the Arabs, who respect the first Jew as Ishmael's patriarch, built the *Ibrahimi* Mosque on the site of the Machpelah cave where Abraham and Sarah are buried. Indeed, Arabs are quick to recall, when Abraham was buried he was interred by both his sons: by Isaac and by Ishmael.

In the 1500s, the Avraham Avinu Synagogue was built in Hebron's ancient center. A Jewish neighborhood was constructed around it, a community that lasted until 1929 when, after the massacre of fifty-nine Jews by an Arab mob, all Hebron's Jews were evacuated. They didn't return until the gaunt, bearded, wild-eyed Levinger came in 1968; first to camp out in the Arab-owned Park Hotel for six months, and then to stage his four-year sit-in outside the military headquarters. In 1972, the Labor government finally caved in: it gave its blessing for Levinger to build a Jewish settlement in the hills above the city. He called it Qiryat Arba—the city of four—the name given to Hebron in the Book of Genesis.

"Go down the hill and to the right," Jared instructed. They were in the center of the city now, moving through crowded streets where vendors jostled each other. The spice-laden odors of cooking meats, falafel and confections drifted from the foodstalls and wafted into the car's air-conditioning system.

"Oh, that smells good, doesn't it?" He began to sing, "In—a little Arab town, 'twas on a night like this. . . ." He rapped his nails on his cast, creating the sound of maracas. "Terrific, huh?" Jared pointed. "Hey—stop. There—"

"What?" She pulled the car to the side of the road and peered out.

"See? Beit Hadassah." He pointed to a two-story stone building into whose facaded front was worked a lattice of Stars of David. It sat behind a mound of rubble. A steel and bulletproof glass guard-house had been pitched in front of its arched gates. Next door was another two-story building, atop which was perched a concrete block-tower with an Israeli flag tied to its radio antenna.

Jared could see soldiers inside, peering through binoculars. "That's one of the first places resettled by Levinger's squatters."

"Should I park?"

"No, we'll come back later. I want to visit the Settlers Association in the market."

"Why?"

"Adrian—"

"It's okay, you don't have to say anything. I forgot—I'm just the chauffeur." She threw the car into gear with a jolt, bouncing Jared off the back of his seat.

"Adrian—"

She tromped the brake. A chorus of strident car and truck horns greeted her action. There were tears in her eyes. "This has to stop, it just has to stop," she said. "I can't stand it anymore."

"Adrian, we're blocking traffic."

"So? What do a bunch of cars matter, J.P.? I'm talking about us."

"You pick the damnedest times."

"When, then? With you lying in bed high as a kite on Demerol? Or when Yoram comes over to gossip with you about what's happening in the Army? When is there a good time? When? Okay—okay, I volunteered to drive you down here. Maybe, I thought, maybe we'd talk in the car. It's a good time. It's private.

"But do you talk to me? Did you talk to me? Not once in fifty kilometers did you talk to me about anything else but politics. All you wanted to do was argue politics. Politics. Politics! It's all *pol-i-tics* to you!"

She rolled down the car window and screamed at the drivers behind them. "*Shekket*—shut up, you stupid idiots!" In tears, she put the car in drive and floored the gas pedal, only to have it stall out. "Dammit." She turned the ignition. Nothing. She turned it again, her foot heavy on the gas.

"Take it easy."

"I am taking it easy. I have been taking it easy. But not anymore, J.P."

"What the hell are you talking—" Jared was interrupted as a dozen Palestinians jumped from the flatbed truck whose bumper virtually touched their own and began pounding on the Chevy's trunk. "Hey, quit that!"

Adrian looked up, panic on her face. She rolled her window up tight and reached around to lock the door. "Jared—"

"It's okay. It's okay." But he wasn't so sure. There they sat, a tiny Jewish island in the midst of a sea of Palestinian faces. Faces, Jared thought, that had hate and resentment and anger on them. Jews had been massacred in Hebron before.

A young man rapped on Adrian's window nastily. "You, missus, move. You block the road."

Jared got out of the car, locking the door behind him. He faced the crowd. "Give her a second. The engine's flooded."

The young Palestinian scowled. It wasn't hate on his face, Jared saw, only exasperation. The Arab looked at Jared's arm suspended in its cast from a sling. He peered inside the car as Adrian, now visibly panicked, turned and turned the key. "Okay—we push you out of the way."

Suddenly the engine caught. Adrian slid the car into gear and, tires squealing, drove a hundred yards down the road. She looked back through the rear window imploringly and Jared ran after her.

"We're all right, it's okay," he shouted over his shoulder at the knot of bewildered Arabs. She reached over and unlocked the passenger door for him. He turned toward the Arabs and waved. "Thanks anyway—*shukran*."

He got in. She looked at him. "That was stupid."

"What was?"

"Getting out. You might have been killed."

"Nah."

"You saw their faces. There have been incidents like that before, Arabs stabbing Jews on the road when their cars break down. Crowds chasing Jews in Arab cities."

"It was okay. They just wanted to help," Jared insisted. But he couldn't say it convincingly. In truth, he had climbed out of the relative safety of the car without knowing what might have happened—and he didn't like the uncertainty one bit.

They drove in silence, Adrian's hands white-knuckled on the

steering wheel, moving at a crawl despite relatively light traffic. On their left, Jared spied the wholesale vegetable market. "Pull in there," he said, pointing at a dusty street.

They crossed two lanes of traffic and stopped. A soldier examined the Foreign Press tags, removed a coil of concertina barbed wire, then motioned them to proceed.

"Good Lord. Look—" Adrian's jaw dropped. "What happened?" What had once been a street of one-story warehouses and loading docks was now reduced to charred skeletons. From makeshift platforms, Arabs loaded their trucks with crates of onions, grapes and melons.

"The aftermath of the Aharon Gross killing. The settlers went on a rampage. They burned the entire area to the ground." Jared pointed to a gap between the vegetable trucks. "Up there," he said.

At the end of the street, beyond the grapes and melons, sat half a dozen mobile homes guarded by two dozen unkempt reservists. An Israeli flag, limp in the heat, sagged from a twenty-foot flagpole. A pair of sweating soldiers in over-hot pillboxes wiped perspiration from their necks and peered at the Arab workers from behind thick panes of bulletproof glass. "We park here," said Jared.

They locked the car and scrunched across newly laid gravel to a trailer. On the door was a sign that read Settlers Association. Jared rapped on the door.

"Come in."

They stepped up and entered. The trailer was air-conditioned, and Jared welcomed the chill. "Hi."

A thin young woman sitting at a messy desk piled high with papers looked up at them. "Morning."

He held out his press card. "I'm Jared Paul Gordon of *World Week* magazine, and this is my friend Adrian Cooper."

The woman smiled. She couldn't have been more than twenty-three or twenty-four. Her dark hair was tucked under a blue and white floral bandanna in the Orthodox manner. She wore no makeup, accentuating the intensity of bright green eyes. "We're honored to have the representative of *World Week* back in Jewish Hebron, Mr. Gordon," she said sarcastically, slipping into English. "I'm Shoshanna. What can I do for you?"

"We'd like to look around, if that's all right. And talk to some of your people. Is Moshe Levinger available?"

"I'm afraid he's not. Not today. He had to go to Jerusalem. But Shmuel Chai is here. He's our spokesman when the Rebbe's unavailable. And as for looking around—you're welcome to go anywhere. We're proud of what we're doing."

"Thanks," said Jared. "You're an American. Where are you from?"

"Qiryat Arba, until we moved here." One of the three phones on the desk rang and she picked it up, cupping her hand over the mouthpiece. "Excuse me." She uncupped her hand. "Yes?" She listened. "Okay. Sure." She hung up the receiver and turned to a typing table on which sat a walkie talkie, its microphone on a short coil of cord. Behind the table a Galil combat rifle, clip in place, sat propped up against the wall. A snub-nosed .38 revolver in a leather clip-on holster lay half hidden by Shoshanna's paperwork. She pressed the transmit button on the mike and spoke rapid Hebrew. "Sector three, Sector three, come in."

Static. Then an answer. "Sector three here."

"Send a patrol over to"—she scanned a map of the casbah on the wall—"location gimmel-two."

"Okay. Gimmel-two. Out."

Shoshanna replaced the mike and turned back to Jared and Adrian. "I'm sorry. Since Aharon Gross was murdered we've had to increase our patrols. The terrorists take advantage of you if you give them half a chance. Now, you were saying?"

"I wondered where you were from—before Qiryat Arba," Jared said.

"I was born in Detroit. I made aliyah six years ago."

"Isn't it hard, your life here?" Adrian asked.

"Yes, but what of it? Physical hardship's not bad if you're fulfilling a dream, fulfilling a *mitzvah*. And that's what we're doing."

Jared nodded. "I gather that most of the settlers here are from the United States."

"Just over half."

"Why? Why so many Americans?"

"Like I said, we're fulfilling a dream. It's so easy to be a Jew in America. You get soft; you forget the commitment your forefathers made to God. Here in Hebron, being a Jew means being an active part of Jewish history. We're following God's instructions here, Mr. Gordon, we're doing God's work."

"How so?"

"God was the first Zionist," she said. "It was God who chose the land of Israel as His seat, as the place where He issued His teachings. His teachings were given to Abraham, whose devotion to God was so great he would have given up his son Isaac to Him, had God really wanted him to do so. Abraham is the father of Judaism; Abraham is buried here. So by re-establishing ourselves in this holy city, we are doing God's work." She smiled beatifically as Jared reached for his notebook, opened it and slipped it under the edge of his cast so he could take notes.

"But isn't your being here a provocation to the Arabs?"

"Every Jew and every Jewish city in Israel is a provocation to the Arabs. Tel Aviv was a provocation. Kibbutz Deganiah, where Moshe Dayan was born, was a provocation. Haifa, Hadera and Zichron Yaakov were provocations. Now, once again, Hebron is a provocation. So what? If Jews hadn't settled in Arab areas there would be no Israel today." She smiled again, an ineffable smile. "We're mainstream Zionists, Mr. Gordon."

Jared nodded. "When can we talk to Shmuel?"

Shoshanna grinned. "Right now." She spoke into her microphone. "He'll be here in a minute. Would you like some coffee while you're waiting?"

"That would be lovely," he said. "Adrian?"

"Do you have any tea?"

"Of course." Shoshanna stood. "I'll just be a second." She stuffed the .38 into the waistband of her long skirt and slipped out the door.

"Reminds me of the old days back out West—pioneer women and their flintstone rifles," Jared said.

"That's flint*lock,* Daniel Boone." Adrian looked over the trailer's interior. "They're well organized, aren't they?"

"Yup. Keep an eye on the door, will you?"

"Why?"

"Just let me know if Shoshanna of the constant smile and lethal six-gun's coming back." Jared went to the desk and looked over the papers on it.

"Jared!"

"All in a day's work." He slid the desk drawer open, examining its contents. There was a bank statement from the Tel Aviv branch of Eagle Intercontinental—Felix's bank. Jared held it up. "Look, you've got a depositor."

"Put it away, J.P. What if she comes back?"

"Okay, okay." He returned the statement and retrieved a Xeroxed list, ran his finger down the column, found what he was looking for, flipped open his notebook and made a quick inscription.

"Here she comes. You ought to be ashamed of yourself."

He replaced the list and closed the drawer. "You've just had a firsthand demonstration of investigative reporting." He turned the notebook page and returned to Adrian's side as the beaming Shoshanna opened the trailer door, carrying a tray with two steaming cups.

Shmuel Chai turned out to be a pudding-faced, transplanted Philadelphian in a knitted *kippa* who enthusiastically recited Moshe Levinger's boilerplate rhetoric by rote into Jared's tape recorder while stuffing his dimpled cheeks with sweet rolls. After three-quarters of an hour Jared had heard enough and excused himself. "It's been interesting. But we want to see what you've done here."

"Wunnerful. T'riffic. I'll take you round." Chai took up a wooden-stocked Uzi and stroked the weapon's snoutlike barrel against his cheek. "Nothing like it," he said. "Shows the terrorists who's boss."

Jared had seen the same gesture before. In 1981. In a hot office in Beirut's Fakhani district he'd sat, simultaneously horrified and fascinated as a young PLO spokesman sat facing him, playing with a loaded revolver as Jared interviewed him. The Palestinian's name was Mahmoud, he was eighteen or nineteen; as he spewed his anti-Israeli monologue into Jared's tape recorder he absentmindedly spun the pistol's cylinder, squeezing back on the trigger while holding the hammer down with his thumb, caressing the .38's short, nickelplated barrel with his cheek.

Where the hell was Mahmoud now? Probably dead. He shot a look at Adrian. "Listen, Shmuel," he said, "maybe it would be better if Adrian and I just walked around by ourselves. You know, like a couple of tourists. Besides, we don't want to take up any more of your time."

Chai protruded a generous lower lip. "But maybe, y'know, you'll have questions."

"If we do, I'll see you before we leave."

"But it's dangerous out there. The casbah is filled with, y'know, terrorists, like the ones who assassinated Aharon Gross—and let me tell you we put them in their place afterward. Well—y'know, not me, but there were some people I know who, y'know, showed the terrorists how Jews fight."

"What did they do?" Jared knew damn well what they'd done.

"They burned about a third of the terrorists' wholesale vegetable market. One of our rabbis even tossed the IDF lieutenant colonel who guards the *shuk* out on his ear. And when the firemen came, we threw stones. It was just terrific. For once we hit the Arabs where it hurt—in the economy."

"And that stopped the terror?"

"Nobody's been killed since. Nobody's even been bothered."

"Don't you think that could be because the Army put two hundred troops and a hundred border guards into Hebron in the past couple of weeks?"

Chai shook his head. "Naw. It's because the terrorists see that we Jews are here to stay. That we mean business."

"Shmuel," said Jared, "could you define what you mean when you say 'terrorist'?"

"Well, y'know, the people who want to kill us."

"The people in the casbah?"

"Well, yes."

"In other words, the Arabs. The Palestinians."

"Well, y'know, they all hate us. Even the ones who smile. Menachem Livni—he's big in the Settlers Association—he says the whole problem stems from the fact that the Army doesn't take a hard enough line against terrorists. You should talk to Menachem. He'll lay it all out for you."

"I've interviewed him before. Where is he?"

"In Qiryat Arba. Wait, I'll call him." Chai spun the dial on his telephone. "Is Menachem around? It's Shmuel Chai. There's a, y'know, reporter here from *World Week* and I thought—yeah. Oh. Sure." He replaced the receiver. "Menachem's not available today. He's got some kind of prior commitment. But you should come back and see him."

"I will."

"In the meanwhile—" Chai rammed a clip into the Uzi. "I'll take you round."

"Don't bother, we'll be fine on our own," Jared insisted. He didn't give the settler time to object. "You've been very helpful." He opened the door of Chai's mobile-home office and nudged Adrian down the steps onto the hot gravel path.

Outside he turned to her. "That was an earful."

"I agree with a lot of what he says. Jews *should* have access to places like Hebron."

"I agree—but what about the Arabs? Levinger and his people are just like Abu Nidal and Abu Musa. They don't want coexistence—they want hegemony."

She nodded. "That is a problem."

"That's the danger of Levinger and Kahane and people like them. They're full of easy solutions to problems nobody's been able to solve for generations." Jared gestured toward the gate of the casbah. "Let's go."

They walked past two soldiers who stood, backs pressed against the low arched stone entrance, and disappeared into the semi-darkness of the marketplace.

"Nothing like Jerusalem, is it?" Jared had to shout over the din that reverberated through the narrow, roofed-in souk. Unlike the boisterous chaos of Jerusalem's Old City Arab market with its domed high ceilings and cut-stone steps, Hebron's smaller casbah was uncomfortably claustrophobic. Its compactness was intensified by the July heat, coupled with the odors of unrefrigerated meats, fly-encrusted fruits and vegetables, and the crush of ripening shoppers who jostled their way from stall to stall, pausing to check the freshness and the price of the merchandise.

The smoke from cooking fires made Adrian's eyes burn. "Do we have to stay long?"

The lack of ventilation coupled with the throb of his arm made Jared queasy too. "Not really." He took out his camera, popped up the flash, and squeezed off a dozen frames, catching two Jewish settlers as, wheeling baby strollers that would have been at home on Madison Avenue through the knots of Arabs, they bought their daily groceries oblivious to the hostile glances.

Behind them, carrying their shopping bags and his own submachine gun, was a khaki-uniformed reservist in knitted skull cap. "Live in Hebron and you get your own batman," Jared said. The casbah's crowded passageways came to a dead end. Jared backed Adrian up against a whitewashed wall as a donkey laden with olive oil in huge cans careened past, whipped by a small boy in sandals and pajama bottoms. He pointed to the passageway on the right. "We'll work our way up to the Machpelah Cave—there's another entrance right next to it—and then you can visit Sarah's grave and the settlers store while I do a little business in the neighborhood."

"With whom?"

"With somebody I have to see. It won't take long."

"You're not telling me very much, J.P."

Jared grunted.

"You used to talk to me."

Jared elbowed through the crowd, trying to protect the cast on his arm.

"J.P.—"

"Later. We'll talk about it later."

She caught his free arm. "There's a lot we have to talk about later."

CHAPTER

He left Adrian sulking over mediocre falafel and indifferent Turkish coffee in a small, dusty Arab café across from the Jewish Settlers store and walked back up the hill on the cobblestoned street that skirted the Machpelah Cave and ran past Abner's Tomb. Instead of re-entering the casbah he turned east, ambled slowly past a yeshiva, then abruptly retraced his path to make sure he wasn't being followed. Then it was back past the yeshiva again, and up a steep hill until he spied a fork in the road. He turned left, climbed a narrow flight of stone steps, picked his way carefully down an alley clogged with refuse, climbed a second set of steps, and finally rapped on the pastel blue wood door of a decrepit, ancient Arab house. There was no answer. He used his fist and pounded. "Hello!"

"Who's there?"

"My name's Shem Tov. I'm a friend of Dvora Lavi."

There was a pause. Two locks were turned and a deadbolt slid from its socket. Then the door opened, prevented by a chain from revealing more than a hint of the dim light inside. A deep voice said, "What do you want?"

"Shimon Levy?" Jared tried to see through the narrow opening but he could not make out a face.

"Who are you? What do you want?"

"I'm Shem Tov. Dvora Lavi's friend. Here, read this." He extracted his folded envelope and handed it inside.

The door closed. The deadbolt was rammed home. Jared waited, his arm throbbing in the hot, cramped alleyway. Finally he heard the deadbolt slide and the rasp of a chain, and the door opened.

The flat into which Jared walked was as tiny as a medieval turret. It was painted the same pastel blue as the door, and received its outside light from a single, small, arched, barred window of thick leaded glass that sat perhaps eight feet above the cool stone floor. The living room walls were trapezoidal, giving the place a *trompe l'oeil* look. Standing in the doorway, Jared felt as if he were peering down the wrong end of a telescope.

Against one wall sat a ratty overstuffed sofa with three cushions, none of which matched. There were two wood chairs and a formica and chromed steel dinette table; a bottle-gas stove with two burners was half hidden by a faded chintz curtain. From the doorway Jared could see a bedroom just large enough to hold a platform double bed.

The door closed behind him. He turned to greet Shimon Levy.

He gasped. Nathan Yaari stood behind the door, his hand extended.

"Hi, Jared. Welcome to Hebron."

"Nathan! Who—?"

"Wait. Shimon, it's okay. It's him."

A tall, thin man emerged from the bedroom, an Uzi on a frayed strap over his shoulder. Like many of the Jewish settlers in Hebron he had adopted the unkempt beard and shaggy hair favored by Moshe Levinger. A blue and white crocheted *kippa* was clipped to the back of his head. His face, arms and neck were tanned the color of roasted turkey.

"Shalom." He offered his hand to Jared. Nathan Yaari motioned the American to sit. He lit a cigarette, then took one of the wooden chairs, turned it around and sat with his arms folded across the back, facing Jared.

"Shimon here is involved in the Shin Bet's investigation of Jewish terror. Except that *he* hasn't been reassigned. He's been working undercover, as you Americans say on your TV shows, for the past year and a half."

"But what are you—" Jared paused as Yaari held up a hand.

"The story so far, as they say," Yaari sucked on his cigarette, "is that we've managed to keep an eye on these crazy Zionist fundamentalist fascist hooligans by maintaining a very low profile within

Shin Bet. And even though I've been reassigned, I still get days off. And I still come to see my old friends."

"I've been trying to get hold of you for weeks," Jared said.

"I know. But after our last adventure it would be—how do you say—inadvisable for me to meet openly with you. On the other hand, one of my better sources told me that you were coming down here today. So I made a point of being in the neighborhood."

"Why?"

Yaari looked in Shimon Levy's direction. "Because I wanted to see you. And because I wanted to make sure you got the proper sort of introduction to Shimon here. If you'd been shown up here on your own, he'd be just another crazy Jewish settler in your book, right? Dvora certainly didn't tell you anything else, did she?"

Jared shook his head.

Yaari dropped his cigarette into a coffee cup. It hissed as it hit the cold liquid. "Since you've been taken in by so many people lately I thought it might be a good idea to get you and Shimon together, so you can deal honestly with each other. It could be mutually beneficial." Yaari peered behind the floral curtain. "Would you like some coffee? There's hot water."

"No thanks," said Jared. " 'Mutually beneficial'—trade information, you mean."

"Yup. What do you guys call it? Quid pro quo?"

"Yes."

"Well, why don't you take my introduction of Shimon as the quid part, and if you find out any pro or quo I'd appreciate if you'd pass it on to him."

"Sounds fair to me," said Jared. "What kind of pro are you looking for?"

"Anything about what the settlers are up to," Shimon said. "I hear things, but sometimes they like to brag to reporters, and even a little detail might be helpful. For example, there are whispers that something is going to happen down here—soon."

"What?"

Levy scratched his beard. "I'm not sure. But there have been rumblings. You know Menachem Livni at the Settlers Association?"

Jared nodded. "I interviewed him for the first Jewish terror piece. He's bright, and eloquent. As a matter of fact, I just came from a meeting with Shmuel Chai. He tried to get me an appointment with Livni today, but it seems he's busy and can't be interviewed."

"Yeah, well we think Livni's involved in whatever they've got planned. He's a real ringleader, that one. Him and his two pals. One is named Shaul Nir, the other is Uziah Sharabaf. Uzi's a real piece of work. And he's got *protekzia* up the ass because he's Levinger's son-in-law."

"So?" Jared reached for his notebook. A look of alarm crossed Shimon's face.

"Jared, please—" Nathan Yaari stood up. "Don't. No notes."

"Just the names, Nathan."

"Be serious. We can't risk it. You know what happened last time."

"But just names—"

"Memorize them. Nir and Sharabaf. Not hard to remember. They're all from Qiryat Arba. All active in the settlers' movement. All Orthodox. I tell you, these Orthodox will be the death of me."

Shimon Levy waved a long finger at Yaari. "Not all the Orthodox, Nathan. What about me?"

"You—you're becoming a Khomeinist just like the rest of them." Yaari pointed at Levy with his thumb. "He's become insufferable ever since he's come down here. Takes all the holidays off. Won't eat *steak levan*. Quotes Scripture all the time. It's sickening."

" 'I command you this day, to love the Lord your God, and to serve Him with all your heart and all your soul.' Deuteronomy Eleven, Thirteen," Levy orated in a basso profundo. "As the prophet says, 'So let it be written, so let it be done.' "

"That was no prophet," Yaari said. "That's Yul Brynner's line from *The Ten Commandments* when he played Pharaoh."

"That's what you say," said Levy. "Hah! When's the last time you went to synagogue?"

"You see?" Yaari interrupted. "You see what I have to put up with?"

"How long have you been in Hebron?" Jared asked Shimon.

"Six months. We still have a place in Qiryat Arba. My wife's there, with the kids."

"What do you do?"

"I work in a garage up there. I'm a mechanic. But as the beloved Reb Levinger tells us, what we're really about is God's work."

"God's work?"

"Displacing Arabs."

"How does your wife feel about what you're doing?"

"Ah, my wife's a lovely, religious woman who believes wholeheartedly in my appointed task."

"Cut the bull," said Yaari. "His wife is a saint named Orna who's put up with his escapades for—what, fifteen years?"

"Does she know?"

"Know?"

"About what you're doing."

"Of course she knows."

"Incredible. So what's going to happen?"

"I'm not sure. After Aharon Gross was killed the settlers torched the Arab vegetable market. But that was just the first shoe dropping. It's been more than two weeks now. The place is too quiet."

Levy looked at Jared. His eyes were penetrating, riveting. "What's your stake in this?"

"I want to own the story."

"Why?"

"I have my reasons."

"Such as?"

"It's a terrific story."

Levy snorted. "Anything else?"

"It's a story that should be told. People need to know the truth."

"Sometimes. What else?"

"My credibility. I almost lost my job."

"Nothing else?"

"Do I need more?"

"Look mister, we've been working this case for more than two years now in the face of considerable interference. It's a no-win situation. If we get the bastards—and we will, because sooner or later we'll catch 'em red-handed and kick their asses—then a sizeable portion of Israel's population will call us traitors to Zionism. In the meanwhile, Nathan was almost canned, and I've been stuck in this shit hole living like a Jewish Shiite. So if all you want's a headline and a raise, do me the favor of walking out the door now and I'll tell you 'Shalom' with no hard feelings."

"Listen—" Jared was incensed.

Yaari interrupted. "Jared's head is in the right place. Believe me, Shimon, he's our kind of Jew."

Levy shrugged. "If you say so." The phone rang. The settler answered quickly. "Hello?"

Jared waited in silence as Levy spoke in hushed tones. There it was again: this time from Nathan Yaari. "Our kind of Jew." What the hell did these people want, blood? He wanted to look Yaari straight in the eye and tell him that he wasn't anybody's kind of Jew except his own. Instead he bit his tongue and waited.

Levy slammed the phone down. "The other shoe," he said. "It just dropped. At the Islamic University—shooting just broke out." He took his Uzi from the formica table. "I gotta move. You'll have to see yourselves out."

"This is crazy. We have no business being here." Adrian pulled at Jared's arm, trying to extricate him from the crush of people in front of the gates of the Islamic University. A wailing mob of Palestinians drowned out the sirens of ambulances taking the wounded to a nearby hospital. Above, two Army helicopters circled the area, their loudspeakers warning people to return to their homes.

"We're staying." Jared pushed his way through the crowd of screaming Arabs to where a line of green-bereted border guards blocking the gates of the dilapidated four-story building held up batons and billy clubs threateningly. He took the press card from his wallet and held it between his teeth. "Keep close."

They struggled through the human gridlock. Jared held his credential in front of a soldier's nose. "Let us through, please."

"No press. The area's closed."

"It's all right—I just came from the Settlers Association. They said it was okay," he lied.

"I said no press." The soldier pushed Jared in the chest with his baton. "Piss off."

Jared backed away. He took Adrian's hand and, together, they squeezed their way to the rear of the crowd. A Palestinian woman in black, a white headdress covering most of her face, tugged at Jared's rucksack. "You—mister—reporter?" she asked in rudimentary Hebrew.

Jared waved his reporter's notebook in her face. "Yes. American press."

"Mister reporter—my son—in there—where he is?"

"I don't know."

"He went to class this morning. I no hear from him now—I come—" She daubed at her eyes with a ragged handkerchief. "You—American. Americans must help Palestinians."

"I don't know anything."

"Jews did this." She spat at Jared's feet. "The Jews came to kill our children. We should kill all the Jews."

Jared handed the rucksack to Adrian and opened his notebook. "What do you mean?"

"Like that one two weeks ago—kill them." She raised her hands toward the sky, clawlike. She raked the eyes of imaginary Zionists. From the back of her throat came ululating Arab keening, the traditional cry of mourning, and slaughter. Other women in the crowd joined her howling.

Jared heard scattered cries of "Kill the Jews!" For an instant he closed his eyes. The shouts, the screaming ululation, the jostle of bodies washed over him, and he began to understand the frenzy of a mob; began to comprehend the kinetic forces that could energize a crowd such as this to rage through the streets.

Had it been like this in 1929? There were no Israeli soldiers then to protect the Jews of Beit Hadassah and Beit Romano. No border guards with M-16s, Galils and Uzis between the Arab mob and the Jewish scholars. Fifty-nine died in 1929. How many would die today?

Someone tapped Jared on the back. He turned to see a middle-aged Palestinian in soiled white shirt, dark trousers and ancient sandals. "I was here," he said. "I saw. It was Jews."

"What's your name?" Jared asked, scribbling.

"No name, please," said the man, his eyes shifting toward the soldiers. "Call me Abu Said."

"How do you know it was Jews?"

"They wore keffiyahs—red keffiyahs, black keffiyahs," the man said. "But they moved like soldiers. Quick—easy. Threw grenade into classroom. Boom—big explosion. Then took machineguns and"—he made a hosing motion with two hands—"killed many people."

"You saw them?"

"I see. I see them run from university. Run into white car with yellow license plates. Jewish plates, no Arab plates."

"Did you see the license number?"

"Not see."

"How many men?" asked Jared.

"Three—maybe four."

"Did they have beards, did they wear"—Jared patted the top of his head—"*kippot*?"

"No see. Faces covered by keffiyah. No see faces. But it was Jews." The man pointed toward the east, toward Qiryat Arba. "From there. Qiryat Arba." He spat on the dusty ground.

"Have you talked to the police?"

The man spat again. "No talk police. Police take you. Beat you. They beat my son for no reason."

"They must have had a reason," said Adrian. "The police don't do things for no reason."

"You no Arab," the man said. "You cannot know."

"Did anybody else see the men—any friends of yours?" Jared asked.

"My friend Mahmoud see too."

"Where is he? I'd like to talk to him."

"He go home. Mahmoud, police, no like. Two years ago police come. Border guard and they blow up Mahmoud house because his son throw stones at settlers. Mahmoud say to me not get involved. Not talk to no one."

"Mr. Abu Said," Jared said, "what do you do?"

"Work." The Palestinian held up gnarled, callused hands. "Carpenter."

"And you live here in Hebron?"

"Always." The Arab jabbed himself in the chest with a tobacco-stained index finger. "This is my city. My father, his father, his father from Hebron too. All far back from Hebron."

He looked Jared and Adrian over carefully. "You look good people. You tell me—why they kill us? Why throw grenade at children, at student?" A tear worked its way from the corner of the Palestinian's eye. "Why Jews come here to take our land, to kill us?"

"I don't know. What do you think?"

"All Jews not bad. But settlers—they bad. Carry guns. Kill Arabs."

"What about the Arabs who killed that student a few days ago?" Jared asked.

"They bad Arabs who kill. There good Jews, good Arabs. There bad Jews—bad Arabs too. Hate breeds hate." The Palestinian threw up his hands in supplication. "When this stop? When?" The Arab turned abruptly and disappeared into the crowd.

"Wait, Mr. Abu Said—" But he was gone. Jared closed the notebook and jammed it into his pocket. He took Adrian's hand. "Let's go."

They worked around the edge of the crowd, watching as more and more soldiers arrived in heavy trucks. Jared made notes of the unit numbers. "They're sending in regular Army," he said. "They expect trouble."

"What'll happen?"

"Probably a citywide curfew. If not, depending on how many people got killed in there, there's gonna be a riot."

They picked their way around the building. The crowd at the rear was big. But at the far side of the rocky hill, where the building sat, the land dropped off steeply. There was a rusty iron picket fence close to the building, below which scrub brush and thorn bushes littered the hillside. The area was empty of people.

Jared picked his way along the fence. "Come on, let's poke around back here." Fifty feet on he saw where the iron pikes had rusted through. He bent two and pried them apart. He squeezed between and called back. "Let's take a look."

"Do you think we should?"

"I want to see inside—see what the damage was."

"But the border guard said—"

"He's not here." He scrambled up to the building, wincing as he pricked his good hand on the needle-sharp thorns. "There," he said, pointing at a ground-level window whose wrought-iron grille had come loose on one side. He peered through the window, reached inside and pushed. It opened. Jared played with the grille, twisting it one-handed until it too came open. He climbed through, dropped four feet to the ground, and reached up for his rucksack. "Give it here."

She handed him the bright orange pack. "You wait here. I'll be back in a few minutes."

"You can't leave me here," she said. "What if you get arrested?"

"I won't get arrested. It's better if you wait."

"Jared, you're not leaving me behind. Not this time." She struggled through the opening. He helped her down. "This is wrong, J.P.," she said. "The soldier—"

"Screw the soldier. Didn't you hear the radio? They've sealed off the entire area. Nobody's getting in or out today. I bet I'm the only reporter in Hebron."

They were in a cramped, book-lined office furnished with two straight-back wood chairs and an aged, nicked desk whose surface was scarred by long, dark cigarette burns. Jared caressed the ancient manual typewriter atop the desk. "A Royal Office Standard," he whispered. "It's gotta be forty years old."

"Where are we?"

"A faculty office, probably." Jared went to the door and cracked it open. He saw the hallway was empty. "Okay," he whispered, "I'm going to take a look around. You stay here and wait for me."

"Not on your life. If you go I'm going too."

"Adrian—"

"You're crazy if you think I'm going to sit here by myself. I don't have a press card. What if you're discovered and they throw you out? What if somebody decides to use this office?"

"Okay, okay. We'll stick together. But you're gonna have to move fast."

"I'll move faster than you."

He opened the door, slid his nose around the jamb and checked the corridor. It was clear. He stepped outside and waved her out. "Let's go."

"Where was the attack?" Adrian asked.

"Front of the building if you can believe what Abu Said said. I'm not sure. So we'll start with this floor, then go up a level if we don't see anything—Whoa!" Jared jumped back into a doorway as the sound of approaching hobnailed boots reverberated off the stone floors. Hebrew-speaking voices grew louder somewhere down the hall. The door was locked. "Come on." He ran on tiptoes to the next door and tried it. It too was locked. The voices and boots grew louder. He put his shoulder to the door and pushed. The fragile lock gave way. "Get in here." He pulled Adrian inside and shut the door, leaving it cracked a hair. The voices passed outside.

"How many?" said one.

"We're not sure, sir." A second voice. "We're getting all kinds of bullshit from the Arabs upstairs. Some of them say it was Jews. Others say it was Palestinians—three of them in red and black keffiyahs and carrying Kalashnikovs. We're talking to the victims now, the ones who can talk."

Jared put his eye to the crack in the door and saw three khaki uniforms. One belonged to a regular Army colonel. The other two were border guard lieutenants.

The colonel asked, "Is Fuad here yet?" Jared knew Fuad was Benyamin Ben Eliezer, a former brigadier general who was now the civilian coordinator of the West Bank.

"He's in the chopper now."

"And Aluf Orr?" That would be Uri Orr, the commander of the Central area.

"On his way."

"What about press?"

"We've got roadblocks north and south, as well as the back road from Qiryat Arba. The American networks wanted to chopper TV crews in. We told 'em to screw themselves."

The colonel nodded. "Right—we keep 'em out until we're in control. All we need is more pictures on TV of the poor Palestinians."

The voices faded. Jared stuck his head out the door. He peered up and down the empty hallway, took Adrian's hand and led her away from the soldiers. They turned left at a corridor he hoped would bring them toward the front of the building. Walking quickly, Jared looked at peeling ceilings and pea-soup green walls that had turned gray with age. There were hand-lettered posters illustrated with doves bearing olive branches.

Turning right into a locker-lined hall strewn with debris they came upon a row of classrooms, schedules in neat Arabic script taped to the doors. Jared eased the first door open. The room was empty. He led Adrian gingerly over piles of books, papers and other educational detritus and tried the one across the hall. "Nothing." Thirty feet on they came to a classroom whose door was open. Jared edged up to it and peered around the doorframe. "Oh, my God."

Adrian looked over his shoulder. "What is it?"

"Adrian, don't—"

She pushed past him. The windows had been blown out by an explosion. Desks were splintered. Blood was everywhere. Puddles of red splattered the floor, furniture, and walls as if put there by an abstractionist gone wild. The bitter smell of cordite hung in the air.

Adrian gasped out. "J.P.!"

"Damn. Adrian—please!" He yanked the autofocus out of his rucksack and squeezed off half a dozen fast pictures.

"How can you?"

"No time. Let's go—quick." He pulled her arm and shoved her out of the classroom, closing the door behind him. As he stepped over a pile of papers something out of place caught his eye, and he stooped to pick it up: a small, blue, plastic-encased card with Hebrew writing. It was a *meluim* identity card, the kind used by reserve officers.

He turned it over and looked at the picture—a bearded man in his late thirties. Jared knew the face—Menachem Livni. Jared sucked in his breath. He cupped the card in his hand and read it quickly. It was Livni's. He jammed it up inside his cast as far as he could. Menachem Livni. The s.o.b. had probably lost it when he shot up the school. So Shimon Levy and Nathan Yaari wanted to deal on a quid pro quo basis? Jared now had the quid pro quo with which to deal. He owned the story.

"What is it?" Adrian saw the strange look on his face.

"Nothing. A twinge in my arm." He took her by the hand and ran her down the hallway away from the destruction. They came to a dead end as he heard voices coming from the corridor they'd just left. Wildly, he sought somewhere to hide. There was a single door fifteen feet behind them, and they ran for it. The door was unlocked. Jared pulled Adrian inside, eased it shut and put his back up against it. The shades were drawn and the room was dark.

There was a light switch by his shoulder and he flicked it up. Adrian screamed. Three blood-soaked bodies partially covered by red-stained sheets lay atop a group of desks that had been pushed together. Hands and feet protruded grotesquely.

"Oh, God, it's—" Adrian began to cry, and was sick.

Jared cradled her head. "It's okay, it's okay." He fumbled in his pocket for a handkerchief. "Here."

She wiped at her mouth. "I'm—"

"You're going to be all right. Breathe deep."

"But they're—"

"They're dead, Adrian." He propped her against a wall, retrieved his camera and shot his pictures. Quickly he rewound the film, opened a fresh package and loaded it into the camera, stuffing the exposed film cartridge into his sock. He took five frames of the bodies, advanced the film another dozen exposures by holding the shutter button down, threw the camera back into the rucksack and grabbed Adrian by the arm.

"We have to move. We gotta get out of here before anybody comes back."

"I think I'm going to faint."

He held her face. "Not now. Now now, kiddo. I'm going to open the door, and then you'll take some deep breaths, and we'll go back the way we came. Smooth as silk—right out the window of that first office and back to Jerusalem."

"I'm dizzy, J.P."

He held her around the waist, his right arm supporting her weight. "Let's go. Just like we used to walk in the Old City. One-two-one-two—that's it. One foot in front of the other—great."

"Stop! You two—hold it where you are."

They froze.

"Turn around. Raise your hands."

Jared swiveled. "Press," he gulped, his slung cast starting to rise involuntarily. Thirty feet down the hall a trio of border guards trained weapons on them. A sergeant, laser-scoped Uzi at his shoulder, held them in his cross hairs. Two corporals with M-16s bolted down the corridor toward them.

Jared ducked instinctively as the soldier closest to him swatted at his neck with the butt of his rifle. It struck a glancing blow and Jared went down, cursing in pain as his cast bounced off the stone parquet. The rucksack was torn from his shoulder and slid toward the Uzi-toting sergeant, who scooped it up by the harness.

Adrian's knees buckled. She sagged to the floor. The second soldier took her by the shoulders and rolled her onto her stomach; roughly he pinioned her arms behind her and secured them with a nylon restraint. He tried to yank her to her feet, but she was limp. So, grasping her by the neck of her T-shirt, he began dragging her down the hallway.

Jared struggled to his knees. "Hey—"

The corporal who had clubbed Jared kicked him in the groin, and he went down again, rolling into a ball to protect himself. The corporal kicked him in the ribs. "Who the hell said you could get up?" He pushed his rifle into Jared's chest. "Just stay where you are."

The sergeant, submachine gun at port-arms, came slowly down the corridor. He stood over Jared and opened the rucksack, examined its contents, then rolled Jared over on his side. Gingerly he pulled the reporter's notebook and wallet out of Jared's right rear pocket. He flipped through the notebook and dropped it into the rucksack. Then he opened the wallet and examined its contents.

He swore when he saw the press credential. Rolling Jared over onto his back, he dragged him by the shirt and propped him up against a wall. "Bring her here too," he ordered, jerking his thumb at Adrian, who lay inert and sobbing. "Keep an eye on 'em. I gotta find the lieutenant. He's a goddamn reporter."

"Press—I told you I was a correspondent, you asshole," Jared gasped, tears in his eyes. "*World Week*. American press."

CHAPTER 16

They were detained in a bare, windowless interrogation room on the second floor of the military headquarters high on a hill northwest of the city. The border-guard lieutenant who brought them—in a closed jeep with red-and-white police plates—from the Islamic University opened Jared's camera and exposed the film cartridge. He confiscated his rucksack, wallet, Adrian's handbag, and their wristwatches, read carefully through the reporter's notebook, ripped out several pages, and stuffed them into the thigh pocket of his faded khaki fatigues.

They were not questioned. They were not searched. Neither were they allowed to use the phones. The lieutenant whispered instructions to a nasty-looking pair of billy-club-toting Druse, who ushered them civilly but firmly up two flights of steps, marched them into an eight-by-ten-foot room whose door had a single knob on the outside, and left them by themselves.

Adrian propped herself up in the corner of the room furthest from the door and cried. Jared lay on his back on the cold concrete floor and raised his legs against the wall to assuage the pain in his privates and the dull ache in his ribs.

Neither spoke for a long time.

"How are you?" Adrian finally whispered.

"Sore as hell."

"Me too. God, those handcuffs hurt." She rubbed her wrists,

which still bore narrow red marks from the nylon restraints. "How could they do that to us?"

"Easy. They play for keeps, our tough Israeli border guards. You've never seen them in action before."

"They were vicious, J.P."

He pulled himself to his knees. "No, they weren't."

"What? They were brutal, the way they beat you. The way they treated me."

He shook his head. "The way they treated us is normal for them. Look, for border guards this is a war. And Yoram once told me you don't fight wars by the Marquis of Queensberry's rules. As I recall, you agreed with him."

She sat silent for some seconds. "What do you think'll happen to us?"

"Oh—I don't know." Jared crawled on his hands and knees to where Adrian sat. He took his pen from his shirt pocket where, miraculously, it had not come dislodged, and wrote on his left palm, just below the cast, "ROOM HAS MIKE. NO TALK ABT FILM." He rubbed his hands together, destroying the message. "Probably they'll hold us for a while, try to scare the hell out of us, then let us go."

"They scared the hell out of me pretty good already."

He slid around Adrian's left side and cradled her with his right arm. "Nah—you were brave back there."

"No I wasn't."

"Sure you were."

"I fainted when you got beaten up. I got sick when I saw the bodies."

"Who wouldn't?"

"You didn't."

"I'm used to it." He thought about what he'd said. "No, I'm not. You never get used to it."

"I've never seen a dead person—murdered person—before. They were so—"

"What?"

"Bloody. And their arms and legs. Jared—the way they were positioned . . ."

"What do you mean?"

"So . . . random. On television when somebody dies, like on 'Starsky and Hutch' or 'Kojak,' they die so neatly. There's no blood. They just fold up, or sprawl on the ground with their fingers tight and their feet straight. Did you see those corpses in there? The way their fingers were spread out? As if they were reaching for something as they died."

"Maybe they were."

"They were so helpless, J.P. There's something obscene about that."

"I know." Jared touched her cheek.

"I mean not *that* way. I mean it's different at funerals. The first dead body I ever saw was when I was eight. It was my cousin, Jerry. Poppa's sister Yetta's only son. He was twenty-three or twenty-four when he died. I loved him, J.P. He was the only one of my cousins who ever took time to be with me when I was a child. We lived in New York and he used to take me to Schrafft's for turkey sandwiches on toasted cheese bread and hot fudge sundaes when he came home from college on vacation. He went to Cornell. He majored in art history. He was going to be a teacher—a professor."

"Toasted cheese bread?"

"Two wafer-thin slices of fresh roast turkey breast, one leaf of iceberg lettuce and cheese bread toast. Russian dressing on the side. Jerry and I went to the Schrafft's on Seventy-sixth Street and Madison Avenue. I remember all the waitresses were Irish and they'd pinch my cheeks. We'd sit at a table looking out on Madison Avenue and people-watch. We'd make up things about the passersby. Tell their whole life story. Jerry was good at that—he'd invent the most fantastic adventures about spies and gangsters and mad scientists. After lunch we'd always walk uptown to the Metropolitan Museum and Jerry would explain pictures to me. He'd show me how the artist painted, and what the picture meant. Then we moved to Washington, and I never saw Jerry again. He lived in New Jersey and it was too far for me to travel."

She toyed with the ruby and diamond ring on her left hand, twisting it in precise quarter-turns. "One day Momma and Poppa told me Jerry died. I don't know from what—I don't think they ever said. We all drove up to New York. The funeral was held at the Riverside on Seventy-sixth Street and Amsterdam Avenue. It was the first funeral I ever went to. Jerry had an open-casket funeral, but my parents wouldn't let me near it. They didn't want me to see him. But just as we were walking out, I broke away from them and ran down the aisle and looked inside. Jerry lay there in a dark blue suit with his hands folded and his skin was as white as our table linen, and for an instant I thought he was only a mannequin made up to look like Cousin Jerry. Then Poppa came running and grabbed me and led me outside, and I cried, and then going home in the car I told them I never wanted people to look at me when I was dead. I told them I wanted to be burned. When I said that—we were in the car on the Jersey Turnpike—my mother slapped me. She'd never slapped me before. How could I know that she was probably thinking about me and where I came from, not about Jerry or those wonderful turkey sandwiches on toasted cheese bread." Adrian sucked air deeply, out of breath from her nonstop talking. She shook, jolted by some unseen tremor.

She was in shock. He cradled her as best he could.

She shivered and snuggled close to him. "Jerry died. I don't think there are any Schraffts left. They're probably all gone. The one where Jerry took me's the Parke-Bernet auction galleries now. The one at Seventy-second Street and Third Avenue's an apartment house. Fifty-seventh Street Schrafft's is a movie theater. On Eighty-fourth and Broadway it's become a Chinese restaurant. Did you know there was a restaurant at Eighty-seventh Street and Broadway called Tip Toe Inn? It was famous for strawberry shortcake and charlotte russe. That's probably gone, too. There used to be ads for it on buses . . . you know the kind of posters they put above the handstraps, and people used to write on them. The big letters read, 'Tip Toe Inn,' and people wrote, 'Flip Flop Out.' "

She tapped his chest lightly with a finger. "That's the depressing thing about going to New York. I don't see the city as it exists now. I see it the way it was when I was five or six. I walk down Fifth Avenue and it's not Gucci or Roberta diCamerino, but Best and Company. It's not Charles Jourdan but DePinna's. It's not Parke-Bernet but Schrafft's.

"They're all gone. Schrafft's, Tip Toe Inn, Longchamps, Best and Company. All dust—like Jerry. I haven't thought of him in years. I haven't thought of turkey sandwiches on toasted cheese bread in years."

She buried her nose in his chest. He could feel the intensity of her tears.

She cried silently for some time. Then without looking up she began to speak again, the breathless torrent of words replaced by a calm, deliberate monotone.

"I don't remember the camps," she said in a whisper. "I was too young. Not more than six or seven months when I was brought to the States. I always thought I was Beverly and Felix's child. Until I was nineteen, when I met Erwin Haberman in Rome and he told me who I was and where I came from.

"It was so—disorienting. I sat in Erwin Haberman's dark apartment on Via Monte Parioli, and my whole life vanished right in front of my eyes. As if, as if I wasn't *me* anymore. It was surreal. I saw Erwin Haberman walking on a street in Rome, and I followed him home. Erwin Haberman—I called him Uncle Erwin—who came to our home, who ate dinner at our table three times a year when I was four or five or six. I thought he was doing business with Felix. But all the time he was checking up on me.

"He's dead now. He was so thin. Beverly used to call him a skinny *marink*. A thin man with terrible eyes and veins that stood out from his forehead and red suspenders. He always wore red suspenders. He worked for the Jewish Agency. Felix and Beverly couldn't have children and Felix's partner Max Grunwald—Felix insists Max was never a Nazi no matter what people said after the war—Max found me in a camp and somehow he got hold of Erwin Haberman and Erwin got me to Beverly and Felix.

"Do you love me, J.P.? I want a Jewish baby. Remember the little man with only one good eye at the *Martef Hashoah*? He gave us an order: 'Make Jewish babies,' he said. He looked at me the same way Erwin Haberman did when he told us about the ones that were lost. 'They could have been you,' he said. 'You could have been them,' he said. God, how right he was."

She put her arms around his neck and held on for dear life. "I went back to the *Martef* when you were in Lebanon that last time, but the old man wasn't there. I asked but nobody knew what had happened to him." She hugged Jared and sighed. "Crazy little man with one good eye."

"I remember him," Jared whispered.

"I confronted them when I got home from Rome. I was nineteen and I told them I knew about them and who I was and where I came from. Oh God, I hated them, Jared. I hated my mother for not having carried me in her body and I hated him for not being able to make her pregnant, not able to pass his genes on to me. I hated them for not having me themselves.

"I came back from Rome and suddenly I felt no part of them, Jared. No connection at all. I felt like a dog or a cat—some stray they'd brought home from the pound to be housebroken and petted, and if things didn't work out, well, they could always return me and get another. God, I despised them."

She unrolled his left shirt sleeve down over the cast on his arm, straightened the cuff, then rolled it back above his elbow in neat folds.

"They planned everything so well, too. That infuriated me even more. When Felix and Erwin Haberman brought me from Germany, from that DP camp nursery, they were living in Great Neck, out on Long Island. It was before they moved into the city. Even then, Felix had clout, because he had a forged birth certificate inserted in the county records. I know that, Jared, because I went out there after I got back from Rome and I looked. 'Adrian Cooper,' it says, 'born April 29, 1945, in Great Neck, County of Nassau, State of New York. Parents: Beverly and Felix Cooper. Place of birth: Great Neck Hospital.' They even paid a doctor to sign the damn thing. If Erwin Haberman hadn't told me about myself I would never have known. All the incriminating evidence had been erased. The records had just . . . disappeared.

"I took revenge. It must have cost them two hundred thousand dollars for my therapy. It didn't help—them or me. Then I smoked a lot of dope. That didn't help either. There was a period—I guess it was my whole junior year in college—when I didn't talk to them. Not at all. Not a word. I'd come home from Sarah Lawrence and I wouldn't say anything. Just go to my room and unpack my bags and dump out my laundry for the maid and then listen to rock and roll on headphones and disappear for days at a time. When they insisted that I go out with them I'd embarrass them in public. They'd take me to Woodmont, to those big country-club dinners where most of their friends would be, and I'd wear all-black clothing and all-white makeup. And say 'fuck' all the time.

"I had such rage inside me. I thought about killing them—I had murder fantasies."

She rolled away from Jared and hugged her knees, staring into space. "Do you understand, J.P.? Not knowing, I mean—"

He looked at her, silent.

"The strain of it. The wear and tear it puts on your psyche; the rage you feel and the emotional energy you expend, simply by not knowing who the hell you are? Nothing matters, J.P. Not people, not sex, not your job—not anything. Because you're so freaking alone.

"I remember when I was in college I took a lit course where I learned that all the great American fictional heroes were like Adam, after he'd been thrust out of the Garden of Eden. They're all a series of symbolic orphans; outsiders who live by their own moral code. Oh, God, how I identified with that theory!"

She got slowly to her feet and walked around the perimeter of the room, trailing a hand along the wall. "I developed my own code, too. I made peace with Beverly and Felix. I adjusted. I found a job. I got married. But I didn't have anything that was mine—not really mine—except my secret."

"You had a life, a husband."

"It was a sham, really. I married Allan to get out of the house. I didn't have the guts to leave without having someplace to go. I couldn't deal emotionally with Beverly and Felix; yet they were the only roots I had. I reached a sort of truce with them just before I got married. We agreed that we all loved each other. But, inside, I wasn't sure. Deep down I still didn't trust them. But the thing is, we were bonded: we shared my secret. No one else knew. Not our friends, not Allan. No one. 'Don't wash your dirty laundry in public,' Felix always says. That's the thing that bothered me. If it was all right, being adopted, why had they kept it from me like it was dirty laundry?

"Anyway, Felix sent us to Israel for our honeymoon. Two weeks at the King David Hotel—a suite overlooking the Old City, of course. The second day, Allan decided we should see Yad Vashem—"

"The Holocaust memorial."

She nodded. "So off we went in our limo, with the guide and the brand-new Nikon and everything. And Allan walked me through the display. Those rooms of relics—uniforms and pictures and barbed wire sections and . . ."

She wiped her eyes with a fist. "I collapsed. I fainted. I couldn't take it. Because those children being herded down the platform at Auschwitz—they were me. And the women standing naked waiting to go to the gas chamber—they were my mother. And the men prisoners—their heads were all shaved—they were my father.

"And all the time Allan was looking and oohing and ahhing and 'Isn't this fascinating, Adrian darling?' and 'Can you imagine such things, dear?' and I was dying inside because I was born from those ashes, those cinders, that dust."

She'd come full circle around the room. She stood next to Jared, her back pressed against the wall. Slowly, she slid down next to him, her thigh touching his. "I hadn't been in Israel since my first trip, when I was nineteen—just before Rome and Uncle Erwin—and still Beverly and Felix's child. On my honeymoon I saw things differently. I saw Israel as a nation of orphans, like those Adamic heroes I learned about in college. They'd been thrust out, and thrust out, and thrust out of different Edens for years—and now they'd come back to claim the original Garden for their own.

"I'm not a Zionist because Felix is a Zionist, J.P. Felix supports Israel for his own reasons—I'm not even sure what some of them are. But I didn't buy a house facing Mount Zion because Felix wanted me to. I did it because of me, because of the way I feel when I'm here—here with history's other orphans.

"It doesn't matter whether we're Jews from Poland or Germany, or Algeria or Morocco, or Yemen or Russia. Here we're all Jews together."

He stared at her. She'd echoed the soldier's very words his first time at the Wall. Had he told her what the man said? He didn't think so. "I was so mad at you," he said.

"When?"

"In New York. I felt so betrayed. Because you hadn't trusted me enough to keep your secrets. When Harriet Mercaldi told me—I could have killed you." He paused. "I understand your wanting to take revenge."

She shook her head. "Harriet Fusco. She used to play with me when I was a baby and Felix took me to the plant. How on earth did you ever find her?"

"Luck. Chance. Happenstance."

"Is that the way secrets get out?"

"Sometimes, I guess. Look at how you found out about yourself."

"I saw Erwin Haberman walking in the street in Rome. If I'd

come out of my hotel thirty seconds earlier or later I never would have seen him. I'd never had found out."

"But you and Felix seem so . . . happy now."

"We're on solid ground these days. He trusts me, and I trust him. I guess trust's what exists between people who love each other. That's why the job at the bank was so important to me. He made me a part of his world. It was the last of the barriers coming down. He trusted me with his business."

"I wish I'd known that at the time."

"I tried to tell you. I started to tell you . . ."

He cut her off. "Trust's what exists between people who love each other."

"That's easy to say, J.P. It's hard to live. It wasn't until after I bought the house in Yemin Moshe that I began to trust my parents again."

"Trust them?"

"Understood they really love me. Love me completely, unreservedly, no quesions asked. It was coming here, to Israel, to Jerusalem, looking across the valley at Mount Zion every day, living as one of history's orphans, that allowed me to see them clearly. To be able to tell them—testify's a pretty strong word but I think it fits—testify how much I love them."

"Strong but the truth. Remember the other thing the crazy little man at the *Martef* said?"

"About having Jewish babies?"

"About our duty as Jews. He said that to be a Jew today means to testify. To bear witness—to what is, and what has been."

"So?"

"So maybe it was time to bear witness. Perhaps—"

He stopped as the door opened. A border guard captain in a pressed uniform, green beret rolled neatly and stuck through his epaulet, strode inside, looking down at the pair of them with ill-disguised contempt. "You can go," he said.

Jared struggled to his feet. He helped Adrian to hers. The captain wheeled. He snapped his fingers. A corporal handed them their belongings. The captain pointed to the door. "Get out. Your car is downstairs. Go back to Jerusalem. Stay away from Hebron. We don't need troublemakers like you."

CHAPTER 17

Summer's last gasp came late, but with a vengeance. *Hamsin,* which Jared insisted on calling Israel's Santa Ana winds, blew westward out of the Judean deserts with biblical ferocity. In Jerusalem, people locked their shutters and closed their drapes, using the natural insulation of the thick rose and gold Jerusalem-stone walls of their houses, villas and flats to keep out the heat. Only in the evenings, when the air in the high city cooled, did they venture onto their terraces and balconies. The hot winds blew unabated for sixteen days, coating the city with a fine layer of gray-tan dust that seeped under doors, into closets and dressers, even settling between plates stacked in kitchen cabinets.

On the morning of the seventeenth day the Unnameable Name relented. The heat ceased as suddenly as it had begun, and the skies over the city resumed their clarity; regained their God-given blueness.

On that seventeenth morning, as if by some pre-arranged signal, thousands of women with thousands of brooms appeared almost simultaneously to sweep stoops, hallways, corridors and balconies clean of the detested dust. Water trucks washed down the streets. Shutters were thrown open; the bright sun, no longer diffused by sand particles, reflected diamondlike highlights off the freshly washed windows. Oriental rugs, beaten free of grit, hung like bright tapestries from terrace railings. From the high-rise splendor of Qiryat Wolfson to the squat squalor of the Turkish Quarter, bedding and mattresses were brought outside to be refreshed by the clean air.

There was an unmistakable sense of change all across the city. From Gillo to Mevasseret Yerushalayim, from Newe Ya'aqov to Mizrah Talpiyyot, the pace and intensity of life increased. Children were readied for school, their parents taking them by the hand to shoe stores on Ben Yehuda Street or braving the crowds to buy book bags, three-ring binders and gym shirts at Mashbir Lazarchan on King George. The knots of people waiting for their buses at rush hour grew less irritable. Even the drivers, whose tempers only days before had been as hot as the oily diesel fumes their vehicles spewed, became pleasant, greeting regular riders and strangers alike with a cheerful "Good evening" as they opened their doors with a hydraulic hiss.

The holidays came and went. In his official residence on Balfour Street, Menachem Begin remained barricaded behind the high stone wall and steel gate, behind the anti-terrorist pillbox with its sophisticated radio equipment and automatic weapons. He became a recluse. He saw no one. Not stirring. Not visible. The most outwardly religious of Israel's prime ministers didn't go to services on Rosh Hashanah. On the fifteenth of September he resigned, eschewing protocol by sending the Cabinet Secretary, Dan Meridor, with the formal letter to President Chaim Herzog, instead of going himself. To the shock of his enemies and supporters alike, not even on Yom Kippur, the year's holiest day, did Begin leave the low stone house to say the mourner's kaddish for his beloved wife Aliza.

The weather began to change. Not drastically, but it could be sensed: the slight but unmistakable fluctuation of temperature, that minuscule atmospheric shift, which sends people to their closets to store the lightest of their clothing and pull out the first wool jacket or find a sweater.

Jared sat at an uneven-legged table at Finzi's café on Ben Yehuda Street's pedestrian mall, sipping a draft Gold Star, a *Jerusalem Post* folded in front of him. From the top of Ben Yehuda, which intersected King George, to the bottom at Zion Square, where vendors set up trays of postcards, people milled aimlessly. The stores were closing up for the afternoon siesta, and the erstwhile shoppers had to make do with browsing or sitting at one of the half dozen cafés that lined the short but crowded hillside street.

Jared perused the paper absentmindedly, scanning the crowds. In the three years he'd lived in Jerusalem, Ben Yehuda Street had been transformed from a thoroughfare to a mall. But with the physical change came a simultaneous identity crisis. Ben Yehuda, once the hub of Jerusalem's middle-class shoppers, was now assuming the look of Rome's Piazza Navone, with its outdoor cafés, ice cream stores, knots of guitar-playing buskers, and handicraft artisans whose cheap leather, brass or silver trinkets were displayed on blankets laid out on the pavement.

He sipped his beer and lit a cigarette, scrunching his chair to the right, when five young men in ersatz designer jeans and polo shirts commandeered the adjoining table. The quintet noisily ordered coffees from a harried waitress.

The leader of the pack was in his mid-twenties. Oriental—Algerian or Moroccan, from the look of his olive-toned skin. Jared snorted inwardly. He'd seen the type before: in Rome, in Florence, in Paris. The kind of petty street-gang hustler who ran errands for second-rate criminals. Now, however, he was beginning to see these hoodlums in Israel, hanging out on street corners in Tel Aviv, in Haifa, even the smaller cities like Herzlyia, Petah Tikvah and Hadera. They finished the Army, and had nowhere to go. No interest in education or the grades to gain admittance to a university. No trade, no experience, and no optimism. So they scrounged, or hustled, or talked about deals; they sat in cafés, sipped coffee and ogled the waitresses. There were thousands of them. According to the heavy ID bracelet he wore, this one was named Gadi. He sported three gold chains and mirrored wraparound sunglasses perched atop his curly, bountiful hair.

Gadi of the chipped front tooth and prehensile forehead. Jared also noted that the second in command was a red-headed stringbean named Yigal who hung on Gadi's every word as if it were being read from stone tablets.

"We got big troubles," Gadi said. *"Godol balagan."* The waitress served coffee. Gadi picked his nose and busied himself staring up the wide armholes of her sweatshirt. "Thanks, sweetie. You busy later? I mean—you and me could have some fun."

"Can my boyfriend come along too?"

"Sure. The more the merrier."

"I tell you what, you ask him when he comes by."

"How will I know him, cutie?"

"He's eighty kilos, a meter-seventy-five, and wears a police uniform."

The other four men at the table laughed. Gadi stirred five packets of sugar into his coffee with the wrong end of a spoon and sipped noisily, waiting until the waitress departed. "Bitch," he stage-whispered to her back, dropping the remaining sugar packets on the table into the breast pocket of his polo shirt.

"What kind of troubles?" Yigal whined.

"The—you know—deal." Gadi held two fingers to his lips and inhaled an imaginary cigarette. He nodded imperceptibly at Jared, engaged with his *Post*.

Jared waved at the waitress. "Could I have another beer, please, miss?" he asked in English.

Gadi snorted. He leaned toward Yigal. "The Lebanese told me he needed money up front."

"But it was all set. He was going to be paid afterward."

"He's getting greedy. Now it's all slipping through our fingers." Gadi slurped his coffee and smacked his lips. "Maybe we'll have to teach him a lesson."

Jared went back to his paper. The children of the generation that made the desert bloom were blooming into a generation of cigarette smugglers.

Yoram had said it, and he was right. Ben-Gurion was spinning in his grave—Israel was moving slowly but inexorably toward the East. It was being Levantinized. Most of the *Mizrahim*—the Oriental Jews from Morocco, Syria, Iraq, Yemen, Algeria and Iran who made up just under sixty percent of Israel's population—weren't adopting the ways of the first, second and third generation Zionist settlers from Russia, Poland and Germany. The Orientals had their own traditions, their own history. Even their own Judaism. Socialism, democracy, freedom of the press and higher education were all, for the most part, outside their experience.

Jared thought about the wedding he had gone to the week before in Binyamina, a farming town roughly halfway between Caesarea and Haifa. Ronny, the son of his friend Aram Yalovsky, had married a girl named Orli, the eldest daughter of a Moroccan family from Afula. Aram and the father of the bride had agreed months before on the number of guests—three hundred—and the fact that they would split the cost of the wedding equally.

The day of the wedding three hundred Moroccans showed up, in addition to Aram's hundred and fifty guests. The caterer went berserk trying to find enough food to feed the last-minute additions. Jared had watched, astounded, as the Moroccans, instead of standing at the buffet tables and filling their plates, carted off serving trays of food for themselves.

To top things off, Orli's father, Yaakov, never paid his share of the costs. Worse, he instructed the bride and groom to pay his share, using their wedding-present money.

"I confronted him," Aram Yalovsky told Jared, "I went through the bloody roof. I had to take a bank loan to pay my share of the wedding because the crops haven't been very good these past two years, and he—the schmuck—said he had no intention all along of paying. It's Moroccan tradition, he tells me, for the bride and groom to assume a share of the wedding—which is bullshit, Jared. And the extra guests? He said it was Moroccan tradition to invite all your friends, and even though he didn't have the money he couldn't leave anybody out. He said he knew he lied to me, but so what?

"So what?! I'll tell you what Moroccan tradition is, Jared—lying is a tradition to them, a bloody tradition. I make deals with a handshake. That's my tradition. All I can hope is that when the kids have their own family they raise their children according to my way of life—not that *putz* Yaakov's."

More than weddings, however, were at stake in Israel, even though one in three of them intermarried Ashkenazim with Orientals. It could be seen all over the country: Israel was moving inexorably eastward in its gestalt. Jared heard stories everywhere. Educators complained that scholastic test scores were down. The Army's chief of training could be heard at parties bemoaning the fact that Zahal's elite units weren't getting the same caliber of recruits. Commanders in Lebanon bitched to their superiors about increased discipline problems, including narcotics use, among the troops. Too many of the nation's young Orientals just didn't seem to care. Not a majority, certainly, but enough to cause concern.

And it wasn't their fault. The Orientals weren't lazy, or stupid. But for years they'd been treated as second-class citizens by European Jews, who considered themselves patricians compared to the down-to-earth, often poor Oriental Jews. Successive Labor governments sent them to live in primitive development towns in the Negev or on the Lebanese border, kept them from the best civil service jobs, promoted them more slowly than their European colleagues in the Army. Only Menachem Begin and Ariel Sharon had courted the Orientals, promising them the majority share of the nation, denied to them for years. And the Orientals responded. Labor candidates were heckled—even roughed up—in places like Afula and Bet Shemesh. When Sharon appeared, the crowds screamed "Arik, Arik, king of Israel," and showered him with rice and candy. Now it was all coming home, coming down around the heads of the Ashkenazim—and the country was suffering for it.

Jared checked his watch, downed the second beer and stood up, dropping a handful of coins on the table as a tip, then thought better of it. He called the waitress over and handed her the money directly. If he'd left it, Gadi and his crowd would have taken it for themselves, he was sure.

He wandered down Ben Yehuda Street to Zion Square. He bought half a dozen postcards from a wizened Iraqi whose stand was made out of TV-set cartons, crossed the Yafo, walked east to Heshin Street and turned north past the Department of Surveys and up the hill toward the Russian Compound and the old Palestine Central Prison, which had been turned into a museum. It was there, during the British Mandate, that Irgun and Stern Gang terrorists were held, although they always were transported to the old Arab prison at Acre for execution. Aimless as a tourist, Jared discarded his newspaper and strolled toward Hanevi'im Street, turned left on Rehov Kook, walked back down the hill to the Yafo and crossed against the light, dodging a bus whose driver shook a fist in his direction. He sauntered west again, turning onto Luntz Street and finally into Rehov Dorot Rishonim.

The restaurant was on his right, a small place whose front was decorated with a rectangular sign in green and gold that read OPHER. He opened the door and walked inside. Amnon Mizrahi, Opher's owner, stood behind the formica counter. He saw Jared and waved. "Long time no see!"

Jared slid onto a stool and clasped Amnon's hand. "Hi, 'Noni. You're right—long time. But it's been busy."

"And hot." Amnon whistled toward the kitchen. "A coffee."

"And hot. How are you? How's your father and mother?"

"Terrific." A cup of Turkish coffee slid over the kitchen's steel counter. Amnon placed it gently in front of Jared. "Salleh's really happy because my sister had another baby. One more grandchild to spoil."

"Mazel tov!" Jared sipped the coffee. He looked at Amnon's round, olive-toned face. It was a classic Middle Eastern face; a face that dated back to Egypt, to Sinai, to Canaan; a face that, Jared imagined, could be seen on hieroglyphic illustrations of the Jews who built Ramses' Pyramid.

"You want to eat something?"

"Absolutely. I'm famished." Jared patted his stomach. The food at Opher was simple fare: grilled meats, Oriental soups, mejadara and Middle Eastern salads. But no one in the city did them better than Amnon. The place was off the beaten track. Most tourists went to Heppner's deli on Rehov Luntz, or the Café Rimon across the street. Still, Amnon had a crowd of regulars who filled the restaurant for lunch six days a week. It was a business Amnon had built slowly; his reputation had come from hard work and good word-of-mouth.

"Okay. Better take a spot while you can." He pointed toward a table of six where a single chair sat empty.

"I'll stay here at the counter," Jared said. "It's less crowded."

"If you like." Amnon scratched his chin. "What do you feel like?"

"Kubbeh soup," Jared said. "Just a tiny plate. And then some kebabs and a big plate of mejadara."

"Only the kiddie portion today, huh?" Amnon swiveled toward the kitchen and whistled.

Jared's hand had no sooner closed over the soup spoon than he felt a gentle tap on his back. "Excuse me, please."

He slid on his stool to the left. Shimon Levy, beat-up Uzi hanging from his shoulder, sat down next to him.

Jared sipped his soup. The bearded Shin Bet agent ordered tehina, Turkish salad and an orange soda. Amnon slapped the plates onto the counter, then went to wipe down a table outside. It was remarkable how so many of Jared's surreptitious meetings took place in restaurants. In Washington leaks took place over cocktails. Here, a good hummus loosened a source's tongue far better than three or four martinis.

Shimon Levy scooped a generous portion of tehina into a chunk of warm pita bread and stuffed it in his mouth. "Tonight," he said quietly. "Come tonight. There's something you have to see."

Jared nodded imperceptibly. Ever since he'd shown up in Hebron with Menachem Livni's *meluim* card stashed in his cast the Shin Bet agent's suspicions about Jared's motives had been allayed, and he'd gone out of his way to be helpful.

Levy's eyes had gone wide when Jared dropped the blue, plastic-coated credential on his dining table. "Where the hell did you find that?"

"Outside a classroom in the Islamic University. Just before the border guards beat the crap out of me."

Shimon had nodded. "I heard," he'd said. "Sorry."

"You've got nothing to apologize for."

The Shin Bet man had squinted at Livni's picture. "Ties him to the scene."

Jared had nodded. "Remember?—I told you Livni's people said he was occupied that day."

"I'll bet he was."

"You owe me a big one."

The Shin Bet agent had offered Jared his hand. "Don't worry, we pay our debts."

"How was lunch?" Adrian grunted as she pulled the Turkish rug off the railing and spread it out on the floor.

"Delicious. Productive." Jared dropped onto the sofa and settled his feet on the coffee table. "And filling."

She nodded. "So?" She wiped perspiration from her forehead with the back of her hand.

He shrugged. "Now comes the hard part."

She headed toward the kitchen. "What do you mean?"

"I've got to go back to Hebron. I'll probably stay the night."

"Why, J.P.?"

"Because it's necessary. Because there's stuff I have to learn." The cat pounced on the carpet's fringe and started to rake at it. Jared picked the creature up and settled it in his lap, stroking it gently behind the ears. "There's still so much I don't know."

She emerged carrying a plate on which sat a jam sandwich. "But it's not safe."

"Safe? Safe is a relative term. Safe from whom? From Levinger and his people? Safe from the soldiers or the border guards? Safe from the Arabs?"

"From everybody." She shuddered. "It's crazy down there."

"Ah," he said in the B-movie version of an inscrutable Arab accent, "zees ez zee mysterious Middle East, my dear Adrian, and what is zee Middle East if not crazee?"

"Don't clown. You know what I mean."

"I'll be careful."

"I worry whenever you go to Hebron. I never believed that Jews could be so brutal. That Jews could do such things. That day—what I saw made me sick."

He nodded. "I know."

"If anybody discovered what you're doing. If that Terror Against Terror group—if they ever knew, who knows what they'd do?"

It was true. Since their arrest and detention together, Jared had made half a dozen trips to the hilly Arab city, and Adrian had fretted each time. She wasn't the only one worried. These weren't rational people he was dealing with. They saw themselves as zealots, as patriots, as nationalists. They had killed innocent people too easily.

"Don't get upset. I'm not going to take any chances, believe me." He patted the cushion next to him and she plunked herself down on it. She put the plate on the table, sat back and rested her head on his shoulder.

"Anyway, you're beautiful when you worry."

"I am? Even when I'm dressed like this?" She looked herself over. T-shirt, jeans, sandals, and a kerchief wrapped around her hair. She frowned. "I'm a mess."

He shook his head. "You're a real *hatti-ha*, my onion." He cradled her. The cat settled between them, purring with pleasure at the closeness of their bodies.

Jared closed his eyes. There was so much still to do. So much he didn't know.

In a small locked steel box under the bed sat his files. What there were of them. There were pictures from Hebron: a collection of snapshots he had taken of the Settlers Association leaders, all labeled with the help of Shimon Levy and Nathan Yaari. Quid pro quo payment for the blue reserve officer's card with Menachem Livni's picture on it. There were other photos, too. Pictures of Qiryat Arba, with its pastel-faced apartment blocks and barbed-wire fences. At Yaari's suggestion he had spent a week sitting in a rented car, a borrowed camera and a telephoto lens pressed against his cheek, snapping off frames of people going and coming from Qiryat Arba's warehouses and machine shops. He made organizational charts of the settlement leadership, and juxtaposed those against Army records that Yaari gave him. He sat over endless cups of coffee in Shimon Levy's apartment as the Shin Bet agent explained the complex series of relationships that intertwined settlement leaders from all over Israel; it appeared to be a loosely knit organization. He took no notes, only committing Shimon's ideas to paper once back in Yemin Moshe.

The time in Hebron and Qiryat Arba was nerve wracking. Sooner or later he was bound to be recognized by someone. Since he'd been wounded in Lebanon Jared had developed a more fatalistic attitude toward his work. But he still walked through Hebron's Arab casbah feeling exposed and vulnerable, sometimes wishing that, like most of the Israeli reporters who covered the West Bank, he, too, carried a pistol for protection. Among the settlers he felt more secure. Not because they were Jews especially, but because they, more than the Arabs, realized the implications of injuring an American reporter.

Jared worked the story on his own time, just as Jerry Atkins had ordered. For Atkins, the subject of Jewish terror was a dead issue. The acting bureau chief had rejected out of hand Jared's photos of the Islamic University corpses from Hebron, and dismissed the first-person account of his treatment at the hands of the border guards as sensationalistic and unnewsworthy.

"I called their commanding officer," Atkins said, a cheap cigar clenched in the center of his mouth. "He told me his men never do anything like the things you're accusing them of. The issue is closed."

Jared's "eyewitnesser" files on Hebron were never transmitted to New York.

On the other hand, the most important element of his life had changed for the better: he and Adrian were back on track. The void between them had been bridged. No longer was she Potemkin Village Adrian.

On the road to Jerusalem that hot summer night, after they'd been released, Adrian drove slowly, shakily, her knuckles white on the car's dark steering wheel. Jared sat, the cannister of film clutched in his fist, staring vacantly out the window as the car, its headlights piercing the unlit road, crawled northward.

Adrian glanced at him. "What are you thinking about?"

"Everything."

"J.P.—"

"Everything. You, me, Hebron." He shook the film. "This. Israel. Us."

"And?"

"And I'm confused. Why the hell does life have so many questions and so few answers?" He laughed. "See? Another question."

He peered into the darkness. "You know, when I was in New York—"

"Yes?"

"I thought you'd told Roger Richards about Yoram."

"Yoram?"

"The commando raid in Syria. The forged file."

"Why would I do that?"

"I didn't know. But you knew the truth. And I—"

She pulled the car to the side of the road, stopped on the narrow gravel shoulder and turned toward him. "Why, Jared? Why would I betray you like that?"

"I couldn't figure it out. But you knew, Adrian. And I'd seen you with Yoram, and Mandy Navor, and you'd lied to me about it. When the whole world collapsed on me . . ." He looked at her in the darkness. Wetness glistened on her cheeks.

"I've always been good at keeping secrets. Perhaps too good."

Clumsily, he held her.

"When you told me about the raid, and the forged file—it was as if you'd finally come to terms with us. You were brave to tell me, J.P. I mean, it was your career. I wouldn't betray your bravery, your trust. Not ever."

"If only you'd trusted me the same way."

"I did trust you, J.P. I do trust you. It's just that some things are . . . hard."

"I understand. I understand. But we weren't supposed to have any secrets."

She slid the car into gear and eased back onto the highway. "What was I supposed to do? Give you my life story the day after we met in Sinai? Open myself up as if you were a shrink? Sit you down the minute we moved into Yemin Moshe and tell you everything that ever happened to me? That's not the way things happen, Jared."

"But it's been three years, Adrian."

"I was married for five. Time has nothing to do with it. It's a feeling deep in your gut, a fear that sat inside me like a cancer; eating away, eating away. You know, when the doctor told me I had a malignancy I thought, I really thought I'd done it to myself. All that worrying, that hiding—and the sickness had taken root in my body as some sort of horrible revenge. It's hard to break through. I was afraid. Afraid you'd find out and you'd leave me. That everything would disintegrate, because I'm not who I say I am, and—"

"That's crazy. You're exactly who you say you are. It's just that knowing, understanding, makes it easier for me to understand."

"Understand what?"

"You. You and Felix. Everything."

"What was I supposed to do, wear a sign?"

"No, but—"

"There are no 'buts,' Jared. Things happen . . . slowly. People expect each other to open up so quickly. No secrets. Everything exposed all at once. Life isn't like that. It's not the same as slicing open a melon and what you see inside is the whole story. It's like an onion, layers on layers that get peeled away."

"And each layer brings tears?"

"Sometimes."

"So you're an onion."

"Something like that."

"But you're my onion."

She smiled for the first time in some hours. "If you say so."

"Oh, I say so. I definitely say so."

"Even if I bring you tears when you peel back a layer or two?"

He'd reached across the Chevy's wide bench seat and stroked her cheek. "Hey, we're Jewish. What would we do without complications?"

CHAPTER 18

He picked up a hitchhiking soldier across from the Jerusalem train station and dropped him outside a military building just south of the Dahisha refugee camp. By the time he reached the Qiryat Arba turnoff four kilometers north of Hebron it was dark. Jared, who wore a knit skull cap clipped to the back of his head, drove the rented car carefully, unaccustomed to the way it oversteered on the two-lane road. He veered left at the settlement's gates, drove past the modernistic Bank Leumi, with its high arched windows, and the squat Hebron Hotel. He continued up a hill, then turned right, past a series of apartment houses, until he came to a wide turn in the road. He parked under a street lamp, locked the car, and continued on foot, climbing a short stone flight of steps and walking through a narrow alleyway between the four-story buildings. A short, bearded man with a mournful Huckleberry Hound face and a Uzi over his shoulder passed him without taking notice.

Jared found the building he was looking for, and pushed open its front door. He pressed the minuterie light, trudged up two flights of stairs before it went out, fumbled in the dark and pressed the button again. He climbed another floor and hit the hall light. At the second door on the right he stopped and knocked softly.

A woman's voice said, "Who's there?"

"Orna? It's Shem Tov."

The door cracked open. "Shalom. Come in."

An attractive woman in her late thirties, she wore the head scarf that was traditional for Orthodox Jews, and a housecoat of chintz-patterned fabric. She closed the door, locked it and motioned the American inside the living room. "Good to see you, Jared. Shimon's in the kitchen," she said. "Come."

"Ahh, you made it. Terrific." Shimon Levy rose from a kitchen table piled with papers and shook Jared's hand warmly. "You want a coffee?"

Jared nodded.

"Orna. Please." The Shin Bet agent watched as his wife put a heavy kettle on the stove. "I'm glad you're here." He took Jared by the arm and walked him out of the kitchen, through the living room and into a small bedroom. From the bedside table Levy took a tape cassette. He inserted it into a minicorder, plugged an earpiece in and handed the machine to Jared. "Here. You listen. I'll get your coffee."

Jared inserted the earphone in his left ear and pressed the play button. The tape was indistinct, as if it had been recorded at a great distance, or through several layers of clothing. There was considerable static, as well as heavy traffic sounds, which punctuated the conversation. Still, he could make out two voices. The first was deep and strangely accented Hebrew—perhaps Turkish or Spanish or Slavic. The second was the reedy, non-guttural Hebrew spoken by many American immigrants—*olim*.

The deep voice was saying, "What's up?"

"I need to do business," the American said, his voice partially obscured by traffic noise.

"Good for me. What this time is it?"

"Dynamite."

"Not impossible. But hard. It's going to cost you."

"Money's no object."

The deep voice laughed. "No, it's not. Not for you people. What quantity we are talking about?"

"Fifty, sixty pieces. Plus the other stuff."

"Other stuff?"

"Fuses. Wiring. I want a complete package."

"Sure—understood. And delivery?"

"Ninety days."

The deep voice whistled. "Tough."

"But you can do it."

"Sure, but—"

"Don't give me 'but.' Either you can or you can't. I'm not going to screw around. If your answer's no, tell me now and I'll go elsewhere."

"Don't worry. I've never let you before down, have I?"

"No, but—"

"So this time you'll take delivery just on the schedule too." There was the sound of someone slurping liquid noisily, then the deep voice again. "Sounds big."

"I wouldn't know. I'm just a middleman."

"Well, mister middleman, what about the money?"

"Three thousand—U.S. dollars."

A pause. The tape hissed. Jared pressed the earpiece tighter so as not to miss anything. The deep voice sucked audibly on a cigarette. "Ten thousand."

"*Goniff*. Robber. Even five thousand would be exorbitant."

"Such big words from the businessman. Look at the risk I'm taking."

"Six thousand."

"If they catch me it's ten years in Ramla prison. Nine thousand. Not a penny less."

"Sixty-five hundred."

"Eight."

"Seven. And it better not be the same stuff you supplied last time. That shipment was so unstable we had to store it on ice."

"Seventy-five hundred. Final. Take it or leave it."

"A deal," the American's voice said.

"Half now, half on delivery."

"Agreed."

"You get the package the last week January."

"Like last time?"

"Yes—your people supply transportation and security."

"No problem."

"So—deal. Money?"

"I'll be back in a minute."

The tape hissed. Jared could make out voices in the background, and car horns. Then: "All there."

The tape went dead. Shimon returned, carrying a steaming mug. Jared put the minicorder on the bed and took the coffee. He blew across it and sipped cautiously.

"That was made in a gas station near Ashdod," Shimon said. "Three days ago."

"Who are they?"

"The big voice is a Turk named Baz. He runs a machine shop near the port. He's into a bunch of things—none of them very legal."

"And the other?"

"We don't know yet. American from the sound of him. He's new."

"How'd you get the tape?"

"By accident. The customs people were on Baz's tail—they made it."

"Can I have a copy?"

"Be my guest."

Shimon watched as Jared pulled a minicorder and set of audio cables from his rucksack, connected the two machines and dubbed the cassette. "Whatever it is it's going to be big."

The Israeli nodded. "A bombing."

"Can you find the American?"

"We're looking. We've got pictures from the customs people."

"Does he live here?"

"Here or one of the other settlements probably. We'll find him."

"Can I get a picture?"

"When I get another. For now, take a look." Shimon slid a grainy black-and-white print toward Jared.

The photograph was an indistinct profile of a man in his early thirties, wearing a blazer and open-necked white shirt, leaning across a table. Perched on the back of his head was a knit skull cap.

"What are you going to do?"

The Shin Bet agent raised his palms in surrender. "We asked for permission to tap some telephones, but it was denied. The Deputy Prime Minister isn't willing to offend his ultranationalist friends from the religious parties by allowing the agency to investigate settler leaders. He needs their votes these days."

"So what do you want from me? Why bring me down here?"

"Because an article about TNT in your magazine would help right now. They read *World Week* in Jerusalem and Washington. The Israeli aid bill will be coming up soon in your Congress—and if a major magazine like yours publishes something on Jewish terror, it could pressure Shamir to act. He doesn't want any embarrassments hanging over his head when he goes to Washington begging for money."

"You remember what happened the last time I wrote about TNT?"

"But you heard the tape?"

"The tape is only a small part of the story. Face it, Shimon, I'm dealing with millions of American readers who don't give a damn about what a couple of people in a gas station near Ashdod say. Now if I could tie this thing directly to the Prime Minister's office, or prove that the Israeli government was suppressing investigations of Jewish terror—then I'd have a story. But right now I've got no names, no specifics, no interviews. What am I supposed to write? That *Shabak*"—Jared used the idiomatic word for the Shin Bet—"has an undercover agent named Levy here in Qiryat Arba? That somebody's ordering a load of explosives? That I found an identity card belonging to Menachem Livni inside the Islamic University the day of the killings? There's not enough hard evidence, Shimon."

The agent pulled at his beard. "Come," he said.

From a cabinet in the living room he took a small flashlight. "I'll be back," he told his wife. Levy led Jared downstairs, walked him up a long hill in the darkness and then into the ground level of another apartment block.

"Quietly," he warned as Jared stumbled on a step in the darkness and cursed. He turned the flashlight on, revealing a steel door. "Bomb shelter," Shimon explained. He opened the door, stepped inside and beckoned to Jared. "Careful."

They were at the top of a long flight of concrete steps. Shimon closed the steel door and secured it. The flashlight probing a circle of light ahead of them, they walked down into the humid darkness. At the bottom of the steps there were two corridors. Shimon took the left one. The flashlight beam picked out a wall switch and the Shin Bet agent flicked it, illuminating the passageway with dim yellow lights.

"Down there's the kids' dormitory," Shimon said. "And next to it's what we want."

Set into the arched concrete passageway was a steel door with a cypher lock set into it. Shimon pressed a combination of buttons and turned the handle. The door opened. The Israeli felt around the doorjamb and turned on a light.

Jared stepped inside. Shimon turned out the passage light and followed him. They had entered a storeroom filled with crates of canned food and bottled water, disposable diapers, crates of crackers, tins of cheese and other edibles. "Everything we'd need for a siege," Shimon explained. "The kids would be safe down here for about four weeks."

"Normal," said Jared. "This is just like the bomb shelters I've seen in Metulla or Qiryat Shemona up on the Lebanese border."

"Right. But we have here—" Shimon pulled a stack of crates aside, scraping the poured concrete floor as he did so. "Here we have an additional supply of goodies."

"Good Lord." Jared bent to inspect an open crate that sat against the wall obscured by the food cartons. It contained half a dozen AK-47 Kalashnikov assault rifles and ammunition clips.

"If I could get these out of here to a lab for a day or so I'd bet we'd find a couple that were used at the Islamic University down in Hebron," Shimon said. "Now, how's this for hard evidence?"

Jared pulled his camera from a pocket, raised the flash and took half a dozen fast pictures of the AK-47s. "It's a start."

Shimon pushed the food crates back in position. He examined the position of the boxes, then escorted Jared to the door. "There are other things here, too. Grenades. Land mines. Extra barrels for the AK-47s, so that they can be exchanged—the better to fool ballistics experts." He extinguished the light and opened the door. "Careful."

They made their way back up the passage to the foot of the stairs, climbed to the top and cracked the door to the outside. Shimon looked around. "All clear." He stuck the flashlight in his pocket and took Jared by the arm. "That's not the only bomb shelter in Qiryat Arba," he said. "There are dozens. Many have similar provisions."

"Specifics," Jared insisted. "I need more specifics. Is there anyone at *Shabak* who would agree to be interviewed on the record?"

"I don't think so. Not now." The Israeli tugged at his beard. "You have enough proof of Jewish terror already, Jared—believe me. You have the organizational charts of the settlers' groups. And pictures of the ringleaders. And you were in Hebron the day the students were killed—you saw their bodies and the classroom. And now you have pictures of an arms cache."

"It's not hard enough. The magazine won't buy it."

The Shin Bet agent shrugged. "I've told you everything I can. Try. At least try."

Jared tried to look optimistic. "Let's see what I can do."

CHAPTER

"The answer is no." Roger Richards's aristocratic drawl hummed over the international line. "We've been down that road once. Look where it got us."

Jared shot Adrian a hapless grimace and paced, phone in hand, up and down the living room. "Roger—look, I can't be specific over the phone, but I've got the goods."

"I've heard that song before, Jared."

"Just let me come to New York and show you. This time it's—"

"The answer is no. How many times do I have to say it, Jared? If Jerry Atkins doesn't like the story, you don't do it. Atkins told me three days ago he doesn't like the story."

"Atkins wouldn't know a story if it bit him." Jared covered the mouthpiece with his palm. "I'm dealing with schmucks."

He put the receiver to his ear again. "Yes, Roger. Yes, Roger. Good-bye, Roger." He slammed the receiver into its cradle. "The man is crazy."

"What's his decision?"

"He doesn't want to see me. He has no interest in the story. He's going to London to tour the bureau and can't be bothered."

Adrian frowned. "That's no way to do business."

"What the hell can I do? Jerry Atkins wants nothing to do with Jewish terror. You know what he told me last week?" Jared mimicked Atkins's broad New York accent: " 'I called Shamir's spokesman himself, and he denied there are any Jewish terrorists.' End of story. And after Hebron, he spiked my eyewitnesses, remember?"

Adrian walked to the window and looked across the valley. The sun had turned the walls on Mount Zion to gold. "You know," she said, "I was always leery of this Jewish terror story."

Jared nodded.

"Until Hebron. Until I saw the bodies. Now—"

"Now?"

"Now I don't know what to think. I've been coming here for ten years, and in all that time I never saw anything like Hebron. *Kibbutzim,* yes. *Moshavim,* yes. Farms in the north, yes. Settlements. But never places like Beit Hadassah or the Hebron casbah. Going there with you, listening to the way Shoshanna spoke, the things Shmuel Chai said. The way the border guards treated us. You used to tell me what was happening, but I never believed you. Now . . ."

"Now?"

"Now, I'm confused. Now, I'm troubled. Israel isn't rotten, Jared. It isn't. But it's changed . . . changing. You know what Felix says, how bad news about Israel is bad news for all Jews? I used to think he was right. Now I'm not sure."

"Comes from living with a journalist."

"Don't be flippant."

He held up his hands. "Okay. So?"

"I hate to admit you were right, but you were. We're such knee-jerkers when it comes to Israel. Lord knows I've been that way all my life. That's the way I was raised, educated, trained.

"It didn't matter who was foreign minister or prime minister, Felix"—she stopped herself—"*we* just supported them. And their policies. I certainly didn't question anything. Besides, there wasn't a lot to question. Israel's wars were a matter of national survival. And Israel's internal policies? When I think about it, we never knew very much about them. We were asked to support Israel—to give money—and that's what we did. You have a phrase for it. What do you call it? Dollar Zionists?"

Jared nodded. "Dollar Zionists."

She made a face. "That's a little harsh."

"Perhaps. But it's the truth. Problem is that dollar Zionism makes it possible for Diaspora Jews to be involved with Israel without really being involved, if you know what I mean. It satisfies all their guilt mechanisms, or their need to be a part of the Jewish state, without having to become intimately involved with Israel on the day-to-day level. Look at Shamir. A former member of the Stern Gang. A terrorist who waged war on civilians, because he thought it was the only way to achieve a Jewish state. Begin was a member of Irgun, which committed acts of random violence against civilians. In 1952 he almost started a civil war over German repatriations. That was terror, too. I'm sorry, Onion, but terror is terror—whether it's Jewish terror or PLO terror or IRA terror."

"And?"

"And look at whose administration it's been under that Jewish terror's become a problem. Not Ben-Gurion's. Not Golda's. Not Rabin's—but Begin's and Shamir's. They may be pals of Felix's, but only under Likud has there been an environment in which organized Jewish terror has become a fact of life. And I can't get the damn story published."

"Maybe Roger Richards is right. Maybe you don't have enough evidence?"

"But I *have* evidence. Pictures, charts—I even got a tape from Shimon."

"Tape?"

"*Shabak* got a surveillance tape from the customs people. It was a buy going down. Explosives. You want to hear it?"

"Sure."

Jared rummaged under the bed, unlocked his metal box and extracted the minicassette. He dropped it into the recorder and pressed the play button. "Listen."

Adrian screwed up her face. "There's a lot of static."

"It wasn't made in a studio."

He watched the expression on her face change as the conversation ran on. She grew serious. "J.P., play it again."

"Sure." He rewound the cassette.

"Do you have earphones?"

"Wait a second." He found a monitoring earpiece and handed it to her.

She plugged the device into one ear and stuck her finger in the other. "Okay—start."

He watched as she listened. "What is it?"

"I think I recognize the voice."

"What? How—"

"Look, Jared, maybe I'm mistaken. But it could be Moishe."

"Moishe?"

"Moishe Halevi. He's one of the assistant managing directors at the bank."

"But Shimon said the voice was American."

"Moishe *is* American. Murray Levy. He got his MBA at Harvard and made aliyah afterward."

"Come on—" Jared took her arm.

"Where are we going?"

"To a public phone. I'm going to call Shimon—he's got a picture of the guy on the tape. If he's home, we're going to Qiryat Arba."

"That's him. That's Moishe." Adrian tapped the photograph with an index finger. They were sitting in the car, parked a discreet distance from Shimon Levy's apartment. Jared had commandeered the picture, slipped it inside his windbreaker, and sprinted back to where Adrian waited in the Autobianchi. There was no need for her to meet the Levys; besides, Shimon was nervous enough that Jared had brought Adrian with him.

"Okay—let me take it back to Shimon."

"Then what?"

"Then I don't know."

"Aren't you going to tell him?"

Jared thought about it. "No. Not yet."

"Why?"

"I want to follow this lead on my own. It could break the case wide open. For God's sake, a Harvard MBA as part of a Jewish terror network? Roger Richards would have to listen to me because of the American angle. God, Adrian, it could get me off probation." He slid out of the auto and ran off. Three minutes later he was back.

"What did you say to Shimon?"

"I told him I thought I had something but it didn't pan out." Jared put the car in gear and drove quickly through Qiryat Arba's hilly streets.

"My God. Moishe," Adrian said. "Buying dynamite. It's inconceivable." She turned to Jared. "Do you realize that it could ruin the bank's reputation? Felix is going to have a heart attack."

"Felix?"

"We've got to tell him, J.P."

"No way. Impossible."

"We've got to! Look—if Moishe is involved in something illegal, that's his problem. If you want to go after him, fine. I'm even glad to help you. But Felix entrusted me with running his operation here, protecting his interests. There are investors—"

"If you tell Felix, he'll go running to the Prime Minister's office. The story'll just—*evaporate*."

"No, he won't, Jared. I promise."

"That's his style, Adrian!"

"He's a businessman," she insisted. "He has responsibilities to the investors. We just opened new branches in New York and Los Angeles. We're turning a nice profit. Felix won't do anything to jeopardize that, J.P., I know him too well."

They sped north on the blacktop road in silence. "He trusted me, J.P. He brought me into his professional life for the first time. I can't turn my back on him now. We've got to call."

Jared swerved to avoid a straggling goat. "Okay—sure—go ahead, call Felix."

"Why the change of mind?"

"It would serve him right," he said self-righteously.

"Jared!"

"I mean it's poetic justice, isn't it? Here's Felix—I like your father, Onion, I really do. But as long as I've known him he's been blind to what's been going on in Israel. 'Is it good or bad for the Jews'; 'Don't wash your dirty laundry in public'—that's what he says. Look at how wrong he was about the Lebanon invasion. And last fall he insisted there was no such thing as a Jewish terror network. And now—we discover a Jewish terrorist operating right under his nose. Maybe even using the bank as cover. Go on—call him. Get him over here. If this doesn't open his eyes nothing will."

CHAPTER 20

Felix arrived in Jerusalem forty-eight hours after Adrian left urgent but cryptic messages at the bank's downtown Washington headquarters and the Coopers' Potomac home. He telephoned from a suite at the King David Hotel, his voice betraying fatigue from the long connecting flight through Paris and tension over the unidentified crisis. "Let me grab a quick nap, Pidge. I'm a basket case. Let's meet at eight. Drinks in the bar first, then we'll go to Chez Simon for dinner."

There was concern on his face as he rose to meet them, enveloping Adrian in a bear hug and pumping Jared's hands in his own. "What's wrong, Pidge? Your message sounded frantic."

Adrian told him about Moishe Halevi. Cooper was stunned and unbelieving. But in the interval since she'd called him, Adrian had driven to Tel Aviv and done some detective work on her own. She'd accessed the bank's computers and found several accounts that troubled her. Now she held out the printouts for Felix to examine.

Jared sat silent, watching Felix's expression change as, reading glasses perched on the tip of his nose, he rapidly scanned the papers.

"I don't want to believe it," he said. "Moishe—I hired him myself. He went to Harvard. He's smart—too smart to get caught at anything like this." He gave Adrian an approving glance. "How did you uncover this?"

"It was Jared," Adrian began. "He—"

"A fluke, Felix," Jared interrupted. He was not about to give

Felix the whole story. Not yet. "I was working on something and Moishe's name came up. By chance, really. Then one thing led to another, and, well . . ."

"This is incredible." Felix paused as a waitress brought their order. He turned the papers face down on the table, picked up his scotch and downed it. "Another, please," he said.

"So soon, Poppa?"

"It's been a long day," Cooper said. "And now, to be hit with this . . ." They waited in silence until Felix's second drink had been placed on the table. "How do you think I should handle it?"

Adrian spoke. "Whatever *we* do, Poppa, we should do it quietly."

Felix nodded, looking intently at Jared. "You're the reporter," he said. "What do you think?"

Jared stared back. What was the guy thinking? He'd reacted coolly, almost too coolly—except for the order for a second drink. Obviously, Felix was shocked. Well, he ought to be. Jared sipped his Campari-and-soda. "I agree with Adrian," he said. "Look, Felix, what you've got is a rotten apple. This guy Moishe is using the bank to funnel funds or launder money or whatever, probably for a Jewish terror group, maybe even the Terror Against Terror network itself. Sooner or later the Shin Bet's gonna find out who he is. He'll be arrested. In the meanwhile, why not just keep tabs on him?"

Felix nodded. "See how he operates . . . how the money gets moved."

"Right. Adrian can keep you posted. She's got access to the computer—she can trace anything she wants to. If it looks like the bank'll be jeopardized, you can call one of your friends in the government."

Felix ran a hand through his hair, careful not to skew the knitted *kippa* he wore in Israel. "This is very unlike you, Jared," he said. "I thought you'd want to jump on this—get the story into your magazine."

"I do, Felix. I want it out—but not until it's ready to be told."

"And when will that be?"

"When I learn more about Moishe—whom he's tied to, what he's doing and how he wants to do it."

Cooper crunched an ice cube. "You're more cautious these days."

"I'm on probation these days."

"I always warned you about what you wrote," Felix said. "I

knew you'd get into trouble, but you didn't listen. You young people never listen—such idealists. Now you're learning, it seems. Becoming more of a pragmatist."

" 'Pragmatist,' Felix? That's a real ten-dollar word."

"Let's say you're beginning to understand what it is to live in the real world. To make compromises."

"Come on, Felix, I've always lived in the real world."

"The hell you have."

"You think I don't see things the way they are?"

"You can afford to see what you want to see, Jared. You've never had to fight to exist."

Jared was furious. "Hey, wait a minute, Felix. I got myself shot up in Lebanon. I've covered the war. I had to fight for stories in Washington . . ."

"I'm not speaking professionally, Jared. But there was always food on your table, you never had to scrape just to survive. You were born comfortable. You've never had to scramble for a dollar. Never had to compromise your precious ideals—"

"Get off it, Felix. I know you worked your way up. You're from a different generation. I respect that. But don't lecture me about ideals or living in the real world. You don't have the right. Besides, I know about your 'compromises' and what they mean. *We* know about you."

"Jared, this isn't the time—" Adrian tugged at his sleeve.

"Know?" Felix sat back in his chair. "What, exactly, do you know?"

"I've been to Frankfurt. I found out. I told Adrian. You were in business with the Germans before the war—right up until the day they invaded Poland. In business with Grunwald, who helped build the concentration camps. And it was Grunwald who bought you out in 1951."

"So?"

"Doing business with Nazis doesn't really seem appropriate for someone like you, does it?" He looked at Adrian. Her eyes told him to stop. But Jared couldn't stop. He smiled. "How many of your friends in Israel know about Grunwald, Felix?"

"They all know, Jared."

Jared was shocked. "What?"

"You schmuck!" Felix pounded the table with his fist. "You

stupid schmuck!" Conversation in the beam-ceilinged room came to a halt as people froze and turned toward them. Felix realized it. His face grew red and he lowered his voice. "How could they *not* know? And I thought you were learning. You haven't learned a damn thing—the world's still all black-and-white, isn't it?"

He waited, staring Jared down. "Well?"

Jared said nothing.

Adrian reached for her father's hand. "Poppa—he didn't mean anything."

"The hell he didn't." Felix crunched another ice cube. "Oh, you're *good,* Jared. Very good. You probably love the idea that some terrorist is working for me. Serves me right, huh? After all—I was in business with *them*—Germans. Right? Lots of guilt for you to probe. Emotional blackmail, perhaps? A little dime-store psychoanalysis, eh, Jared?" He turned toward his daughter. "And you were probably taken in by his—his discoveries. You, of all people, Adrian!"

Abruptly, Cooper stood up, pulled a wad of shekel notes from his pocket, and tossed them on the table. "We're getting out of here."

"Where are we going, Poppa?" Adrian asked.

"Upstairs, where I can give you two a history lesson in private."

They sat there as Felix, his back to them, stood watching the walls of the Old City, brilliant under the clean white light of halogen lamps. He hadn't switched the chandelier on, only closed and locked the door behind them and motioned Jared and Adrian toward the couch. "I owe the two of you," he said, his hands clasped behind his back. "You didn't have to call, to tell me what Moishe's been doing. What you did is going to save the bank a lot of embarrassment. Maybe save the state of Israel some embarrassment, too. And that's important—to me. And to the two of you, despite what you may think."

He turned and faced them, a silhouette framed by the terrace door, the walls bright behind him across the old no-man's-land. "You have to understand that the world's never been a nice place for Jews, an easy place for Jews to exist . . ." he began.

Jared's eyes grew accustomed to the darkness as he watched Cooper's lips, the words washing over him and Adrian in an uninterruptible torrent. "You don't understand," Cooper told them; "don't understand, or remember, or have the slightest idea what it was like before there was a state of Israel.

"I was born in 1908," he said, "in a poor, wooden house in Cracow's ancient ghetto. Yes—ghetto. My father was a fishmonger who pushed a wooden cart with heavy, solid wheels, for twelve hours a day. You should have seen his feet on winter days—toes so frozen my mother would massage them for an hour before he could feel anything. Sometimes he brought home money, sometimes he didn't. But we lived. Existed. Just like the other poor Jews. It was always cold in Poland. That's what I remember most, the cold. Bone-chilling cold and never enough coal or wood and me shivering to stay warm. Our lives were a constant series of escapes. From the tax collectors. Or the *goyim* who, if they caught you after they'd been drinking, would beat the hell out of you just because you were a hebe, a sheenie, a kike. Oh, how we prayed. We prayed every day to be in Jerusalem, we prayed every day to be left alone, and we prayed every day that our rich cousins in America would send us enough money so we could escape from Poland.

"Somehow, the dollars finally arrived. And in 1913, while the British and Germans were trying to come to a strategic accord and debated the numbers of battleships—something we, of course, never knew at the time—we sailed for the United States. We were among the lucky ones. We got out before the war. They changed my father's name at Ellis Island from Koplik to Koopler. My roots were severed with the stroke of some Mick immigration officer's pen. But what the hell—who needed roots? We were in America.

"We moved in with our rich cousins on Rivington Street on the Lower East Side. Rich—hah! That was a laugh. They were poorer than us. But we lived. We survived. Three rooms for nine people, and the toilet out in the hall, shared by twenty more. But only Jewish behinds sat on the seat. Back in those days there were a third of a million Jews living in two square miles on the Lower East Side. Nobody called me kike anymore, at least not in my neighborhood. I was a Jew in a Jewish city. My father found work in the fish markets. Worked all day up to his hips in ice, schlepping fish. He was still always cold. Me—I used to sit next to the stove and do my homework and thank God to be warm. I had it easy. I was going to be an American.

"My parents never learned English. They spoke Yiddish and prayed in Hebrew. They didn't need English. Then my father died, in 1923. I was fifteen and I never went back to school.

"I haven't told you this, Adrian, but it's something you should know. I worked for gangsters. That's how I made my living when I was fifteen. Running messages for gangsters who had a social club on Essex Street and took protection money from store owners."

Felix turned his back on them and walked out onto the small terrace, looking down onto the Old City walls.

"Oh, how we prayed in Cracow. Prayed to be allowed to see Jerusalem. The songs we sang. The prayers we offered. I forgot them for a while, but I've learned them again."

Felix turned back, his hands massaging the bridge of his nose. "Gangsters," he laughed. "The Kosher Nostra. I knew what they were doing. But I had sisters to support, dowries to earn. You do what you have to do to survive.

"History teaches us that. The Marranos, the secret Jews of Spain. They were forced by the Inquisition to convert—but they kept their faith behind closed doors. They survived. In Russia and Poland there were pogroms. We learned to live with them. To hide, to run away—and we survived. Even after the Romans burned the Second Temple and sold the Jews of Jerusalem into slavery we survived. In Yavneh, where the rabbis gathered and taught and kept the spark of Judaism alive. History teaches us, and by instinct I, too, did what I had to do, whatever was necessary.

"I won't bore you with details. Suffice it to say I made money. There was a world beyond the Lower East Side and I discovered it. I took care of family business—my sisters' dowries—they're all dead now, God rest their souls. I buried my mother next to my father. I was street-smart—the gangsters taught me well. And I saw the way the winds were blowing and changed my name to Felix Cooper because it was good for business. You know how it is. Behind every Robinson there's a Rabinowitz; meet a Manning and he turns out to be Mendelsman. I did it in self-defense. I became Felix Cooper, American.

"I worked hard at it, too. Lost my New York accent. Ate bacon and ham. Sent Christmas cards to my clients—religious ones with the Virgin Mary and the baby Jesus. I was more assimilated than you, Jared. And in the mid-thirties I met Grunwald. Werner Grunwald. Oh, he was a man with vision. I was making appliances then.

Irons, heaters, toasters. I sold them myself to small chains of stores in the Midwest and the South. I was on the road most of the time in those days—I learned about America. America wasn't the Lower East Side. It was filled with *goyim* who would have called me hebe if they'd known I was a Jew.

"I met Grunwald in Chicago—a chance meeting on a train. I couldn't afford to travel Pullman and he, he liked riding in coach. We rode back to New York together; talked the whole way.

"He was fascinating. He was just my age—we'd been born within a week of each other. But how different we were. He had charisma, the kind that comes from knowing exactly who you are. His name was never changed by any immigration agent, believe me. He was a man with a birthright—a man who could trace his roots back eight, nine, ten generations. He was so aggressive, so powerful. I remember he wore custom made gray double-breasted suits of hard worsted fabric; his tie had a university crest on it. His uncle had built the company—it was getting successful, beginning to compete with Telefunken and Grundig, making radios and other consumer electronics. But Werner was a dreamer. He believed that Grunwald should expand its market—make a foothold in America. So he'd learned English and come to study the American marketplace.

"It was 1934. Hitler was dreaming about the invasions of Austria and Czechoslovakia. Grunwald was already building military radios. Werner wasn't convinced about Hitler—not totally. But he was optimistic about the business environment Hitler encouraged. He loaned me fifty thousand dollars to expand Felco. To make not irons, but military equipment. He bought twenty percent of the company for his money. I was happy to give it to him. We did business together three years before he discovered I was Jewish. That came as a shock, believe me. But he was a pragmatist. He kept it quiet at home.

"No—don't interrupt. I know what you're going to ask—what about the German Jews? Didn't we know what Hitler had in store for them? Couldn't we see how bad it was going to get for them?

"If you think that you're wrong. There were rumblings. But no more. No pressure on Washington, no mass evacuations. You may not believe this, but between 1933 and 1939 only fifty thousand Jews left Germany. The Nuremberg Laws were passed in September 1935—German Jews lost their citizenship. Even then they didn't leave. So I myself had no idea what was going to happen. Did Werner? Maybe.

Who could tell. Frankly I didn't care. I was making more money than I'd ever dreamed. I met your mother—Beverly—and we got married. A civil ceremony—we didn't stand under the *chuppa* until five, six years later, when we were remarried by a rabbi because her parents insisted. I expanded my business. I began making photoelectric cells. Resistors. Other electronic equipment. I was well positioned for the war, believe me. And that was Werner's doing.

"He knew I was Jewish, although he kept it from his family. But he wasn't altruistic: we each had a stake. By 1938, after Czechoslovakia, we both realized there'd be a war, even though we—like most people then—chose to think America wouldn't become involved. I was pragmatic. If Germany won, then I'd have a new market. If it lost, then Werner had a toehold in America, a place to start fresh.

"You think that's immoral, don't you? You think what I did was evil, that I turned away from the truth. But I did what I had to do. I had responsibilities. And I did well for America during the war. Felco won six War Department citations for production excellence. Beverly and I were invited to the White House—two hundred of us on the lawn, receiving our citations. I felt like a real American. It was only afterward—in 1945—that I began to learn. Grunwald used slave labor. From Germany. From Poland. Erwin Haberman told me. Erwin Haberman. Before the war he was part of an operation that tried to send Jews to Palestine. *Ha'avara* they called it, the transfer agreement. Afterward, he joined the Jewish Agency. He sought me out, gave me the files on Grunwald—on the company that owned twenty percent of Felco. He knew exactly who I was, he'd done his homework, although God knows how he'd found out. He called me Yankel Koplik. A name I hadn't heard in more than thirty years. Koplik, he said, you're a Jew—although you certainly don't make much of a point about it—what are you going to do about this?

"What could I say? I told him I'd do what was necessary. I put pressure on Werner. Got him involved. Werner went to the DP camps. He had money—the family stashed much of its assets in Swiss banks before the war. Now Werner siphoned it back into Germany and used it to help Jews. So long as the Grunwalds helped, Erwin kept the authorities away from their door. Erwin told me what he wanted, I told Werner, and Werner got it done.

"Werner found you, you know? Found you in a camp—I don't even remember the number of the place—and you had no one. Both your natural parents dead. He wrote me how beautiful you were. Eyes as big as saucers even then. You were supposed to go to Palestine. But we brought you to America, Erwin and Werner and I.

"After the war, I sold the company to Werner. There was no challenge for me any more. The memories weren't good. You need good memories from your work and Felco held none for me. Not after I learned about Werner and his family and what they'd done to Jews—Polish Jews to whom I could have been related.

"Besides, it was Werner's more than it was mine. Electronics was his idea. You might not believe me but I liked making those irons and toasters. They were tinkerer's toys; I loved the road, the selling, the deals. So I sold out, and took the money and moved to Washington. There were deals to be made in Washington back then. Real money. And there was Israel. Israel needed friends back then. Needed money, political support. Needed people like me—realists.

"Do my Israeli friends know? You asked if they knew—Begin and Shamir and Sharon and even your pal from Washington, Yoram Gal. Yes, they all know. But they're not like you, Jared. They live in the real world. They understand that sometimes you have to do business with the devil in order to survive. Israel's survival is what's important. Because with Israel intact and strong, the long hunting season for Jews—that's what one writer called it just after the state of Israel was founded—the long hunting season for Jews is over. Nobody's going to call us hebes and sheenies and kikes anymore and not suffer for it. Never again."

Felix slumped into an armchair, exhausted. He wiped his eyes with the back of his hand. Adrian went to him. She kneeled by his side, weeping.

He put a hand to her cheek. "There's so much . . ."

Father and daughter embraced. Jared watched, wanting to say something but stunned into silence—an outsider. Damn Felix. Compared with Felix, Jared had grown up in a cocoon. No one had ever called him names. Hebe and sheenie and kike were words he'd read in books, not experienced personally. He'd taken his Jewishness for granted, accepted it without any thought of what it meant. He was a Jew. Okay. Big deal. "The long hunting season," Felix said. Jared had no comprehension of what the long hunting season might have been. His parents and both sets of grandparents had been born in America. His paternal great-grandparents had emigrated from Russia more than a century ago; on his mother's side they'd come even earlier. He didn't even know their names. It wasn't anything he had ever bothered to ask about, nor anything that had ever been explained.

Not until he'd come to work in Israel had he begun to read Jewish history and philosophy. Not until he woke up every morning and looked out on Mount Zion had he begun to feel a part of collective Jewry; sensed the historicity that bound him to his ancestors. And yet there was a gulf that separated him from Felix; a generational, emotional gap wide as the one that divided the Old World's Jews from the Israelis—the world's new Jews. Now, for the first time, he understood why Felix supported Israel, right or wrong. The reason Felix insisted on asking "Is it good or bad for the Jews?"

He watched as Felix and Adrian clung together. He'd misjudged the man—read him incorrectly. Felix was right, perhaps he didn't live in the real world.

Sometime later, Jared and Adrian took the long way home from the King David Hotel. Footfalls crunching, they walked without speaking, without the need to speak; arm in arm, their shoulders touching, they paced one-two-one-two along the Hativat 'Ezyoni, below the walls of the Armenian Quarter, staring up in silence at the silent stones. They crossed onto the Hebron Road, climbed Mishkenot Sha'annim's narrow paving-stone street and turned to look at Mount Zion in the darkness as the monastery bells tolled their hollow sound. They cut up the rough-hewn steps to the house in Yemin Moshe, locked themselves behind the security gate and wood door, fed the cat, then unmindful of its mewing they left it outside the bedroom door, peeled off their clothes, climbed into bed and clung to each other, mixing whispered conversation with kisses and tears.

That night, Adrian and Jared conceived a child.

PART

FIVE

April 1984

CHAPTER 21

It was a wet, cold winter, but a happy one. The doctor confirmed Adrian's pregnancy in January. They celebrated with a long weekend in Eilat where they pulled some strings and stayed in the same room they'd shared more than four years earlier. At home they splurged on two forced-air heaters for the cold bedroom that faced away from Mount Zion. Felix visited later in the month, bringing Beverly, who clucked and cooed and talked incessantly about how wonderful marriage was, while Jared and Adrian held hands and tried unsuccessfully to change the subject.

At the bureau, Jared kept a low profile, writing only what Jerry Atkins assigned. He visited the Israeli-controlled sector of Lebanon and interviewed IDF troops on their reaction to the impending American pullout from Beirut. He scoured the Knesset for one-liners denouncing Lebanese president Gemayel's renouncement of the May, 1983, peace accord between Lebanon and Israel. In his spare time he expanded his files on Jewish terror, meeting at irregular intervals with Shimon Levy. The problem was that there seemed to be less and less of a story. The Shin Bet, according to Shimon, was making progress investigating the Islamic University killings in Hebron, but the undercover agent gave Jared few new details. And if the agency had uncovered anything more about Moishe Halevi, he wasn't saying anything about it.

For her part, Adrian monitored Halevi as best she could. But, so far as she could tell, the American did nothing out of the ordinary.

He handled his job with efficiency; came and went on time. The accounts she had given Felix showed no new activity. And a team of independent auditors that visited Tel Aviv to check quietly on the books came up with nothing amiss. Adrian was puzzled. Jared counseled patience. Besides, he admired her ability as a quick study on the computer. A neophyte to bits, bytes, binary numbers, BASIC and Pascal, Adrian quickly turned into an accomplished hacker, adept at playing with a sophisticated system Jared found all but incomprehensible. She even talked of installing a terminal at Yemin Moshe so she could access the bank's computer without having to make the drive to Tel Aviv, but decided against it after the local IBM representative explained that the security level wouldn't be adequate because she'd be using public phone lines.

Their lives settled back into a comfortable routine. They spent their weekends in the Old City, or drove to the West Bank where they bought antique terra cotta Arab olive jars and a hundred-year-old wooden plough, which Jared painstakingly mounted on their living-room wall. They spent a weekend in Zefat, venturing down to the dude ranch at Vered Hagalil, where they rode horses along well-used trails. Even though he was on probation, Jared began to find his job tolerable. Without the bureau chief's responsibilities he worked only an eight-hour day; had more time for Adrian.

By mid-March the weather began to change for the better. Jared exchanged his *dubon* for a sweater and sportcoat. Soon the three hundred thousand tulips from the government of Holland would blossom and their plots, in Jerusalem's parks and along the walls of the Old City, would come alive with color.

Jared sat in his office, his feet on the desk and the keyboard of the Kaypro on his lap. He had just come back from lunch with one of the few Mossad operatives who still spoke to him, having tried—unsuccessfully—to pump the man for information about the three Moslem gunmen who the day before had kidnapped a political officer, William Buckley, from the U.S. Embassy in Beirut as he left his apartment in the Western section of the ruined city.

He was spell-checking the memo when Adrian burst into his office. "Moishe's gone," she sputtered breathlessly. "He's disappeared. Cleaned out his desk. I tried calling his flat, but there was no answer."

"Damn." Jared smacked his palm against the desk. "Does Felix know?"

"I called him from the bank as soon as I found out."

"What did he say?"

"He says he'll make some inquiries."

"What about the accounts Moishe handled?"

She plopped herself onto a straight-back chair. "I don't know. I didn't check—"

"Can you go back and run through the computer?"

"J.P., it's an hour's drive to Tel Aviv, and the traffic's horrible."

"It's important."

She sighed. "I guess so, then."

He snatched his sportcoat from where it hung on the door. "I'll go down to Qiryat Arba."

"But why?"

"It's time to let Shimon know about Moishe. Maybe Shin Bet can do some spadework. Look, you go back to the bank. I'll see you at the house later."

When she hadn't arrived at home by nine, Jared called her private line. "What's going on?"

"It's all screwed up."

"What?"

"The computer. Everything. I can't get access to Moishe's files."

"All of them?"

"No, just a couple. But they have to be, you know, special ones. You know what I'm talking about." There was a pause on the line. "J.P.—come take a look. There's something terribly wrong."

Forty-five minutes later she let him in in her stockinged feet, carefully closing the glass doors of the bank's executive offices on the building's second floor, locking them, and turning the security system back on before she led Jared down a carpeted hallway into her office.

It looked like a war zone. Lined computer printouts lay strewn on the floor. Legal files, opened, were stacked in piles. Adrian wheeled an ergonomic chair to where her computer terminal sat on its customized stand. Jared plunked himself down and watched as Adrian hit a series of keys. She worked quickly and efficiently, her toes wrapped in a prehensile grasp around the footrest bar underneath the terminal table.

"Now—look."

"What?" Jared stared at the screen.

"See, where the cursor is." She pointed at the top line. The name of the account and the column where numbers should have appeared at the top of the electronic spreadsheet were blanked out. "I can't bring anything up."

"Why not?"

"I don't have the access code. The password. Look—" She hit another series of keys and one spreadsheet was replaced by another, also blanked out. "You remember the account we opened for the Phalange?"

He nodded.

"Okay. Now to open the file—" The screen went blank. A line of electronic type appeared: ENTER ACCESS CODE, followed by a row of X's. She hit seven keys, and the blank spaces were replaced by names, addresses, financial information and neat columns of figures.

"See? And to follow the transactions, I hit this . . ."

He watched as the screen changed and a series of names and numbers scrolled past his eyes. "What are those?"

"The checks they've written. The deposits they've made. Okay—I'm supposed to be able to monitor any account. I keep the list of access codes in my safe. But now, here's one I'm positive Moishe handled. It's got his codes and annotations, but I can't get into it. And he's gone." She tapped at the keyboard and the screen went blank.

He shrugged. "So?"

"I don't know what to do. Maybe if I played with it." She stretched. "Boy, I'm tired. Did you find out anything from Shimon?"

He shook his head. "Shimon's mad."

"Mad?"

"He says I should have told him about Moishe three months ago."

"Is he right?"

"Probably. But we decided to keep it quiet, remember?"

Adrian nodded. "There's got to be a way to break the code."

"Tell me about it." He put a hand on her shoulder. "Come on, Onion—we're out of our depth. Let's go home."

She shrugged him away. "No, not yet. There's a way, J.P. There's got to be a way inside."

"But it could take weeks."

"Maybe. But it could also take an hour or less."

"Look," he said, "you do what you want. I'm exhausted."

She pointed at the couch across the room. "So lie down."

He stroked her neck. "I'd rather go home."

"Not yet, J.P. I want to work on this. I'm the managing director, dammit. Nobody's supposed to have any secrets from me. You go close your eyes for a few minutes. I promise—we'll leave soon."

Jared swept the piles of papers off the couch, rolled his jacket into a pillow, and lay down, covering his eyes with a forearm. "Wake me when you get tired." She grunted in response.

He was walking through the Old City with Adrian. She was eight months' pregnant and they were striding in one-two-one-two lockstep unison, unmindful of tourists and vendors and young Arabs bearing tarnished brass trays of sweet mint tea. They were on their way to Shahin for kebab and salad. Except they couldn't find the restaurant. The streets they knew so well had turned into a maze. Finally, in desperation, they walked into a courtyard in the Jewish Quarter to ask directions and discovered Yoram, the big dog Othello at his side, playing backgammon with the little one-eyed man from Martef Hashoah. *The wooden board was set atop a display table filled with War Department citations and sections of barbed wire. Felix sat in the corner crunching ice cubes between his teeth and speaking German. Yoram unrolled a Torah scroll and gave them a map, which they followed. Up the alley, down the stairs, across the Temple Mount, past a roadblock manned by Koby One, Yom Tov and Sergeant Yossi, where a green Datsun smoldered—and all of a sudden, right next to a mobile home where Shoshanna stood, a rifle at port arms, there was Shahin. Fuad the owner stood waiting for them, wearing a red, green and black* keffiyah *and holding a Molotov cocktail. He bowed, said,* "Ahlan W'asahlan," *beckoned them to enter and opened the door. They walked into the bloody classroom at the Islamic University of Hebron, face to face with Moishe Halevi, dressed in an academic robe and crimson Harvard hood, a mortarboard on his head, armed with an AK-47, and smiling. Adrian screamed and screamed and screamed his name and threw computer paper at Moishe. He fell on top of her and tried to wrestle the rifle from Moishe, who pulled and tugged and tore at his jacket sleeve.*

He opened his eyes to find Adrian shaking him.

"You're not—" she was screaming. Jared sprang to his feet, still not awake, and took her hands in his.

"What is it?"

"I—it was just a joke—didn't mean to—you—" She made a conscious effort to calm herself, then took a deep breath and pointed at the computer terminal.

Jared tried to rub the sleep from his eyes. He walked across the office and peered at the screen. Rows of incomprehensible figures peered back at him. "What is it?"

"Account."

"The one you were trying to access?"

She shook her head. "Yes—no—another. I was just playing around. I—"

"You got in—terrific. That's wonderful. How did you do it?" Then he turned and saw she was crying. He went to her. "Onion—what is it? What's wrong?"

She shook her head, unable to speak.

"Adrian—"

"Access," she garbled. "Access code."

"What about access code?"

Tears running down her cheeks, Adrian sat down again at the computer. She erased the screen and brought back the blanked-out spreadsheet. The cursor blinked, a dot of green light on the black tube. She pecked at the keyboard. Instructions came up: "ENTER ACCESS CODE" and a row of X's.

She typed six letters, and the screen came alive with figures. The letters she had typed were KOPLIK.

"Oh, God," she said. "Don't you see? I was just playing around, and it's Felix's name. It's Felix's code." Then she fainted.

CHAPTER

They made printouts and took them back to Jerusalem, Jared driving the wide, rolling highway at high speed in stunned silence, Adrian slumped against the opposite window. There was no doubt: the bank was a conduit for money flowing to a secret organization—probably a Jewish terror group, perhaps even TNT itself. Tearfully, Adrian had dredged up the information bit by bit, following the paperless train of deposits made at Eagle Intercontinental branches in New York and Los Angeles—more than one hundred and sixty thousand dollars in all—and followed them through a maze of electronic transfers snaking through off-shore corporations in the Bahamas and trust accounts in London. It was a trail designed to mislead and bypass the bank's usual logging processes. Moishe—or whoever—had designed it well. It took her some hours to decipher the complex system. But when she did, the pieces added up together—damning, overwhelming evidence.

The numbers were not huge compared to the more than fifty million dollars the bank had invested in Israeli industry. But it was there, inescapably, an account that could not be accessed or examined. It didn't exist; appeared on no balance sheets or accounting statements; and could be monitored only by someone who knew the password: Koplik.

Jared's knuckles were white on the Autobianchi's steering wheel. Adrian hugged the sheaf of papers to her stomach. Just past the Latrun salient they began to climb into the foothills, the night air turning clean and cool. They'd be approaching the memorials now—primer-painted skeletons of armored cars and trucks that sat above the road, grim relics, silent reminders of the convoys that had braved Arab ambushes during the War of Independence.

There were hundreds of similar sites throughout the country. Burnt-out tanks and armored personnel carriers from the 1967 and 1973 wars sat along roadsides. Fragments of planes, flowers carefully planted next to them, served as living memorials for pilots who had died defending Israel. On the highway from Tel Aviv to Haifa a rotting black-and-white wooden boat not much bigger than a Boston Whaler sat on an embankment above the east side of the road just south of Herzlyia, evidence of the days when Jews risked their lives to run the British blockade and settle in their ancient homeland. Shrines of recent history alongside shrines pilgrims had traveled to for centuries.

What purpose did they serve? Jared thought about it. To link past and present, perhaps. To teach lessons. To instruct. To remind. The act of reminding was an integral part of the Jewish state. Indeed, Israel was a state bound up in its own history. For centuries, Jews were, as Adrian called them, history's orphans. They lived outside history; outside the mainstream of society—although they affected that mainstream wherever they touched it. But the Jews had always been forced to create their own history. Look at the Age of Enlightenment. Enlightened for whom? Not the Jews, certainly. Voltaire? Goethe? Diderot? All anti-Semites. What did they teach? The bottom line was that they'd discovered it was possible to be enlightened and still hate Jews. Only with the creation of Israel had Jews finally brought themselves back into the mainstream of history. And so they created shrines to connect themselves to that history.

Did they teach lessons, those shrines? . . . that evidence? He downshifted, gathering speed as the road climbed up toward Jerusalem, the car's engine straining with the effort. The Autobianchi's headlights picked up the road signs; new names and old flashed by as Jared floored the accelerator: Zomet Shoresh; Qiryat Ye'arim; Abu Gosh; Yad Ha-Shemona. Old names and new names. A merging of past with present. On the horizon, the dark sky began to tinge with light, black turning to purple above the ragged silhouettes of evergreens and the rough Judean hills.

Did they teach lessons, those shrines? Israelis believed so. The country was a nation of amateur historians and archaeologists. Despite internal dissension, the memorials, the cemeteries, the shrines would all be filled on Memorial Day, on Independence Day. Tourists thought so, too. The buses would pass the skeletons, the fragments, the relics, and pictures would be snapped. Evidence of Israel's birth and survival for the scrapbooks at home—tangible reminders of the Jewish homeland. Other pictures, too: Jews somber at the Holocaust memorial; pensive beside a remnant of an Israeli Mirage; eager, happy faces smiling as they stood alongside charred Syrian armor. Tanks for the memories.

Oh, lessons could be learned. From the stones of the city of David. From Yad Vashem. From the *Martef* where urns contained the ashes of Jews turned to ashes by the Nazis. From the Western Wall, where all Jews could confront their history, their historicity. From the two-thousand-year-old vineyards where Koby Naiderman planted his Carignan grapes. From the stark, prehistoric peaks in Sinai where the Unnameable Name forged and tempered His people on an anvil of hot stone.

And yet it was . . . was . . . mystifying to Jared how the same people who had established the code of ethics that formed the basis of Western civilization, who had finally brought themselves back into history's mainstream, could reject history by accepting fundamentalism and terror. Not that Jewish terror could be equated with Arab terror—it could not. But it was accepted. Accepted by American Jews who gave money to organizations that condoned violence against Arabs. Accepted by Israeli reporters who turned their backs and censored themselves when it came to exposing the cancerous growth of TNT and the fundamentalist religious groups. Accepted by the silence of American Jews. Jared knew: in Jewish tradition, silence is akin to approval.

How could Felix have done it? What perverted sense of fundamentalism, of . . . Jared couldn't come up with a word to describe it . . . had convinced Felix to channel money to a group whose values contradicted virtually everything in the Torah and its commentaries. What—

Adrian stirred. "I would have helped him."

"What?"

"I would have helped him. If he'd trusted me, if he'd told me."

"Helped him?"

She shook the papers and dropped them in her lap. "With this. Not that it's right, but as a daughter I would have."

"How could you?"

Her tears came again. "Because he's my father, dammit." She sat silent for some time, her shoulders heaving. "But—you see—now . . ."

He waited.

"Oh, God," she said. "It's like that moment in Rome all over again. That instant in Erwin Haberman's living room when I discovered I was . . . all alone. God dammit, Jared, he's orphaned me again. Cut me out. Left me by myself."

He glanced at her. His hand slid from the gearshift to her hand and clenched it tightly. "You're not alone this time, Onion. This time you have me. You have the baby."

She nodded. "I know." She sat back, one hand clutched around the seat belt that ran across her chest, the other holding onto Jared for dear life. "What are we going to do?"

He shook his head. "I don't know. But we have to do something."

They'd crested the last of the hills now and in the early-morning half-light Jerusalem lay before them clean and bright. The jewel in God's crown. They slowed at the police roadblock until the officer saw Jared's Foreign Press sticker and motioned them through with a smile and a good morning wave.

"It could ruin the bank. Ruin him."

He kept his eyes on the road. "I know."

"Jared—"

"You've seen the files. You've seen my files. This thing is coming together. What am I supposed to do? Come on, Adrian—we've got to let the chips fall. We can't be silent. It's not right to be silent."

"What if it was your father, Jared?"

He sighed. She was right. To implicate Felix would be to betray Adrian. And yet not to implicate him would be to betray himself and everything he stood for; to do those same things he castigated others for doing. And yet he'd done it before: traded some stories for others—with Yoram, with Nathan Yaari, and with other sources.

But somehow this was different. Before, he'd always censored himself in exchange for something better. This time he would be giving up a crucial element for—what? For silence. For Adrian. It violated every value he felt important.

The city was sunlit now. Streets beginning to come to life. Jared took the long way home. He drove down the Agrippas, along the southern edge of the Mahane Yehuda, moving at a crawl as he watched the shopkeepers throwing open their metal security grates and getting ready for the day's business. He swung south on King George until it intersected Keren Hayesod, then swerved left across Plummer Square and drove around Mishkennot Sha'annim. He parked by a low wall and turned off the ignition. But neither of them moved.

"The problem is there's no one to talk to," he finally said. "I can't call Roger Richards. I don't want to go to Shin Bet, so Nathan and Shimon are out of the question. But—damn it, Adrian, the bank's *involved*. And if I'm ever going to get off probation I've got to be able to prove that what I wrote last year about Jewish terror's correct. But I've got nowhere to go."

He rolled up his window, unlatched his seat belt and stepped outside the car, locking the door behind him. He held Adrian's door for her, then locked it, too. They stood facing the Old City across the valley, silent as the bright sun, risen, began to bleach the roofs of houses. The air was clean, the sky a flawless azure. In the distance they could make out the Old City minaret called David's Tower in the guidebooks. Adrian perched on the wall, clutching the printouts. She looked down. "I wish I'd never done these. Maybe it would be better just to destroy them, Jared."

He stood silent, thinking. About himself, about Adrian, about their unborn child, about the values he wanted to instill in it. Jewish values.

"I mean," she said, "with these or without, there's a story. Oh, dammit, J.P., I hate Felix for this—I do. I hate him for getting involved, for whatever reasons he got involved. And I hate him for hiding it from me. But for God's sake, he's my father—I can't see him destroyed, I can't. It would kill me, too."

He looked at her. He loved her, that he knew. But until that moment, he'd not known how much. He took the papers from her hands and flipped through them. Figures flicked before his eyes. Evidence: damning and overwhelming. He looked up, looked at her, and Mount Zion. The bells tolled. He said, "We'll burn them."

"Oh, J.P.—"

"I'll get the story," he said. "I know I'll get it anyway—it's only a matter of time. And your father . . ." He paused. "Your father's the one who's going to have to live with himself, with this. Sooner or later he's going to discover we've seen his files, we know his secret—it's a sword we're holding over his head."

"Discover? How?"

"I don't know—maybe we'll tell him, some day. Maybe there's something in the computer that logs its use—maybe there's another security system you didn't find. But he'll find out—and he'll try to get even."

"He wouldn't, he couldn't," she said. "You're wrong, Jared. He's my father. He loves me."

"He's a survivor," Jared said. "He's always done what he has to do to survive. That's not going to change."

"You're wrong. I know you're wrong," she said.

He kissed her. "In my heart of hearts, I hope I am," he said. "Let's go home."

The call came unexpectedly, shortly after one in the morning. The incriminating ashes were cold, covered with an inch of water in the metal trash can that sat in the gully behind the house. He answered the phone on the second ring, cupping the mouthpiece in the darkness so as not to awaken Adrian, who groaned softly and reached for him. He tucked her arm under her chin, rolled to his left and sat on the edge of the bed.

"Hello?"

A woman's voice said, "Jared Paul Gordon?"

"Yes?"

"Do you remember where you and the general first talked about TNT?"

"Huh?" Jared struggled to clear his head.

"You and the general. TNT. Do you remember?"

He thought, then remembered. "Yes—at—"

"Say nothing now," the woman's voice interrupted. "Just be there in an hour." The phone went dead.

Jared rubbed his face with both hands. Adrian stirred, half asleep. "Who was that?"

He leaned over and kissed her neck. "Somebody." He rubbed her back. "I have to go out."

She came awake. "Now? It's so late!"

He caressed her. "I know. I know. Go back to sleep. I'll probably be home by the time you wake up."

He dressed hurriedly, pulled a knit cap on, grabbed his parka from the hall closet and started down the stairs. Halfway to the door he stopped. Climbing back to the living room he went to his desk and took a minicassette recorder from the second drawer, checked the battery level, slipped a fresh tape inside, and dropped it into the breast pocket of his parka.

He locked the outside doors of the house, scampered up the cut-stone steps to the Autobianchi, checked underneath the car, and then climbed inside. Without lights, he U-turned and drove off, up the hill toward the Tel Aviv highway.

The road was empty. From the darkened gas station at Lifta until he reached the Ben-Gurion Airport turnoff, Jared didn't see another car. If anyone was following him, he decided, they were doing it without lights. Just to be safe, he took the highway into Tel Aviv instead of heading north at the Gannot interchange, cutting back and forth on a series of one-way streets until he reached Ben Yehuda. Then he swung north again, drove through Old Tel Aviv, past darkened restaurants and nightclubs. He swung east, then north, skirting Sede Dov airport.

He circled Tel Aviv University, drove west on Rehov Einstein as if heading toward the sea. Then abruptly he pulled over and parked at a corner where he could see anyone who approached from either direction, turned his lights off, and waited five minutes. There was no one on his tail. He turned the ignition, popped the car into gear without turning his lights back on, screeched around the corner onto the Haifa Road and floored the accelerator. At Herzlyia he crossed the highway against the light and drove west, circling through streets where half-built villas stood skeletonlike in the darkness. On Rehov Kedoshai Hashoah he parked, waiting out a large dog behind a heavy iron gate who began barking. He reached inside his breast pocket as if fumbling for keys, and turned on the tape machine. He'd do nothing suspicious where he could be observed. He had an hour's worth of recording time. Then he locked the car and, shoulders hunched against the wind, walked down the narrow street toward the Daniel Tower Hotel.

At the hotel he turned south, crossed the four-lane street, and found a gate house. He pushed on the rusted, spiked gate; it opened creakily. Carefully, in the darkness, he started down a set of concrete steps that led toward the beach, his footfalls masked by the sound of the surf.

At the bottom he turned and scrunched across damp sand. There was a fine mist in the air and the scent of the sea, and he pulled the parka zipper up under his chin. Ahead, in the hazy moonlight, he could make out two shadowy figures hunkered at Daboush's deserted tables. He waved.

Nathan Yaari stood up. "We'd almost given up hope."

Yoram Gal rose, the huge dog, Othello, muzzled at his thigh. Jared took Nathan's hand, then Yoram's. He reached down and ruffled Othello behind the ears. "Nathan. Yoram. What's up?"

Yoram Gal motioned to Jarad to sit. "There's been a break in the case against TNT," the general said.

"Terrific." Jared edged closer. He sat with both elbows on the table. "How? What?"

The Israelis glanced at each other. Jared waited.

Nathan Yaari stretched and yawned. "We've got an informer," he finally said. "A guy—a reserve officer—whom Yoram tracked down. We put pressure on him and he went to work for us."

"What kind of pressure?"

"That's not important. Thing is, he's been convinced to give us names and dates—specifics. The things we've never had before."

"So why do you need me? You've solved the case. Go arrest the sons of bitches."

"We can't. Some of the higher-ups in the Prime Minister's office say it's too political. There'd be an uproar in the settlements. These aren't PLO terrorists or Arabs from Nablus, Jared. We're talking about heavy people."

"Like who?"

"Like Moshe Levinger's son-in-law, Uzi Sharabaf. He was one of the gunmen at the Islamic University in Hebron. Like Menachem Livni, the guy whose card you found. He's a battalion commander in the reserves. He did more than participate in the Hebron raid. He organized it. There are more than a dozen of them in all. We're talking about the elite of the settlers' movement."

Jared whistled. "Political dynamite."

The Shin Bet agent nodded. "It could tear the country apart. Think of what it does to the Army—field officers as part of the Jewish terror movement." He shook his head sadly.

Yoram lighted a cigarette and inhaled deeply. "The Prime Minister's office is against arrest and prosecution. Their argument is that these guys are basically patriots—misguided patriots but loyal Zionists nonetheless. So instead of arresting them, it would be more, ah, positive, to put quiet pressure on them to stop killing Arabs."

"Look, Jared," said Nathan, "Shamir's in bed with the ultranationalists. He's supported by the religious right. He can't offend settlement leaders like Moshe Levinger or Elyakim Ha'etzni or the guys who run Gush Emunim. Because if he did—if he came out strongly against Jewish terror—the National Religious Party and one or two others would defect from the coalition, and Shamir would be left holding his limp you-know-what in his hand."

"The people who run this country are more worried about keeping political power than whether some West Bank Arabs get blown away," said Yoram.

"So we've been told to lay off," said Yaari. "The word's come down from on high: do nothing unless TNT does something so outrageous that even Shamir can't ignore it."

"Oh, Christ."

"Hey—it's the truth. Look, Jared, I put my job on the line when I told you about Begin's interference in our investigations. Look where it got me—"

"Look where it got *me,*" said Jared.

"Okay, okay—Begin screwed you. The Prime Minister's office cooked the records. But now . . . this—"

Yoram interrupted. "We have to get something into your magazine. Except for a few scattered stories the Hebrew press won't touch the issue. Besides, even if it tried, it would be censored. But if it's published outside Israel—then *Maariv* and *Yediot* and *Davar* and the rest of the newspapers would have to follow up. It could cause the government to collapse. It would be good for Israel, Jared."

"Good—bad—that's not my concern," Jared said. "Besides, what the hell can I do? As usual—there's no documentation. I have no papers, nothing. I can't publish a damn thing without evidence. And my damn bureau chief won't look at a Jewish terror story. I couldn't even get an eyewitnesser from Hebron into the magazine."

"There's more," Yoram said.

"What?"

The two Israelis glanced at each other nervously. Jared put his elbows on the table and leaned toward them. "Come on," he said. "Tell me what the hell is going on."

"A decision has been made. A political decision."

"You said that."

"No." Othello laid his head on Yoram's lap, and the general stroked the dog's neck gently. "A different decision."

"What?"

Nathan Yaari took a deep breath. "We know what Livni and the rest of them are planning. We know what, and when, and where, and how."

"And?"

"And the decision's been made to let them do it and then make the arrests."

Jared sat up straight. "What's their plan?"

"They're going to bomb the central bus station in East Jerusalem next weekend."

"What?!"

"It's the truth. At the height of rush hour. A minimum of five bombs on the buses."

"That could kill hundreds of people!"

"Easily," said Yoram. He threw his cigarette toward the water, watching it arc onto the sand.

"That's horrible. That's murder—with government complicity."

Nathan Yaari nodded. "Precisely. But the logic is that once TNT has acted, once they've committed wholesale murder, we can go in and arrest them because they'll lose public support."

"It's insane. All those people killed."

Yoram shrugged. "People? They're only Arabs. That's how the government thinks these days."

"Can you prove you've been ordered to let them commit murder? Is there any evidence?"

Nathan Yaari shook his head. "Nothing. All our discussions have been verbal. These guys are too smart to leave a paper trail."

"So what the hell do you want from me? To publish another 'leak'?" Jared slammed the table with his hand. " 'Israeli intelligence sources say . . .' " He shook his head. "I can't do that, Yoram. The last time I took you at your word I was nearly fired. So was Nathan. I'm not going to risk my career again."

"We owe you, boychik," Yoram said.

"You gave us the wedge that opened the door," Yaari added. "You gave us Menachem Livni's identity card. You didn't have to do it."

"And we didn't have to do this," Yoram said. "But fair's fair. What was it you and Nathan said? Quid pro quo. Here's the quo." He dug into the pocket of his windbreaker and retrieved a fat envelope. "Maybe this will help."

Jared took it and tore the end off. Inside were six sheets of paper, each with the date stamp of the Prime Minister's office embossed into the paper. "What is it?"

"Three days ago there was a debate about the Shin Bet's findings during a cabinet meeting. Even though nothing specific about the bombings was mentioned, the gist of the conversation substantiates what Nathan's told you. These are the original minutes of the pertinent portion of that debate. Each page is signed by the Cabinet Secretary and stamped by the Prime Minister's confidential secretary."

"Good God."

"They're yours," said Yoram. "A gift. I'd suggest you get them out of the country as soon as you can."

Jared's mind was spinning. It was possible that he could bring down the government. It was at least a lead story—perhaps even a cover. It could mean the end of his probation—the end of Jerry Atkins in Jerusalem. He hefted the envelope and stuffed it inside his parka. "I'll get on this tomorrow."

"You don't have much time," said the Shin Bet agent.

Jared looked at the two Israelis. "This could be dangerous for you."

"We'll take our chances," said Nathan.

Yoram stroked the dog. "You do whatever you have to do."

Jared stared at the general. "Are you sure?"

Yoram returned Jared's gaze evenly. "Whatever you have to do, boychik."

Nathan stood up. "I've got to be going," he said. "See you in print, Jared."

The American waved and watched as Yaari trudged across the sand and up the steps. Yoram pulled a cigarette from his pocket and offered it to Jared. He unmuzzled Othello, who sniffed Jared's hand, put his paws on the reporter's knees and licked his ear. Cigarette clenched in his teeth, Jared ruffled the dog's neck.

"Let's take a walk," Yoram said. He rose and stretched, lit Jared's cigarette and started north, the dog at his thigh.

"We want this story out," he said.

"I'll bet you do."

"Israel's been taking it in the press," Yoram said. "The American networks jumped all over us in Lebanon—for the most part unjustifiably. And now, with the Marines gone from Beirut and Syria taking control up there we're being blamed for a lot. It doesn't do us much good, Jared."

"I understand."

"I wonder if you do."

"Huh?"

"You're sophisticated, Jared. You speak Hebrew. You've got good sources here—including me." Yoram laughed. "But you still tend to see things like any other American."

"How's that, Yoram?"

"Idealistically. To you American Jews Israel is a state of mind. The problem is—we're not."

"I know that."

"I'm not so sure. For you it's all black and white, boychik. You're like an adolescent in your mood swings. First you loved us because we made the deserts bloom and beat the crap out of the Arabs at twenty-to-one odds. Now you hate us because the country's moving away from your idealized concept of what Israel should be. But it's not your country, Jared—it's mine."

"What're you getting at?"

"I'm trying to tell you to be flexible. To remember that Israel isn't a state of mind. It's a state, period. Take Jewish terror. It's a good story for you. And, ultimately, it's good for Israel to crack down on these bastards. They're not helping us preserve the Jewish state—they're tearing it down the middle. If we allow this government to get its way here, Israel would suffer. We'd suffer in your Congress, where we've got a four-billion-dollar aid package sitting in committee. So it's good for us when you publish. The Americans see we're cleaning our own nest, and the money comes in. We'd suffer in world opinion, too, although that doesn't mean anything."

"You can't be serious."

"But I am." Yoram gestured out to sea. "*They* won't like us—the rest of the world. So what? The fact is that *they've* never liked us. Jews. *Yehudim.* To most of the world we're still kikes—outsiders.

"In the long term, Jared, Jewish terror doesn't mean a goddam thing. We'll survive Jewish terror and our own Nazis like Kahane, because we've always survived our zealots. Painfully, sometimes, but we've survived."

Jared followed at Yoram's side, the envelope tucked inside his parka, uncertain where the general was leading. He was anxious to get back to Jerusalem, to go through the material, to show Adrian that the story was going to come out despite what they'd done earlier.

"That's the important thing—to survive. Israel as a reality is important, Jared. The survival of the state itself. Because Israel exists, Jews all over the world feel safer. So your story about TNT doesn't really matter."

"But—" Jared was confused.

"It matters to you, professionally. And it satisfies your reporter's sense of outrage. And in the long run, I'm happy to see it published because it helps the state of Israel survive. Look—we have different agendas, you and I. Today they run parallel. So we help each other—and I'm happy to do it." The general ruffled Othello behind the ears. "But you have to be careful. You have to temper your outrage, Jared. You can't publish everything you know."

"Everything?"

"If certain facts were to come out, it would be bad for Israel's survival."

Jared stopped, and planted his feet. The dog sensed a change in him and looked up, its snout nuzzling Jared's dangling hand.

"Speak more plainly, Yoram."

"I will." Before Jared had time to react, the Israeli had run his hands along the front of Jared's parka. Instinctively, Jared reached for the pocket where the tape recorder sat. With lightning speed Yoram knocked his hand away, reached inside and extracted the recorder. He turned it off.

"Goddammit, Yoram—" Jared tried to snatch it out of Yoram's hand; he got the Israeli's shoving palm on his chest in return. It was not a hard blow but it landed Jared on his rump on the sand.

He scrambled to his feet and launched himself at Yoram. "For chrissakes—"

Yoram sidestepped, twisted, and caught the American's feet with his leg. Jared went sprawling again. The dog barked and growled. Yoram snapped his fingers and Othello sat in place, staring at Jared. "Just stay where you are," Yoram ordered.

Breathless and furious, Jared obeyed. He watched Othello watch him.

The Israeli examined the machine. Then he extended his hand and pulled Jared off the sand, and with a flourish handed the recorder back.

"Don't worry, boychik, I'm not going to erase your precious tape."

"Then why—?"

"I don't give a shit about what you and Nathan and I said to each other. But this is private."

"What is?" Christ, the man had been quick.

Yoram plucked a cigarette from his pocket and lit it. He slapped his thigh and the dog rose off its haunches, stood and yawned. "There's been a breach of security at Eagle Intercontinental."

Jared's face flushed. He hoped the Israeli couldn't see it. His pulse began to race. "I don't understand what you're getting at."

Yoram flicked cigarette ash toward the surf. His tone was ominous. "Don't lie to me, Jared."

"Lie?"

"Let's just say that all computers have security systems, okay?"

"What the hell are you getting at?"

"Israel," the general said. "The survival of the state of Israel." He blew smoke through his nose. "You have to understand things, Jared."

"Such as?"

Yoram shook his head. "You haven't been listening, have you? Go write the Jewish terror story. But leave Felix out of it. Leave the bank out of it. We've given you more than enough evidence—a smoking gun even. I told you, Israel will survive Jewish terror. It's just a phase we're going through. It'll pass. But Felix . . ."

"What about Felix?"

"Felix is good for Israel, boychik. I don't give a shit about his motives. Guilt, whatever—they don't matter. But he's well-known. He has access. To your President, to important people. He represents American Jewry—represents American popular support for Israel. We can't lose that support—not for your story, not for anything."

"I'm not confirming anything you say," Jared said. "But for argument's sake let's say I had something. So what? There are others like Felix." Jared extracted the envelope from his pocket and shook it in Yoram's direction. "Why the hell are we playing games, huh? Screw it, Yoram—the man's supporting the same people you want me to incriminate."

"They don't count. He does."

"That doesn't make sense."

The Israeli sighed. "Don't look for logic here, Jared. Don't make this harder on me than it already is."

"Harder?"

"Remember Syria, boychik? I told you then—and I'll tell you again—that sometimes we do things we don't like to do. Except they're necessary. I don't follow orders blindly. In fact, I was brought up to question orders. But if it's important—" Yoram paused and looked out to sea. When he turned back to the American there was sadness in his eyes.

"Leave Felix out of it," he said. "It could get dangerous if you don't."

Jared was incredulous. "You're threatening me—I don't believe it."

"I'm not making threats. I'm telling you the truth."

Jared kicked at the sand. Fists clenched, he looked at Yoram—the soldier, friend . . . stranger. He'd already burned the printouts, eliminated Felix from the story—except Yoram didn't know that. Yoram hadn't trusted him enough to make the right decision. "The truth?" he asked. "What the hell is the truth, Yoram?"

"You have a woman who loves you. You're expecting a child. Things are more complex now than they were before. You don't want complications, Jared. An easy pregnancy. A healthy birth. A good baby. Think about it. Things can . . . happen. That's the truth."

"You bastard. You *ben-zona*. Leave Adrian out of it, goddammit. This is between you and me."

"And that's the way I want to leave it. Believe me, Jared, telling you these things doesn't give me any joy. But we have to understand each other."

Jared stared at Yoram. "I understand you."

The Israeli's face was a mask. He took the envelope from Jared's hand and stuffed it back inside the American's parka. "Go," he said. "Write your story." He snapped his fingers and turned, scrunching off on the sand, the big dog at his side.

Without looking back he raised his hand and waved at Jared. "Bye-bye, boychik. Be careful."

Jared watched them go. It was chilly now and an early-morning mist had begun to cover the beach, a haze of fog into which Yoram and Othello disappeared.

Yoram—goddamn him. He knew the threat was safe with Jared; knew Jared was incapable of ever sharing this particular secret with Adrian. Yoram knew—knew he loved her too much ever to tell her. "Goddamn you, Yoram," Jared screamed into the darkness. "Goddamn you to hell you sonofabitch." He turned and walked south, tears in his eyes.

Yoram was right. He was a naïf when it came to Israel. Yoram was right. Israel wasn't a state of mind, the idealized Jewish homeland envisioned by American Jews. He'd known that all along; looked cynically at the tour buses and their tagged occupants as they visited Potemkin Village Israel. But it went deeper than that.

Once, perhaps, there had been an ideal, an idea, about a Jewish state. Herzl had it. So did Weizmann. Then came Ben-Gurion, Polish-born Palestinian Jew, to whom the elder Zionist Weizmann represented Old World Jewry—the Diaspora. Ben-Gurion had even refused to let Weizmann sign Israel's Declaration of Independence. Now, Ben-Gurion's values had been transmogrified by a whole new generation of Jews. These new Jews—Jews like Yoram and Nathan Yaari, Jews like Moshe Levinger, Jews like the Orientals who lived in Bet Shemesh and Afula—they had changed Israel, too. It didn't matter whether it was for better or for worse. The fact was that they'd changed it into their own kind of state. And unless he was going to stay and fight them on their own turf, he couldn't do a damn thing about what they'd done—what they were doing.

He climbed the concrete steps, patting the bulges in his parka where the tape recorder and envelope sat secure. He walked to his car, unlocked it, and sat inside, thinking about what to do next.

It was half an hour before he turned the ignition and started the long climb back to Jerusalem.

CHAPTER 23

SWWM: JERU/5 NYK 18 APRIL 1984
TO: NEWSDESK FOR: WORLD
FROM: JERUSALEM BY: J.P. GORDON
SLUG: GOVT DEBATES JEWISH TERROR NETWORK

—MILITARY CENSOR HAS NOT CLEARED THIS COPY—

CONFIDENTIAL CABINET DOCUMENTS OBTAINED BY CORRESPONDENT AND ALREADY IN POSSESSION OF MAGAZINE'S CHIEF OF CORRESPONDENTS ROGER RICHARDS FOR AUTHENTICATION INDICATE THAT DESPITE AN EXTENSIVE INVESTIGATION OF A WEST BANK BASED JEWISH TERROR NETWORK KNOWN AS ≪TNT≫—TERROR AGAINST TERROR—BY THE SHIN BET, ISRAEL'S INTERNAL SECURITY ORGANIZATION, THE ISRAELI GOVERNMENT IS TAKING ITS TIME ACTING AGAINST TNT, WHOSE MEMBERS REPORTEDLY INCLUDE LEADERS IN THE ULTRA-NATIONALIST ≪GUSH EMUNIM≫ SETTLERS MOVEMENT, AS WELL AS OFFICERS IN UNITS OF THE ISRAEL DEFENSE FORCES (IDF).

ACCORDING TO THE SHIN BET'S INVESTIGATION, TNT HAS BEEN INVOLVED IN A NUMBER OF TERRORIST ATTACKS DIRECTED AT ARABS ON ISRAEL'S OCCUPIED WEST BANK, INCLUDING THE 1980 BOMBINGS THAT INJURED THE WEST BANK MAYORS KARIM KHALAF OF RAMALLAH AND BASSAM SHAK'A OF NABLUS AND, MORE RECENTLY, AN ATTACK ON THE ISLAMIC UNIVERSITY OF HEBRON WHICH KILLED FOUR STUDENTS AND INJURED THREE DOZEN MORE.

BUT THE CABINET, AWARE THAT TNT ENJOYS ENCOURAGEMENT FROM A SUBSTANTIAL NUMBER OF ISRAELIS, AS WELL AS TACIT SUPPORT FROM A FEW RIGHT-WING MEMBERS OF THE KNESSET, IS REFUS-

(MORE)

PAGE TWO JERU/5 NYK 18 APRIL '84

ING TO ACT AGAINST THE TERROR ORGANIZATION UNTIL IT COMMITS AN ACT SO OUTRAGEOUS THAT PUBLIC OPINION WILL FINALLY SUPPORT DECISIVE ACTION AGAINST IT.

THE CABINET'S THINKING REFLECTS A RECENT PUBLIC OPINION POLL TAKEN BY THE RESPECTED ISRAELI NEWSPAPER ≪HAARETZ,≫ WHICH SHOWS THAT THIRTY PERCENT OF ALL ISRAELIS FEEL THAT VIOLENCE DIRECTED AGAINST ARABS—INCLUDING TERRORISM—IS JUSTIFIABLE.

THAT POLL REFLECTS ISRAEL'S SHIFT TO THE POLITICAL RIGHT SINCE THE ELECTION OF MENACHEM BEGIN IN 1977, WHICH CULMINATED IN THE JUNE, 1982, INVASION OF LEBANON, A MILITARY CAMPAIGN FOR WHICH THERE REMAINS STILL TODAY NO BROAD PUBLIC CONSENSUS.

HIGHLY PLACED AND WELL CONNECTED INTELLIGENCE SOURCES HERE BELIEVE, THEREFORE, THAT THE GOVERNMENT WILL ALLOW TNT TO COMMIT A MAJOR CRIME BEFORE ARRESTING ITS LEADERS, WHOSE NAMES ARE ALREADY KNOWN.

THE SHIN BET HAS DISCOVERED THAT TNT PLANS TO PLACE BOMBS AT AN EAST JERUSALEM BUS STATION NEXT WEEKEND, BUT HAS—SO FAR—NOT ACTED AGAINST THE TERRORISTS. THE LEADERS

(MORE)

PAGE THREE JERU/5 NYK 18 APRIL '84

OF THE PLOT INCLUDE QIRYAT ARBA RESIDENTS MENACHEM LI*****************THIS IS IDF MILITARY CENSOR TEL AVIV. YOUR TRANSMISSION HAS BEEN INTERRUPTED FOR REASONS OF NATIONAL SECURITY. WORLD WEEK CORRESPONDENT JARED PAUL GORDON CONTACT CENSOR'S OFFICE IMMEDIATELY. NO TELEX OR TELEPHONE CONTACT WITH LOCATIONS OUTSIDE THE STATE OF ISRAEL WILL BE ALLOWED BY WORLD WEEK MAGAZINE PERSONNEL UNTIL CENSOR HAS BEEN CONTACTED.**

CHAPTER 24

Jared and Adrian spent the hours until Roger Richards arrived from New York in a state of unofficial house arrest. Their home was not searched; but their phone service was cut off and, looking out the front windows, they spotted at least two teams of Shin Bet agents in the narrow street below. At first Adrian thought it was coincidence, that the surveillance was intended for someone else. But the first time she tried to leave, a net shopping bag rolled up under her arm, a young man in jeans and a plaid short-sleeved shirt showed her a *Shabak* credential and instructed her politely but firmly to stay inside.

At seven-thirty Thursday evening the doorbell rang. Jared went down to answer it and found Roger Richards standing outside. The Chief of Correspondents looked grim.

Jared invited him inside. Richards ducked under the low doorway and trudged up the stairs behind Jared, set his briefcase on the Turkish rug, gave Adrian a perfunctory hug, and sank onto the sofa.

"You look as if you could use some coffee," Adrian said.

Richards rubbed a hand over his face. "I'd prefer something stronger if you've got it."

"Scotch? Gin? Vodka?"

"Gin—gin with a little ice."

She went to the kitchen. Jared heard her rummage through the cabinets.

He peered at the Chief of Correspondents. He'd never seen Richards when the man hadn't been immaculate. Even, Jared recalled, when, as an intern, he'd worked for Richards in Los Angeles during the Watts riots back in 1965. Every other newsman Jared had seen during that week of violence had been grimy, soot-covered and red-eyed from the tear gas. Richards had worked the streets for five days without stop, somehow managing to change his shirts twice daily, and never lost the crease in his trousers.

Now, however, Richards's suit was rumpled and he had a haggard look. But it was more than that. The youthfulness, which, to Jared, had always been Richards's most memorable feature, was gone. Disappeared. Vanished. The Chief of Correspondents had a reputation at the magazine as a boy wonder. Even now, at the age of fifty-three, he was perceived as one of *World Week*'s young turks by both staff and outsiders. But Jerusalem, Jared noted, does strange things to perception. The crepuscular light had metamorphosed now from warm golds and reds to early evening blue. And in the fading light of the living room, Jared began to see clearly the creases around Richards's mouth and the crow's-feet around his eyes. The boyishness entirely disappeared. In its place sat a babyfaced man of middle age; a man whose lined face, a mask of surface composure, reflected strain and pressure, coldness and cynicism. It suddenly dawned on Jared that Richards had probably been a tremendously effective CIA agent.

The mood was broken as Adrian returned with Richards's drink, pausing to turn on the one big lamp in the living room. The natural light now gone, the Chief of Correspondents' face regained its normal, juvenescent patina. He grinned gratefully as he accepted a small glass of gin in which a single ice cube floated. He raised it in Adrian's direction, said, "Cheers," downed it in a single gulp, and held it up. "Please," he said, "another."

Richards sat in silence until he received the liquor, took a sip, then carefully set the glass atop the coffee table. "Thanks."

Jared cleared his throat. "We didn't know when you'd get here."

"I've been on the go since yesterday," Richards said. "Never even got home to pack a change of clothes. I went straight to the airport—caught a flight to Paris, then changed planes and ran from Ben-Gurion straight to the Prime Minister's office. I've been cooped up there for hours." He took half-frames out of his jacket pocket and slipped them on, giving the room a wide, sweeping glance that ended with Adrian, who was just about to make herself comfortable in the armchair.

"I don't want to sound abrupt," he said, "but Jared and I have things to talk about."

"There's nothing Adrian can't hear."

Richards shrugged. "Whatever you say, Jared." He sipped at the gin, then reached for the briefcase, which he pulled onto his knees and opened.

Jared understood what was coming. He had discussed the probabilities with Adrian in the hours before Richards arrived. He realized that *World Week* was going to have to transfer him out. He felt ambivalent about leaving. On the one hand, his position as a reporter in Israel was untenable now. The government had no doubt already revoked his press credential permanently. On the other hand he wished there were some way to stay. After all, he'd finally vindicated himself: sent Richards undeniable proof about a Jewish terror network and the government's reluctance to act against it. His telex might have been interrupted. But the tape he'd made of the conversation on the beach and the documents Yoram and Nathan had given him were safely in Richards's hands, sent by courier. The story was rock-solid; hard as concrete.

They'd concluded that it wouldn't be so bad after all. *World Week* would transfer him back to Washington, or to New York, where he'd find a quiet, anonymous slot reporting on innocuous subjects, maybe writing something for the back-of-the-book: lifestyles of the rich and famous, or the new "Trends" section. He'd worked as a low-profile correspondent before, now he'd do it again. He had Adrian—and they'd have the baby. That was what counted.

Richards riffled through a thick sheaf of papers, found one and looked at it. "As I said, I've just come from the Prime Minister's office," he said. "When I was there, I signed this agreement." He held the document with two fingers in Jared's direction.

Jared, settled on the floor by the armchair, took the paper and read it; Adrian scanned it over his shoulder. "Oh, God."

Jared couldn't believe what he was seeing. He rolled over onto his belly as if he'd been gut-punched. He rolled back and read the single sheet a second time.

It was an agreement to return the Cabinet papers to Yitzhak Shamir's office without using any information contained in them. It stated that *World Week* had obtained the exclusive property of the state of Israel through error, and that the magazine was giving them back to the government in good faith. In return for which the magazine would be allowed "uninterrupted access to bona fide news stories within the State of Israel."

"You blew it, you sonofabitch," Jared exploded, tears in his eyes. "We had them by the balls and you blew it, you gutless—"

Richards's eyes, which had been following Jared's as he read the agreement, glazed over. His tone turned professional. If he was ruffled by Jared's accusation he didn't show it. It was as if he'd thrown an internal switch and turned off his emotions. "There are things," he said, "you don't understand."

"I understand, I understand," Jared's voice rose in anger. "You sold me out."

"We have to live in the real world, Jared."

Jared looked up at Adrian. He'd heard the phrase before—from Felix. "What the hell does that mean?"

Richards sighed. He rose, shot the grimy white cuffs of his red-white-and-blue-striped English shirt, and straightened his tie. "*World Week* is very much like a small country," he began, somewhat pedantically. "Our capital is in New York. But we have diplomatic outposts all over the world. You—the correspondents and bureau chiefs—are our journalistic ambassadors. You send back your files—just like diplomatic cables—and we translate them into stories. The magazine's foreign and domestic policy studies, if you will."

"Isn't that a little high-flown?" asked Adrian.

"I don't think so," said Richards, finishing off the gin. "We visit the world's capitals. The managing editor and I meet with leaders of the free world regularly. *World Week* has its own summits with the General Secretary of the Soviet Union and the President of the United States. We interview them—and they interview us. Those people look to us for advice and guidance, Jared. Indeed, one of *World Week*'s duties is to forecast trends so the world's leaders can make educated decisions about how to govern."

"Okay," said Jared, rising to his feet and shaking the agreement under Richards's nose, "so we're like a little nation-state. What the hell does that have to do with this—or with me?"

"We need our . . . diplomatic posts intact. We have to maintain a bureau in Jerusalem so we can continue our mission. But *World*

Week journalists, just like other diplomats, must be vetted—credentialed—by the host country. Now, we have to maintain our access here for the good of the magazine, and so it's been necessary to practice some quiet diplomacy so we can keep that access uninterrupted."

Jared realized what the Chief of Correspondents was saying. "You schmuck!" he shouted. "They got you to kill the story."

Richards went on, unperturbed. "We had to make an accommodation, Jared. The Prime Minister's office assured me that otherwise *World Week* would not be allowed to work in Israel for the foreseeable future."

"Don't you *understand,* you ass? We had them by the short-and-curlies. They'd never lock *World Week* out. They can't afford to. They need us, even when the magazine's hostile, because we're one of their major conduits to American public opinion."

"That was something I couldn't risk, Jared."

"Then you're a coward, Roger—you're all cowards. For God's sake, just think for a minute, look at the scenario. The magazine's bureau is shut down by the government. It's front page news in *The New York Times*. It's on all the American television networks. And in *Time* and *Newsweek*. And that's just the American press. It would make the Israelis look like some third-world dictatorship. They don't want that—for God's sake, Roger, they were bluffing."

"They sounded serious to me, Jared."

"That's because we had the goods. They couldn't deny anything. We have the names, the time, the place—we had the truth, goddammit."

"We had your version of the truth. And by the time we hit the newsstands it might have been incorrect. It was made clear to me that if we published this story we would be wrong," Richards insisted. "I've been told—on the highest authority—that arrests will be made before the bombings. That the bombs will be defused. What you gave us, Jared, was technically incorrect."

The Chief of Correspondents held out his hand. "I'll need the agreement," he said.

Jared surrendered it. "So you keep your 'diplomatic immunity.' "

Richards nodded. "Yes." He paused. "Look, Jared, this isn't easy. I hired you. I shepherded you. I protected you."

Jared saw what was coming. And yet he wanted to be the one to say the words. "And now you're going to can my ass," he said. "Because the Israelis want you to."

There was a resounding silence in the room, broken only by Pilgrim's quiet breathing. Somehow, the cat managed to sleep atop the Turkish carpet that sat on the still-warm marble floor. Jared stared out toward Mount Zion. He walked to the window, looking north to where the lights shone on David's Tower and the Old City walls. It had been almost a year since he'd sat in Richards's office, shaking in fear of being fired, of suffering the stigma that went with it. All those phrases he'd heard his entire professional life: career track; exclusive byline; publisher's page citation—he suddenly found them empty and meaningless. He'd always believed the worst thing that could ever happen to him was being fired. Now, the moment at hand, it wasn't as bad as he'd thought. He turned, framed by the window, and waited for Richards to continue.

" 'Can your ass' isn't quite the way I'd put it," the Chief of Correspondents said finally. "You've been with the magazine for eighteen years. There're your stock options, and your pension—you're vested, Jared, and that's quite a quantity of cash, if you know what I mean. But I'm sorry—"

Jared raised his hands. "Shove it, Roger. Spare me your commiseration."

"We'll pay to move your belongings back to the States," Richards continued as if he hadn't heard. "You'll get a generous severance package. And you can resign. Trust me, Jared—nobody will ever know."

Could the man be so naïve? "Nobody will ever know"? Jared remembered his ordeal at the Knesset months earlier, even if Richards conveniently forgot about it. The public accusation by Begin. The search at the gates. The television cameras. Israel was a small country—it would take only hours for the whispers to start, for the word to get out.

And yet, undeniably, he felt a sense of profound freedom. He was light-headed, giddy as the time he'd smoked his first cigarette and it had made his head spin.

"Get out, Roger."

"Jared—"

"You've said what you have to say. I'm grateful you took the time to do so. But there's nothing left to say. So get out of our home."

Richards was caught off guard. He'd expected a different reaction. He covered his surprise by fumbling in the briefcase and withdrawing a typed statement.

"I'll leave after you sign this," he said, proffering the sheet to Jared, who took the paper, laid it on the coffee table, and read it quickly. Simple, declarative sentences.

"What is it?" Adrian asked.

Jared cackled. " 'I, Jared Paul Gordon, being of sound mind . . .' " He laughed again. "It's my letter of resignation." He patted his breast pocket for a pen but found none. Richards plucked a vermeil Dupont from his suitcoat and handed it over. Jared went over the document line by line twice, the second time drawing heavy black lines through two sentences and initialing the margins on each side.

"What are you doing?" Richards said.

"I've deleted the part about not ever revealing the reasons for my resignation."

"You can't do that."

"Listen, Roger—I can do what I damn well please. *World Week* may consider itself a sovereign nation, but it's not. It's only a magazine. Like *Time*. Like *Newsweek*. Like *The Economist*. No—not *The Economist*—you're not as good. You're not Mossad or the CIA. I don't have to sign any secrecy agreements with you."

"You do if you want your financial settlement."

Jared snorted contemptuously. "You'll pay me off anyway. You want me out of your hair, Roger—you and your colleagues. Face it—if I signed this thing the way it was I could take you to court. I'd just love to see your deposition—'The Magazine Seen as Nation-State.' That would look good in the *Columbia Journalism Review*. Forget it, Roger. You can't hold me to this. Let's just sign it as revised and we'll be finished."

The Chief of Correspondents nodded solemnly. "Done and done, boy." A flash of a smile crossed his face for an instant. "You can't blame me for trying, Jared."

Jared almost laughed out loud. Since when could a stripe-shirted WASP from New York outhaggle a prince of the desert, a vulpine Semite, a man who'd been bargaining in the souk for years? Without responding, Jared attached his signature to the bottom of the page.

Richards took the paper and his pen and slid them into his briefcase, which he locked. Then he rose. He offered his hand to Adrian. "I'm sorry you had to—"

She stood, her arm around Jared's shoulder. "Please just get out of our house now," she said. She picked up Richards's empty glass from the coffee table and headed toward the kitchen.

Richards, on his way to the stairs, turned when he heard the sound of shattering glass. "What's the matter?"

Adrian stood in the kitchen doorway. "I didn't think washing would remove the stain," she said.

Jared locked the door behind Richards, listened to his footfalls recede along the rough stone pavement, then climbed the stairs again and sat in silence for some moments. Adrian pulled the cat onto her lap and sat next to him. She smiled. She laughed. He watched her. It was contagious and he broke out laughing. It was all so goddam . . . hysterical, somehow . . .

Some moments later, tears of relief still in his eyes, Jared picked up the phone receiver and listened. For the first time in a day and a half he heard a dial tone.

Their mornings began early, because it is at dawn and dusk that Jerusalem is at its best. So by five on this Memorial Day they were awake, wrapped in flannel robes, their feet snugly encased in zippered shearling booties. They sipped thick, unsweetened Arab coffee from a tiny store on al-Rashid Street where the son of the owner bore a U.S. Marines tattoo, spoke openly of Palestinian rights, and swore the phone was tapped by the Shin Bet. Shutters open, they shivered in the spring chill and watched the skies turn from black to indigo, purple to carnelian, ruby-red to rose, finally brightening into burnished hand-wrought gold over Mount Zion.

They munched on toast spread thick with strawberries grown in the Sharon Valley, and listened to the monastery bells (bells whose dull, metallic thuds had neither the sonorous toll of Notre Dame nor the deep peal of St. Paul's but a sense of ineffable, atonal historicity).

At six he scampered up the three flights of cut-stone steps and across the wide street to the Sheraton, cadged a *Jerusalem Post* and *Davar,* tucked them under his arm, and trotted back to Yemin Moshe. Together, they read the headlines. Today's said: "Major anti-Arab terror cases cracked by security services." The arrests of TNT's leaders had been front-page news all week. Richards's predictions had come true: five bombs had been discovered and defused at the East Jerusalem bus station. Hundreds of Arab lives had been saved. And the leaders of TNT had been arrested. In the settlements, there were protests against the government's actions. On the streets, Israelis debated the identities of the terrorist leaders, kept secret by the authorities.

Word of Jared's firing had indeed spread through Israel's tight-knit journalistic community. But he discovered that the fact he'd been forced to resign because of government pressure also got around. Friends, sources, and acquaintances called to tell him he'd been on the right track about Jewish terror. By the end of the week after the arrests he found, both surprisingly and gratifyingly, that his former sorry standing among his colleagues had evaporated. Indeed, the day of the TNT arrests he was invited to appear on Israel Television's news magazine show, and was interviewed by the anchorman about the aborted telex he'd tried to send to New York. A *Ha'aretz* editorial mentioned him favorably as one of the few reporters to cover Jewish terror on a continuing basis. The *Jerusalem Post* sent a reporter and photographer around, and a flattering profile appeared two days later. He appeared for twelve seconds on ABC's "World News Tonight," described by the correspondent as a well-known writer on the subject of Jewish terror, looking into the camera and saying, "We accept Arab terror as a political reality—we've come to expect no less from them. But terror from Jews is contrary to our whole moral history." He'd begun the week as a pariah. He ended it as a minor celebrity.

World Week's severance check arrived by messenger. Ninety-eight thousand dollars in all, along with a twelve-page form letter describing the intricacies of shipping a household furniture container back to the United States, and a thick packet of official forms. The money Jared posted to his Washington bank. The shipping forms sat on the coffee table, still blank.

Felix telephoned almost every day. Adrian refused to speak to him, so he made uneasy small talk with Jared, trying to wheedle out of him any nugget about his daughter's pregnancy. He wanted a grandchild desperately, Jared thought, wondering if Adrian would ever let her father see the baby, wondering if he would allow it, too.

Friends called. Nafta Bar Zohar, *World Week*'s photographer, invited them to an Independence Day eve dinner at his home, which they accepted. But for the most part they puttered around the house, took long walks, or sat in the cafés on Ben Yehuda Street. They didn't speak a lot. Not that there was nothing to say. But somehow Jared couldn't find the words. Financially, they were in good shape. They could live for more than a year on Jared's severance pay while he tried to find a job in Washington, or New York, or wherever. But there was still . . . something missing. Neither Jared nor Adrian called the shippers to come and begin packing up the house in Yemin Moshe. The forms sat in their envelope on the coffee table untouched and unread.

Early one morning they climbed into the Autobianchi, now denuded of its Foreign Press stickers, and drove aimlessly toward the north. They stopped in Ramallah for coffee, then took the narrow, dusty, sometimes unpaved road through the rough Samarian countryside, driving past terraced Arab olive groves, herds of goats and sheep, and sparse, small fields of crops. They drove slowly through the villages and settlements: Ofra, Mughaiyir, Duma, Gittit, Beqa'ot, Mehola, all seen as if for the first—or last—time.

Jared had done something similar before. The week he'd left Detroit for a new assignment in Atlanta he drove aimlessly through the Motor City's streets, up and down, so as to set the place in his memory. Now he was doing the same with Israel. Each visit to the Old City was as if his last; on each careening drive down to Tel Aviv he fixed the memorials in his mind, so as not to lose them. On each excursion to the West Bank he made mental notes, took pictures with his eyes. It was as if he was seeing the country for the first time again. As a journalist he'd looked for certain things. Now he was discovering a different place; taking pleasure in the very land itself. He discarded his professional observer status in favor of another, more passionate identity.

Finally they reached the main road at Bet She'an and turned west toward Afula. On a whim—and as though they were being drawn there—they turned west and south, through countryside that looked like Switzerland, rich in evergreens and rolling foothills, to Zichron Yaakov; there they wandered hand in hand, their faces turned toward each other in muted conversation, through Koby Naiderman's Carignan vineyards while the strong, silent farmer watched them from a distance and kept his counsel.

He sent them home with six bottles of wine and three kilos of eggplants, living souvenirs. They'd looked exhausted, emotionally spent, like men he'd led in combat. Yet there was, to his practiced soldier's eye, a steely reserve of strength within them. Adrian kissed him as she stowed his presents in the car.

"*Litrahot*—see you later," she said, hugging the huge man.

"God willing I'll come to visit you in America," he said, knowing it was virtually impossible. The crops hadn't been good. There was too much work to do. He waved as the little car shot off down the hill. He prayed they'd be all right.

They finished their toast and coffee. Today was Memorial Day, so after reading the papers Jared had brought home they went to the Old City, walking past shuttered shops, their arms around each other's shoulders, one-two-one-two up the narrow, dusty alleys in lockstep unison. They meandered through the Cardo, with its new art galleries and restaurants, now closed and locked. Just before eleven they reached the Western Wall's wide, sunswept plaza, now clogged with thousands of people.

Drawn to the Wall as if by a magnet, Jared clapped a cardboard skull cap on his head and walked inside the barriers. He stood in front of the cool stones and said words, while tears came to his eyes, then threaded his way back through the crowd to Adrian. He looked at her swollen belly, touched it gently, then kissed her.

Sirens wailed. It was the instant of remembrance; the entire country was coming to a complete halt. On the highways, traffic stopped, drivers standing silent next to their cars. On the beaches, surfers stood clutching their surfboards, heads bowed. In the streets, people stopped whatever they were doing and remained in place. In the midst of the huge, silent throng crowded and frozen in place in the wide plaza, Jared clutched Adrian's hand in his own, the two of them staring at the Wall.

A body pressed up against theirs. They could feel its heat; smell its odors: sweat, dust, ashes and old tobacco smoke. Two hands clasped their clasped hands from behind.

Alarmed, Jared started to wheel about but a low voice, commanding through the sirens' wail, said, "No—don't look. You must not look. You must not move."

It was an old voice, a tired voice, a voice he'd heard before. The voice from the *Martef.*

They obeyed. They stared at the Wall, the heat from the old man's body hot on their backs.

"You know already what I will tell you," the old man wheezed, his voice a hoarse whisper behind their heads. "That you must stay here now. Stay here with us, with history's orphans. To testify. To fight. To make your Jewish baby."

His hands left theirs and went to Jared's shoulders. Their imprint was intense—searing, almost.

"Still young and in love," he said. "No—don't turn, don't turn. Look at the Wall. Look at the Wall and learn its lessons. Learn, and hope is possible. Forget, and despair is inevitable.

"You must stay, and you know it. You have no place to go—orphans must stay with orphans. To fight, to testify. To be a Jew today means to testify."

Adrian's hand was moist in Jared's. He leaned toward her, brushed her cheek with his lips and tasted salt tears. It was inevitable—the decision to stay, to fight, was something he'd known all along, but hadn't been able to face.

The country, after all, was his, was Adrian's, as much as it was Begin's, Sharon's, Kahane's or Yoram's—but only if he stayed, if they stayed. To fight for the kind of Israel they wanted. The battleground wasn't in Washington or New York or Los Angeles. The war wasn't going to be fought at temple fund-raisers, Hadassah book sales or UJA young leadership missions, but in Jerusalem, Hebron, Afula, Tel Aviv, Beersheva and the West Bank settlements. It was going to be a guerrilla war, a dirty war—a bitter war. But it had to be fought, for the sake of all Jews. Ultimately, Yoram was wrong—Felix didn't count. Not really. What really counted was what took place here—the real fight was here, a battle for the soul of the country.

The old man was right. There could be only one answer, and so Jared found his head nodding in assent. Yes, they would stay. Yes, they would fight. Yes, they would testify, they would not surrender. Somehow, they would do it. Adrian's hand squeezed his tightly. She, too, nodded: yes.

The sirens' wailing stopped and, for the briefest instant, absolute silence reigned in the crowded plaza, thousands of Jews standing statuelike in the bright sun. Jared took Adrian into his arms and held her tightly. They wept tears of deliverance and joy.

When he turned, some seconds later, his shoulders still felt the heat and pressure of the unseen hands, but the little man himself had disappeared.

ACKNOWLEDGMENTS

This book could not have been written without the help, encouragement and cooperation of scores of friends and colleagues in the United States, Israel and Europe.

My agent, Knox Burger, believed in the project when even I was skeptical. His associate Kitty Sprague's editorial comments kept the book on the right track. My editor at Viking, Charles Verrill, tempered hard-nosed criticism with careful, incisive, thoughtful guidance. My good friends Roderick Townley, Richard Barber and Dirck Halstead were generous with both their support and their advice. *TV Guide*'s Editorial Director, Merrill Panitt, and the magazine's Editor, David Sendler, allowed me a generous amount of time off for research and for writing.

In Israel, I am grateful for the friendship and counsel of Brig. Gen. Menachem Eini and his wife, Esther, and Reuven and Chaya Sharoni, whose hospitality and guidance were invaluable. I am indebted heavily to Koby and Ziva Naiderman; Maj. Gen. Uri Simhoni and his wife, Elana; Itamar Siani; Amos and Gail Aricha; Amos Ettinger and *Maariv* columnist Tamar Avidar; *Davar*'s Amir Oren; Israel-TV correspondent Elimelech Ram; Nachman Shai, former Israeli Embassy spokesman in Washington and now in charge of Israeli Army Radio; Dr. Ami Gilladi; Ze'ev Chafets; El-Al Israel Airlines Washington manager Michal Guttman; National Public Radio Jerusalem correspondent Jim Ledderman; Salleh and Hannah Mizrahi; Brig. Gens. Fuad Ben-Eliezer and Yalo Shavit; Maj. Gen. Yanouch Ben-Gal; Shmulik Askarov; Dax Dekel; *Time* magazine Jerusalem bureau manager Jean Max, and especially to David and Anni Rubinger.

Ari Rath, editor of the *Jerusalem Post,* gave me access to the newspaper's encyclopedic archives. I am also grateful to a long list of correspondents from the American television networks, who shared with me their experiences while working in the Middle East during the past decade, and members of various branches of the Israeli security forces, who all, by their choice (and for their security), must remain anonymous.

In Europe I spent hours in conversation with Patrick Seale, the longtime Middle East correspondent of the London *Observer,* and with various American Foreign Service, military and intelligence personnel who were generous with both their time and their frank, off-the-record analyses of Israeli politics.

Most important, this book could not have been written without the constant support of my wife, Susan, who endured long, solitary hours while I flailed over a hot computer. It is she, more than anyone, who has made these last three years of work possible.

August 1983–May 1986
Herzlyia/Jerusalem/Washington

June 22. 1991